Praise for Jenn Bennett and *Kindling the Moon*

"The talent pool for the urban fantasy genre just expanded with Bennett's arrival. This is an impressive debut, which opens the door for a series that promises to be exceedingly entertaining. . . . Plenty of emotional punch, not to mention some kick-butt action. . . . Bennett appears to have a bright future ahead!"

—RT Book Reviews

"Without a doubt the most impressive urban fantasy debut I've read this year. . . . The writing is excellent, the characters are charming, and the romance is truly believable. . . . Flawlessly original!"

—Romancing the Darkside

"For the love of things that go bump in the night, this book was FABULOUS! It was the perfect blend of action, intrigue, tension, and the supernatural."

—Reading the Paranormal

"I was hooked from the first page. . . . The story was fun and original. . . . The twists and turns came at every intersection. . . . I can't think of one thing I didn't like about the book. I didn't want to put it down."

—Urban Fantasy Investigations

"I was smitten with this book right from the beginning. . . . A fantastic debut to a new series I am very excited over, and a must-read for all lovers of urban fantasy."

—Wicked Little Pixie

"Debut author Jenn Bennett takes the familiar ideas of magic, demons, and mythology, and she gives us something sexy, fun, and genuinely unique in *Kindling the Moon*. Arcadia Bell is a sassy, whip-smart addition to the growing pantheon of urban fantasy heroines, and Bennett is an author to watch!"

—Kelly Meding, author of *Three Days to Dead*

"Fantastic magic, non-stop action, and hot romance make *Kindling the Moon* a not-to-be-missed debut. Arcadia Bell is a tenacious and savvy heroine who had me hooked from the start."

—Linda Robertson, author of *Arcane Circle*

"Delicious characters, fun twists, and fiendish risks. . . . This smart, stylish debut really delivers. Loved, loved, loved it!"

—Carolyn Crane, author of *Double Cross*

This title is also available as an eBook

Don't miss the first Arcadia Bell novel . . .

Kindling the Moon

SUMMONING
THE NIGHT

AN ARCADIA BELL NOVEL

JENN BENNETT

POCKET BOOKS

New York   London   Toronto   Sydney   New Delhi

Pocket Books
A Division of Simon & Schuster, Inc.
1230 Avenue of the Americas
New York, NY 10020

First Pocket Books paperback edition May 2012

POCKET and colophon are registered trademarks of Simon & Schuster, Inc.

For information about special discounts for bulk purchases, please contact Simon & Schuster Special Sales at 1-866-506-1949 or business@simonandschuster.com.

The Simon & Schuster Speakers Bureau can bring authors to your live event. For more information or to book an event contact the Simon & Schuster Speakers Bureau at 1-866-248-3049 or visit our website at www.simonspeakers.com.

Designed by Esther Paradelo

Manufactured in the United States of America

10 9 8 7 6 5 4 3 2 1

ISBN 978-1-9821-3489-1
ISBN 978-1-4516-2055-9 (ebook)

To my Aunt Erin and Aunt Kitty,
who famously blackened out anything objectionable,
wicked, or filthy in their fiction.
Their Sharpies would've run dry before they finished my books.

1

Jupe pinched himself on the arm and grinned from the passenger seat of my Volkswagen. "Yep, I definitely feel different."

I swiped my monthly pass through the card reader at the parking garage entrance down the street from my bar. It buzzed in acceptance, and the gate's striped barrier arm rose. "Well, you sure do *look* it," I agreed, stowing the pass in a pocket on the sun visor.

"Different how?" Jupe tugged at one of the long espresso curls jutting out around his face. Like other Earthbound demons, his head and shoulders were crowned by a swirling halo of hazy light. His was an alluring spring green that matched his unusually pale eyes and gave off a lightning-bug luminescence in the shadowed interior of my car.

"You look older . . . more sophisticated," I teased.

"Really?"

I rolled my eyes and pulled through the raised gate into the dark garage. "No."

He punched me in the arm.

"Dammit, that hurt," I complained in the middle of a

laugh, rubbing my shoulder. "See if I ever give you anything again, you ungrateful punk."

Jupe snickered as he stretched out long, wiry legs and examined the savings deposit receipt perched on his knee, thoughtfully tracing his finger along the indented ink. The deposit was for $15,000, originally in the form of a check, made payable to me from Caliph Superior, the leader of my esoteric organization back in Florida. The money was payment for the black-market glass talon Jupe's father, Lon, had bought to help me out a few weeks ago. My magical order was rolling in dough, so I didn't feel guilty that they had offered to reimburse Lon. But when he refused their check, I couldn't keep the money for myself, so the only logical solution was give it to his son . . . while Lon was away in Mexico on a three-day photo shoot. Sneaky? Sure. But if you're going to lie to Lon, you have to do it while he's away on business. Otherwise he'll just sense it before you can make it out the door. Jupe taught me that trick. He should write a book, *How to Outsmart an Empath*. The boy has skills.

But who knew giving money to an underage kid would be so hard? Jupe and I spent almost an hour arguing with tellers inside my credit union: no, I did *not* want to put it in some giftable trust fund that Jupe couldn't touch until he was twenty-one. He already had a fat college fund and enough bonds and CDs to start a third-world country.

Problem was, the credit union didn't allow minors on a joint savings account without a parent or legal guardian co-signing, and I was neither. Girlfriend of the Boy's Father didn't qualify, apparently. The branch manager couldn't understand why I wouldn't wait until Lon was back in town to get his signature. I wasn't about to tell the manager that Lon would refuse—which he would. After a blue-faced argument, the manager finally, inexplicably, gave in.

"By the way, I know you still don't believe me," Jupe said as he snooped inside the glove compartment, "but I really *did* do it. Me. I got the manager to make an exception and let us open the account."

God, he really wasn't going to give that a rest. I swatted his hand away from the glove compartment and steered the car down the ramp to the next parking level; the Metropark garage sticks the monthlies in the dregs on the bottom floor. "You're a charmer, don't get me wrong." And he was. Witty, geek-smart, almost annoyingly outgoing, and well on his way to becoming drop-dead gorgeous. Just yesterday he bragged that he'd overheard some girl in his class referring to him as "totally hot." Did I mention he was cocky?

"I'm serious, Cady. I concentrated with my mind and twisted his thoughts around. I think it's my"—he leaned over the armrest and spoke in a lower voice, as if someone could hear us outside the car—"knack."

Knack. Slang for a preternatural ability possessed by an Earthbound demon. Most Earthbounds have one, but many knacks fall short of spectacular. A little foresight here, a little nighttime vision there. A whole hell of a lot of psychokinetics, most of them no more than bland party entertainment, unable to lift anything heavier than a freaking spoon a couple inches off the table. Don't get me wrong: the occasional impressive ability *does* exist. I've met Earthbounds who could pick a lock with a touch, and others who could curse your unborn child. Those weren't exactly commonplace, though.

"You're crazy," I said, waiting for another car to back out. A large, sparkling jack-o'-lantern clung to the top of its antenna—less than two weeks to Halloween. "For starters, you've got a couple more years before your demonic ability will start expressing. And second, you'll inherit it from your mom or dad. It's genetic, you know—you don't just get a new ability out of thin air."

"I know all that," Jupe complained. "Who's the demon here, me or you?"

"You are. I'm mere human." Well, human magician with a few extra skills, but still human.

"Yeah, and I got the stupid 'knack' speech with the 'birds and the bees' from my dad when I was eight."

"Poor, poor Lon," I murmured. The car windows were fogging up; it was going to rain. I turned the defroster on and cranked up the compressor fan.

"All I'm saying is that I know about what's *supposed* to happen. But I'm telling you, Cady, I can make people do things. I can get inside their minds and change their thoughts."

"*Pfft.* I've never even heard of a knack like that." Well, Lon could influence thoughts when he was amped up into his transmutated demon state, but that's nothing Jupe knew about, or would ever know. Not from me, anyway. Besides, Lon's influence was temporary, and he had to be touching the person. Plus, it was more common for the inherited knack to be weaker than the parents', not stronger.

"I think my knack is like"—he paused, as if he knew what he was about to say was going to sound ridiculous, but he just couldn't stop himself—"a Jedi mind trick."

I snorted.

"I'm serious!"

"Dream on." I shot him a sidelong glance as he snuck a couple fingers just beneath the waistband of his jeans and scratched—vigorously, with a teeth-gritting, pained look on his face. That was the third time today I'd caught him scratching. "What the hell is wrong with you? You have ants in your pants?"

SUMMONING THE NIGHT   5

He scratched harder and groaned. "I've got an injury."

Dear God, have mercy. I held up my hand to stop him from saying more, waving away any mental images before they had a chance to pop into my head. "I don't *even* want to know."

Affronted, he made a face at me. "Not *there.* It's . . . nothing. Never mind."

No need to tell me twice. He could discuss it with the school nurse or his dad. Not my job description. I promptly changed the subject. "So, what was all that jibber-jabber earlier about you wanting an Eldorado?"

He'd talked the branch manager's ear off, telling him what he was going to do with the savings account. Jupe swore to the guy—who couldn't have a given a rat's ass—that he wouldn't touch his new money until he turned fifteen and could apply for a driver's learning permit, and buy a car. That's right: a year from now this ADHD mess of a boy would be plowing down the same roads I drove on. Heaven help us all.

"Umm, *Super Fly*, duh. The Cadillac Eldorado is only one of the greatest cars in movie history—the original pimpmobile." He waggled his eyebrows. "Driven by Youngblood Priest, played by Ron motherfucking O'Neal."

I didn't even bother to curtail his obscenity-rich language anymore. Getting honey out of a hornet would be easier. When I was his age, my parents would've slapped me for talking like that. Then again, my parents turned out to be evil, power-hungry serial killers, so what did they know? I mean, these were the people accused of murdering the leaders of rival occult organizations when I was seventeen. They swore they were innocent, and because I believed them, they were able to persuade me to assume a fake identity, separate from them, and hide from the FBI for seven years. When they resurfaced

a couple of months ago, Lon tried to help me prove their innocence, but we discovered that they actually *had* murdered
several people and were planning to kill one more: me. They'd
conceived me during some crazy sex ritual that granted me
the title of Moonchild and enhanced magical abilities that
lay dormant inside me until I turned twenty-five—and they
wanted to steal those abilities through ritual sacrifice. But I
escaped and they were spirited away by a demon into the
Æthyr, where, I hope, karma bit them both in the ass.

So, yeah, compared to them, Lon was parent of the year.
That's why I just stuck to the Butler house rule: no swearing
around strangers. Unless Jupe was making an ass of himself in
public, he could knock himself out.

"Yuck," I complained. "Didn't Boss Hog drive an Eldorado in the *Dukes of Hazzard*?"

His wince told me that I was right.

"Anyway, I seriously doubt your dad's going to go for a
pimpmobile."

He clicked the release on his seat belt several times.
"Then how about a 1977 Firebird Trans-Am?"

The boy was obsessed. He knew the make and model of
every car produced in the last fifty years—at least the ones
featured in movies or on TV.

"Oh, *hell* no," I said. "Not a Trans-Am."

"That's the Bandit's car. What's wrong with that?"

I puffed my cheeks out and made a puking noise.

"Hey, you're talking about Burt—"

"Yes, I know. Burt motherfucking Reynolds. Put your seat
belt on, Snowman—we've still got two more levels to go."

He refastened the buckle. "Holy shit! I've never been this
far down underground. There'd better be an elevator. This looks
like the kind of place where you get stabbed and left for dead."

Ugh. Tell me about it. Parking here was the worst part of owning my bar, but it was better than leaving my car on the street. I once had my window broken and my car stereo stolen while parked in front of the bar. At least the garage had cameras and a guard on-premises 24/7.

"If I had to choose, I guess I'd go for the Eldorado," I said, trying to distract both of us from the sight of a homeless guy sleeping in a dark corner by one of the stairwells. "But I'm kinda doubting that fifteen thou is going to buy you one."

"My dad knows a ton of car collectors. He'll get me a deal."

Mmm-hmm. Sure he would. We headed down the final ramp onto the monthlies' level. I spotted a tight corner space, not too far from the elevator.

"We're parking here?" Jupe asked, wiping away fog to peer out the window. "Gross."

"Welcome to glamorous big-city life."

"I bet the Snatcher would have a field day down in this dump."

"Who?"

"The Sandpiper Park Snatcher," he repeated, as if I were the dumbest person in the world. When I shook my head in confusion, he explained. "Some kid went missing in La Sirena a couple of days ago. Everyone at school says the Snatcher's back."

I grunted and warily glanced out the window. Leave it to me to get spooked by a teenager inside my own parking garage. "Look, you said you wanted to see my bar before it opens today."

"I do, I do!" he confirmed, throwing off his seat belt.

"Then help me haul this shit out of the car and let's get going before the rain starts."

I popped the trunk as Jupe slammed his door shut and jogged around to meet me. The restaurant supply guy had screwed up our delivery yesterday, so that meant I had to take care of this weekend's garnish supplies by tracking down mondo sacks of lemons, limes, oranges, and pineapples. Jupe and I made a quick trip to the wholesaler's warehouse before the whole savings account fiasco earlier in the day. Along with the fruit, I let him pick out Halloween candy both for home and the bar, so we also had enough Tootsie Rolls, Pixy Stix, and severed gummy body parts to feed an army of demons.

While we unloaded the trunk, Jupe started in again about the Snatcher. In the oceanside Northern California town where he and Lon lived, this was apparently a local urban legend: a bogeyman whom no one had ever seen. When I pressed Jupe for details, all he could give me was a tangle of motley stories about young teenage Earthbounds who were picked off one by one at Halloween in the early '80s.

Great. That was the last thing I wanted to think about. Several weeks had passed since Jupe had been held hostage and his arm broken, but those memories continued to send a familiar pang of guilt through my gut. And from the worry shading his eyes right now, I guessed he wasn't all that keen on pondering the possibility of getting kidnapped again, either. Best not to talk about it.

"Smells like someone's been pissing all over the walls," Jupe complained, wrinkling his nose in disgust as we toted the bags of fruit and candy to the elevator.

"Someone probably has. Lots of someones." I glanced over my shoulder and scanned the dirty garage. The concrete floor shook with the dull boom of a car on the level above us driving over speed bumps. Otherwise it was quiet. Usually was during the daytime on weekends. "Inhale through your mouth," I suggested. "And stay sharp."

He followed my instruction as I stopped in front of the elevator and used a knuckle to press the cracked plastic button to go up. I started to ask Jupe a question but was interrupted when something hit me in the shoulder, knocking me sideways. My cheek smacked into the concrete above the elevator button panel. Pain flared. A bag of limes fell out of my hand as Jupe yelled behind me.

"Against the wall! Move!" A man in a bright blue hoodie towered in front of us, his face shrouded in sharp slices of shadow under the dim garage lights. No halo, so he was human, not Earthbound. His blond hair was shaggily cropped. He carried a curved hunting knife in one hand and stood with his legs apart, bouncing on the toes of his tennis shoes, ready for a fight.

I dropped the other bag I was holding and backed into Jupe. The scrape on my cheek was on fire. My heart galloped frantically inside my chest.

"Money. Now!" the man shouted. As he did, his head shifted out of the shadows to reveal a mouthful of yellow, rotting teeth. Meth head, I assumed, pairing his dental issues with the twitchy way he moved. Not exactly a man in his prime, that's for sure. On one hand, I might be able to take him down with a swift kick to his balls. Then again, I might get stuck with that dirty-ass knife.

"Credit cardth too," the man added with a lisp, looking me over with nervous eyes. He turned the knife over in his hand and blinked rapidly. His erratic, drug-primed pulse was probably a few pumps away from causing his heart to explode. I wished I could will it along a little faster.

Jupe made a mewing noise behind me as his hands

gripped the back of my jacket. I thought of the magical seals on my inner forearm, white ink tattoos etched into my skin. I could charge one of them to make Jupe and me seem to disappear, then we could run to the car and escape. But most of the seals require blood or saliva to activate—both rich with Heka, the magical energy needed to power spells—and my jacket sleeves were stiff. The meth addict could easily shiv me in the gut while I fumbled to get to the seals.

What else? Not enough time to break out a hunk of red ochre chalk and scribble out a spell, and I couldn't very well knock the guy out with a sack of limes. There was my new ability, the so-called Moonchild power. The last time I'd used it, I'd given up my serial-killer parents to an ancient Æthyric demon in payment for their crimes. Not exactly something I wanted to dwell on . . . or remember at all, frankly. Regardless, the ability only worked on demons, and the man standing in front of us was human. So what the hell was I going to do?

"You got a wallet, boy?" the mugger asked.

"No way," Jupe whispered in my ear. "I'm not giving him my money."

"What did you say? You got money?" The man twisted his head around, scanning the garage as another car drove through the level above us.

I didn't answer. Like Jupe said, no way.

"I don't mind hurtin' either one of you," the man warned. "Eat or be eaten. A big, bad thtorm's a-comin'. Can't you feel it in the air?"

From the psychotic glint in his eyes, I didn't think he was talking about the afternoon rain forecast. Stupid bastard was out of his ever-loving mind. Dirty, diseased, high, and crazy.

A fluorescent light shone above the elevator. I was going to have to shock him. Why was my last resort always my only option? Best not to kick a gift horse in the mouth, I supposed. Most mages would probably give their right arm to be able to kindle Heka like I could. My sensitivity threshold to electrical shock was pretty high. "Stay away," I threatened, "or whatever god you pray to better help you, because I'm going to fry you to hell and back."

"Say what?" He narrowed his eyes and visually searched me for a weapon.

I tapped into the electrical current. My skin tingled with the familiar flow of foreign energy as I spooled electricity into myself. No time to be gentle about it, so I pulled fast. Lights flickered. The descending elevator groaned in protest. Within a couple of seconds, my body hummed with enough charged Heka to shock the guy pretty badly. But I'd have to get close enough to touch him. The concrete floor was a poor conductor.

"Let go," I growled through gritted teeth, trying to shake Jupe off. He was gripping my jacket like death and if he didn't let go, I couldn't do this. Without a caduceus staff to even out the release, it was going to hurt all of us when I let go of the kindled Heka.

The garage elevator dinged.

The mugger yelped and swiveled wildly, searching for the source of the sound.

The elevator doors parted.

"Police are coming! Run!" Jupe shouted near my ear. I jumped in surprise, nearly losing control of the Heka.

Spooked, the mugger cried out incoherently, turned on his heels, and fled from Jupe's nonexistent police in the empty elevator car. We watched in disbelief as he raced his own heartbeat up the parking garage ramp toward the next level. As he barreled around the corner, a large blue minivan sped down the ramp and slammed on squealing brakes when Methbrain ran out in front of it. The disconcerting thump of metal on flesh echoed through the garage. Then the man's body jerked and he crumpled on top of the minivan's hood.

Jupe gasped.

The doors to the elevator closed.

Unable to hold the Heka any longer, I shoved a shaking hand into my inner jacket pocket until my fingers wrapped around a pencil. I pushed Jupe away forcefully, then thrust the pencil into the concrete wall, releasing a substantial volt of charged Heka through the small graphite point. The wooden caduceus staves I normally used for magical work contained fat graphite cores that allow smooth releases of kindled energy. This puny pencil? Not so much. It immediately overloaded and shattered, wedging a yellow wooden splinter into my skin.

"Shit!" I stuck my injured finger in my mouth as a wave of post-magick nausea hit me and I swayed on my feet. The sound of car doors opening drew my attention to the minivan. Three people were running to help the meth head—but he popped up from the hood like an unkillable video game character, briefly shook himself, and tore off, further up the ramp and out of sight.

Jupe's eyes were two brilliant circles of leafy green surrounded by white moons. "You okay?" I asked, putting my hands all over him like an overanxious soccer mom. Panicked thoughts of his needing another cast ran through my head.

"Whoa . . ." He was just shaken, but otherwise fine. His eyes darted between me and the minivan. "We almost got mugged."

"Oh, God, Jupe. I'm *so* sorry." I wrapped my arms around him. A dark laugh vibrated his shoulders. I released him to study his face. He wasn't smiling.

"Do you believe me now?" he said. "I did that, Cady. Like I convinced the manager at the credit union."

"Jupe—"

He shook his head, dismissing my lack of belief, then said firmly, "I just made that mugger believe the cops were coming."

2

The bottom fell out of heavy clouds during our half-block trek to the bar. As rain poured from a dark sky, we dashed down the sidewalk with the bags of bruised fruit, darting through umbrella-carrying crowds. All I could think about was getting Jupe the hell out of that garage, dropping off the bar supplies, then hightailing it back to my house without anything else happening.

I'm not the only magician in town, so there's likely plenty of warded places scattered throughout the Morella and La Sirena area, but only three that I trust: my house, Lon's house, and my bar, Tambuku Tiki Lounge, where neither supernatural attacker nor crazy, meth-addled human mugger could get inside without setting off several protective spells. Safe as milk, especially when it was closed.

A short length of steps flanked by waist-high tiki statues led us down to the door of the underground bar. The neon signs were off. It was around noon, and even though we didn't open until two on weekends, my business partner, Kar Yee, usually came in early to work on the previous night's receipts in the back office. I pounded on the locked door and peered through iron bars into the stained glass. Its red hibiscus design obscured the view when the inside lights were off, so I couldn't see much. Maybe she wasn't there after all. Cold, pooling rain dripped from the thatched awning above the entrance. Jupe huddled next to me as I fumbled with my keys and got the door open.

"Your sign says 'No One Under 21 Allowed,'" Jupe noted with a devious smile.

"If anyone asks, you're on official delivery business." I pushed him inside and locked the door behind us. The motion-sensor toucan that Kar Yee had recently installed by the front door chirped to announce our entry. Hearing the damned thing go off every minute during my shifts made me want to hex somebody.

A thick cloud of worry settled in my lungs and tightened my throat as the weight of the situation settled on me: we almost got *mugged*. I pushed away gruesome thoughts of Jupe dying in an ER from a dirty knife wound. Lon was going to freak when he found out. Maybe I could persuade Jupe to keep his mouth shut about it.

"It smells like pineapple in here," he remarked cheerfully, as if the events from the parking garage were already forgotten. His head turned in circles as he strained to see the long, narrow bar in the diffused light shining in from the red window.

"Hold on." I shucked my coat, shaking out the raindrops, and flipped three switches that turned on the ambient lights: multicolored glass Japanese fishing floats hanging above the bar, Easter Island lamps at the booths, and thousands of stringed white lights.

"Whoa!"

I'll admit, even with my shot nerves, it made me a little proud to show off Tambuku to someone who appreciated its kitschy charm. His father, who is uncomfortable in small, crowded spaces, had only ducked inside a couple of times after closing to pick me up, and he'd pronounced it "nice"—Lon's all-encompassing adjective for anything that he doesn't hate.

Jupe, however, proceeded to bounce around the bar with enthusiasm, noting details. "Those are the binding seals around the tables that you told me about?" he said, eying the booths and tables with curiosity. Beneath each one, magical snares were hand-painted onto the floor. A local artist altered the designs to fit in with the Polynesian feel of the place without corrupting the authenticity of the symbols. "You really use them to keep drunk-ass Earthbounds in line?"

"Yep."

"Every night?"

"Depends on the night."

"Oh, man," he pined, "would I *love* to see you do that."

"It's not that exciting, I promise."

"You designed this place all by yourself?" Jupe dropped three battered sacks on top of the bar and stared up at the wooden tiki dolls dangling from the ceiling.

"No, she didn't." Kar Yee padded out from the office, the door slamming shut behind her. "If Cady had her way, we would have installed too many booths. At least one of us has good business sense."

"Oh, so you *are* here," I complained. "Didn't you hear me banging on the front door? It's pouring outside."

The lithe Hong Kong ex-pat shrugged, her sleek black bob rustling as she passed under a ceiling fan. She was wearing a thin, white cowl-neck sweater that fell mid-thigh and clung to her petite figure, and below it, a pair of black leggings. "I was listening to music. Why are you so grumpy?"

"We almost got mugged in the Metropark."

"Almost?"

"The mugger ran away." I darted a glance at Jupe. He wasn't listening. He was too busy staring at Kar Yee.

"No one was hurt?" she asked, studying the scrape on my cheek.

I shook my head.

"We need more cops in this area," she snapped. Her tone was high-pitched and brusque, like *I* was the reason for the lack of police presence.

"We're fine," I said.

Her face softened. "I called that big man to come guard the door next week during Halloween business."

"Who? Charlie?"

She ignored me, stopping a couple of feet in front of Jupe to dart a critical eye up and down his lanky form. "So . . . you are the kid?"

Jupe froze, a deer in headlights, while taking off his rain-drenched coat. Kar Yee had that effect on people. I'm not sure if it's her gratingly honest demeanor or the bored-but-dangerous look in her eyes, but most of our regulars steer clear of her.

"This is Jupiter Butler," I said. "He goes by Jupe."

"Tall," she observed.

Jupe remembered how to move and cleared his throat. "I've grown three inches this past year." He lifted both eyebrows expectantly, waiting for her to be impressed by this tidbit.

"Hmm . . ." Kar Yee took a step closer and measured him with her outstretched hand. "Just how tall are you? It's hard to tell under all this hair."

"Five-nine and three-quarters," he said very seriously. "My dad says I'll be way taller than him by the time I go to high school. That's next year, by the way." Without looking, he reached behind him to set his coat on a bamboo barstool and missed. Neither of them seemed to notice when it hit the floor. I grumbled as I picked it up, then hauled a bag of lemons behind the bar.

Jupe eased onto a stool with the smarmy pizzazz of a Wayne Newton impersonator. He braced his arm against the edge of the bartop as the two Earthbounds examined each other's halos, hers more an aqua-blue compared to his pale green. "I've talked to you on the phone a couple of times when I've called here for Cady," Jupe pointed out. "You were kinda mean, but I didn't mind. I don't like weak women. I like warriors."

Kar Yee leaned against the bar, hand on hip. "Is that so?"

"Yep. My dad says that if you want to be a warrior, you should be able to take care of business and not be afraid to speak the truth."

"Oh, *really*? Is that why he's hot and bothered for Arcadia here?" Kar Yee tossed an accusatory glance my way. She was well aware that honesty wasn't one of my strong suits.

"Probably," Jupe confirmed. "My dad says he likes her so much that if she kicked him in the balls, he'd just thank her."

I groaned at Jupe and struggled with the plastic netting on one of the lemon bags. Kar Yee laughed for the first time in . . . weeks, actually. Loud and genuine.

"Sounds like your dad is pussy-whipped," Kar Yee said. "Do you know what that means?"

If he didn't have firsthand experience with the term, he damn well knew what it meant, all right. His nostrils widened as a lurid smirk transformed his face. And just like that, my world crumbled. The kid I'd played video games with after school yesterday was suddenly a horny teenager. And he was crushing on my best friend.

"Holy Whore, Kar Yee," I complained. "Shut the hell up, would you?"

Too late. He was already moonstruck.

"What's your knack?" he asked.

"Do you want me to tell you or show you?"

"Kar Yee!" I snapped.

"I was just teasing," she said to me, then leaned closer to Jupe. "I can make people afraid."

"Really?"

"Really. My knack increases anxiety." Very effectively, in fact. Though it didn't last long, she could scare the bejesus out of an entire room with a little bit of effort.

"I can make people do what I want," Jupe blurted.

"Is that right?" Kar Yee said, as if he'd just told us he was an astronaut. "Aren't you a little young to have a knack?"

"Yes, he is," I said.

"I'm an early bloomer," he argued.

Kar Yee smiled and poked a slender finger into his bony chest. "I like you, Jupiter. You're tall, good-looking, and you make me laugh. When you're older, give me a call."

Jupe tore his cell out of his jeans pocket. "Why wait? What's your home number?"

I reached over the bar and smacked him on the arm. "Don't do it, Kar Yee. He'll be texting you from school every half hour. Trust me." Yesterday's smorgasbord of texts from Jupe included three general requests about what I was doing, one urgent message begging me to help him cheat on his English test, and two musings about possible magick spells I should work on (i.e., supercharging his dog, Foxglove, so she could run faster). If I didn't respond right away, he'd text twenty more times to ask if I'd gotten his original message. When I couldn't reply with a proper answer, I'd somehow agreed to use Lon's generic text reply: LUBIB. That was shorthand for "Love you but I'm busy." Jupe said the "love you" part was his personal addition to Lon's former canned response of BUSY, insisting that it detracted from the sting of being snubbed.

Before Kar Yee could debate whether it was a wise idea to give a teenage kid her digits, someone pounded on the door and Amanda's shadowy face pressed against the window bars. Kar Yee sauntered away to let her inside.

"Whew! What a storm." Amanda closed her umbrella and shook out her long, sun-drenched locks as Kar Yee locked the door behind her. "Oh, hey, Cady. I didn't know you were working today."

"I'm just dropping off fruit. Toni's tending bar tonight. This is Lon's son, by the way. Jupe, this is Amanda, our senior server."

"Oh, I know who he is!" she said brightly. "You go to school with my cousin, Rosy. I'm from La Sirena, too. My parents own Three Dwarves Pottery Studio in the Village." The Village was the tourist center of the small beach community, and Amanda's family's studio one of the busiest spots—less to do with their pottery skills and more because Amanda and her parents gossip like it's an Olympic sport and they're going for the gold.

"Rosy's pretty cool," Jupe confirmed casually, "and I know your parents' place. Next to the crappy ice cream shop that serves freezer-burned Rocky Road."

Amanda laughed. "Yeah, not my favorite either. Are you spending the weekend with Cady?"

"Lon's out of town," I answered. "Jupe's staying with me tonight."

He leaned against the bar, readying himself to charm girl

number two. At least he didn't seem traumatized by our run-in with Methbrain in the parking garage.

Amanda set a tinkling box on the bartop—new mummy mugs that her parents had designed for our two-day Halloween promo. Kar Yee came up with the bright idea to charge patrons twenty dollars for an exclusive holiday drink served in collectible mugs that customers could keep. If we could unload all three hundred mugs, we'd make a nice haul.

"So, *huge* news from La Sirena." Amanda pried up the edge of the box tape with her fingernail. "Another kid went missing. Dustin Chapman—fifteen-year-old son of a wealthy broker."

"What?" Jupe said. "I know that guy!"

Amanda's brow furrowed. "Oh, honey, I'm so sorry."

"I mean, kind of know him," he admitted. "My dad knows his dad. He goes to private school. What happened?"

"His parents said he was taking out the garbage last night. When he didn't come back in the house, they looked outside and found trash scattered all over the yard. Dustin was gone." Amanda ripped the tape off the box with a violent pull. "There was blood on the driveway."

"Blood?" Jupe squeaked.

"Yeah. So awful. He's the second kid to go missing in La Sirena. You've heard what everyone's saying?"

He nodded seriously. "The Snatcher."

Kar Yee frowned. "Snatcher?"

"Some guy who kidnapped teens thirty years ago around Halloween," Amanda explained. "He took seven kids in a couple of weeks. The day after Halloween—All Saints' Day—their names were found carved into a circle of trees in Sandpiper Park—just outside the Village—down on the beach. The cops never uncovered who did it, and the kids were never seen again. No bodies ever found."

"Is this a real crime, or just an urban legend?" I said. "It sounds made up."

"Oh, it's real," Jupe assured me.

"Look it up on the internet," Amanda challenged. "Sometimes you can even find the original police photos of the circle of trees, but most of the sites that put them up get pressured by the families to take them down. They closed the park after it happened. Ten years later, they leveled the trees and installed a stone memorial. Families of the kids still bring flowers and candles there on Halloween. Totally spooky."

"It's supposed to be haunted," Jupe added.

I rolled my eyes. "You know damn well there's no such things as ghosts."

"Are you sure?" Wary eyes slid toward Amanda. I could easily guess his thoughts—he was questioning the fact that she was the only person in the room without a halo.

"She's not a savage," I said. Savages are humans who don't believe in the existence of Earthbounds, magick, or anything else supernatural. Most humans can't see halos—with my preternatural sight, I was an exception—but some, like Amanda, take our word for it.

In Amanda's case, she had an extra push from an early age. "Ugly Duckling," she announced with a raised hand, using the Earthbound term for nondemonic offspring. Her mother is human, father Earthbound. And, like other kids born from an Earthbound-human couple, Amanda is 100 percent human: no halo, no knack.

"Oh, cool. Anyway, I still think ghosts exist," Jupe said stubbornly. "My dog sees things that I can't. None of the Earthbounds at my school have seen ghosts, but everyone says you get a weird feeling around that memorial stone in Sandpiper Park."

Amanda nodded. "You need to be careful, Jupe. Don't go anywhere alone. You could end up like Dustin—one minute you're hauling out the garbage, the next you're gone. Poof! Until Halloween's over, you better make sure you've got someone with you at all times."

"Damn. It's not safe *anywhere*." Under the bar lights, the faint smattering of freckles over Jupe's nose and cheekbones seemed to darken against his pebble-brown skin.

"That is, *if* there's a Halloween," Amanda amended. "Some crazy civic watch group is trying to get Halloween festivities canceled. They're gonna be on the morning news tomorrow, trying to scare the public into supporting them. And not just in La Sirena. Morella, too. They want to cancel the Morella Halloween Parade and ban trick-or-treating throughout the entire county."

"What?" Jupe and Kar Yee said in chorus.

"No way! I've been wanting to go to the city parade for years and Cady promised to take me! They can't do this! My birthday's on Halloween!"

"I don't give a damn bout the parade," Kar Yee said, "except that it's bad for business and I've just paid for three hundred mummy mugs!"

"Nobody's canceling Halloween, for the love of Pete," I said.

"They'd better not." Kar Yee scowled at Amanda, as if it were her fault for bringing bad news into the bar. Still, she had a point. For demons, Halloween was like St. Paddy's Day or Cinco de Mayo. Last year we cleared almost $10,000 on Halloween night alone—not to mention the considerable upswing in profits the week before. And that was *without* the mummy mugs.

Amanda toyed with the braided hemp bracelets on her

wrist. "Whether they cancel it or not, it's still scary that kids are being taken. I wonder if it's some copycat crime?"

Whatever it was, she needed to shut the hell up about it in front of Jupe. Tonight was the first time he'd be spending the night at my house, and I just wanted to have a normal, problem-free weekend with the boy while Lon was gone, but that was looking like a pipe dream at this point. Let's see: nearly mugged in parking garage, check; minor in bar, check; underage lust kindled by best friend, check; scary child-snatcher rumors, kaboom.

Good job, Arcadia Bell.

3

I spent the rest of the day doing my best to keep Jupe's mind off the Snatcher, which is probably why he was able to sucker me into hauling him to a downtown comic book shop, where he managed to drop his entire weekly allowance in five minutes. We spent the rest of the night at my place watching movies and playing with my pet hedgehog, Mr. Piggy. I finally got the two of them to conk out in my guest room sometime after three in the morning, and gladly succumbed to exhaustion myself shortly after.

But sleep didn't last long.

I sat up in bed a few hours later, groggy and disoriented. Steamy light floated out from the cracked door to the master bath. Someone was in the shower. My momentary panic cleared when I noticed a suitcase on the floor and one of the drawers in my bureau standing open: Lon's drawer. Our big commitment step. I cleaned it out for him a couple of weeks ago. Though he'd only stayed over once, it still felt satisfying that he kept a few things at my house. In turn, he generously gave me an entire side of his walk-in closet. Walk-in "room" was more like it—the closet was big enough to hold a dressing bench and built-in wooden island in the center with a thousand drawers. *My* closet had louvered doors circa 1975 that were covered in dust and constantly falling off the track.

I laid my head back down on the pillow and stretched my toes. Even without the suitcase and open-drawer evidence, Lon was the only other person with a key to my place, and the house wards hadn't alerted me to an intruder. But why in the world was he home so early? I hadn't expected him back until well after my shift started at the bar later in the afternoon, and the alarm clock read 9 a.m.

The shower faucet squeaked off. Seconds later, a wonderfully wet and very naked man emerged from a transitory cloud of steam like a scene out of a '70s porno flick. He was beautifully built, all lean muscle and golden skin—more golden above the waist than below, I noticed. His outdoor shoot in Mexico must have been spent sans shirt. Good thing he was shooting travel ads and not women in bikinis, or I might've been jealous.

My eyes lingered over his taut stomach and followed the enticing dip of muscle curving over his hipbone, then lower. When he stopped toweling his hair, I glanced up, meeting his gaze. My heart hammered and a warm happiness spread through my chest. An easy grin parted his lips, outlined by the thin pirate mustache that trailed down past the corners of his mouth and matched a roguish triangle in the center of his chin. When he smiled, small wrinkles at the outer corners of his eyes deepened. I found this strangely enchanting.

"Morning, witch."

"Hello, devil." I raised my head and leaned on my elbows. "If this is a dream, it's a pretty good one," I rasped, clearing my throat. "What's going on? Why are you here early?"

"Caught a red-eye," he said, sounding weary.

"What about your shoot?"

"I got all the night shots before I left."

"Why?" I repeated.

He finished drying his shoulder-length light brown hair. "Why what?"

"Why did you come back early? You look exhausted."

"I caught a couple hours of sleep on the plane," he said with a shrug. "I came home because I got a call from Ambrose Dare."

That took a couple seconds to register. "Dare? The head of the Hellfire Club?"

"Mmm-hmm." He flung the wet towel on the floor and stepped to the edge of the bed. I reached out to run my hand over the soft hair on his thigh, still damp from the shower. He smelled good. He looked good. I'd missed him in all sorts of ways.

He made a small noise, one that told me he was listening to my emotions with his empathic knack. Until I met him, I paid little attention to my own feelings. But he did. He often pointed out nuances I'd never considered . . . like arousal. He said that my accompanying emotions sounded like a song going up an octave, and he could identify it even when I was ogling him from several feet away.

"Dare wants to see us," he said.

"Us," I repeated languidly. My wandering hand stilled. "Wait, *us*?"

"About those missing kids."

"Huh?" I tried my damnedest to process this information. What in the world did we have to do with two missing kids in La Sirena?

"Tomorrow afternoon. Wants some favor from you. Probably magick. He wanted us to come today, but I told him you were working a shift later." His eyes flicked to Mr. Piggy curled up by my feet. He scooped up the sleeping hedgie, toted him across the room, and set him down inside his open suitcase.

"You could've called. And if the meeting's tomorrow, then why did you leave the shoot early?"

In answer, he returned to the bed and lay down on top of me over the covers. The box spring groaned with his added weight, dipping lower when he shimmied to wedge his thighs between mine. He immediately kissed me several times in quick succession before I could protest.

"Do I have disgusting morning breath?" I asked after the assault, slightly breathless, but unable to stop smiling. Damp locks of wavy hair fell around his face. I tucked it behind his ears.

"No worse than your evening breath." As I laughed, he slipped his arms around me, gathering me close to bury his face in my neck. "God, I missed you," he murmured near my ear in a voice that was alluringly deep.

Tiny jolts of happiness surged through me. His warm weight resting on me felt so good. He was startlingly firm between my legs, even through the heavy quilt between us. His beautiful halo swirled in my vision, forest-green flecked with bits of golden light. When he held me close like that, our halos mingled around the edges. I wrapped my arm around his broad shoulders, holding up my hand in the middle of the cloudy haze. Gold, silver, and green lazily curled around my fingers like smoke.

"You kinda look like a sexy Jesus," I whispered, running a slow hand down his back.

"Would you like to reenact the Gospels?" His mustache tickled the sensitive skin behind my ear. "You could be Magdalene and wash my feet with your hair."

"*Pfft*. You could wash mine instead."

"Or you could pretend to be paralytic. I'll heal you."

"With what? Your cock?"

He pulled back to look at me, slitted green eyes shining as he grinned. "The night before I left for Mexico, you said it was a gift from God."

That coaxed a laugh out of me. "Hmm . . . this *does* sound better than Nurse and Doctor."

"How thin are the walls here?"

I sighed. "Paper."

"Your Silence spell?" he asked with hope.

He referred to a handy sigil that, when charged, would create a field of white noise a few feet around a door. It was too small to help here, and not worth the trouble to set up several in a perimeter along the wall. I'd be so tired by the time I finished, I'd be too nauseous to do anything else. I shook my head no.

"Damn. I was looking forward to hearing you wail."

My jaw dropped indignantly. "Wail?"

"Mmm-hmm. Like a cat giving birth."

I squeezed one eye shut, considering. "Wow . . . *that's* what I call romantic. I guess I should thank you for choosing cat over hippopotamus or some other sort of extra-degrading analogy."

"You're welcome."

"Is that why you came home early?"

"Maybe."

It totally was. I grinned up at him. "For the record, I like it when *you* sound like a dying horse."

His hips rocked against mine in one slow but insistent push. "First Jesus, now a stallion? You've really got it bad for me, don't you."

"I'm not the one who took an early flight home," I said as I smacked him on the ass with the tips of my fingers.

He retaliated by running his teeth over my neck and making a humorous growl that sounded neither holy nor horse. "Goddamn, it's cold in your house, Cadybell. You gonna let me inside the sheets?" He hooked a finger over the bedcovers. "Hold on just one minute . . . are you wearing"— he tugged at the quilt, trying to pull it down—"a nightgown?"

Crud. I'd forgotten all about it.

I didn't own much lingerie. Before Lon, I slept in a T-shirt. After Lon, I mostly slept naked. But this was the first time Jupe had spent the night at my house, and all of my acceptable lounge pants were dirty or at Lon's. I didn't want to be surprised in the middle of the night if the kid couldn't sleep, which is why I was wearing the ugliest nightgown known to human- or demon-kind. The printed design was scattered with cupcakes, hearts, and the word *HUGS!* repeated on a Pepto-Bismol-pink background. Kar Yee gave it to me in college as a prank. Hard to believe at times, but she really did have a sense of humor.

"Cupcakes?" His nose crinkled and he struggled to yank down the covers while I slapped at his fingers. I couldn't have been more embarrassed. This was *so* not helping my ongoing anxiety over our age difference. He knotted his fingers into my sides to tickle me. I jumped and squealed. He redoubled his effort. I tried to buck him off of me, half laughing, half yelling in protest.

Without warning, the door to my bedroom was flung open and slammed against the wall with a loud crack.

A throaty "Hey!" boomed from the open doorway.

Lon and I yelped in surprise.

"Goddammit, Jupe!" Lon bellowed.

"Dad?" Squinting away sleep, he stood in the doorway with his hand over his heart and his shoulders sagging in relief. No shirt, barefoot, army-green drawstring pajama bottoms, his hair a frazzled electric mess. "I thought maybe that mugger from the parking garage had followed us and broken into the house or something."

"Mugger?" Lon said.

I jerked the edge of the quilt up and wrapped it around Lon's hips as he rolled off me, settling against my side. "We didn't get mugged," I said quickly. We *almost* got mugged. Completely different. And Jupe was supposed to keeping quiet about it, the little traitor.

"What are you doing back so soon?" he asked his father.

"I just am," Lon grumbled.

"You were both screaming pretty loud in here. . . ."

"Laughing," I corrected.

"Go away." Lon buried his face in my hair and draped his arm across my waist.

"Wait!" Jupe pleaded. "I've got twelve things to tell you!"

"Twelve? That's twice as many as usual," Lon remarked, pushing my hair out of the way so that he could scoot closer to better share my pillow.

"I've been busy." Jupe shuffled over to the bed and plopped down near our feet. I pictured him lying in bed and counting all twelve things out before he went to sleep. He claimed to struggle with history dates at school, yet he had memorized the original release year for every horror movie in existence and was excruciatingly exact with numbers in his daily life. "And some of it's *really* important," he insisted. "I haven't seen you in three days."

Total guilt trip. Well played, Jupiter.

Lon moaned and consented. "Five minutes."

I braced myself, debating what riveting news he could possibly lead off with. He'd already blown his promise to keep the mugging secret and I wasn't eager to rehash the Snatcher rumors.

"Okay, the number one most important thing: I met the hottest woman in Morella. Her name is Kar Yee, she's Cady's best friend, and she promised to give me her phone number when I turn sixteen."

I should've guessed.

"Number two: this hippie waitress at Tambuku gave me an awesome tiki mug shaped like a mummy. It's worth twenty dollars. Col-*lect*-ible." He'd obviously bought into Kar Yee's promotional scam. "Number three: Cady's crazy next-door neighbor, Mrs. March—"

"Mrs. *Marsh*," I corrected.

"Whatever. More like Mrs. *Hag*."

"Jupe!" we both scolded.

"That's not very nice," I added. Kind of accurate, but still.

"Well, it sure wasn't very nice when she gave us those nasty homemade cookies, and mine had a big orange cat whisker baked into the middle of it. Not a hair, Dad—a fucking *whisker*."

Lon made an appreciative retching noise.

"I wasn't letting him have sugar or anything—we just accepted the cookies to be hospitable and threw them away when we got in the house," I added quickly as I sat up in the bed and slid out from underneath the sheets.

"You mean those Pop-Tarts were sugar free?" Jupe asked seriously. "They sure tast—"

I gritted my teeth and sliced my fingers across my throat repeatedly. "Ix-nay on the op-pay arts-tay."

Something close to a smile crept over Lon's face. The jerk was enjoying seeing me squirm.

Jupe continued. "Anyway, number four: today I became independently wealthy. . . ."

Uh-oh. Time to make a run for it before he ratted me out for the savings account. I mumbled an excuse about getting a drink downstairs in the kitchen and scampered out of the bedroom. As I did, Lon chuckled at my nightgown and made some comment about licking frosting off cupcakes while Jupe continued jabbering. Halfway down the stairs, I heard Lon say, "She did *what*?" So I took my time getting water. About twenty minutes' worth, in fact. But long before their voices died down, my thoughts drifted back to the Snatcher. I wanted to know how Lon really felt about the missing teens, whether he was concerned about Jupe's safety.

On top of all that, I was anxious about meeting Ambrose Dare for the first time. My last experience with the Hellfire Club wasn't something I wanted to repeat. Lon assured me that Dare was made of better stuff than most of the other heathen Hellfire officers, but I didn't know if I totally believed this. Regardless, why in the world would someone like Dare insist on speaking to *me* of all people about these missing kids?

4

Midday sun spilled over Ambrose Dare's perfectly manicured lawn, which Lon and I could just glimpse as we drove onto the elegant estate through wrought iron gates. Gnarled Monterey cypress trees and palms lined a long, curving driveway that occasionally branched off to a small guest villa, gardens, and a pool. We headed to the main house, a multilevel Mission-style home with thick, white stucco walls, arched windows, and a red tile Spanish roof. The grand arcaded entry was studded with curving palmettos and housed a deep-set porch. Underneath its shelter, two rustic church pews flanked the massive wooden entry doors.

A petite housekeeper in a gray uniform led us through a two-story foyer with polished terra-cotta floor tiles, her voice echoing off the high ceiling as we followed. The scent of rosemary wafted from an enclosed atrium in the center of the mansion.

An hour before we'd arrived, Lon dropped the bomb on me that in addition to our meeting, Dare would be hosting a small brunch party during our visit. Casual, he insisted. I seriously doubted that my idea of "casual" jibbed with that of the wealthy La Sirenians who'd be attending. Then again,

Lon had only bothered to upgrade to a nicer pair of jeans and donned a charcoal sport coat over a beloved T-shirt that was older than me and so well worn, the green cotton had faded to a soft gray. He told me that he'd learned a long time ago not to bother trying to please these people.

Dare's atrium was overflowing with food, drink, and a mingling crowd. Money, and lots of it, as far as the eye could see. I glanced down at myself and winced. My fitted black shirt wasn't living up to its enticing "no- iron" promise.

Lon slid a hand around my waist and pulled me closer, probably sensing my anxiety with his empathic mojo. "What's that?" he whispered, feeling the top of the portable eight-inch caduceus I'd stashed inside my thin leather jacket.

"Insurance."

Sure, Dare might be Good Guy of the Year, but a month or so ago, his club members had been prepared to feed Lon to a summoned wild Æthyric demon while considering ways to rape me on the sidelines. One thing I'd learned from all my recent woes was that trust had to be not only earned but also proven, on a regular basis. The Hellfire Club had a long way to go before I would ever trust them again. Not that I ever had. It's hard to put your faith in a cabal of elite demons whose idea of relaxing involves commandeering Incubi and Succubi as entertainment for secret monthly orgiastic parties in caves along the coast.

I scanned the crowded atrium for club members. An older woman who'd tried to feel me up in the Hellfire caves was chatting near a buffet table, and a couple of others looked vaguely familiar. Now, instead of inhaling strange drugs and engaging in group sex, they were transplanted into a Bizarro World setting, eating finger food and discussing city politics while irritatingly smooth jazz drifted from hidden stereo speakers.

"Lon Butler." A too-handsome blond Earthbound about Lon's age stuck out his hand in greeting. His halo was blue. His teeth, bleached. "Where've you been hiding yourself?"

"Mark." Lon flipped into defensive mode, narrowed eyes and stony jaw.

"Talkative as ever, I see." Mark laughed, then slapped Lon on the shoulder before glancing my way. "And you must be his new girl." He smiled like he was getting ready to sell me something and make a fat commission. "I'm Mark. CEO of Dare Energy Solutions."

"Arcadia Bell. Bartender." I declined to shake his hand, crossing my arms over my middle. Last week, some dickish Earthbound in Tambuku shook my hand and made me sick for several minutes, a lame attempt to force me into giving him free drinks. I doubted this guy would sink to something so low, but I didn't know what his knack was. I also didn't like him much.

He shot a wary glance at Lon and immediately evened himself out with a forced chuckle. "That's right," he responded cautiously. "I believe someone mentioned that you owned a wine bar in Morella?"

"Something like that." Tambuku stocked one chardonnay and one cab sauv. I went through a bottle of each per shift, if that. People don't come to tiki bars to drink wine; they come to get plastered on flaming rum and fruit juice, but clearly this cultural phenomenon was below Mark's CEO caste.

When Mark introduced his wife, she hung back and gave Lon a tight smile. A well-toned beauty in her forties, she had glossy black hair that shone under the daylight that poured in from the glass ceiling above. She held a full wineglass in one hand, and on that hand was one of the biggest diamonds I'd ever seen outside of a cartoon. Blister-blue mist swirled inside—a sliver of Mark's halo. Mark had a smaller diamond embedded into his wedding band that was tinged with the green of her halo.

Earthbound couples who could afford it hired a gemplexer when they got engaged, a demon chemist who could siphon off a bit of halo and bend it into certain gemstones. *Very* expensive.

Mark's wife took her time studying me with hooded eyes. Judging. No doubt she saw me as some barely legal gold digger . . . Lon's midlife crisis. Her gaze lingered on my head. For a second, I thought she was staring at my dual-tone, Bride of Frankenstein hair. Strands of bleached platinum white from the nape of my neck were loosely braided into the dark brown bulk that hung down my back. I had hoped wearing it this way would make me look a little older. But Mark's wife couldn't have given two hoots. She was checking out my unusual silver halo as if it marked me as some sort of terrorist in a sea of green- and blue-crowned demons. She'd probably also heard what I did in their Hellfire caves, banishing their incubus sex slaves to the Æthyric plane—an accident, to be fair—and busting up their underground demon mixed–martial-arts ring.

Once her critical assessment of my halo ended, she glanced at Lon and took a step back. It took me a few moments to realize why. Lon's knack. They were moving out of his empathic range, nervous because they knew that *he* knew how they really felt. He'd told me when I first met him that other demons shied away from him when they found out about his ability. He's not the person you want to be around when you have something to hide.

The awkward small talk didn't last long, thank God. A couple of other people said hello, but didn't stop to chat.

When Dare finally walked into the room, I was actually relieved.

"Ah, Miss Bell." His booming voice filled the atrium. Everyone turned. He grasped my hand heartily and whispered, "Our little wolf in sheep's clothing. It's delightful to finally meet you."

Dare was in his early seventies, of average height, physically fit but for a slight paunch around his middle, and completely bald. His dark eyes twinkled as he looked me over. Lon seemed to relax in his presence, so I tried to do the same. They greeted each other, then Lon and I followed Dare out of the atrium to speak in private.

His home office was dark and comfortable, part Spanish baroque, part English drawing room. He encouraged us to take a seat on an antique sofa in front of an unlit fireplace, then settled in a leather wingback across from us. His knees creaked as he sat. "Parts of your body start giving out when you're my age," he admitted while straightening the crease in his dove-gray slacks. "You can take pills for some of them, but others . . . well, you're just screwed."

I smiled in response. "I'm glad to finally have the chance to thank you in person for the caduceus you sent me a few weeks ago." Unlike my others, which were cheap knockoffs, his gift was the real thing, hundreds of years old, with a nice, fat plug of graphite and a small precious stone on the end. Most of my staves were simple poles with the two entwined snakes molded around the top half. Not this one. The staff was intricately carved into the elongated form of the god Mithras, and the snakes were replaced with basilisks, one carved from dark wood, the other pale. The wood was smooth and worn. Practically humming with residual Heka, it was an esoteric collector's dream.

Dare smiled thoughtfully and nodded his head. "As I told Lon, I hope you find it to be an acceptable peace offering for the buffoonery to which you were both subjected on club night last month."

Lon grunted.

"Sure," I said. "As long as you keep David and Spooner the hell away from us, then yes. And, for my part, I apologize for busting up your glass summoning circle."

He shrugged. "We'll have it replaced before the annual solstice celebration in December."

"Nothing says happy holidays like being slaughtered by a pissed-off Æthyric demon in front of a cheering crowd."

Dare tilted his head to the side and held his palms upward, pretending to weigh the air in front of him. "Participation is supposed to be voluntary. It was designed for entertainment, not punishment."

Entertainment, my ass. It was dangerous, is what it was. Summoning Æthyric demons is always risky, but it's downright suicidal if you don't have the skills to keep them leashed. Relying on vermilion-filled glass binding circles is a cheat. Good magicians depend on their skills, not on objects.

"So, Arcadia," Dare said with a gentle smile, "you might be interested to learn that I've known Lon *literally* since the day he was born—visited his parents in the hospital. Lon's father and I were close friends for many years. Dear old Jonathan Butler. I still miss him." His gaze unfocused for a few seconds as he recalled some memory or another. I was beginning to think he might be a bit senile until he spoke up again. "And Jonathan was present for the birth of my son two days later—Mark. You met him and his wife in the atrium."

I blinked away my surprise. "I . . . didn't realize he was, uh, your son."

"Some days I wish he wasn't," Dare replied dryly. "We had a falling-out several years ago. My son is a bit of a prick, you see."

"Oh . . . ?" I didn't know whether to laugh or fidget.

Dare chuckled softly. "It's okay, my dear. If you feel the same way, and I can see that you do, it just means you have good sense. Lon will testify to hating Mark's guts. Sometimes I wish I had switched you two in the hospital," he said to Lon affectionately. "Would've saved myself a hell of a lot of grief."

Lon inclined his chin in answer, nearly smiling, but not quite. He'd obviously heard this joke before.

"Well, it doesn't matter. I'm getting too old to fight, and it's not worth the stress on my wife. For her sake, I made up with Mark recently and gave him the CEO position at my company. The point I'm trying to make is that despite the bad first impression you got of the Hellfire Club, we are, at heart, an extended family.

"All of us have roots in La Sirena," he explained, lounging in his seat. "Roots that stretch to the time the community was founded, after our ancestors fled the Roanoke Colony and settled here. We've taken care of one another for centuries, long before the Hellfire Club ever existed. And even if some of us fight or bicker"—he threw a gentle look to Lon—"or drift away from each other, we still take care of our own. And now we're facing a danger that threatens the core of our community—our children."

I uncrossed my legs and sat up straighter. "The missing kids."

"Yes. Both were children of Hellfire Club members."

"What?" Lon said in surprise. "Rick Chapman's kid this weekend, sure, but—"

"The first was Thomas Jones's boy."

Realization settled over Lon's features. "I haven't seen Tom in years," he admitted. "I didn't even know he had a kid."

Dare slumped in his armchair and swooped an open palm over the top of his bare head. "Tom's kept to himself over the last few years, but he's still one of ours."

"It's certainly a terrible thing," I agreed, "and I'm sorry to hear that they were both part of your . . . community, but I don't understand why you wanted to talk to me about it."

"You've heard the rumors about this whole thing being a replay of the Sandpiper Park Snatcher, yes?"

I nodded.

"I have reason to believe that this madman is still alive and targeting Hellfire children out of revenge."

Goose bumps rushed over my arms as a hollow silence filled the room.

"I'll explain," Dare said. "Thirty years ago, during the original abductions, Lon was just a boy himself—twelve or thirteen, I believe?"

Lon nodded in agreement and absently rested his hand on my knee. It hadn't even crossed my mind that Lon would have lived through the first snatchings. Sometimes I forgot how much older he was than me.

"Anyway, I'm sure you've heard the story. Seven teenagers went missing during the days leading up to Samhain, one taken every day or so, and the last child was abducted on Halloween night. The police chased their tails trying to find the person responsible, just as they're doing now, and the Snatcher was never caught, nor identified."

Dare explained that a month before all of this occurred, he'd been embroiled in a yearlong dispute with a club member named Jesse Bishop, who was challenging the Body, the thirteen ruling officers of the Hellfire Club. Bishop wanted something exclusive that only Body members were allowed—transmutation, a secret initiation spell that made a permanent change to their demonic natures. Members who underwent this spell—like Lon and his ex-wife, Yvonne—were able to shift into a half-human, half-demon form at will. In this state, their demonic abilities increased considerably. But the club limited initiates to thirteen seats at any given time. Until an officer left or died, no one else could undergo the secret spell.

"I was convinced that Bishop wasn't a bad person," Dare said. "Believed that his intentions were good, and he had reasons for wanting the transmutation ability beyond mere power. But the Body stood by its rule. Only thirteen." He smiled at Lon. "Your father persuaded me to put my foot down. We made a final ruling. Bishop left. A month later the abductions started."

"Why would you assume he had anything to do with them?" I asked.

"I didn't at the time. The abductions were frightening—the talk of the town. But after Halloween, the circle of trees was found with the children's names and the kidnappings stopped. It was terrible, but nothing led me to believe Bishop was connected. That is, until a few weeks later. I called him several times to check in, see how he was doing. But I couldn't get him on the phone, so I drove to his house. . . ."

Through a window, Dare observed that a pile of unread mail had collected inside the front door. He became worried that Bishop was dead inside, so he broke into the home and discovered it had been abandoned. The electricity had been shut off—for nonpayment, Dare surmised from the late notices piling up. Bishop's car was gone, but a pot of sludgy coffee sat on the counter with the remnants of moldy food, as if he'd run off in the middle of breakfast. A newspaper on the table was dated ten days before Halloween . . . the day the first teen went missing.

And ten days before Halloween now, I realized.

"But what interested me the most wasn't in the kitchen," Dare said. "It was what I found spread across the living room floor. Stacks of old grimoires and journal pages filled with handwritten notes containing bits of spells. I think he was researching transmutation. Trying to figure out the spell on his own."

"Did he manage it?" Lon asked.

"We wondered at the time. Your father and I searched for him for several months. But it was as if he disappeared without a trace."

"Why would you suspect that he took the kids, though?" I asked.

A pained look crossed Dare's face. It took him a moment to answer. "The children's names were written in his notes. They were cross-referenced with spell elements."

"Jesus." Lon shifted uncomfortably in his seat.

"I think he was experimenting on them with magick," Dare said. "There were notes regarding adolescent Earthbounds being stronger than adults for magical takeover. He called them 'vessels.'"

"All seven kids taken in the eighties were Earthbounds," Lon noted.

"Yes," Dare confirmed. "I think he performed magical experiments on them on Samhain—the veil between earth and the Æthyr is thinnest then, you know. A good time for magick. So that's probably what he's planning again this time. I don't know why it took him so long or where he's been all these years, but he must have failed the first time around—and now he's started up again. It's no coincidence that both kids taken this past week are ours, Lon. It's revenge. All the Hellfire teenagers are moving targets. My grandson, your son . . ."

A clammy chill slithered down my spine. Lon and I looked at each other, and I could see the cracks forming in his defensive facade, the fear behind his eyes.

Not Jupe. I'd be damned before he'd get taken again. I yanked out my phone and checked for my daily flood of texted Jupisms. There were three, the last one fifteen minutes ago. I exhaled in relief.

"He's in social studies right now," Lon murmured.

"School's probably one of the safest places he can be," Dare said, startling us. "The original kids never got snatched from public places. It was always when they were alone, and *always* at night. However, my grandson—Mark's son—goes to Meadow Rue Academy." The private school north of the Village. "Both of the children who went missing are students at the academy, so Mark and his wife are taking extra precautions when they pick him up from school. Even though Jupiter is attending public school, he's still a Hellfire descendant, so I'd advise you to be cautious. Better safe than sorry."

Lon's leg bounced anxiously. Now I knew where Jupe got this nervous tic. I didn't like seeing Lon scared. He was supposed to be the rock in this relationship, not me.

"Mr. Dare?" I asked, pulling myself together. "Did you call us here to warn us?"

"Not exactly. I called to ask for help. Yours, specifically."

"Why?"

"I've heard what you can do, from my club members. Heard what you do in your bar, binding Earthbounds in public."

I stiffened and glanced at Lon. Had Dare heard about my

newly acquired Moonchild ability? Lon promised he would never reveal that secret to anyone, but Spooner had seen me use it in the Hellfire caves to free an incubus. I wasn't ready to rent this ability out. It was a huge unknown—if I began using it, would I go crazy like my parents? Did it have a physical backlash I hadn't yet discovered?—and I needed to figure it out for myself. Which I would. Soon. I just wasn't quite over my parents' betrayal . . . nor the loss of them, if I was being honest.

Dare's words snapped me out of my thoughts. "If the police couldn't find Bishop in the eighties, they're probably not going to find him now. He's had thirty years to tinker with experimental magick. He's out of their league. Probably out of mine, too. But if what I've heard is even half true, then he's not out of *yours*." Dare leaned forward. "Do you know what my demonic ability is, dear? My knack?"

Lon had told me. "Rally," I said quietly. To inspire groups of people and bring them together. An ace up the sleeve for someone in his position, no doubt.

Dare nodded. "I'm getting old. My ability isn't what it once was—not even when I'm transmutated. When I die, my seat in the Hellfire Body will be offered to my family before it's given out to the next member on the waiting list. My wife doesn't want it, so that leaves my son, Mark. And though I'm trying to make amends with him, if he took my place, this club would fall into ruins."

I cleared my throat. "You'll have to forgive me when I say that the Hellfire Club disbanding wouldn't be the worst thing to happen in this town." It would surely cut down on illegal drug use and sexually transmitted diseases.

"See, that's where you're wrong," Dare said. "The Hellfire Club *is* La Sirena. The mayor, city council, and all the major business leaders that funnel money into this community are all Hellfire members. We aren't just decadents, Ms. Bell. We are the pillars holding up this town. Did you know that the largest population of Earthbound demons in the entire world lives within a sixty-mile radius of La Sirena?"

When I lived in central Florida as a teen, I'd run into a random Earthbound once or twice a week. Later, when I moved to Seattle after my parents and I split and I was on the run, I saw Earthbounds every day. But after college, when Kar Yee and I moved here to California? As many Earthbounds as humans. Still . . . the largest demon population in the world? I wondered if this was true, or if he was just bullshitting.

"My point being," he said after a pause, "the Hellfire Club is far more influential than you're aware. And I'd like to live long enough to see my grandson grow up to be a better person than his father, so that I can rest in peace knowing that my life's work wasn't a colossal waste of time. But I can't do that if Bishop abducts the boy. And likewise, none of it will matter if Bishop's able to successfully complete the transmutation spell on himself and decides to massacre the entire club."

I started to speak. He cut me off.

"Listen to me, Arcadia Bell," Dare said firmly. "I'm asking you this as the leader of this community, and as a family man. I'm also asking honestly, without using my ability to influence you. But if I wanted to . . ."

His eyes narrowed and he trailed off. The veins in his hands stood rigid on the surface of his papery skin. The air rippled, and just as I realized what was happening, a small groan flew from Dare's pursed lips as he transmutated right in front of us. His ears elongated to points, his brow shifted forward. Two small ridges plumped up the sides of his head, right above his ears. They didn't quite make horns—just bumpy bands of thickened flesh with deepened furrows above them. But the most impressive change was the halo, which morphed from a luminous green cloud to a fiery oval that flickered high above the center of his head.

Like an echo, Lon shot up out of his seat and put himself between us. If Dare's transmutation was a ripple, Lon's was a storm. It thundered in my ears and threw my balance off. His halo flamed up into a golden pyre, brighter and bigger than Dare's, dancing high around the majestic pair of spiraling auburn horns that nearly took my breath away every time I saw them.

The men glared at each other like snarling dogs. Hello, testosterone. I slipped my hand inside my jacket and touched my caduceus, just in case. Not the best weapon, but at least it wouldn't explode in my hand like the pencil in the parking garage when Jupe and I were getting almost-mugged. And even though I didn't have time to draw a proper binding triangle, I could still shock the hell out of Dare, if need be. I was wary but not excessively worried, which was probably foolish. You know you've been spending *way* too much time with demons when two of them standing before you transmutated and ready to fight were preferable to a weak human mugger afraid of his own damn shadow.

"Now, Lon—" Dare started, his voice slightly altered by his transformation.

"Out of respect, I'm giving you a warning," Lon rumbled, his own voice noticeably deeper, dangerous enough to raise the hairs on the back of my neck. "If you even *think* about charming her into doing your bidding, I'll stop you—family or not."

A spark of affection lit me up from the inside. Was it wrong that I found his show of loyalty toward me incredibly romantic? Probably. I chastised myself and pushed away those thoughts—he could pick them right out of my head when he was transmutated.

"All right, son," Dare said. The tension between them calmed. I peeked around Lon's legs, watching as Dare let go of the transmutation and shifted back to human. He closed his eyes and held the side of his head as if in pain, then exhaled dramatically. "Give an old man a break," he said between breaths. "I was just trying to prove a point."

Lon stood still for several seconds as flames leapt around his head. He was listening to Dare's thoughts. Whatever he heard must have satisfied him, because a few seconds later, he shifted down. The spiraling horns and pyrotechnic halo faded and disappeared, as if they were never there. Clash of the Earthbounds avoided.

I released my caduceus and removed my hand from my jacket as Lon ran a hand through his hair where his horns had just been. He often complained that they left a strange itchy sensation behind, like a phantom limb.

"Okay," I said after a few moments. "Now that we're all best friends and trusting each other again, what exactly is it that you want me to do?"

Dare grimaced and shook his head, probably fighting off a post-shift headache. Then he looked at me very seriously. "I want you to find Jesse Bishop and stop him from taking our kids. I want you to trap him and bind him with magick, and then I want you to banish him to the Æthyr."

5

Executioner.

That's what Dare wanted from me. The same role I'd been forced to play with my parents. Icy shock froze my tongue as this realization dredged up guilty feelings that I logically shouldn't have, but did. Damn them for forcing me into that role, and damn Dare for asking me to repeat it.

I didn't say yes, but I couldn't very well say no, either. Dare thanked me, nonetheless, assuming my silence was agreement. I guess it was. Who was selfish enough to refuse to help innocent kids? I might have been a few months ago . . . before my parents' betrayal. Before Lon. Before Jupe.

But things had changed, and so had I, I supposed.

Lon and I exited Dare's house with a shoe box of paperwork in tow, filled with information he'd amassed over the years regarding Jesse Bishop. Unfortunately, Dare had burned most of the incriminating papers that he'd found in Bishop's home thirty years ago—the stuff that matched up the children's names with spell elements—so all we had now was a fairly useless stack of Hellfire Club photos, a few yellowed newspaper clippings about the Sandpiper Park Snatcher case, and a list of the original missing children with addresses.

At the very bottom, below the paperwork, was a blue velvet ring box. Inside lay a small metal key about two inches long on a tarnished silver chain with a broken clasp. Dare said he'd found it at Bishop's house beneath the kitchen table after they'd discovered Bishop missing. Dare and Lon's father had searched the place for anything it could've possible fit, but came up empty.

None of this seemed useful in helping us locate Bishop, and to add to our frustration, Dare suspected the man had done some sort of cloaking magick in the '80s, so he might be hard to find using normal methods today. Normal methods for *me* meant constructing a magical servitor—a roving ball of energy that fetched information. However, the last time I used a servitor to find another magician, it came back and bit me on the ass, and that's when Jupe got hurt and kidnapped. I didn't want to take that chance again until I was able to teach myself more advanced servitor techniques. Better to exhaust other methods first.

Lon put his SUV in gear and jerked the wheel to head down the long driveway. We stopped in front of the entrance gate and waited for one of Dare's employees to open it and let us through.

"You didn't tell Dare about my Moonchild ability, right?" I said.

The iron gates ground open in a slow arc as Lon fished his valrivia case out of his jacket pocket and speared me with an irritated glance. That was a no. A small relief.

I took one of the hand-rolled herbal cigarettes he offered. "I just don't understand why he assumes I can banish an Earthbound. No one can. Unless you can find a way to travel in time to the Roanoke Colony," I said with sarcasm. "Then maybe you could locate the magician who conjured your demon ancestors from the Æthyr and shoved them into their original human bodies."

Lon lit up and passed me the lighter. I cracked the window as he headed out of the estate and onto the main road. "Seems to me you've banished all sorts of things you haven't conjured lately."

Sure, things in their original Æthyric bodies, like imps. Not humans or Earthbound demons in human bodies. Then again, my human parents had been sent into the Æthyr . . . but I hadn't banished them outright—an Æthyric demon named Nivella took them. I just gave Nivella permission. It occurred to me, of course, that I might bargain with another Æthyric into taking Bishop if we were able to find him, but I didn't say it out loud.

"Earthbounds can't be separated," I argued stubbornly. "Your demon nature has integrated with your human DNA. It would be like asking me to separate soul from body. Unless I could piece together some sort of antispell for the original Roanoke Invocation—which has been lost for hundreds of years—it's a no-go. I've got skills, but I'm not God."

"All I'm saying is that you don't really know the extent of the Moonchild ability. You haven't even used it since San Diego."

I mumbled a noncommittal response. Call me a chicken, I don't give a damn. My ability was unnaturally created by two homicidal maniacs masquerading as parents. What good could come of using it? Too much magick could make even the gentlest of magicians go nutso, and I had crazy genes working against me. If I started experimenting with the Moonchild ability, I was worried some sort of insanity clock would start ticking inside me. How long would it be before it went off? A month? A year? A decade? My parents weren't even fifty when they started to go banana-boat. For all I knew, I might not even make it to thirty.

"I can do magick the old-fashioned way just fine," I finally said.

He grunted—something I interpreted to mean "We'll see about that." He dropped the subject. "We need to find Bishop first."

"Maybe there's someone in La Sirena who knew him back then," I suggested. "That might be a good place to start."

"I just want to get Jupe home first." Lon swerved out of a bicyclist's path while trying to manipulate his cell phone.

"Stop," I complained. "I'll do it."

I got out my phone and sent Jupe a message: WE ARE PICKING YOU UP TODAY OUT FRONT. It was 2:30; Lon's housekeepers wouldn't have left the house to get Jupe from school yet. I'd call them and tell them not to bother today.

Jupe's reply came almost instantly: SWEET!!!! TONIGHT IS MOVIE NIGHT #3, DONT FORGET.

Groan. A few days ago, he'd emailed Lon and me a list of twenty "must-see" movies to watch before Halloween and pressured me to plan my work schedule around the monster marathon.

"He's okay?" Lon asked, trying to hide his anxiety as he strained for a peek at my phone.

"Yep. I hope you're ready for *Gore-met: Zombie Chef from Hell.*"

Lon didn't laugh. Horror isn't as appealing when it's happening in your own life.

Though it was somewhat comforting to listen to Jupe's account of his day as we drove from La Sirena Junior High to their place, it wasn't enough to stop my mind from wandering to Dare's request. Lon's either, I guess, because he kept glancing at me while Jupe spiritedly yammered away from the backseat.

It took us fifteen minutes to reach the ocean cliffs at the edge of La Sirena where they lived, another five to climb the winding road up the mountain. Towering redwoods, pines, and cypress trees blocked out the October sun until we ascended to the very top. Lon owned ten acres of prime Big Sur coastal land: part hilly forest, part clifftop beauty, and a short stretch of rocky beach about a quarter of a mile drop below it all. Amanda, in full-blown gossip mode, once told me that it was some of the most expensive real estate in the country. All I knew was that it was lush and beautiful and private, and that I'd spent so much time there recently, it was starting to feel like home.

The house stood in a cleared section of land overlooking the blue Pacific, a blocky modern home with long horizontal lines, stackstone walls, and enormous plate-glass windows. Expensive and stylish, but not showy. I liked the way the stone and wood made it seem as if it was an organic part of the land.

I also liked the acre-sized ring of stones that we crossed to get there—Lon's house ward, the same one that he'd helped me build around my house, strengthened with strong protective magick. It kept out imps, potential robbers, and any other miscellaneous intruders. Most people intending harm wouldn't be able to cross the ward. Anyone strong enough to manage it would be dropped to their knees by a debilitating, high-pitched noise, and we'd be alerted.

As the car's tires crunched over the circular gravel driveway in front of Lon's house, I spotted two figures with aqua halos standing together at the front doors. Mr. and Mrs.

Holiday lived in a small house at the edge of Lon's seaside property. When his parents died nine years ago—just before his divorce—he hired them full-time to help take care of Jupe and tend to the house and land.

I was a little shocked the first time I met them. "Mr." and "Mrs." were, in actuality, two women in their late sixties. They'd been together for forty years and married in the Netherlands before it was legal in the States. Jupe was the one responsible for nicknaming them Mr. and Mrs. when he was younger. They found it endearing, so it stuck.

"Oh, damn," Mrs. Holiday called out to Jupe as we exited the SUV. "I was hoping you'd been kidnapped again. Then I could set fire to your room and be done with cleaning it."

"Dream on, woman."

"Jupe," Lon complained crossly.

"Dream on, old lady," Jupe amended with a teasing smile.

Mrs. Holiday tried to swat at him, but missed when a dog barreled from behind her and lunged for Jupe. Foxglove was a sleek chocolate Lab with a purple collar, and she spent half her time patrolling the clifftop property, the other half trailing Jupe.

"Managed to survive the school day, Jupiter?" Mr. Holiday inspected Jupe's face while her partner reached for his backpack. They sported similar short, silvery hairdos and looked a bit like Martha Stewart circa 1995, dressed in khakis and billowing, long-sleeved shirts with the collars extended.

"Where's Mr. Piggy?" Jupe asked as Foxglove gave him one last lick on the cheek.

"Probably burrowed inside the garbage dump you call a dirty clothes pile," Mr. Holiday said.

I glared at Jupe. "He's loose?" The last time Jupe let my hedgehog roam free in their house, Lon stepped on a shed quill with his bare feet. He was not happy.

"I closed him up in his crate before school, I swear!" Jupe's eyes darted between me and Mr. Holiday.

"He must've picked the lock with his tiny claws," Mr. Holiday suggested dryly.

"I don't think he's gone far," Mrs. Holiday added. "He seems to enjoy the smell of your soiled underwear, and God knows there are plenty of pairs scattered around your bed."

"God, Mrs. Holiday!" Jupe snatched the backpack out of her hand. "Do you enjoy embarrassing me?"

"I live for it, darling," she answered, gripping the sides of his face long enough to plant a kiss on his nose before he squirmed away and ran inside.

Mr. Holiday waited until he was out of earshot, then turned to Lon. "Anything we should know about your visit to Mr. Dare?"

He crossed his arms over his chest and kicked a chunk of gravel. "Both of the kids taken were Hellfire."

Mr. and Mrs. Holiday murmured in surprise. They knew about the Hellfire Club. They weren't members themselves, and I don't think they quite knew everything that went on during their monthly bacchanales inside the Hellfire caves, but they knew about Lon's transmutation ability.

"Do you remember a Hellfire member named Jesse Bishop?" Lon asked. "He disappeared after the kids were taken thirty years ago."

Mr. Holiday thought for a moment. "Doesn't ring a bell."

"For me, either," her partner agreed. "Why?"

"Dare wants Cady and me to find out if he's still alive— wants us to track him down, but didn't give us much to go on."

Much? Try anything. Dare's box was full of useless paperwork.

"Well," Mr. Holiday said, "if the man was a Hellfire

member, you might try looking through your father's things. Your mother always complained that he could fill a warehouse with all the garbage he hoarded."

Lon grunted. "That's not a bad idea."

Jupe's muffled voice called from within the house. It sounded like he said, "I found him." I hoped that meant my hedgie hadn't been eaten by the dog.

"Where do you keep your dad's stuff?" I asked.

"In the Village. If we leave now, we'll be back before dinner." He lifted a brow at Mr. Holiday. "Can you make sure he doesn't leave the house ward?"

"If you'd let me install that padlock on his bedroom door like I wanted, we wouldn't have to worry about the ward."

The corners of Lon's mouth curled. "Don't tempt me."

Lon's mother died of cancer around the time that he and his then-wife, Yvonne, were splitting up. His father died a few months later, of loneliness, Lon thought: cause of death was never determined. His parents weren't rich exactly, but they had a respectable amount of property, including the plot where Lon's house was built. They also owned a couple hundred acres of farmable land outside the city limits, which Lon sold, and his parents' home in the Village, which he didn't. The plum-colored Victorian house sat on a quiet block, snug between two other newer homes that would've dwarfed it if it weren't for the trees standing between the properties. Their extensive canopy enveloped the home, adding to the privacy that a tall iron fence provided.

Four gas-burning lamps bordered the crumbling sidewalk, and another hung near the painted front door. The fence locked behind us with a weary squeak as we headed inside.

"I keep the utilities on," Lon said as my eyes scanned the pale light glowing through the covered first-story window. "Most of the residents in this neighborhood know it's empty, but I don't want it to look abandoned and vulnerable to prowlers."

"You grew up in this house?"

"Yeah."

Kind of spooky, if you asked me. Like an overgrown gingerbread cottage with lacy decorative trim around the eaves, spindly banisters, and crescent moons punched out of the black shutters—the complete opposite of Lon's modern house. Like other Victorians on the block, his childhood home fit right in with the fairy-tale vibe of the Village, but the fact that it was empty gave me the creeps. When we stepped inside, the dry, dusty smell that permeated the walls didn't help, nor did the creaking wood floorboards.

Most of the furniture had been donated to charity, and what little that remained was covered in sheets. I sneezed several times as we headed up three flights of stairs to a locked attic door.

He clicked on a bare bulb that hung from the rafters. I looked around. It wasn't a finished attic. A ten-by-twenty strip of plywood had been hammered down over ceiling joists and exposed pink insulation, creating a runway of sorts leading away from the stairs. Boxes and wooden crates lined both sides.

"Over here," Lon instructed, leading me to a separate stack of boxes. We sat on the plywood walkway and sifted though several boxes of paperwork, mostly photos and old Hellfire bulletins. The esoteric organization I grew up in, Ekklesia Eleusia, more commonly known in the occult community as E∴E∴, printed up bulletins that were passed out during classes and meet-and-greets. They mostly advertised things like equinox energy raisings, rituals for members moving up a grade in the order, and the monthly performance of something called the Sophic Mass: think Catholic mass with a naked priestess on the alter while a quasisexual magical play is being reenacted. It's more pompous and less interesting than it sounds. Drinking wine and gagging on a dry homemade wafer while staring at untrimmed pubic hair and sagging breasts isn't exactly my idea of holy—and you don't even want to know what's in the wafer.

The Hellfire bulletins, however, were a thousand times more amusing. I thumbed through a colorful stack of them from the 1970s and '80s. They featured inventive Masonic-like symbols, weird drug-fueled poetry, interpretive cartoons of demons in silly Kama Sutra positions, and local restaurant reviews based on the sexual attractiveness of their servers. I noted that the chain fondue restaurant in the Village rated only two smiling penises, but the Alps Fondue Chalet inside Brentano Gardens got an enthusiastic five. That was an awful lot of proverbial dick—we were *so* going to eat there.

While leafing through one of the old bulletins, a small picture slipped from the pages. It was a group photo of three men and four children. Three smudged names were written on the back: Dare, Merrimoth, Butler. I flipped it over and recognized Dare and a teenager who clearly was his son, Mark. Standing beside him was Lon's dad, Jonathan Butler. Lon definitely favored his father in the broad build of his shoulders and the way his eyes were eternally creased into slits. And speak of the devil . . . Jonathan had his arm around a wickedly attractive teenager whose light brown hair fell halfway down his back. He was skinny and long, his arms tight with sinewy, lean muscle. No trace of facial hair. A Black

Sabbath *Heaven and Hell* T-shirt clung to his torso. He scowled at the camera like he was trying to break it. A total badass.

"*Lo-o-on,*" I purred, biting my bottom lip as I flipped the photo around in my fingers to show him.

He tried to take it away from me, but I wouldn't let him have it.

"You were all kinds of adorable," I said.

He grunted.

"How old were you?"

"Fifteen, I think."

"Fifteen?" I repeated in disbelief, turning the photo back around to inspect it. "Were you still a virgin at that point?"

"Mostly." A playful smile tugged up one side his mouth.

"Man oh man, my fifteen-year-old self would have been all over that."

He snorted. "When I was fifteen, you weren't even born."

I stuck my tongue out, then fought him off while pressing the photo to my breast as he tried to pry it out of my hands again. "Stop! This picture makes my heart flutter. Can we take it with us, please?"

"There's several photo albums' worth of the same thing at home," he said.

"You promise?"

He nodded and gave up the fight, returning his attention to the pile of papers in front of him. "I can't believe Jupe hasn't forced them on you already."

"Any from the time you were in the seminary?" I asked.

"That sexy Jesus thing again?" he teased without looking up. "You're a filthy girl, you know that?"

"I'm being serious."

He grunted, then answered after a time. "Maybe. My hair was short in the seminary."

I tried to imagine a devious nineteen-year-old Lon with short hair, playing at being pious. What a shock it must have been for his instructors to realize what Lon really was.

I slipped the photo into the stack of bulletins as he stared at a photocopy he'd found inside a file folder. A strange look bloomed on his face. "Read this list and tell me what's wrong," he said as he handed the piece of paper to me.

It was a wrinkled copy of a handwritten journal entry dated October 29, the year the first group of kids was taken. A few things were illegible, crossed out. Seven names were written in bold caps. "Jesus. These are the original kids' names. Do you think this is a copy from Bishop's journal? I thought Dare burned all that stuff."

"Could be. What about the last name on the list?"

"Cindy Brolin . . ." I read. "Wait, that's supposed to be—"

"Janice Grandin."

He was right. According to old newspaper articles we'd perused in the banker box Dare had given us, Janice Grandin was the last kid taken, not this Cindy person.

"The other names are all the same, right?" I asked.

"Yeah, I think so."

"Did you know Cindy Brolin?"

"No. I didn't know any of the kids. I went to private school. Back then, all the missing kids were from the public school."

A reverse of what was happening now. After a few moments of staring at the piece of paper, I noticed something. "Janice Grandin was taken on October thirty-first. This was dated two days before."

"Huh." Lon pushed the box away and looked at me, his brow knotted. "If Cindy Brolin was originally on the Snatcher's wish list, what happened to her?"

6

Moved out of town.

Cindy Brolin apparently left La Sirena shortly after the original seven teens disappeared. Lon made some phone calls to the La Sirena police, but they didn't have a crumb about this mystery girl in their records. She was never part of the original investigation, and there was no mention of her in any of the newspaper clippings—nothing online either.

We almost chalked her up as a dead end until a broader search uncovered one Cynthia W. Brolin listed at a downtown address in Morella. Before my 4:00 shift the following day, Lon followed me into the city in his SUV and parked at my house. We took my car and headed downtown.

Morella is a sprawling, flat city. La Sirena's coastal cliffs are only about ten crow-flying miles to the west, and the Santa Lucia Range cradles the land to the southeast. On a clear, smog-free day, you can see beautiful crinkled mountain peaks stretching around the city in the distance. Most days, however, all you see is concrete and steel.

Cindy didn't live in the best part of town. On her street, we drove past abandoned storefronts plastered with sun-bleached posters for psychic phone readings, two sketchy

Circle Ks, and a rim shop with barred windows and doors. If I thought the Metropark garage near Tambuku was bad, the one attached to her high-rise apartment building was downright sinister. It reminded me that I needed to rework the temporary wards on my car. And maybe it was time to start investing in something more longterm on the underside of my hood.

We found a space on the second level. After parking, I reached over Lon's knees to the glove compartment box and pulled out a silver plastic angel that fit in the palm of my hand.

"A wind-up parking goddess?" Lon read from the discarded packaging.

"She doesn't wind anymore. I stripped out her insides and stuffed her with powdered angelica root." On the flat base was a simple warding sigil. Nothing fancy, but effective. I dug out a piece of gum from my purse and chewed it until it was soft. Mumbling a quick spell, I pressed the chewed gum, now chock full of Heka-rich saliva, over the sigil. A brief wave of dizziness passed over me. I exhaled slowly until it passed, then stuck the newly charged angel on my dash. "It won't last long," I explained, "but I'd rather not get my car out of impound after hoodlums decide to take it on a joyride."

Lon narrowed his eyes at my low-rent magick and made a little noise of appreciative surprise. "You're kind of turning me on."

"Just wait until you see what I can do with a balloon and some consecrated Abramelin oil," I said with a wink.

His low laughter reverberated through the garage as we exited the car.

In the '70s, Cindy's building had probably been a swinging bachelor's dream home. Orange shag carpet lined the lobby and cracked mirrored tile ran down the center of the walls. Whatever it was in its glory, it was just depressing and dirty now.

Cindy's apartment was on the sixteenth floor. Lon and I exchanged leery glances as we paused in front of her door, listening to the sounds of daytime TV roaring from the apartment to the right, and an angry domestic dispute in the one on the left. Stale cigarette smoke and rancid cooking oil permeated the hallway. A dark spot the size of a basketball stained the carpet near our feet.

After ringing the doorbell twice, the door finally creaked open. Female eyes peeped through two cheap chain locks.

"Cindy?" I asked.

"Yeah?" Her voice was wary.

"Hi," I said brightly. "My name is Cady and this is Lon. We're from La Sirena Historical Preservation. We're writing a book about the history of schools in La Sirena, and we've been tracking down alumni for interviews. We were wondering if you had a few minutes to talk to us about La Sirena Junior High?" Probably not the best lie we could come up with, but it was better than our original plan, to pose as cops.

As if it would help prove our story, I held up a copy of the society's book about coastal farming in the 1800s, taken from Lon's library. Why Lon owned it, I had no idea. He owned a lot of strange books—and I'm not talking about the ones on demon summoning, either; his avid interest in irrigation and composting was far more peculiar, if you asked me.

Confusion swept over the sliver of Cindy's face peeping through the door crack. "I haven't even stepped foot in La Sirena in thirty years."

"Even better," I chirped, smiling as big as I could. "You'll have a different perspective. We've talked to about ten people so far, and the interview only takes five minutes."

"I don't really remember much—"

"You'll get credited in print," I suggested.

"No. Sorry." She started to close the door.

"Or you can be completely anonymous," Lon offered quickly.

The door stilled.

"It would mean a lot to us if you could help us out," I added. "We drove all the way out here."

She blinked at us for several seconds, giving my silver halo a suspicious glance, then shut the door and slid both chains off the locks. When the door reopened, a thin woman with dyed red hair, a dark green halo, and leathery skin stood in front of us. Dressed in a blue Starry Market shirt with a red name tag, Cindy gestured for us to come inside.

Her small apartment was cluttered with small porcelain figurine animals with big eyes: owls, cats, and dogs lined cheap brass étagères along the walls. Two variegated spider plants hung from beaded macramé holders, blocking the view from a single dirty window.

"Hope we're not catching you on your way to work," I said, nodding at her name tag as we sat down on her couch. "We'll only be a second."

"No, I'm just getting home. I usually work nights, but I had to pull a double."

"Night shifts for me too," I said, hoping to make some sort of connection. "My day job is a night job—bartender."

This seemed to put her at ease. She nodded and sat down. "Working nights is exhausting."

"Sure is," I confirmed.

"So what do you want to know?" she asked as she whipped out a red leather cigarette pouch. After popping the clasp, she paused and asked an obligatory, "You don't mind?"

before tugging her lighter out of a small pocket. We didn't, but I was surprised by the scent of tobacco smoke. Not many Earthbounds preferred it over valrivia.

After a prompt, she talked reservedly about the elementary school she attended as a child. We weren't really interested in that, of course, but I encouraged her to reminisce, trying to loosen her up. But once we moved on to junior high, any progress we'd made immediately receded. I worried that we'd never get to the Snatcher, so I pushed a little harder.

"You were attending junior high when your family moved here to the city?" I asked.

She paused, then nodded. "I was fourteen at the time. Ninth grade."

"When was that, year-wise?"

"Early eighties," she said, dropping her eyes. "Can't remember exactly."

"I bet it was hard to leave friends behind."

She shrugged. "I didn't have a lot of friends."

"Me either when I was that age," I said. This was true, but my attempt at solidarity didn't even register. "So . . . why did you move?"

She blew out a cone of smoke and ran her fingers over a crocheted doily that covered her chair's armrest. "My father got a job in Morella."

"Do you happen to remember the month you left?" Lon asked.

Cindy gave him a strange look, then crossed her legs and blinked rapidly. "It was in the fall, I think. Why would that matter?"

"Just judging from your age"—which was the same as Lon's? Dear God, he'd fared better—"you may have lived in

La Sirena during a well-known child abduction case. Do you remember hearing about the Sandpiper Park Snatcher?"

Lon pressed his thigh against mine in warning, but I could already tell by the way Cindy's shoulders tensed that I'd pushed too far. She sniffed a couple of times, then wiped away a bead of sweat from her brow. "What does this have to do with historical . . . what did you say you belonged to?"

"Preservation Society. We're interested in how the cultural climate of the town influenced the experience of attending school there." Pretty good improvisation, I thought, but not enough to quell her nerves. Her countenance shifted from wary to full-on suspicious.

Lon immediately took over the interrogation, attempting to calm her with a softer voice. "All of us have memories that we'd prefer to forget, but sometimes good things can come from remembering the past—even the bad parts. Your memories might help someone today. Were you aware that two kids went missing last week in La Sirena?"

Her breathing stilled momentarily. She blinked several times. "No, I hadn't heard. I don't keep up with La Sirena anymore."

"The police think it might be the same person taking kids again," he said.

The hand holding her cigarette shook. Ashes fell onto the crocheted armrest, but she didn't notice. We all sat in silence for several seconds, then Cindy suddenly stubbed her cigarette and stood. "Look, I'm sorry, but I can't talk anymore. I've got to go to work, so you need to leave."

"But you said you just got home from work—"

"I'm tired!" she shouted. Her hands were shaking badly now, and she backed up to the window.

"We didn't mean to upset you," I said quickly. "We don't have to talk about that. Let's talk about something else."

She shot me a steely look. "Get out, or I'm calling the police."

Lon picked up his farming book, handed me my purse, and pushed me toward the door. Clearly he was reading Cindy's emotions and knew that we weren't going to get anything else out of her. He dug inside his jacket pocket and retrieved a small blue business card. "If you change your mind and want to talk—"

She refused the card and pointed toward the exit. "Get out. Now."

The door slammed behind us right as we made it into the hallway. Locks clicked and chains slid into place. We stared at the door for several moments, then walked to the elevator in silence.

Disappointment and frustration flooded my thoughts as I watched a hobbled elderly woman using a walker at the opposite end of the dim hallway. Cindy definitely knew something about the original abductions. More than something. "You read her feelings. Tell me what you think," I said.

Lon pressed the elevator button and pocketed his business card. "She was scared out of her mind. Someone wouldn't be that afraid just casually remembering a town terror from childhood."

"Someone would be terrified, however, if they'd encountered the town terror," I said.

Lon nodded. "She was on the original list and was replaced at the last minute. She could've been captured by the Snatcher and either escaped or was released."

"If that's true, why didn't she go to the police?"

"Too scared, maybe? I'll tell you what, though—she was lying about her father getting a job. My guess is that her folks moved away to get her out of town and protect her from the Snatcher . . . maybe also to spare her from being in the public spotlight."

"If any of that's true, then she might know stuff, Lon—where the Snatcher took them the first time, what he did, what he said. We've got to get her to talk. She might be the only person alive with firsthand knowledge of all this."

"She won't talk," Lon said shaking his head definitively. "We scared her, and she doesn't trust us. If we want to get information out of her, we're probably going to have to use magick—maybe one of your medicinals."

I grimaced. "That seems icky. If she's been through some sort of torture, I don't want to traumatize her again."

Lon sighed, heavy and deep. "You're right. Maybe we can come up with a better way. In the meantime, I'm thinking we should find a death dowser."

"A what?"

"An Earthbound who can find dead bodies."

"Dead bodies . . . You want to find the original group of kids?"

"I don't *want* to, but it might help. Might lead to Bishop or give us some clues. The bodies of the original kids aren't at Sandpiper Park—we know that much. Police dug up the whole park looking for them. So if they aren't there . . ."

"Then maybe wherever they are will lead us to Bishop," I finished. "But what if they aren't dead? What if they're alive somewhere and have had their memories stripped or something?"

"It's possible, but unlikely. But we have to try, and a death dowser would help. Earthbounds with that knack are extremely hard to find, though. Haven't heard of one in La Sirena, so we'll need to put some feelers out here in Morella."

And by "we" he meant *me*. Seeing hundreds of Earthbounds walk in and out of Tambuku every week, you'd think that I'd have heard about somebody. I strained to recall any customers who'd mentioned a knack like this in the past. Though I was coming up blank, I could, however, think of one person who might be able to help track someone down. And unless hell froze over, I'd see him later tonight at the bar.

7

My shift dragged. During a lull, I found myself staring at a sign behind the bar. Two hooks on the top held changeable plastic numbers, and the bottom read ___ MORE DAYS TILL HALLOWEEN in orange and black script. Since it was after midnight, and therefore officially a new day, I swapped out the 9 for an 8. Eight days remaining until Halloween, nine until All Saints' Day, and three since the second kid went missing. My mind kept churning up images of Cindy Brolin and how she acted when we brought up the recent disappearances. She looked so . . . haunted. What did she know, and how could we persuade her to tell us?

As I was pondering this, a regular entered the bar, his arrival announced by the squawk of the motion-sensor toucan.

Bob.

Just the Earthbound I wanted to see. Well, the Earthbound I was *forced* to see every bloody night I worked. With slicked-back dark hair and an endless supply of short-sleeved Hawaiian shirts—tonight's was blue, with Sailor Jerry–style pinup girls—Bob waved to a few other regulars before bellying up to the bar. I prepped his drink before he got there: a Singapore Sling with extra Cherry Heering. If I needed an important favor from any of the other regulars, I might have considered slipping in a drop of one of the magical medicinals that I kept hidden in a small compartment behind the bar, a little something to make them more compliant. Bob, however, was my number one fan. No push needed. A few weeks ago, he was depressed for days when I told him I was serious about Lon.

"Cadybell, Cadybell, trap me in your sweet summer spell," Bob said dramatically as he spun toward me on the barstool. He drummed his hands on the bamboo edge, then dug into a wooden bowl of rice crackers.

"It's autumn, you know. Not summer," I said. "You need a new poem."

He offered up a lopsided grin in response. One of Bob's eyes was a wee bit lazy. You didn't notice it right away; it was only after chatting with him for a couple of minutes that you realized something just didn't quite focus on you. Even so, it was his bulbous, red drunkard's nose that stole all the attention.

He wasn't the easiest guy to look at, and he was mildly irritating to talk to. But he seemed to know just about every Earthbound in Morella, and I trusted him. After two years of hearing about the minutiae of his daily life, it was kinda hard not to.

"Bobby boy," I drawled affectionately, laying it on thick as I poured his drink from the shaker into a hurricane glass. "I've got a weird, yet extremely important favor to ask."

His grin faded as he glanced from side to side, making sure I wasn't talking to some other Bob. "Really?"

"It's on the down low," I said, putting a silent finger to my lips.

He leaned low over the bar and spoke in a soft, conspiratorial voice. "Anything, Cady. Name it."

"I need to employ the services of a death dowser. Ever heard of one?"

A couple of seconds ticked by until he finally answered. "Umm . . . yeah, I know a guy."

Good old Bob. For a moment there, I'd wondered if he was going to hold out on me. "Is he reliable? He can really find dead bodies?"

"Yeah, I think so."

Better sweeten the pot, I thought. He was a sucker for freebies, so I quickly constructed a fruit extravaganza on an extralong umbrella skewer—lime wedges, cherries, orange segments, and four pineapple slices—and settled it horizontally across the rim of the glass.

"O-o-oh," he said appreciatively, holding out both hands to cradle the ridiculously top-heavy concoction.

"Tell me more about this guy."

"The death dowser hasn't done any work for me personally." He pulled fruit off the umbrella and popped it in his mouth as he reached for the right words. "He's a little, well, out there. Not exactly someone you'd want to take home to Mom, you know?"

I washed my sticky hands at the bar sink. "I don't care about that. Is he good?"

"People say he has skills. He brags that the Morella police have paid him under the table a couple of times to find bodies. I can't verify that, but I did hook him up with someone a few months ago, and they said he completed the job."

"Awesome. Can you set up a meeting? It needs to be fast."

"How fast?"

"Every day counts."

He slurped his drink. Pale pink foam stuck to his lips.

"How 'bout later tonight?" he finally asked, wiping his mouth on the back of his hand.

"Really? Yeah, absolutely."

"I'll make a phone call. He's a night owl. Has a couple of side businesses. . . ." Bob's mouth puckered slightly. I probably should've taken note of this at the time and asked more questions, but I didn't. "Anyway," he continued, "I'm sure he'll agree to meet. He doesn't live far from here. Maybe ten minutes? He's skittish about visitors, but he trusts me. I can take you there when your shift is over."

The last thing I wanted to do was tool around the city with Bob in the wee hours of the morning, but I put my feelings aside and merely said, "I'm counting on you."

That's all he needed. His good eye fixed on me with saint-like devotion. "I won't let you down, Cady."

I finished up all my closing duties and locked up the bar around 2:30. Bob offered to drive, but I declined, knowing exactly how much alcohol he'd consumed the past couple of hours. He wasn't drunk—I'd never seen him cross the line into sloppy—but no need to chance it.

He gave me directions along the way. The drive was a *lot* longer than he'd promised, nearly a half hour, and Bob fidgeted in the passenger seat the entire way. Turned out the dowser lived on the outskirts of Waxtown, a former industrial neighborhood in southeast Morella that was in the middle of a painful gentrification. Converted lofts, upscale bakeries, and trendy restaurants had driven up property taxes—and driven *out* most of the original residents from the center. On the outskirts of the neighborhood, however, blocks of small apartments, once home to factory workers, were now occupied by a motley mixture of art-school idealists and some of the

displaced residents who could no longer afford the skyrocket-
ing rents further in.

I parallel-parked outside one of these old brick apartment
buildings, which Bob said was a few blocks away from the
dowser's place. Headlights from the occasional car whizzed
past as we navigated around prostitutes and late-night club-
bers stinking of beer. Instead of heading to the entrance of
the building where the dowser lived, Bob led me to a rusting
chain-link fence on the side. As I looked on in bewilderment,
he quickly foraged around the crumbling sidewalk for a small
pebble, then reared back into a pitcher's stance and lobbed it
in a high arc to ding against a second-floor window.

"What the hell, Bob?" I whispered.

"Sorry. He's weird about too many phone calls."

"*Great.* That sounds on the up-and-up," I muttered as
I folded my hands around my middle and shivered. A few
seconds passed before a girl with a dark green halo leaned out
the window. Bob announced himself in a loud whisper. Without a response, she left for several seconds, then returned and
tossed down a single key on a large silver ring, which turned
out to unlock the front entrance. We headed up a couple of
flights in a depressing stairwell straight out of Soviet-era Russia, with concrete steps lined by flaking metal handrails. Every
surface of the stairwell was smothered in a thick coat of cheer-
less, glossy gray paint—even the dust on the exposed pipes.

We made our way to the last apartment at the end of
the hall. The same girl who'd thrown us the key answered
the door. With sugary-red dyed hair, she looked like a Latina
Raggedy Ann doll. Dark circles hung beneath dull eyes that
wanted us out of her sight. She held out an impatient open
palm to Bob. He set the key in her hand and mumbled a timid
hello as we entered.

The apartment was filthy. A cramped kitchen overflowing with trash and dirty dishes funneled into a narrow dining room. As we passed into a larger living space, the smell of damp hamster cage transitioned into a vinegary, burning-soil aroma: sømna, an opiate derived from the dried gills of a mildly toxic Pacific Northwest fungus. Like valrivia, it was smoked mostly by Earthbounds. Unlike valrivia, it wasn't a mild, legalized smoke you enjoyed on your afternoon coffee break, but rather, a highly addictive and highly *illegal* narcotic.

"Bob, you asshole," I mumbled.

He shot me a nervous sidelong glance. A thin sheen of sweat covered his forehead.

An Earthbound with a large, bright blue halo sat on a striped couch at the far end of the living room, near a curtainless window. Two humans were hunched over a coffee table in front of him, their backs to us. One of them bent to inspect something on the table. The Earthbound on the couch glanced over his head and caught my eye. "Take it or leave it," he said to the men. "Makes no difference to me."

"It's not what I expected," one of them said.

"Not my problem. You paid, I provided. Get out. I've got company."

Both men turned to look at us, fear pulsing in their eyes. One grabbed the mystery item off the table, stuck it in his jacket pocket, then slapped his mate on the shoulder. Both kept their eyes on the floor as they marched out of the room, parting like a wave around Bob and me. The apartment door slammed behind them.

"Robert," the blue-haloed Earthbound said, "introduce me to your friend."

"Cady Bell, one of the Tambuku owners. Cady, this is Hajo."

"A pleasure." The Earthbound stood up, unfolding a frame well over six feet. He was dressed in jeans and a slim, black leather racing jacket with a mandarin collar and three silver stripes on one sleeve, zipped all the way up to his throat. He was about my age, I guessed, mid- to late twenties. Short dark hair and darker eyes. Long, thin sideburns styled into diagonal points. Smoldering good looks.

"Bob failed to mention that the death dowser he knew was a sømna addict," I said.

He emitted a rough chuckle as he looked me over a little slower than I liked. "No worries. My willpower is rock solid."

If you had self-control, you could supposedly use the drug in small amounts for years without much backlash to your health. Problem was, once you crossed the line and upped your intake, you hit a no-return point, referred to as tribulation. Past this, you were pretty much screwed. Dead man walking. Medical rehab success was slim, and if you couldn't stop, toxicity levels stacked up exponentially. A state law passed five years ago was one of the harshest in the country: possession of any amount was a felony that got you an automatic ten years in prison and a $20,000 fine. But half of those imprisoned died within a week of being denied the drug.

"I don't give a damn what you do on your own time," I said. "I just don't want to be in your home when the cops catch up to you."

"Oh, I don't live here." He unzipped his jacket to reveal the suggestion of a well-defined chest beneath a shirt that clung to his skin. "This is Cristina's place. I don't shit where I eat."

So *very* classy. You know how people get better-looking the more you know and like them? That applies in reverse too. The smolder was dying.

"I've seen you at your bar a couple of times." He sat down and spread his arms over the back of the couch. An upturned Ducati motorcycle helmet teetered near his thigh. His voice was low and hard to hear over the volume of the flat-screen TV across the room.

I perched on the edge of a stained La-Z-Boy recliner. Bob stood next to me, cracking his knuckles nervously. "Don't remember you," I said, "but I serve a lot of people."

Hajo shrugged. "Too crowded for my tastes. So, Bob tells me you need to find something in La Sirena."

"Yes," I said reluctantly. *Please don't let this be a mistake.* "What do you need for tracking?"

"Bare minimum? The name of the dead person, a photo, some facts about them. But to save time, I need to get on the same path they were on before they died."

"What does that mean?"

"It means I could drive around all day randomly trying to pick up on a thread, or I can cut corners and line myself up to a marker that will lead me to the thread. There are a few ways to do this. If you know the exact place they died, that's best. I can track a body from place of death really fast."

I shook my head. "No clue where the actual death occurred."

"Okay, then what about the last person to see them alive?"

That would be Bishop, I supposed; however, if we knew where Bishop was, we wouldn't be tracking down dead bodies. "No again. What else?"

"Last place they were seen sometimes works, but it's tough. Depends on what the person did before they died. Grandpa Joe might've been last spotted at the local diner, but he could've tooled around town before driving off a cliff."

"You're a cheery person to be around," I grumbled.

"I'm Captain fucking Kangaroo. You try wielding this knack and see how cheery it makes you."

He had a point, but not my sympathy. I wasn't all that thrilled with the lot I'd been dealt, either, so I just ignored his bad attitude and tried to focus on why I was there.

Maybe he could track one of the original abducted kids from the place they were last seen. But it had been so long, and I didn't want to tell him exactly *how* long, because I didn't want him guessing who we were tracking.

He scratched his chin. "There's always objects. You have anything the deceased might've touched right before they died?"

I wondered if Lon could get in touch with his police buddies and find out if they still had anything in evidence. We could contact the parents of some of the original missing kids, but most of them were scattered, and several were dead themselves—it had been thirty years, after all, and they were all in their seventies.

Then I thought of one thing we *did* have: Bishop's key, the one on the broken silver chain that Dare gave us. "What about an object from the last person to see them?" I asked. Right away, I could tell by his reaction that it was a long shot, so I ponied up and added, "It probably belonged to the killer."

"Oh? Yeah, that should give me a strong lead." Hajo stroked the raised velour striping on the couch with his thumb. "What kind of object is it?"

"A key. A small one. On a necklace."

Hajo's brows lifted. "The killer wore it, then? Like jewelry?"

"Maybe," I said.

His head quickly bobbed up and down. "That's good. Very good. If it's been worn on the body, it's a good tracker. I like working from jewelry." He considered this for a moment, staring off into the distance, then he focused on me again. "La Sirena is a smaller town. Much easier to track bodies there than in the city. Yeah, I can probably do it."

"Great," I said, with trepidation. Because finding a bunch of dead bodies wasn't exactly my idea of good time. After a few seconds of uncomfortable silence, I asked him about his success rate.

"Pretty high," he answered in a noncommittal tone.

"'Pretty'?" I repeated.

"I don't keep a fucking pie chart on my jobs," he said sourly. "If you know another dowser, feel free to hire him instead."

Point taken. "How long will this whole tracking thing take?"

He shrugged. "A couple of hours to all afternoon. Maybe longer. Depends on how fast I can catch the thread."

That gave me hope. I relaxed a little. My eyes wandered to the TV. *Metropolis*, 1927. The scene where the robot is seated in front of a pentagram.

"One of my favorite movies," Hajo said.

"How do you watch something with no sound?" Bob asked, piping up for the first time since he'd introduced us.

"It's got a score," Hajo said. "Are you deaf?"

"I meant talking," Bob said, wiping sweat off his brow.

"I've seen it several times," I admitted, then nodded at the screen. "The restored version is so much better. Easier to see all the details in those elaborate sets." Funny thing was, Jupe and I had talked about it a couple of weeks ago. I was so proud to be familiar with a movie that he hadn't seen and memorized already. So I bought him the DVD, one of the birthday presents I was planning to give him next week.

Hajo smiled, his eyes gentler. Almost merry. "You have good taste."

Common ground with a junkie. Good taste, indeed.

His smile withered as he addressed Bob. "Cady and I need to discuss payment arrangements. Would you please join Cristina in the kitchen?"

As Bob stuttered a vague response, Hajo called out for Cristina, who promptly appeared and herded Bob through the dining room, closing a heavy curtain over the doorway.

I glanced at Hajo. An uneasy chill slid down my spine.

"I don't have money on me," I warned, suddenly acutely aware of his expensive drug habit and all the news reports featuring desperate sømna addicts who'd passed tribulation and were stealing or killing for money.

Hajo chuckled. "I don't want your cash, calm down."

"What do you normally charge?"

He didn't reply right away, his attention momentarily distracted by the movie. "I make all kinds of alternative arrangements," he answered at length. "My other jobs provide me the cash I need."

My pulse spiked. "And what other jobs would those be?" I asked.

"Nothing to worry about," he said. "For dowsing, I prefer the barter system."

"Free drinks at Tambuku for a month?" I offered.

He shook his head very, *very* slowly. His eyes trailed over me again, languid and dangerous. "Maybe you and I can negotiate a mutually beneficial . . . *intimate* arrangement," he suggested in a low voice.

"No thanks. I'm taken."

He glanced at my hand. "Doesn't look that way to me."

"Sorry, try again," I said as my phone chimed. I tugged it

out of my pocket and glanced at the message on the screen. It was from Lon, asking for an update, as if he sensed something wrong all the way from the coast. "Like I said, taken." I held up my phone and wiggled it as proof.

Hajo made some indecipherable noise as he observed me for several seconds while I stuck my phone in my jeans pocket. "Bob says you were a great piece of ass."

I nearly choked. "*What*?"

His eyebrows lifted in challenge.

"You've *got* to be joking." Not if he was the last lazy-eyed demon on earth. And after I got Bob out of this dump of an apartment, he was going to get a swift kick in the balls for lying. As Jupe would say, gross.

Hajo let out a single "Ha!" and slouched into the couch. "That makes much more sense now. I couldn't understand why you'd—"

"I wouldn't."

"Got it." After a few seconds of silence he cleared his throat. "Regardless, we were discussing an arrangement." He stretched out his leg and slipped one very big boot between my feet.

I pushed it back with the toe of my shoe. "Your girlfriend is in the next room, or have you forgotten?"

"We have an open relationship."

"Oh?" I stood up from the recliner. "Then I'll just go make sure it's okay with her, shall I?"

Hajo jumped off the sofa and grabbed my wrist. "All right, all right," he growled. He tugged me closer until I was standing in front of him, his body inches from mine. "You did say you wanted to keep this dowsing job under the table." His hushed voice was graveled with darkness. "I'm sure you wouldn't want it to get around town that the girl with the silver halo is slumming east of Eden." His head dipped low as he fingered a lock of white-blond hair from behind my ear, sending a flurry of unwanted chills down my neck.

"I don't think anyone pays much attention to what I do."

"Everyone pays attention," Hajo replied. "You're a local fairy tale. People brag about being bound in your bar like it's some sort of masochistic merit badge." His finger left my hair and trailed across my jaw. "You know, even though I can track death trails of strangers, once I've met someone in person, I never forget live energy. Like a fingerprint. No two alike. And I'm finding your energy to be especially unique, because your halo looks demon, but you are . . . a little different." His head dipped lower. I couldn't move. I felt his lips skimming the outer shell of my ear as his voice dropped to a whisper. "So different, in fact, that I'm betting I could track you halfway across the state."

A warning blared in my brain. Conditioned to run and hide from anything or anyone that could sell me out down the line, I had to remind myself that my murderous parents were long gone. Even if the feds found me, I had nothing they wanted anymore. Then again, they didn't know that. What would I say if I got arrested? *My psychotic parents were using an Æthyric demon to siphon energy from people they killed. The demon demanded their lives as payment and I gave them up.*

Right.

I did my best to calm down, but something near hysteria rose up in me like a geyser. My pulse pounded in my temples. The sigils on my arm called out, begging to be charged. Worse, the Moonchild ability, stagnant and unused for weeks, flared up somewhere deep in my mind. It was like a chiming doorbell, but I didn't know who—or what—was on the other side of the door, asking to be let inside. And it terrified me, almost worse than Hajo's threats.

What the hell had I gotten myself into by coming here?

My phone chimed in my pocket again.

"Appears that your boyfriend is worried," Hajo murmured, pulling back. "I don't blame him. I would be worried too if you were mine and alone with someone like me."

"He doesn't worry." I came to my senses and pushed away the flicker of Moonchild power. Then, without any more hesitation, I grabbed the portable caduceus from inside my jacket and shoved the blunt end into Hajo's windpipe.

He retreated in surprise, but I followed. My head was clear. He was demon; I was magician. I held the power—not him. He seemed to be thinking the same thing as he tucked his chin and peered down at the caduceus, raising his hands in surrender.

"Hold on, now," he said, "I thought you needed symbols to bind us."

"Not to blow a hole in your larynx." A bluff. At most I could shock him enough to scare him, but he didn't know that.

He lowered his hand to rest beneath the caduceus and gently pushed it away from his throat. I let him.

"Maybe my proposal was too much, too soon," he said. "After all, you barely know me." The corners of his mouth curled into a slow smile. "I'm a patient man. Like I said before, rock-solid willpower."

In answer, I pointed the caduceus lower.

He laughed nervously and cupped himself with one hand. "How about another proposition?"

"I'm listening."

"Bob says you make a strong vassal potion."

What? My momentary bravado wilted.

I scrambled to remember how Bob would know that. I brewed lots of medicinals, and used them freely in the bar when I needed to maintain peace, but I only used the vassal when milder medicinals failed and binding wasn't a practical option. Just a drop. Once dosed, the person who swallowed it would be putty in my hands, agreeable to sitting still and turning things down a notch. Agreeable to whatever I asked. It was a powerful tool. In the wrong hands . . .

Then I vaguely remembered mentioning the vassal medicinal around Bob several months ago. It was late and I was pissed off and tired, and making threats under my breath about a table of smart-aleck Earthbounds. Bob had asked me what I was talking about, and I dismissed it. He never asked again.

So, innocent little Bob wasn't so innocent. Dear God, was everyone really only out for themselves? Could I trust no one?

"I'm going to assume from your silence that Bob wasn't lying," Hajo said. "I'll take an ounce of the vassal as payment for this job. But I want it in hand tomorrow before we start."

"I'd rather pay cash."

He shook his head. "I won't take it. Vassal or no deal. How bad do you want to find this body?"

That was a good question. And I hadn't told him it was multiple bodies, rather than just one.

I felt woozy. That much vassal would be worth thousands in esoteric circles. It wasn't an easy medicinal to make. One of the herbal components was rare, and the spell to transform the brew was tricky and required finely tuned skills. Making magical medicinals was one of the few talents that I was able to learn successfully on my own, and I was good at it, but it still wasn't easy.

My phone chimed again. Lon was probably having a panic attack at this point, wondering why I wasn't answering. I thought of the glass talon he'd bought to save me in the incident last month, and the $15,000 he'd shelled out for it. Fifteen thousand dollars that now sat in Jupe's new savings account. But even if I could somehow negotiate a cash price for Hajo's services, I couldn't afford them, and I couldn't ask Lon to pay up again. He'd helped me when I needed it, and now it was time for me to return the favor. It killed me; went against everything I knew, deep within, was right. But I obviously wasn't about to consider Hajo's original barter, and I didn't have much more to offer.

"I only have half an ounce," I said.

"Can you brew up more by tomorrow?"

I shook my head.

"No deal," he said.

I gritted my teeth in frustration. "What about half an ounce, and I'll bind an Earthbound for you."

His eyes widened in surprise. He studied my face, thinking. "I'll take the half ounce and three bindings. Night or day, I call and you come. You keep your mouth shut and don't ask questions."

I hesitated. Hajo's quiet threat of being able to track me down added to the pressure.

"Two," I said. "And no weird shit—I'm not binding someone for you to molest, rape, torture, or kill."

He laughed brightly, with far more casual happiness than I was feeling at that moment. It was the laughter of someone who'd just won and knew it. "I'm not a monster, Cady. Just an entrepreneur. I'll gladly agree to your terms. Deal?"

His hand extended. I lowered my caduceus, but I didn't

shake. "You'd better track down what I need, or the deal is off."

"I'll find the dead body for you. And in the meantime," he added, "we'll get to spend some quality time getting to know each other."

My phone rang. "Meet me at the Singing Bean in the Village tomorrow at two."

"No can do," he said. "I've got another job. Day after tomorrow is the earliest I can do it."

I started to argue, but he cut me off.

"I really can't," he said firmly. "Day after tomorrow. Same time and place. And just to put you at ease, I'll even bring Bob along," he suggested, zipping his racing jacket back up to his throat. "Besides, I'll need a test subject for your vassal potion, just to verify the quality."

Fine by me. The rat fink deserved it for selling me out.

"I'm so sorry," Bob called out behind me as he ran to catch up outside Hajo's building. "You've got to believe me."

Lights from a city bus danced across the sidewalk as it passed. I turned the corner and headed in the direction of my parked car. A man had already yelled at us from a second-story apartment window to shut up. Last thing I needed was for someone to call the cops, so I increased my stride.

I was furious. At Bob, at Hajo, and at myself for caving in to Hajo's bartering. For feeling terrified that he could track me one day. My parents were dead, but I was still the same scared girl I was when they were alive, hiding in shadows. You'd think, at the very least, that their deaths would release me from the lie I'd been living on their behalf for the past seven years. That I could relax and be normal. That an idle threat from a junkie wouldn't rattle me.

But it did. Because I was still living under an alias. Still on some FBI list or another.

Still afraid.

"Please listen." Bob's hand gripped my shoulder. I pushed it off and spun to face him.

He launched into a rapid explanation. "Hajo asked about the vassal when I called him earlier to set up the meeting. He'd heard stories about you. I tried to tell him that I didn't know anything, but he hung up on me. So I called him back. I told him that I remembered you mentioning it, but I didn't know what it was. I still don't." He wiped his hand on the front of his blue Hawaiian shirt and looked at me with pleading eyes. "I swear, Cady. You've got to believe me. Please!"

"But you told him you've slept with me?" I said, my voice a higher pitch than I intended.

"What?" His hand stilled in the middle of running it over his slicked-back hair. His mouth opened. He was genuinely taken aback. "Did he say that? I never said that. Never! He's lying, and—"

"All right, all right," I grumbled, waving him away. I don't know why I even cared. It wasn't important.

"I wouldn't talk trash about you—I mean, we're friends . . . aren't we?"

"I thought so," I snapped. But when he flinched in response and his face fell, guilt wormed its way into my chest. "We are," I amended after a pause. "Friends, that is. So don't sell me out to someone like Hajo again."

"Never. Give me a lie detector test. I'll do anything."

I stopped in front of his car, suddenly bone-weary.

Bob pulled his car keys out then paused in front of me. My gaze rose from the hula-girl print of his shirt until I met his eyes. They were tight with grief or regret. Maybe both. "I'm *so* sorry, Cady."

He wasn't the only one. I shouldn't have agreed to give Hajo the potion. God only knew what despicable things he'd end up doing with it.

8

I wasn't the only one upset about the bar-
ter with Hajo. Lon was livid, more at Hajo—and Bob—than at
me, he said, when I called him on my way back to my place
with a report of what had transpired. He didn't say much,
but he never does on the phone. I could hear the anger in the
loaded combination of grunts and poignant silences. And it
was still bugging him the next day when I drove to La Sirena
to meet up with him for some reconnaissance.

Bishop's former house address was in Dare's box of paperwork, so we decided to check it out. Maybe we'd see something useful, some clue that pointed to where he would've
corralled seven teens in the weeks leading up to All Saints'
Day. Dare said that he and Lon's father found no indication
that they were kept inside the house when they searched it
thirty years before, but at least we'd have a point of reference
from which to start.

"Do you have Hajo's phone number?" Lon asked as he
made a turn into a small neighborhood on the east side of La
Sirena, a few miles inland from the coast. Traffic hummed in
the distance on the main highway leading to Morella—the one
I drove back and forth to work.

"Bob has it."

"What if he doesn't show tomorrow? We have to send Bob to track him down?"

I pressed the button to lower the passenger window so I could see the houses we were passing. "I suppose. But he'll show. He wants the damn vassal medicinal."

Two slits of green slanted in my direction. "I still can't believe you promised him that."

"Me either, but my options were limited." No way was I telling him about Hajo coming on to me. I squelched that thought before Lon had time to figure out what was on my mind. "He's not country-club material, Lon. He's a junkie. You wanted a dowser, I got you a dowser. If you want someone more respectable, Bob says you'll have to go out of state."

"'Bob says.'" His hand hung loosely over the top of the steering wheel as he slouched in his seat and stared straight ahead like he was daring the road to piss him off. "I must remember to thank Bob and his big mouth."

"He's excited to meet you, too."

No answer. A muscle in his jaw flexed. The long hollows under his cheekbones deepened.

Two blocks of crowded, boxy homes sailed by my window before he spoke again. "I wish you'd driven to La Sirena last night after all that."

I blinked several times, trying to decipher what he meant, which was often more than what he said. "I was tired. And mad at myself. I didn't need you mad at me too."

"I wasn't mad. Not at you. I was worried."

"No reason to be. I could've shocked him if I had to. But I didn't."

Another grunt. Another block driven. "I don't like sleeping alone anymore."

I glanced at him, but his concentration was on the road. Stoic. "Me either," I admitted.

The tight angle of his shoulders loosened. Just slightly.

As he rounded a corner onto Dolores Street, where Bishop used to live, I said, "Look, I'm over being mad at Bob, but if you want to challenge Hajo to a duel when we're finished with him tomorrow, I'm totally cool with that."

That got me a light grunt. Then another askance look. Then the tiniest twitch of mustache at the corner of his mouth. Finally. I grinned back.

Bishop's one-bedroom house clung to a steep hill in the middle of the block. The siding looked brand-new, and the inclined driveway was darker than the street, freshly resurfaced. Public records said it had been empty for nearly twenty years before it was resold several times, bank-owned, then purchased earlier this year by one Simon Cleeton.

We parked on the street and glanced around before exiting the car.

"These old houses are being bought and fixed up by people who work in Morella and commute," Lon noted. "Easy access to the highway on-ramp, cheaper property taxes than living in the city, low crime rates."

"Except for that pesky child snatcher."

"Except for that."

Lon exited and set the car alarm. I sniffed the air. Burning leaves somewhere nearby. I always liked that smell. Sort of comforting and pleasant. As I walked around the SUV, I eyed the houses on either side of Bishop's place, then the ones across the street. Cute, well-kept. We'd looked up the property owners of those, too. Everyone who'd lived here thirty years ago had long since sold their homes. No one left with memories of their neighbor at 658 Dolores Street. A pity.

"Nothing unusual," Lon noted as he stuffed his hands in the pockets of a tailored brown jacket.

"No deserted playgrounds or creepy ravines," I agreed. The house itself was small and square. "One bedroom. He never married or had kids, huh?"

"Nope."

We climbed stone steps that cut up the hill to the front door. Lon peeked around the side, over a shoulder-high wooden fence, which still had lumber tags stapled to several boards. "Tiny backyard. Barely worth owning a lawn mower," Lon said.

I stood on tiptoe and peered over the top of the fence. "No ominous old shed back there. No John Wayne Gacy crawl space under the house."

Lon pivoted and surveyed the block. I did the same.

"What's that at the end of the street behind the fence? Looks like a parking lot."

Lon squinted. "If I didn't know better, I'd say that's the back of La Sirena Junior High."

"Really?" I must've been turned around. I didn't know La Sirena all that well, but I'd dropped off Jupe at school on occasion. And there was, of course, the time when Jupe had been held hostage by a rival magician, Riley Cooper. But I wasn't paying much attention to the school's location that night.

"We normally come from the other side," Lon said. "This whole area's changed. I didn't realize this street butted up to Madison."

"Was the junior high here thirty years ago?"

"Yep. The same one Cindy Brolin attended."

"You mean to tell me that Bishop lived a block away?"

"It looks that way. Come on."

We walked back down to the sidewalk and headed in

the direction of the parking lot, crossing over Madison, and stopped at the chain-link fence. It was Jupe's school, all right. And the bit we could spy from Bishop's old house was faculty parking. The roots of a knotted cypress had buckled the sidewalk here. An old cement bench sat beneath the tree, its back touching the fence. The parking lot exit was only a few feet away.

"Jesus, he probably scouted out his victims from here," Lon said.

The hair on my arms rose at the thought. But the new missing kids didn't go here. They attended the private school across town. I was reminding Lon of this when a woman with a pale blue halo exited a door at the back of the school. An alarm beeped. She was heading toward a car parked nearby, on the other side of the fence.

"Ms. Forsythe," Lon said in greeting.

She glanced up, confused, then smiled and stepped up to the fence, speaking through it. "Mr. Butler. I was just headed out to lunch. There's nothing wrong, is there?"

"No, we were just in the neighborhood and thought we'd walk by the school." He put his hand on my lower back. "This is my girlfriend, Arcadia," he said, then turned to me. "This is Grace Forsythe, one of Jupe's teachers."

She was Earthbound, both a couple inches taller and decades older than me. She wore no makeup and was dressed in a flowing poncho-style shirt over polyester pants. Her hair was in a long, dark bob with straight bangs that covered her eyebrows. A little frumpy, a little flower-power. Exactly as I'd pictured her. Not only was she Jupe's science teacher but also his homeroom teacher *and* his favorite. He talked about her all the time.

I held my hand up and waved once. "Nice to meet you."

"Cady, right?"

"Yes."

She smiled. "Oh, yes. I've heard *all* about you from Jupe."

Uh-oh.

"I expected you to be wearing a rubber catsuit and wielding a sword."

Errr . . .

"He's got a big imagination," she explained with a smile.

"And a bigger mouth," Lon grumbled.

Her laugh was confident. "Better than being afflicted with shyness." She turned to me. "You're the one who's been teaching him about constellations."

The way she said this, I felt like I was in trouble. "Is that a bad thing?"

Her face brightened. "Oh, no. It's good. Though he's gotten a few wrong, and insists on correcting me in front of the class."

"That's Jupe's short attention span, not her lessons," Lon said with a hint of a smile.

"Oh, I never doubted that. You know, I think it's wonderful that he has a new female role model in his life. I've noticed a real difference in him recently. He's much more positive."

"Thanks, but I doubt that's because of me." I shifted uneasily on my feet.

"Don't be so sure. He's more focused. Scoring better on exams, too. Confident—though he's never really had a problem being sure of himself," she said with a wink.

Lon crossed his arms over his chest. "He's been more confident than usual around the house. Seems to think he's coming into his knack."

Ms. Forsythe's eyebrows raised. "Oh, really? I haven't heard this tidbit. He's too young, don't you think?"

I nodded. "That's what we've been saying."

"I once had a female student who came into her knack early, maybe ten years ago. But it's rare. And I haven't noticed anything unusual going on with Jupiter."

"Well, if you overhear him claiming to be able to persuade people with the sound of his voice, please do me a favor and tell him he's full of it," Lon said. "He'll listen to you."

She chuckled. "That Jupiter. So wonderfully dramatic!"

Lon's expression said that he did not quite agree with that assessment.

"I overheard him saying in homeroom that he was going to the carnival tonight," she said, tugging her purse onto her shoulder as she stepped back to unlock her car door.

"We're going to try to make it over there after school, before it gets dark."

She opened the car door and braced her hands on the top edge. "That's probably wise, with all the Snatcher talk floating around town. The kids are starting to invent danger around every corner. I don't normally allow negative talk in my classroom, but I do encourage them to stay alert. Better safe than sorry, I tell them."

Lon mumbled an agreement. But I couldn't help but wonder if the teachers who worked here thirty years ago had recited the same adage to their students . . . while Bishop stood in the same spot where I stood now, making a mental list of his potential victims.

9

"How many times have you been here?" I asked Jupe as the three of us approached the entrance of Brentano Gardens amusement park later that afternoon.

"This year, or my whole life? 'Cause if you just mean *this* year, then that would only be three times, but if you mean since I was born, then, uh, let's see—"

I whistled and drew my fingers across my throat. "Never mind."

"But—"

Lon reached over his son's shoulder, clamped his hand over Jupe's mouth, and pretended to punch him in the stomach. Jupe's muffled cry of laughter echoed off the pavement. They wrestled the entire way inside.

Brentano Gardens sat opposite the boardwalk in the heart of La Sirena, just across Ocean Drive. The brick wall surrounding it stretched over several outlying blocks of the Village and was shaped like the crenellated wall of a European castle, the rooftop outlined in white lights. It originally opened in the early 1920s, and its claim to fame was having one of the oldest American wooden roller coasters still in operation.

During the last two weeks of October, the park stayed open nightly until midnight for their annual Spooktacular carnival. When we arrived, would-be revelers were already lined up shoulder to shoulder at the ticket booths.

The park was sweetly old-fashioned, with bales of hay and pumpkins stacked around small kiosks shaped like overgrown toadstools. A tree-lined promenade filled with quaint restaurants and shops welcomed us at the entrance. Good thing, because I was starving. However, my excitement over the possibility of dining at the smiling-penis-rated Alps Fondue Chalet was trampled when we discovered the wait was well over an hour. We decided to skip it and go for bad carnival food instead. No one was happier about this development than Jupe, who happily polished off an entire corn dog and a fat pile of cheesy fries in a few short bites.

As we sauntered further into the park, Jupe hammed it up as our tour guide. Sure, the park brochure might tell you that the Whirling Wammie ride was built in the 1960s, but did you know that Jupe had thrown up after riding it—not once, not twice, but five times? He proudly pointed out all five vomit spots. There was also Thor's Lightning, on which Jupe lost a flip-flop when he was seven, and the Black Forest Water Flumes, the ride that "almost drowned" him the following year when he wriggled out of his seat restraint and tried to go overboard while waiting for the ride to start. Lon rolled his eyes and silently shook his head behind Jupe's back as his son related the dramatic event in stunning, high-def detail.

Two Spooktacular attractions were set up in the center of the park: the unfortunately named Jack-O-Land—which Jupe, and probably every other kid under eighteen referred to as Jack-Off-Land—and our intended destination, the Spirit Cove ride.

"Eye of Horus, the line is long," I mumbled in frustration.

"It's a Butler family tradition," Jupe said brightly. "We have to ride it."

"No, *you* have to ride it."

"Dad said we can't separate tonight," Jupe argued.

Yeah, but I wasn't in danger of being kidnapped by some elderly ex-Hellfire member with a chip on his shoulder.

"Buck up, witch," Lon said. "I hate crowds. If I have to endure it, so do you. What's two hours out of your life?"

"Two hours?" I glanced at the the queue area. It snaked around a dozen or more handrails. Hundreds of people shuffled along a few inches at a time.

"It looks like a cow pen," I protested.

"*Moo*-ove," Lon wisecracked as he urged me into the line behind Jupe. It kind of smelled like a cow pen, too. Someone needed to pass a law forcing people to use antiperspirant. I would vote for that; moreover, I would happily stand in line for two hours to do so.

While Lon checked his phone, I busied myself with thinking of ways that he was going to repay me later. We'd been in line only a few minutes when Jupe spotted someone he knew ahead of us and leaned over the rail to chat. While doing so, he conducted some discreet scratching beneath the waistband of his jeans. "Look," I whispered to Lon. "Did you see that? What's going on with that? He told me it was an injury."

"Hmph. I'll bet."

"Is this a boy thing? Did you injure yourself when you were his age? Being . . . overenthusiastic?"

"More chafing than I care to admit . . . the occasional carpal tunnel flare-up," Lon said with a self-deprecating shrug. As I bit back a laugh, he assured me, "I wouldn't worry. He'll be fine."

"But will *I*? Now I'm gonna have to scrub those images out of my brain. I liked it better when he was sweet and innocent."

"You're a little late boarding that train. He hasn't been innocent for years. He's had his hands in his pants since kindergarten."

"Stop!" I protested, covering my ears.

Lon laughed heartily and tugged me against his side. "Parenting sucks in all kinds of ways." He followed Jupe's movements with his eyes, shaking his head at his son's obvious discomfort. Then I noticed someone from Dare's brunch party walking past the ride queue.

I elbowed Lon. "Look. Isn't that Dare's son, Mark?"

At the sound of his name, the blond man looked up and spotted Lon, then me. The wince was barely perceptible, but it was pretty clear that we were the last two people he wanted to see. He pasted on a polite grin and stopped outside the rail near us. "Lon . . . Arcadia. Twice in one week. Imagine that."

"Small world," Lon agreed.

"I'm here with the family," Mark said, lifting up the collar on his jacket to shield his neck from the wind. "My wife is waiting with my son to get a pumpkin carved. I'm surprised the crowds are so large tonight. A pretty big turnout for a town fighting against Halloween right now. Did you see that civil action group on the news this morning?"

"Yep."

"Maybe they'll have better luck in Morella."

"Maybe."

"Can't keep down the Halloween spirit here. Too much money to be made." He laughed, rubbing his hands together, then blew into them to keep warm.

Lon nodded absently, as if he couldn't possibly care less.

"Hey . . . I was wondering about why you two were visiting my father the other day. Everything okay?"

Dare hadn't told Mark that we were trying to track down Bishop? Guess he really wasn't lying about all the animosity between them.

"Everything's fine," Lon said, avoiding Mark's original question.

Mark waited for more, then tried another tactic. "No one from the club sees you much anymore." He paused, then added, "Though I did hear you brought Arcadia to the last Hellfire event at the caves . . ."

"Mmm-hmm," Lon answered. Blank, cool. No emotion whatsoever.

"You two coming again for Samhain?"

"Not if my life depended on it."

Mark's chuckle was dry and awkward. He cleared his throat. "Don't see you around the Village these days either, but I've been busy working long hours and I hear you're always out of town on those photo shoots of yours. Still the big celebrity, I guess. Life in the fast lane, all that. Speaking of celebrity, how's Yvonne? Heard from her lately?"

"She's fine." Lon wrapped an arm around my waist and herded me forward to catch up with the now-moving line. "Nice to see you again, Mark. Take care."

Mark's jaw flexed. He wasn't happy about being dismissed. He mumbled a good-bye, adjusted his jacket collar, and continued on his way.

Half an hour after our encounter with Mark, we finally made it through the queue. A park employee dressed in a black-and-white striped chain-gang-prisoner costume herded the three of us into a staging area. Groups of people ahead of us entered the four-person boats on one side of a small canal filled with blood-red dyed water.

"Huh. I could swear that this thing used to go faster," Jupe said to the man as we watched a seashell boat emerge from the indoor ride and glide to a slow stop.

"It's an older ride. We had some minor track problems at the higher speed, so we switched to a slower setting about a month ago," the park employee explained in a professional voice, straightening his name tag. It read *Henry* above chipped gold stars and what seemed like an afterthought, *20 Years of Service*. "You may not know this, but this attraction originally started out as the popular Beach Fun Party ride in the 1970s. Back then, they operated the ride at an even higher speed so that the two waterfall drops would splash the riders. It was changed to Mermaid Cove in 1980s, and then Spirit Cove ten years ago."

"Yeah, I know all that," Jupe said with breezy immodesty. "My dad rode it when he was a kid. He said it was better because the animatronic mermaids used to be girls in tiny bikinis." He waggled his eyebrows suggestively to underscore his words.

Both Lon and Henry looked simultaneously embarrassed about this factoid.

"Uh, yes, I suppose," Henry said before composing himself to continue the history lesson. "It was fast enough to require belted lap restraints, which they later removed when they revamped to the Halloween theme and slowed the ride down. As for the ride's speed this season, it does make the wait longer, and we apologize for that. But the tradeoff is that you can enjoy the Spirit Cove experience for a full nine minutes instead of the normal four and a half." He smiled encouragingly at Jupe, then called for the next group of people.

"Damn," Jupe muttered under his breath. "That's almost twice as slow."

"That's *exactly* twice as slow," Lon said.

"Whatever. It might as well be It's a Small World. This blows."

"Is it scary?" I asked. "I'm not a fan of people jumping out at me."

"Nah, it's kinda lame." His eyes darted to the side.

"That's not what you said three years ago," Lon said.

"I was just a kid, and thanks for bringing that up, assbag."

"*Father* Assbag," Lon calmly corrected. "And you're the one who was bragging earlier about vomiting. So go on, tell Cady all about how you weren't scared that time."

"If you think it's so funny, *you* tell her."

"Did he cry?" I asked, making a pouty face.

"Worse," Lon said.

Jupe groaned, letting his head loll backward as he squeezed his eyes shut. "I pissed my pants, okay? Are you happy now?"

"What? Shut up! You didn't!"

"It was the worst day of my life," he admitted.

"Mine too. I nearly froze on our way to the car," Lon said. "I had to give little Pee-Pants my jacket to cover up."

I snickered and poked Jupe in the ribs. He giggled and tried to tickle me.

"Next," Henry said loudly, interrupting our horseplay. "Hurry up. Others are waiting."

Lon helped me into the teetering boat. We settled together on the long planked seat behind Jupe, who twisted around to peg us with a cocky grin. "Let's make a bet. I'll bet you five dollars out of my new savings account that I can use my knack on Henry to speed this ride up."

Lon rolled his eyes. "Not this again."

"Doubt all you want, haters. I'm going to be unstoppable when I master this thing. You just wait."

"Oh, I'm waiting."

"Does that mean you're taking my bet?"

"I'll bet you're going to turn around in your seat before I change my mind and haul you off this thing."

Jupe grinned. "I'll take that as a yes."

Henry pressed a large red button on the control panel behind him. With the blare of a buzzer, the ride jerked, then settled into a lazy trajectory, clinking along the metal underwater track. "Knack my ass," Lon muttered, drawing me closer in the boat's backseat. "You better hang on so you don't fly off when we go down that second waterfall."

Jupe snorted. "At this speed? We won't even get a drop of water on us."

"I think you mean drop of *blood*," I said, leaning over his shoulder to make spidery fingers in his billowing curls. He laughed and grabbed my hands as an atmospheric Halloween soundtrack crackled over hidden speakers.

Two doors opened, allowing the boat to float into the first section of the dark ride. A cloud of dancing red lights was rigged to mimic evil eyes winking on the edge of a bog. It smelled strongly of chlorine and the soundtrack was so loud it almost hurt your ears. The costumed people posing on the ride's shores looked more bored than frightening. Even the fog was cheesy. The whole production was an insult to both haunted houses and amusement park rides. Walt Disney would've rolled over in his grave.

When the ride ended, I leaned over the handrail and whispered into Jupe's hair, "Stupidest ride ever."

"It's better when it's faster," he complained. "You

couldn't even tell when we went down the second waterfall drop."

"There was a second drop?" I teased.

"See! So lame. I'm going to make this thing go faster."

"Uh-huh, get right on that," Lon encouraged sarcastically.

As a family with a small child boarded the boat in front of us, Jupe closed his eyes and white-knuckled the handlebar. "There he goes," I whispered to Lon. "How cute is that?"

Suddenly Jupe popped up from his seat and cupped his hands around his mouth to yell. "HENRY! Turn it up to the highest speed and let us through one more time!"

"Goddammit, Jupe!" Lon snapped, yanking on his son's jeans, which were so loose that they nearly slid right off his hips. With his retro "Let's Go Out to the Lobby" cartoon theater-concession-food boxer shorts on display, Jupe grabbed the waist of his jeans just in time and tugged them back up. "The ride's better faster," Jupe called out again to Henry as all three boats glided forward. "Like the good old days!"

With apple-red cheeks and a confused look on his face, Henry took out a key and unlocked a door on the control panel. He switched something inside before slamming his palm over the big red button. "Hang on to your seats!" he warned.

And he wasn't kidding. Our boat squealed on the track, parting the red water as we vaulted forward. I clung to the handlebar as a surprisingly strong gale of musty air hit my face. Jupe's puffy mass of corkscrew curls blew back. A chorus of shouts rang out around us inside the dark tunnel.

The soundtrack was deliriously off-kilter as we buzzed by the first batch of ghostly animatronic mermaids. Lon swore indecipherably at my side, something grim and colorful about murdering his son, who twisted in his seat to yell, "Do you believe me now?" I thought he said, "motherfuckers" after that, but it was lost under the disconcerting squeal of the boat as it roughly chugged along the underwater track.

The first waterfall came way too fast. I heard the cries of the family ahead of us and braced myself for the drop. Cold, red water splashed over the sides, soaking half my hair and the entire right leg of my jeans as I cried out.

The drop propelled us faster through the tunnel. Bone-shaking fast. My teeth clacked together and the little girl in the boat ahead was crying. As the glow-in-the-dark Halloween scenery blurred by, the whole thing spiraled into some warped Willy Wonka nightmare.

The second, steeper drop was just around the corner. The boat ahead creaked and groaned as it tilted down into the darkness. Lon threw one arm around me and the other around Jupe. I clung to the handrail as the boat plunged over the falls. My stomach lurched. A surge of water flew over us in an arcing sheet that crashed behind our heads.

Soaked from crown to sole. Every goddamn one of us.

Worse, the boat made a horrible cracking noise when it realigned at the bottom of the waterfall, rocking as it screeched along the rails through the final straightaway.

The ride's exit doors arced open, but not fast enough. The family ahead ducked down low in their seats, covering the head of their child as they passed through. *Crack!*—the front of the boat clipped the doors and splintered a couple of inches off the edges.

As we whizzed through behind them, light erupted from the loading area. Three park employees were clamoring around the control panel. A buzzer sounded. The family in front of us came to a grating stop. Screams ripped through the air.

Now us, now us. . . . I blinked. We weren't stopping.

Our boat zoomed, splashing red water onto the people at the front of the ride queue. My mind went blank as I prepared to crash. I closed my eyes and steeled myself.

The buzzer sounded.

Our boat skidded to a jolting halt, metal shrieking in protest, water splashing. The teens' boat slammed into ours. My body whipped forward, then back. We all sat in the boat, dazed, for several beats before coming to our senses.

Lon and I pulled Jupe out of the boat at the same time the teens behind us jumped onto the platform. Half a dozen park employees flocked to the platform to check on all of us. It was the little girl in the boat ahead that I was concerned about, but she appeared to be okay. Just scared out of her mind.

"Oh, God, I'm sorry . . . so, so sorry!" Jupe said to the parents as the little girl sobbed in her father's arms. The mother patted Jupe on the shoulder. She then turned to the park staff and launched into a tirade against poor Henry, using words like *irresponsible,* phrases like *could have killed us all,* and ended with a rousing "demand that he be fired or we'll sue your asses to the moon."

To our surprise, the formerly dour and rule-abiding Henry argued back vehemently, yelling that the ride was better faster.

10

Somber and weary, we drove out of the Village to the outskirts of town and made the steep climb on the private back road to Lon's clifftop home. No one said much. Lon asked Jupe a few restrained questions, like exactly how long he'd known about his knack, and who he'd used it on, and whether he could also hear people's emotions (which he couldn't). I was prepared for Lon to lay into the boy—and prepared to stop him—but he was surprisingly calm. Defeated, I supposed.

After a shower, Jupe curled up in my lap on the couch, with Foxglove tucked into the empty space behind his knees. His hair smelled pleasantly of chamomile and coconut oil. I gently detangled his stubborn curls in sections with a wide-toothed comb while the TV chattered in the background. Apart from a few mumbled words, he was quiet—the quietest I'd ever seen him. I tried to cheer him up, but he just clung to my leg and sighed. It hadn't been so long ago that I'd been uncomfortable with Jupe's huggy-touchy lack of boundaries. Now, with his head heavy in my lap, it seemed like the most natural thing in the world. To him, too, I suppose. He fell asleep on me long before his usual midnight bedtime. Lon had to wake him up to get him upstairs into bed.

"What the hell am I going to do with a kid who can manipulate people to get whatever he wants?" Lon asked me a few minutes later as he padded into the kitchen.

I opened the dishwasher and flipped my glass upside down on the top rack. "*You* can manipulate people."

"Only if I'm transmutated. Only if I'm touching them. And changing someone's emotions isn't half as dangerous as being able to walk around in broad daylight, making people do your bidding."

"I'm not sure it's quite that dramatic," I said.

"And my emotional influence only lasts for a minute. I can't permanently alter people's feelings. Did you see the look on that ride operator's face when we left? He still believed the stuff that Jupe had pushed inside his head."

"Yeah, that the ride was better faster. But you don't know how long Jupe's influence lasts. Maybe it wore off Henry an hour later?"

"Maybe."

"I thought Earthbound kids always inherited one of their parents' powers."

"Me too."

"This isn't from Yvonne, then?"

His shook his head slowly and sat down on one of the barstools at the kitchen island. I dried my hands on a towel and leaned against the countertop a few steps away. Waiting. When Lon and I first became involved, he told me he didn't want to talk about Yvonne's knack. He said he would, in time, but I'd definitely waited long enough. I watched his face as he wrestled it out of his mouth.

"Allure."

"Allure," I repeated. "Like a glamour kind of thing, or . . . ?"

After a few moments, he spilled the rest of it. "Yvonne always claimed that she didn't have a knack. I met her on a photo shoot in Antigua. I guess she was a year or two older than you at the time. She was at the height of her modeling career, and I'd heard stories about her from other photographers. It was no secret that she was wild. Liked to party. So I knew better than to get involved with her, but when I met her . . ."

He paused, remembering. The look on his face unnerved me. It was as if he was recalling some life-changing experience that could never be repeated. A sublime meal, or the perfect sunset on a romantic vacation. I'd never seen him look that way when talking about Yvonne. All I'd heard were horror stories. How she'd neglected Jupe. Flirted with drug addictions. Cheated on Lon. Sliced him open with a knife before his divorce trial. Of course, I knew there had to be good times, too. But the way his eyes glossed over as he relived one of these memories made my throat tighten and my stomach queasy.

"She was . . . exquisite," he reminisced. "Not just her looks. The whole package. Her knack didn't only affect how people saw her on the outside, it made you believe that she was kind and funny and caring. Charming. And I wanted her." He blinked, and the memory faded. "I knew that she was lying about something. I knew it was big. But I didn't know she was hiding a knack until after I'd knocked her up." He paused. "Jupe was an accident. We'd been seeing each other on and off for several months. She didn't want to keep the baby. It complicated her career and she wasn't ready to settle down. I was pretty sure the baby was mine, based on her emotional reaction when she first told me, but I didn't know for sure. I followed her to an abortion clinic. I had to transmutate in order to talk her into keeping him. She was the first non-Hellfire person to see me do that."

I stared at the floor, a little shocked by the story. A little sad, too. "I guess she was pretty surprised by the transmutation."

"Not as surprised as I was when I later overheard a phone conversation with her mother, a few months into her pregnancy. That's when I knew I'd been duped." He looked up and gave me a tight smile. The overhead lights in the kitchen were off. A single bulb over the sink created shadows under his eyes. Low voices and music droned from the television in the living room.

"But my finding out didn't change anything. She was still using her knack, and I was still crazy about her, even though I knew better. Told myself that I could see her for what she really was because I could hear her emotions. I asked her to marry me a couple months before Jupe was born. She refused. Twice. She only caved a couple of weeks before her delivery when her pregnancy got difficult. After she had Jupe, she still kept her ability turned 'on' all the time. Persuaded me to take her to the Hellfire Club and get her inducted when one of the thirteen in the Body died. A mistake, of course. When she's transmutated, she could make the Pope himself renounce God, fall to his knees, and worship her."

"Damn."

His finger traced out a pattern on the counter. "That's when things began disintegrating between us. We moved to Miami for a few years. She quit using her knack on me. Just didn't care anymore. I couldn't believe how different she was without it. I knew in my head that I was being manipulated the whole time she was using it, but when she stopped . . . I was suddenly living with a stranger." He shrugged. "And you already know the rest of it. The drugs, the parties, the cheating. Her mom and I became closer the second time Yvonne got out of rehab. She was the one who convinced me to leave."

"Hold on. Yvonne's own mother persuaded you to leave her daughter?"

"She flew down from Portland one summer and told me stories about Yvonne's childhood. Up until that point, I was convinced that I could save her, if I was patient enough. Tried hard enough. But I couldn't. I took Jupe and moved back home. My parents died, I built this house. And now we see her at Christmas. Usually."

Jupe never mentioned her, except in the broadest sense. All his retold childhood memories included Yvonne's family— her sister, Adella, and his grandmother, who were both still actively involved in his and Lon's lives—but never Yvonne.

A long moment ticked by. "Do you think the fact that you'd undergone the transmutation spell before you got Yvonne pregnant—"

"—has something to do with what's manifesting in Jupe?"

"Well, yes."

"Possibly. He hasn't inherited someone else's knack. Despite my doubts before he was born, he's clearly not the milkman's kid."

"He's definitely yours," I agreed with a smile.

He pressed the heel of his palm over a brow, deep in thought. This wasn't so bad, Yvonne's knack. Definitely not as bad as the nightmare knacks I'd dreamed up for her. I could see that it upset him to admit the whole messy story, but it didn't make me think any less of him. He must've thought it would, otherwise he wouldn't have keep it quiet until now.

But something was still bothering me. Anxiety twisted inside my stomach—the source of it just out of reach. My thoughts tumbled and churned.

"What's wrong?" Lon said, startling me.

"Hajo came on to me," I blurted. "He wanted me to sleep with him as payment for the job. The potion was a compromise."

Lon's eyes tightened, searching my face.

"Nothing happened, of course. He tried to kiss me, but I stopped him. I just wanted you to know."

His expression was unreadable, so I immediately felt a little silly for confessing. It's not like I did anything wrong. Why was I telling him this now? My heart pattered a nervous rhythm as I struggled to sort it all out. "I guess if the situation was reversed, and someone had tried to kiss you, I'd be pretty pissed if you kept it secret. Does that make sense?"

He slowly shook his head up and down, then reached for me. His hand slid around my neck. He gave me a gentle smile as he stroked my ear with his thumb. It felt good. Relief rushed through me. I let out a long breath and curved my hand over his, holding it still against my neck.

"I don't want secrets between us," I said. "Not ones that matter, anyway. I keep secrets from everyone all day long. But not you. Okay?"

He tugged me toward the bar stool, closing the remaining distance between us. "I've been waiting for you to say that for weeks," he whispered.

"You have?" I whispered back.

He pushed my hair back over my shoulder to expose my neck. His eyes wandered there. "Sometimes I think I might die if I can't touch you." He said this with great seriousness, his voice suddenly much lower.

A fire sparked inside my chest and lit a path downward. "Is that right?"

"I swear."

"On what, holy man?"

"Guess the Bible's out."

"Whose fault is that?"

"I swear on *Liber Magica Daemonica*." He grinned sweetly, then gave me three kisses, placing one at the cleft above my lip and the others at each corner of my mouth. Delicate, lingering, drugging kisses. So very good.

His head bowed. He went straight for the sweet spot behind my ear. I shivered with pleasure, then reached between us and skimmed my palm over the front of his jeans. He made an appreciative noise. His hands skated up under my shirt, then dropped to unfasten my jeans.

"If he wakes up and catches us in here—"

"He's asleep. I'm listening," he assured me as he tugged my jeans over my hips, rocking them until they dropped to the floor. My panties followed. He barely gave me time to step out of them and kick them away before his hand slid between my legs. I yelped in surprise.

"Shh," he warned playfully. His fingers smoothed, flicked, and rubbed. My breathing quickened. God have mercy, but the man had serious skills. I could hardly do better myself. He hadn't memorized what I wanted—or what he *thought* I wanted. He listened to my emotional responses and made adjustments in his explorations. I sagged against him and muffled soft moans against his chest. Ten points for the empathy knack.

I somehow summoned the wherewithal to push his hand away. He smiled down at me with heavy-lidded eyes as I yanked his shirt up. He raised his arms briefly. I pulled the fabric over his shoulders and off his head, tossing it somewhere behind me with my discarded clothing, then reacquainted myself with the delightfully warm, rock-solid wall of his golden chest. So beautiful. I scored a fingernail down the golden trail of hair that bisected his torso and bent to kiss the scar over his ribs. He shivered violently. I couldn't wait any longer.

Breathless, I pushed aside the nearby stool, then turned around and bent over the stainless steel countertop. The metal was cold against my stomach as he slowly smoothed a splayed palm down my spine. "Hurry," I instructed, but I really meant, *I need you right now*. The metallic jingle of his belt buckle unfastening behind me made my breath hitch. A second later, there was heat and a familiar, insistent pressure . . . and with one long push, he was inside me. Every cell in my body suddenly roared to life.

"Holy Whore of Babylon," I swore, clinging to the sides of the counter for support.

His pace was fast and hard and hyperventilatingly wonderful. Between a couple of hard smacks on my ass, I was thanking both him and every saint in the Bible. Even a few more that weren't in it. I glanced over my shoulder so that I could watch him through jostling vision.

Unexpectedly, he pulled out with a groan. I cursed at him, then squealed when he flipped me around to face him. He slung an arm around my waist to haul me up until I was sitting on the edge of the counter. It was a good height for us. His jeans hung around the middle of his thighs, threatening to fall down to his feet any second. "Yes," he whispered as he entered me again. "Just like that."

I stretched a leg out and pressed my toes against a stool, struggling for leverage. He dug his fingers into my hips as they lifted off the table to meet his. Our pace increased. We gave each other no quarter—it was furious, breakneck, bruised-and-sore-later sex. My pulse jackknifed and sped up. The stool under my straining toes clinked against the counter. I became increasingly sure that I was going to have a heart attack or an aneurysm. Maybe my bones would snap from the strain. But I didn't care, because it was *just there*, in the distance, so close.

"Look at me," Lon growled.

"I can't . . ." do two things at once.

"Yes, you damn well can."

A strangled laugh caught in my throat, then I groaned in frustration.

One of his palms slapped down on the counter behind me. The other gripped the back of my neck. He lowered my hips back down on the table and pressed his forehead against mine again. Our labored breath mingled. I wrapped my legs around his waist and dug my heels into his ass. "Yes, yes . . . God, yes. Hold on—"

The transmutation roared in my ears and sent chills dancing across my skin. His horns brushed my hair as they spiraled into place. I curled my fingers around them like handlebars on a bike.

"Look at me," he said, a breathless, gentle command this time. And I looked—I couldn't *not* look. His eyes were a lush, dark forest, his lashes guarding the only entrance; everything I wanted was inside. He kissed me like he was staking a claim. His wavy hair and fiery golden halo fell around my face, blocking out everything but him. "No secrets."

No secrets, I agreed in my head. He could hear my thoughts now. No need to speak. Slick and swollen, I constricted around him as the vanishing point flickered and the distance gave way.

"Christ!" he murmured in amazement, his grip on me tightening in response.

Thank you, thank you, thank you, I thought in my head as my muscles slackened one last time, ebb and flow, so close now . . . just needed to catch it.

"My pleasure," he confirmed between huffed, short breaths.

Now, Lon, now, I encouraged, quivering madly, squinting my eyes shut to make it over the last peak.

"Look at me," he pleaded one final time.

And I did.

Several minutes later, both exhausted and happy, we pulled each other's clothes back on and made our way upstairs. I hadn't crashed before midnight in weeks, but I was fully prepared to collapse on his bed and drift into a beautifully deep sleep, nestled up against him. I could think of nothing better. Tomorrow I'd deal with Hajo's search and Jupe's early-blooming knack, but tonight I was done. The world could just go to hell, I didn't care.

As we shuffled through the living room, shutting off lights along the way, Lon picked up the remote to turn off the TV, then halted. "What the hell?" he mumbled, turning the volume up.

The 11:00 news was broadcasting live from Brentano Gardens. Tension flared as my mind jumped to what had happened there earlier. Jupe must be in more trouble than we'd thought.

But the panning Channel 7 camera was nowhere near the scene of Jupe's mind-crime. On the opposite end of the park, the news was reporting that while the Spirit Cove ride had been temporarily closed due to a mechanical malfunction, another La Sirena teen had gone missing. He was last seen by his friends before he left to buy a bag of hot churros. The remnants of the fried dessert were found behind the Sweety Tooth carnival booth . . . next to three crumbled dollar bills spattered with blood.

11

"Is that him?" Lon asked, peering out the window of the Singing Bean Musical Coffeehouse the following afternoon.

"No. And we still have ten minutes. I told them two o'clock."

Lon quietly fumed as he glared out the window and sipped tea from a paper cup.

A few minutes passed before Hajo sped up to the coffee shop on a green-and-silver Ducati that looked more like an insect than a motorcycle. Sounded like one too. I doubted it was street legal. Nothing about Hajo was.

"That's the death dowser," I said, tapping twice on the window with my fingernail.

Lon watched Hajo as he took off his helmet, then murmured, "You've *got* to be kidding me," before crumpling his cup and hurling it into the trash.

I adjusted the loop of the skinny black-and-white-striped knit scarf around my neck as I headed outside to greet Hajo. He looked much the same as he had the other night, including the simmering, lusty look in his eyes as he smiled at me. I wondered if he was high. His smile flattened when he saw Lon over my shoulder.

I made introductions. No one bothered to shake hands. Part of me almost regretted that I'd confessed all that stuff about Hajo last night. Lon looked as if he was considering the best way to murder him. Before the situation plunged into a dank pit of awkwardness, Bob drove up. His Hawaiian shirt reflected his oh-so-repentant mood: a somber brown background speckled with black bongo drum silhouettes. He looked up at the darkening stormy sky as he exited his car, then reached through the open door for an umbrella.

Lon followed my line of vision to Bob and promptly headed toward the Earthbound before I could stop him. He held up a casual hand to the oncoming car while he crossed the street, not bothering to look up when the car slammed on brakes and honked.

With a neon-orange umbrella in hand, Bob closed his car door and turned around to find Lon headed right for him with a deathproof swagger and an intent to do some verbal damage.

"Poor Robert," Hajo sympathized as he saddled up to my side. "Glad that's not me."

Lon wasn't saying much, but he was awfully close to Bob's face. Bob backed up and flattened against his car, talking rapidly and waving the orange umbrella in front of him to indicate his innocence. A few people gawked as they walked past them.

I should've known Lon would be angrier about Bob's betrayal of my vassal potion than about Hajo's stepping over the line. Hajo was a stranger. Bob was a friend. Treachery was far worse when it was personal. Lightning cracked through gray sky in the distance. *Please let this day be over soon.*

With his eyes forged into a single dark slash under a rigid brow, Lon trailed Bob as he scurried across the street. Bob's round face was flushed beet-red. Dammit. Now I felt sorry for him again. I couldn't help it. He looked like a kicked dog. When his eyes met mine, I mouthed "sorry." Then I quickly took control of things before the three of them ended up pounding each other's heads into the sidewalk.

"I've got the tracking object on me," I said to Hajo. "Do you do this on foot?"

"Usually on my bike."

"I'm not letting the tracking object out of my sight," Lon said without emotion as he stuffed his hands into his pockets. "No offense, but I don't trust junkies."

Hajo was momentarily taken aback. He composed himself, smiled, and said coolly, "None taken."

"If you have sømna on you now, I'm not getting into a vehicle with you," Lon said. "I'm not going to chance getting pulled over and arrested."

"I'm not carrying," Hajo said.

Lon didn't press it, so I assumed he read Hajo's answer as honest. "All right. Let's go."

We piled in Lon's SUV. I drove. Death Boy and Lazy Eye sat in the second row behind us, their feet wading in Jupe's pile of comics. Lon sat in the passenger seat with a short-barreled Lupara shotgun in his lap, like some Sicilian mobster. I wanted to ask him who he planned on shooting, Hajo or some dead bodies, but he was in a black mood, so I let it go.

Before I put the car in gear, Hajo spoke up from the back. "There's the little matter of payment before we start." I glanced at him through the rearview mirror and pulled the brown, half-ounce bottle of the potion out of my jacket pocket, handing it to him through the front seats. Then I pulled out onto the street and headed toward Ocean Drive.

Hajo held the tiny bottle up against the window, checking

the level of the liquid in the dimming afternoon light. He un-screwed the dropper top and sucked up the medicinal.

"Bob?" Hajo prodded.

"Is this really necessary?" Bob asked. "I told you, I can vouch for her."

"Open wide," Hajo insisted.

"Only one drop. No more. It's brewed from a mixture of calamus root and *Atropa belladonna*."

Hajo paused.

"Deadly nightshade," I clarified. "One of the most toxic plants known to man. One too many drops could cause heart palpitations and blindness. A few more could kill."

"One drop. Got it," Hajo said. "Open."

Sour and depressed, Bob opened his mouth and allowed Hajo to drop the liquid on his waiting tongue. Bob made a face and swallowed.

"How long for it to take effect?" Hajo asked.

I waited as Bob's pupils dilated into enormous black holes. "Now," I said.

Hajo studied Bob. "How long does it last?"

"Thirty minutes. An hour. Depends on the person."

"Have you dosed me with this before?" Bob asked me nervously. He was starting to sweat again; he was quite pos-sibly the sweatiest demon alive.

"I never thought I needed to," I replied.

He sighed and swallowed hard. "Go ahead and do what you're gonna do, Hajo."

Hajo spun the bottle in his hand, thinking for a short time before he spoke. "I can't ask you to do something you wouldn't mind doing. That proves nothing. It has to be some-thing that you would only do against your will or better judg-ment."

I didn't like the sound of that. Lon and I glanced at each other.

Hajo settled on his test. "Since you and Mr. Butler aren't the best of friends, Bobby boy, I'm guessing you wouldn't be eager to piss him off any more than you already have. That would be the last thing you want right now."

Bob panicked, reacting to the vassal effect and Hajo's suggestion as Lon turned to glare at them, unhappy about where this was headed.

"Even though you're deathly scared of him, you'd do anything for Cady, wouldn't you?" Hajo said. "Why don't you show Cady how you really feel about her. Kiss her. Now."

Lon and I uttered a series of outcries that quickly erupted into random angry shouts as Bob unbuckled his seat belt and stuck his head between us. He was mumbling as he reached for me—saying that he was sorry, that he had to do this.

"Sit down!" Lon barked, shoving at Bob.

Hajo laughed as Bob pressed forward. For several seconds, the front seat was a mass of tangled arms and Bob's clammy lips trying to make contact with my face, then Lon stuck the antique sawed-off shotgun into Bob's chest. "Sit the fuck down."

Bob wailed, but tried to push the gun away, undeterred. I cut the wheel harder than I expected—I was unaccustomed to driving something so big. The SUV swerved violently, hit the curb, and plowed over it. Bob's head slammed against the side of seat. Lon grabbed the *oh-shit* handle and braced himself while cussing me out. I got control of the car, but not before a couple of drivers honked, and not before my heart rate tripled.

Bob moaned and gripped the side of this head, trying to catch his breath. This had gone too far. Nobody could stop Bob but the person who dosed him.

"Hajo!" I bellowed into the rearview mirror. "Make him stop!"

Lon twisted in his seat, shoved Bob roughly, and pointed the Lupara at Hajo. "Now, you son of a bitch."

"All right, all right!" Hajo said, still fighting back laughter. "Bob, stop trying to kiss Cady. Sit in your seat and be a good boy. Simon says."

Bob whimpered as Hajo pocketed the little vial, pleased as pie. "You brew good stuff, Cady," he concluded. "Now let's hunt your dead body. Where's this tracking object you promised?"

We drove around La Sirena with the rear windows cracked while Hajo held Bishop's key in his hands and went into some sort of mild trance. One hour passed, then another. On occasion, he mumbled a quick direction: "Turn right," or "Trail's gone cold. Loop back around." Compliant but depressed, Bob was crumpled in the seat next to Hajo, wedged up against the door.

Lon and I sat in silence as rain drizzled, the wipers keeping a steady rhythm on the windshield. Worry stalked me from a distance. I wasn't sure what I wanted more: for Hajo to find some thirty-year-old mass grave, or for him to fail and find nothing. Either prospect was undesirable, and both made me anxious.

Nightfall approached. As we curved around the shore outside the city limits, Lon sneaked his hand over the leather armrest and gently prodded my arm. When I glanced over at him, he was resting the side of his head against the seat, a tender look on his face. He tucked his long hair behind one ear, then ran his knuckles over the elbow of my jacket. I switched hands on the wheel so that I could link fingers with him.

With a sudden cry, Hajo woke up from his stupor. He'd caught the thread.

His directions became increasingly frequent and urgent. Bob perked up and watched with interest as Hajo guided us down an unmarked rocky side street that meandered around the coast. It was hard to see much of the terrain under dark skies and dreary rain. The headlights illuminated a thicket of evergreens on the left that blocked our view of the main road and, as I steered the SUV around a sharp curve, a row of concrete buildings stacked up in the distance, clinging to the shore. From a rickety post, a metal sign hung sideways, riddled with rusted-out holes. It read: PACIFIC GLORY TUNA CANNERY.

"Huh," Lon murmured. "I remember touring this place on a school trip when I was a kid. It used to rival Bumble Bee until it was shut down in the late 1970s. Botulism outbreak. Put hundreds of locals out of work."

"We're close," Hajo said. "Really close."

I slowed the SUV as the bumpy road became covered with creeping bramble and downed tree branches every ten feet or so. Across the water, white-purple lightning struck on the edge of the horizon as darker storm clouds gathered. Angry waves crashed against the shore below us as we drove further down into the small peninsula where the cannery sprawled. Sections of the buildings transitioned from land to water with the aid of stilts. A long dock with missing boards wrapped around the Pacific edge of the buildings where tuna boats used to empty their catches.

"*Stop.*"

I braked in front of one of the cannery buildings.

"Inside there," Hajo said, flinging off his seat belt.

I switched off the ignition and exited the SUV under a smattering of cold rain while Lon dug around in a seat pocket for a flashlight. He flicked it on and followed Hajo to a large loading door at the end of the building. Waist-high weeds, dead and brittle, blocked the door. Lon and Hajo worked together silently to stamp them down until they revealed a vertical door handle chained with a blackened padlock.

"You know how to pick locks?" Hajo asked Lon.

Lon shone the flashlight on the padlock, studied it for several seconds, then beckoned for me to take the light from him. "Hold it right there," he instructed. He fished out his father's old pocketknife and dug rusted bolts from the metal plate holding one side of the chain. Within seconds, the entire plate fell away with the chain still attached.

"Don't get your fingerprints on anything. Just in case," he said. He retracted his hand inside the edge of his jacket sleeve before sliding the large door a few feet to the side, and one by one we slipped into darkness, shaking the rain off as we entered the crumbling warehouse.

A shallow ramp led into a cavernous empty room. Everything was concrete—the floor, walls, rows of columns, even the ceiling. Only a narrow, rectangular band of windows broke the monotony. Stormy twilight passed through busted glass and illuminated an impressive display of faded graffiti that tagged the walls. Near the entrance, wooden crates were stacked high, a make-do ladder leading up to one of the broken windows, presumably used by graffiti artists to get in and out of the building. A pile of rusted spray-paint cans lay nearby.

We walked in, wet shoes squelching as we avoided rubble and some foul-smelling standing water that ran through the center of the room. At the end, we continued through a passage into a second area filled with tables and long metal tanks. Abandoned machinery was choked with weeds that snaked in through the broken windows. The graffiti tags tapered off here.

"So strong . . ." Hajo mumbled. "Keep going."

Something stirred in the darkness to the side. I started and Lon herded me in closer to his hip. "Just rats," he assured me, "or bats. Or maybe seagulls." Any of them would explain the strong, acidic smell of animal droppings that stung my eyes.

"People get sick from breathing in pigeon shit," I complained, eyeing the darkness with trepidation. "Like, hospital sick."

Lon grunted. "Isn't your buddy Bob here a healer?"

"I'm not good with disease," Bob argued in a loud whisper behind me. "Just minor injuries. My father's knack was stronger. He was a well-known GP in Morella before he died."

He was right about that. Earthbounds with healing abilities were fairly common, and those with substantial skills usually made a career of medicine. Their high rate of success gave them a sizable advantage over human doctors and also gave them access to the highest-paying jobs. In fact, Bob lived off his father's inheritance. I often wondered if Bob felt overshadowed by his father's success—he talked about the man a lot, especially after a few drinks.

"It's just on the other side of that hallway," Hajo said.

We all looked where he was pointing. "That hallway" was long, narrow, and echoed with the sound of water dripping from broken pipes running along the ceiling. Every fiber of my being screamed a warning *not* to step into it. If Jupe were there, he would tell me that people too dumb to live did this kind of thing all the time in horror movies.

"Can you track more than one body at a time?" Lon asked.

Up until now, neither of us had brought this up. We couldn't very well just tell Hajo that we were hunting the remains of the abducted children from the original Snatcher case. We might be too dumb to live, but we weren't dumb enough to trust Drug Lord Hajo with that information.

"Naturally," he said. "You wanna know how many bodies I sense on a daily basis? Thousands. Humans, animals—even insects, if they're big enough. Death is everywhere, man. I can't walk by a graveyard or I'll pass out. And, yeah, there's a boatload of dead things up in here, as if you can't smell that yourself."

I tried not to gag and inhaled with my mouth instead of my nose.

"You think I enjoy having this knack?" Hajo continued, his tone abrasive. "Would you? Why do you think I smoke sømna and just about anything else I can get my hands on? Anything to make me forget about it, or I go crazy."

Lon grunted and aimed the flashlight at Hajo, who shielded his eyes.

"Come on," I coaxed. If the children's bodies were here, we were about to find out.

Single file, Hajo leading the way, we marched down the dank hallway. He stopped in front of a thick metal door. "Inside here."

"Open the door," Lon instructed.

"I can't."

"Why not?"

"I don't know," Hajo admitted. "I just . . ."

I stuck my head around Lon's arm and guided his hand to aim the flashlight on the door handle. A diffused wedge of pink glowed between the frame and the door. "It's secured by a spell," I said. Weird magick. Temporary spells fade, but

stronger magick cracks. The pink glow here was riddled with
fine lines, which meant that the spell must've been set a long
time ago. Years and years . . . maybe even *thirty* years.

Lon bent low to inspect the glow, reaching, then suddenly withdrew his hand. "What are we looking at here? A
serious ward? A warning?"

I examined the markings. They weren't anything I'd seen,
but on closer inspection, they followed a familiar pattern. "I
think it's just a deterrent. A trick to keep people out. Move
away."

We shifted positions. I tried to open the door myself,
but my hand wouldn't grasp the handle. What a clever spell;
I wished I knew how to do it. In order for us to get inside, I'd
have to short it out. I retrieved a short stick of red ochre chalk
from my jacket and drew a sloppy circle around the handle,
then marked it with three sigils. I would've preferred to use
a better spell, one that required kindled Heka, but we were
sans electricity, so I had to use simpler magick. I mumbled a
dissolving spell and spat on the sigils. The red ochre markings
crackled with a brief flash of light, then popped and died. The
old pink haze disintegrated.

I stood and started again to open the door, but Lon's arm
hooked around my waist and pulled me backward. "Let him
do it."

Hajo balked. "You paid me to dowse, not lay a red carpet
down for you."

"Open it." Lon wasn't asking.

Hajo muttered to himself but complied as Bob scooted
closer to cower behind me. I think he was sniffing my hair—
probably still experiencing lingering effects from Hajo's vassal
suggestion—but I was too anxious about finding dead bodies
to care.

The door creaked open and a foul, musty odor wafted out. We turned our heads away and moved back, waiting several moments for the stench to dissipate. This couldn't be good.

The golden arc from Lon's flashlight drifted over a square, windowless room. A bulky piece of broken conveyor machinery with several cranks and ceiling exhausts jutted out from the left, taking up a third of the area. Near the far wall, sketched onto the floor, I could just make out a row of mandalas: holy squared circles. Large ones. They are most commonly found in Buddhist and Hindu spiritual art, filled with delicate patterns and used for meditation and trance induction to focus energy. The outer circles of these were much simpler in design. But it was the size that caught my attention: three or four feet across. Inside the outer rings, a strangely patterned square was drawn, then another smaller circle inside the square. Four simple sigils rimmed the outer boundary. None of it was chalked. The designs were etched into the concrete. Serious stuff.

"I need to look at the symbols," I said.

We moved as a unit and stepped inside the room.

"Stay here and guard the door," Lon instructed Bob.

"In the dark?"

Lon dug a silver Zippo out of this pocket, snapped open the cover, and flicked it on. "Don't lose this—it's vintage. Speak up if you hear anything coming."

"Oh, God," Bob mumbled breathlessly, accepting the lighter with fearful reluctance. The blue-and-yellow flame bounced up and down in time with the Earthbound's shaking hand.

"The spell on the door was old," I assured Bob, putting a steady hand on his elbow. "No one's been here for years."

Lon picked up a rusted piece of piping off the floor, shook off cobwebs, and gave it to Bob. "Just in case."

Bob whimpered.

We left him at his post and walked toward the mandalas. My stomach twisted as I counted them. Seven. Probably not a coincidence. And when I stepped closer and got a good look at the first one, I mentally changed that "probably" to a "definitely not."

They weren't charged—no Heka glowed within the lines—but, like the pink spell on the door, there was something achingly familiar about the patterns around the inner square of the mandalas. I knew it well. Change the square to a triangle and you had practically the same markings that were painted beneath each of the tables in Tambuku.

"Binding magick," I whispered to Lon.

The magical artwork surrounding the mandalas was unique. Each of the four sigils was drawn with clean lines, and all were scored with letters in a sophisticated, evolved alphabet that wasn't earthly.

I squatted and looked closer. "Something Æthyric, maybe."

"I've never seen anything like it," Lon mumbled.

No sign of old blood, Heka, bones, or anything else around them. I took out my phone and snapped a quick photo of each one, trying not to think about terrified kids being held here. If there *were* such things as ghosts, as Jupe stubbornly believed, I couldn't imagine anything worse than their being trapped in a place like this for eternity.

Lon shone the light around the room after I'd finished taking pictures. "I don't see any remains."

"That's because the thread's not connected. Those are clean." Hajo pointed to the far side of the conveyor machinery, away from the mandalas. "The thread ends over there."

My heart sped up as we treaded across the room. Hidden from view between the wall and a broken machine, an oblong oval stretched across the cement floor—not carved like the mandalas, but drawn with a dark pigment.

Outside the oval was more of that strange alphabet from the mandalas.

And inside the oval was a single skeleton.

An *adult* skeleton. Not a child.

The arm and leg bones lay in a pattern that suggested the body had been splayed out. The skull was still connected. In the middle—where the torso should have been—a pile of splintered bones radiated in a rough circle, as if a bomb had gone off inside the body. A dark spatter stained the concrete beneath, stopping abruptly inside the edge of the oval. No trace of any clothing whatsoever.

A gruesome sight. But what was written on the cement above the skull sent an army of chills down my spine:

JESSE BISHOP

Shock swept through me. I stood frozen for several moments, then pushed it away and focused on the details. The writing was definitely inscribed by the same hand who'd carved the mandalas, and, like the strange alphabet on those, the letters here were evenly spaced.

Like a child practicing block letters. That shook something loose in my brain. An image from an old newspaper clipping in the bottom of Dare's banker box. I was no handwriting expert, but even I could see that Bishop's name was written in the same manner as the names of the seven kids that were carved into the trees at Sandpiper Park.

Oh, Christ . . .

Bishop wasn't the Snatcher.

Bishop was *killed by the Snatcher.* The key on the necklace had provided Hajo with a direct thread to its owner's remains—not the children.

A dry croak stuck in my throat as I tried to say this out loud, but Lon immediately hushed me. "Take a picture," he commanded softly.

With shaking hands, I pressed the screen on my phone to enable the camera function. It was all I could do to focus long enough to get a partially blurry shot, so I took a second one, but it didn't turn out much better. One thing was obvious: though the seven mandalas were well planned and precisely executed, the oval holding Bishop's bones was an afterthought. It was set off in the corner, the angle slightly askew. Drawn quick and rough. In a moment of anger?

"So, this is the guy you're looking for, yeah?" Hajo said. "Looks like he was involved in some heavy occult shit. Remind me not to cross a magician."

"Damn straight," Lon muttered.

Hajo squatted down near the circle and pointed. "What's that? There's something behind the jaw. Looks like he swallowed it."

Lon shifted the flashlight's beam to illuminate the skull, while Hajo leaned over the skeleton to reach for it. When his fingers almost made it, he leaned in farther, taking a step inside the oval, and a tinge of dull red light, barely perceptible, washed over his shoe.

"No!" I shouted. But it was too late.

The red light sizzled around the oval and brightened. Another spell. It wasn't a deterrent this time. Not a warning, either . . .

A deafening blast cracked the concrete beneath the

skeleton and the whole room shook. An unseen force rushed at us, knocking Hajo against the wall and slamming Lon into the conveyor machine. My back hit the concrete floor. Pain ripped through my lungs. Lon's flashlight flew from his hand and ricocheted off the wall. It blinked a couple of times as it spun on the floor and rolled somewhere near me.

"Cady!" Lon bellowed in the darkness.

Before I had time to answer, "What happened?" echoed in the distance and I saw Lon's golden Zippo flame flickering, floating through the air like a yellow fairy as Bob ran toward us.

I pushed myself up, scanning the dark for the flashlight. It was pointed at the wall. I touched the handle with my fingertips, accidently pushing it away as a strange scuttling sound vibrated through the air, somewhere off in the corner.

Scritch, scritch, scritch, scritch, scritch.

"Be quiet!" I yelled. Bob's running feet stopped abruptly.

My hand stilled as I strained to listen to the bizarre scratching sound. It multiplied and moved, and my heart nearly stopped.

Scritch, scritch, scritch, scritch.

What was that? Claws? Something small was clicking on the concrete, moving closer.

12

Bob shrieked and the Zippo flew through the air, the flame extinguished before the lighter clinked on the floor. Sounds of a struggle broke through the darkness, then Bob shouted, "Get it off me!"

My fingers gripped the handle of the flashlight. I swung it madly, bouncing the cone of light around the room. Lon, Hajo, Bob, surrounded by shiny things. Moving things. Birds?

I shone the light on the skeleton. The tripped spell that knocked us off our feet had furrowed the concrete floor and part of the wall and left a gaping inch-wide crevice. It had also cracked the skull—cleaved it right in two, from crown to jaw. And in the center of the split skull, like a sprout emerging from soil, the moving things slithered out and made a thumping noise as they hit the floor.

Not birds.

Bugs.

Enormous goddamn cockroaches.

Ribbed, shiny, flat bodies. Spiny legs that clicked on the cement like claws. Twitching antennae as long as my fingers. Beady eyes that glowed turquoise under the flashlight's beam. *Eyes?* I'd never seen a roach's eyes. I'd never seen roaches this big. They looked like terrifying prehistoric bugs from another planet.

Bugs from the Æthyr.

One extended a pair of shiny wings the color of burnt sugar. Then it made a hissing noise, buzzed its wings, and took off several feet into the air . . . and landed on Hajo's leg. He kicked it away. It made a queasy crackling sound when it landed, then a scraping noise as it skidded on its side across the floor.

Okay, make that *flying* bugs from the Æthyr.

Screams cut through the room. Mine. Hajo's. Maybe Lon's. I'd never heard him scream, but who could tell. I nearly wet my pants in a moment of hyperventilating revulsion.

"Help!" Bob fell to the floor, reaching for his leg. Nearby, a trail of light brown goo dripped from the conveyor machine. A squirming bug carcass lay upside-down at its base, its spiny legs twitching violently. "It bit me!"

I scurried on hands and knees to help him while Hajo defended himself against the oncoming horde, kicking away the bugs as they emerged from the skull.

"It bit me," Bob repeated in near hysteria. "It burns—" He hiked up his pant leg. Blood streamed from a jagged mark on his ankle. But that wasn't the problem. The "bite" was swelling, and way too fast. A series of black rings already ridged the flesh around Bob's ankle and advanced one by one up his leg.

"What the hell?" Hajo bellowed. "What are these things?"

Another bug skittered up behind Lon, its spiny black legs clicking on the cement. I called out a warning. Lon swiveled in time to raise his foot and stomp. The awful sound of cracking exoskeleton filled my ears, followed by a splatter of brown bug guts across my jeans.

A gurgled cry of fear bubbled up from Bob. The black lines ringing his leg had disappeared past his pushed-up pant leg. He gripped his stomach. I pried his hands away and wrenched up his Hawaiian shirt. The rings had already made it up there, too.

The bugs were venomous.

"Can't . . . breathe," Bob choked. "My heart—"

"A little help over here!" Hajo shouted frantically. He'd found another piece of pipe and was swatting at the bugs with savage swings. Squishy, crackling roach deaths echoed off the walls, but the bugs didn't stop coming. They were still pouring from the cracked skull like brown lava.

I blocked out the scuttling and the hissing and the horrifying flitting of wings to concentrate on a solution. Hajo had definitely tripped a spell when he entered the oval around the skeleton—some kind of magical ward, something big and nasty that I'd never seen before. But if it was just a ward, then these bugs weren't real. They were thought-forms; illusions designed to instill fear. That seemed more reasonable than a spell that opened up a hole in the cosmos into a nest of Æthyric cockroaches.

"It's just magick," I said. "Not real. The pain is psychosomatic. Listen to me, Bob. It's not real."

Lon bent over Bob and ripped his shirt open. The black rings were inching up Bob's throat. His face was dark red. He couldn't breathe.

"Real or not," Lon said, "he's going to have a goddamn heart attack."

"The bug juice is burning my skin," Hajo yelled from somewhere nearby.

I glanced at my jeans. He was right. Like acid, the roaches' pudding-like innards were eating away holes in the fabric.

"Aagghh! Shit!" Lon kicked out, then fired a booming shot, so loud I recoiled in shock.

He dropped to his knees and let the Lupara clank against the floor.

"Lon!" I jerked up the hem of his jeans as he groaned in pain. A craggy puncture wound on his leg, a little higher up than Bob's. The damn bug had bitten right through his jeans. A moment later, the first black ring circled his skin.

"Counterspell," Lon shouted at me, gripping his leg in pain.

Meanwhile, Bob was going into convulsions, the heels of his shoes rapidly banging against the floor. I tried to steady him, but it was useless. Nearby, Hajo continued to scream for help as he played baseball with the bugs. I forced myself to focus, reaching inside my jacket for the red ochre chalk. If this was a tripped ward, then I knew exactly two spells that could possibly negate the magick. One of them I'd used several times successfully in the past. The other spell, *Silentium*, was more powerful, but I'd never used it. I only knew that it required a huge blast of Heka to power it. Kindled Heka—my natural magical mojo reinforced with outside energy. Bodily fluids weren't going to be enough. I needed electrical current for the kindling, and the cannery had probably been dead for years. . . .

Bob's convulsions picked up speed as Lon gripped his own thigh, gritting his teeth and squinting into the harsh glare of the flashlight. In the distance, I could feel the rumble of thunder outside. The storm—I wondered if it was close enough for me to pull down lightning.

All I could do was try.

I began sketching the *Silentium* seal on the floor in front of me, holding the flashlight in my other hand, but before I could even form a small circle, the chalk broke. I was bearing down too hard. I scrambled to retrieve a nub, but one of the bugs dove out of the darkness and lunged for my fingers. I beat it back with the flashlight. As metal collided with cockroach, its glossy brown body cracked . . . and so did the glass lens. The flashlight bulb broke with a pop, and the precious cone of white light sizzled out.

Darkness blanketed the room. Anxious shouting broke out around me. Bob was going to die. Lon was groaning in pain. Hajo was fighting for his life.

Scritch, scritch, scritch, scritch, scritch.

I opened myself up and reached for any current—battery, electricity, lightning. *Come on, come on*, I thought. As I strained to ferret out a source of energy, something dark stirred inside me. The air shifted. The sounds in the room slipped away, replaced by an unearthly hum. A cold power poured from me into the darkness. The familiar blue pinpoint of light.

My Moonchild ability.

The one bred into me by my psychotic parents. The one I hadn't used since that horrible night in San Diego weeks ago. The one that tempted me the other night with Hajo. *No, no, no!* My body shuddered as I desperately tried to shove it back down. But it was like trying to abstain from sneezing. No matter how hard I tried, no matter how much I wanted to reign it in, I just couldn't. It was too strong.

Death by magical roaches or use the Moonchild power? Wait, why was I fighting it? I couldn't remember. It didn't matter, because I wasn't going to be eaten alive by creepy brown bugs the size of rats. I stopped pushing the power away and let it come.

The pinpoint of light grew into a flat blue disk, begging

to be used. The *Silentium* seal crowded my thoughts, then the sigils and lines transferred from my mind to the blue light in front of me. Negative space fell away and the seal glowed in the darkness.

It felt . . . good. Heka was being funneled from me in a small stream. I could feel it leaving, but where was it going? Was my body using it to kindle moon energy? I couldn't grasp how it worked, but I sure as hell felt it when it rushed back through me like fire and overflowed into the blue seal, charging it. On instinct, I pushed the silver seal with my mind, slamming it down to the floor while shouting the arcane words to complete the *Silentium* spell.

A spark blossomed into an explosion. For a lingering moment, the entire room was alive with white light. Bob's convulsions halted; Lon and Hajo craned their necks upward. The silver seal bounced off the floor, expanded around all of us into a glittering cloud, then imploded.

Darkness dropped from the ceiling. The room fell silent. No more tickity-tick, scritchity-scratch of tiny feet. No more squishy crackles. No more buzzing wings.

"Are they gone? Are they?" Hajo said.

It took me several moments to get my balance. I braced for post-magick nausea, but it never came.

"Cady?" Lon's voice broke with emotion.

I reached out for him, our hands colliding as Bob moaned.

"You okay?" I asked.

"Pain's gone," Lon answered as he wound his fingers around the back of my neck and pulled me close. "You used it?" he whispered.

"Not on purpose," I whispered back.

Quick and rough, he kissed the side of my head. "I

thought . . . Never mind." He kissed me again, then released me.

I bent down to inspect Bob, my fingers still wary of colliding with bug exoskeleton, but all I felt was warm skin. Bob whimpered in relief and clamped his sweaty hands around mine as Hajo mumbled exclamations behind us between labored breaths.

Metal scraped over cement. After two flicks, a soft, orange glow ballooned from the Zippo, which Lon now held. He moved it over Bob's skin, then his own leg. The black rings were gone. Bite marks too. Even the holes burned in my jeans by the blood had disappeared. He inspected the floor around us. No trace of the magical cockroaches remained. No smear of bug pudding, no twitching legs. Nothing. Only the wildly scattered bones of Bishop's skeleton and the monumental crack running the length of the room remained as witnesses.

Lon crawled to the shattered skeleton and reached for the skull, grabbing the object that Hajo had first spotted, the one that started this whole damn mess. He inspected it under the Zippo flame, then handed it to me.

It was a rolled-up Polaroid photo. The backing was peeling away, the image was dark and indiscernible. I shoved it into my pocket and hoarsely said, "Let's get the hell out of here."

No one disagreed.

It took us half an hour to get to the Village. I shook the entire way. Prickling terror still lingered under my skin, and my muscles twitched with the memory of the blue-eyed bugs. In the moments when I was able to push away images of the abhorrent bugs and the realization of just how enormously powerful that old magick had been—*We could have died!*—I mused on the Moonchild ability and how good it had felt. I didn't have any regrets. I thought I might, but I didn't. At least not right now.

After we made back to the Singing Bean and watched Bob and Hajo walk to their vehicles, Lon and I sat alone in his car till the rain tapered off a little.

"Good goddamn riddance," Lon complained, shoving the Lupara under my seat. "If I never see either one of those idiots again, it'll be too soon."

Unfortunately, I couldn't hope for the same. Once Bob got over all this, he'd be back at Tambuku. And Hajo, well . . .

"I can't believe you're going to have to bind someone for that piece-of-shit junkie dowser," Lon mumbled.

Two someones, actually, but a deal was a deal. And asshole druggie or not, I'd give the guy one thing: he didn't cut and run in the middle of the hissing cockroach fight.

"I thought you were dead," Lon said.

"Me? Why?"

"In the cannery, when you stopped the bugs. I . . . couldn't hear you."

"You couldn't read my emotions?"

He shook his head quickly. "No. They were there, and then they were gone. Like listening to a radio that suddenly gets turned off."

"That's strange."

"It's never happened to me before. Not even when you've used the moon magick. Definitely not in the Hellfire caves when you banished that incubus. And even though things were crazy at the time, I think I would've noticed if it happened in San Diego, when your parents . . ." He gestured with his eyes, as if to say "you know."

"Tried to sacrifice me?"

He grunted affirmatively. "Anyway, it doesn't matter. At least your magick scared the piss out of the death dowser," Lon said. "Bob too. They'll think twice before crossing you."

Maybe, but we had bigger problems.

We now knew Bishop was dead and his body entombed in that warehouse. But if he'd been killed by the Snatcher thirty years ago, that raised a whole new set of possibilities. Had Bishop helped the Snatcher and later been betrayed? Or had he been trying to stop the Snatcher and gotten caught in the crossfire?

As Hajo sped by us on his green motorcycle, Lon and I reviewed the photos I'd taken with my phone. The seven binding mandalas clearly served a different purpose than the oval seal around Bishop, but what, exactly? Containment? A magical cage? Hajo had confirmed that there weren't death-threads around the seven carvings, so they hadn't been used in ritual sacrifice. If Lon could track down that Æthyric alphabet in one of his goetias—assuming that it *was* Æthyric— maybe we'd understand.

We attempted to smooth out the crinkles in the old Polaroid. I wondered if Bishop had swallowed the thing, or if it had been shoved down his throat. Either way, we couldn't make head or tail out of the image. It looked like it might've been taken at night. Somewhere with trees in the background. Hard to be sure, though. It would take some time and patience, but Lon said he could scan it and find out more. He had a few professional Photoshop plug-ins that would help restore the image.

Until then, we needed to figure out what we were going to do next. Because if we weren't looking for Bishop anymore, just who the hell were we tracking?

13

The day after the cannery incident, we still didn't know. Discussing the situation with Dare gave us no further insight. While Lon worked to decipher the image on the old Polaroid, we waited for Dare to discuss the Bishop development with his "people" and get back to us. Until we could all agree on what to do next, life went on. Lon still had a kid with a knack he shouldn't have, and none of us knew how or why. So we drove to Jupe's school, just shy of noon, to take him out of class and bring him to someone who might have some answers.

Dr. Spendlove's office was across town, on the other side of the Village, in a quaint two-story Tudor with stucco walls and decorative half-timbered wood detailing. Bold orange and yellow chrysanthemums were planted in green window boxes below narrow leaded-glass panes. His practice was quietly announced in medieval lettering on the sign that swung from a protruding iron rod next to the door: RED SKY WELLNESS CENTER—COUNSELING, THERAPY, PSYCHIATRIC CONSULTATION. Carved into the cornerstones above the door was the same interlocking circle Nox symbol that's printed on Tambuku's sign—indicating that the business was demon-friendly.

Inside, what was once a home had been converted into a business. A desk near the door greeted patients for the three doctors who shared a practice here. After Lon filled out several forms and checked Jupe in, we sat together in one of two waiting rooms decorated with Colonial American artwork, much of it featuring subtly haloed Earthbounds. I looked around at the other people waiting: not a single human in the entire office. A few people glanced up at my silver halo, as demons always did, but soon returned to their magazines and mobile phones, unconcerned.

Jupe, nervous and fidgety, was swept away to the second floor. The doctor kept him up there for almost forty-five minutes, and when he returned with one of the center's assistants, he was all smiles.

"Dr. Spendlove will see you now to complete Jupiter's file," the blond assistant said to Lon with a polite smile.

"Why don't you do your homework while we're seeing the doctor?" I suggested to Jupe, gathering up my purse to follow Lon. Maybe I really *could* live up to the whole "positive female role model" thing his teacher was talking about.

"On it." He formed his hand into a gun shape, pointed at me—"*Pow!*"—then snapped open a gossip magazine and slouched into the lavender waiting chair.

Dr. Spendlove's upstairs office was spacious. More Early American artwork hung on the navy blue walls, along with several painted vases, tools, and a small collection of wooden tobacco pipes in glass cases. A few chairs were grouped together on one side of the room, but no psychiatric fainting couch, to my disappointment.

The doctor stood up from behind a large desk that sat between two narrow stained-glass windows on the far wall. "Lon

Butler, how wonderful to see you. Come in, come in," he said enthusiastically, waving us inside. The assistant softly closed the door behind us. "It's been ten years? Is that what we were saying on the phone earlier? Goodness."

Dressed in a black corduroy blazer, Dr. Spendlove was a trim man sporting a gray mustache twirled into points at the corners. He wore his silver hair pulled into a short, tight braid at the base of his neck. His deep blue halo nearly matched the wall color.

"Guess I've been busy," Lon replied, shaking his hand.

The psychiatrist turned to me, smiled, and offered his hand. "Lawrence Spendlove."

"Arcadia Bell."

"Lon mentioned you on the phone. So wonderful to meet you. Please, sit."

Lon and I settled into two chairs in front of the desk as Dr. Spendlove unabashedly stared above my head. "I'm sure you get asked this all the time," he said, "but would you mind telling me about your halo? It's quite intriguing."

Lon rushed to speak. "Cady, wait. Dr. Spendlove is—"

"I'm not demon. I'm a magician," I blurted out over Lon's words, fast as a snakebite.

"O-oh," Dr. Spendlove cooed with excitement. "Fascinating."

"He's a truth sayer," Lon finished. "I forgot."

"Oh, God," I moaned. I'd heard of that knack but had never been on the receiving end. "You can force the truth out of people?"

"Not 'force' exactly. My patients just open up a little more for me. Don't feel uncomfortable. I promise not to ask anything about your sex life," he said good-humoredly.

That was the least of my worries. "You . . . *forgot?*" I

murmured to Lon. Dear God. I was going to murder him when we got out of there.

"Please don't push her about her background," Lon said.

The doctor raised his hands in surrender. "Not here to judge. But I am interested in your halo. Can we talk in generalities about it? Knack free. Cross my heart. It's just that I don't meet many magicians. Certainly none with halos."

"Demons and magicians, natural enemies," I said lightly.

"You're certain you don't have any Earthbound further back in your bloodline?"

I nodded.

"Hmm. Well, you've got something rather Æthyric bonding with your DNA or you wouldn't have a halo." He tilted his head to the side, pondering. "You were born with it?"

"Yes."

"I have seen one or two anomalies in my thirty-some years of practice. Tell me this: have you yourself conjured anything Æthyric?"

Of course I had. It was just oddly chilling to talk about it with someone outside the occult community. "A few Æthyric demons, a Hermeneus spirit." Poor Priya, my lost connection to the Æthyr. The Hermeneus spirit who was once my guardian promised that it would regenerate and link itself to me again, but it could take years. . . .

Dr. Spendlove crossed his legs and leaned into one side of the chair. "Fascinating! So you know firsthand that there are indeed other Æthyric beings besides demons."

"People in my esoteric order believe there are multiple Æthyric planes and that demons inhabit only one of them," I said. "Then again, who knows how accurate that is. Most magicians don't even believe that Earthbounds exist, because they can't see halos."

"But *you* can," he stated, studying my face.

"Yes."

"She co-owns the tiki bar in Morella," Lon said.

"Ah! So you're *that* girl. Yes, I've heard people make mention of you from time to time. Beat and bind, as they say in fencing, yes?" His cheeks were ruddy with interest.

"En garde," I replied flatly.

He laughed like Santa Claus, minus the jiggling belly. "Indeed, indeed. Lon's always shown a sharp interest in magick—since he was a small child, in fact. So it doesn't surprise me that he'd connect with someone like you."

A thrumming panic was surfacing. Not out-of-control panic, but it was there. Sweat was beginning to make my hair itch at the nape of my neck. Lon reached for my hand and threaded his fingers through mine.

Dr. Spendlove didn't seem to notice my fear. "I once had a young patient from a small town in northern India with a dark orange halo," he said, circling his hand in the air around his own in demonstration. "Never having seen another person with a halo, he lived his whole life thinking he was mentally ill. Had been prescribed antipsychotic medications. When he was eighteen, he came to the states for a job, right here in La Sirena, and *voilà*!" He clapped his hands together then spread his arms dramatically. "Halos, as far as the eye could see. He began seeing me to wean him off his medications, which I did. But I was never entirely convinced that he was *demon*. Earthbound like the rest of us, yes, but Earthbound *what*, exactly?"

He paused dramatically, arching a brow, as if reading the tagline for a movie featuring a nefarious conspiracy theory.

"That's . . . interesting, but I think my halo is related to magical ability," I said, "and not some long-lost Æthyric race."

"Have you met other magicians with halos?"

"No," I admitted.

"You know," he said, "many ancient cultures didn't believe in a distinction between demons and gods. They saw them as a higher level of beings. About twenty years ago, I read an essay theorizing that the origin of magick stemmed from godlike beings called Sekhmets, who taught their skills to a select group of ancient Egyptian priestesses."

"Sekhmet is an early Egyptian war goddess," I corrected.

"Or"—he leaned low over the desk, eyes dancing with intrigue—"was she merely named Sekhmet after another race of beings? A race who shared with humans their specialized knack for harnessing Heka, to prepare them for a prophesied future war between the planes?"

He slowly nodded his head, as if he was certain that he'd just blew my mind. He hadn't. I'd already heard every crazy crackpot esoteric theory out there. Most of the people in my order went a step further, proclaiming that magicians *were* gods, or at least descended from them. A King Kong–size ego was necessary for at least two positions of power in this country: presidential candidates and upper-echelon officers in any magical organization.

I shrugged my shoulders high. "I doubt it's something we'll ever know, but I didn't mean to get us sidetracked," I said, generously, since I wasn't the one who'd gotten us on this tangent. "I'm sure you're busy, so let's talk about Jupe."

Dr. Spendlove grinned, then enthusiastically slapped his palm on the edge of his desk. "Yes, certainly, my dear." He pulled the computer keyboard toward him and typed as he talked. "So, the last time I saw Jupiter, he was three years old—but little Jupiter isn't so little anymore, is he? I ran a few standard tests on him . . . coaxed some truth out of him . . . and it appears his knack is manifesting a year or so early. Not unheard of. About ten percent of Earthbound children manifest before the age of fifteen. On the other hand, a quarter of all Earthbounds never even manifest a talent at all—did you know that?"

I certainly didn't know the percentage was that high. Lon didn't either, from the way he shook his head.

"These figures are based on my own studies, mind you, combined with figures from a few of my colleagues." Spendlove typed, squinting at the screen in front of him. "However, what's more interesting about Jupiter isn't the timing but rather the knack itself. Now, you are an empath, Lon. And according to Jupiter, his mother was a beguiler." He paused and looked up. "I do remember her. Was she really that lovely, or was it all 'allure'?"

Lon grunted.

Spendlove didn't seem to notice. "Well, as you know, Earthbound offspring almost always manifest one or the other parent's knack. But there are rare cases in which this doesn't occur. In those, the anomalous knack can usually be traced further back on the family tree. Let me just look at your records. . . ."

"My parents were both empaths, though not as strong as me," Lon volunteered.

"Yes, I'm well aware of that," he said with gentle amusement. "Your father and I were friends, you'll remember. I was looking up your in-laws. The Giovanni family, from Oregon . . ." he read off the screen.

"On Yvonne's side, her father had no ability. Sister doesn't either."

"Yvonne's mother?"

The woman who talked Lon into leaving her own daughter. Ballsy. And kind of awesome that she was still actively involved in Lon and Jupe's lives after all these years.

"Her mother is clairaudient."

"Oh? That's not common. What kind of range?"

"About ten feet or so, but she can hear through walls."

Wow. I was certainly glad Jupe hadn't inherited *that* knack. According to Jupe, Gramma Giovanni was the bees' knees and could do no wrong—same as her other daughter, Jupe's aunt Adella. Jupe talked to them every Sunday and saw them several times a year, apparently. Multiple photos of them were scattered around Lon's house.

"Hmm. Interesting, but that doesn't give us Jupe's knack, does it? What about great-grandparents?"

"I'll ask Yvonne's mom."

"Yes, good idea. Let me know when you find out so I can update Jupe's file." He swung the computer screen around to show us a color-coded diagram. "I've divided up all known knacks into seven main families: sense, transform, move, repair, destroy, illusion, and miscellaneous."

I saw abilities I knew, and many more that I'd never heard of or could even begin to guess. All told, he'd documented more than fifty verifiable knacks. Most of those had varying levels of skill, including Jupe's—persuasion.

"I've only run across persuasion twice in my practice, and neither manifestation was quite like Jupe's. One patient was only able to persuade other males, and another was able to influence people only temporarily. Based on Jupe's answers to my questions, his influence appears to be lasting. However, to determine exactly *how* lasting, I'd suggest that you do some supervised experiments with him at home. If you aren't comfortable with that, he can undergo some tests here, of course. But it's less stressful in an environment where he's relaxed and comfortable. It's important that children coming into their knacks are encouraged to use them in a positive, healthy manner, without shame or pressure."

"What kind of experiments?" Lon asked.

Spendlove shrugged. "Ask him to use his knack to influence your favorite color, perhaps. See how long you continue to believe it. Things like that."

Lon grunted again, this time more thoughtfully. Changing someone's favorite color sounded far less stressful than forcing a carnival ride operator to put people in danger.

Spendlove continued. "Persuasion is grouped under the 'Sense' family of knacks, you might be surprised to learn. Which makes it related to abilities like your empathy. I believe it to be the next step up, so to speak. For example, if you can *sense* people's emotions, the natural progression is the ability to *manipulate* emotions. Just as being able to sense honesty is a step below those who can foster honesty, like me."

"Yes," Lon said quickly, dropping his eyes.

We both knew Spendlove's theory was on the mark because of Lon's ability to transmutate. Speaking of which, neither that nor the bloody Hellfire Club had come up yet, so I was assuming Spendlove didn't know about either.

"Anyway, that's why I'm more inclined to think Jupe's knack is something inherited from your side." Spendlove settled back into his chair. "Still, it's hard to be certain."

"I'm worried about it going to his head, getting out of control," Lon said.

"Sure, that's a legitimate concern. It certainly has more potential for greater consequences than psychokinetics, say. But it's like anything else that can be abused—money, good looks, status—all you can do is teach your kids right and wrong, provide positive reinforcement, and lead by example. The rest is up to them."

This seemed to calm Lon's nerves. He unlaced his fingers from mine, rearranging our hands to clasp palm to palm, and gently stroked my knuckles.

"Jupe's ability might undergo some changes as it manifests," Dr. Spendlove said. "Growing pains. It's not uncommon for a young knack to be easy one day, harder the next, and for the results to vary wildly. He might experience headaches or other side effects after using it."

I could relate to that. I knew all too well about side effects and varied results from using magick.

"By the way, he has a bit of a 'tell' when he's using his knack," Dr. Spendlove said.

"Squeezing whatever he's holding in his hands with a viselike grip?" I guessed, thinking of how he acted at the carnival.

The doctor laughed. "That will pass when he's able to better master it. I'm talking about the rapid eye movement— REM, like when you're dreaming. If you watch his eyes, they flick like this." He moved his finger back and forth like a pendulum to demonstrate.

Lon and I looked at each other and nodded. Good to know. Very good. Worth the whole damn doctor visit, if you asked me.

"The best advice I can give you is to be patient, and to pay attention to him," he concluded. "Have him practice the right and wrong way to use it around you, and monitor his behavior carefully. Severe shifts can be warning signs. If he becomes withdrawn and depressed for no reason, or if he becomes inappropriately wild and begins taking too many risks, you might want to bring him in to talk to me."

I wondered if the incident on the amusement park ride would be considered "inappropriately wild," but said nothing while the appointment concluded. On our way downstairs to retrieve Jupe from the waiting room, Lon stopped short in front me.

"What's wrong?" I said.

"Nothing's wrong. I just had an epiphany."

"About Jupe?"

"About the Snatcher investigation."

I paused. "About the image in the Polaroid?"

"No. Something better."

I watched him stare at the wallpaper for a long moment, then leaned in and whispered against his ear. "Tell me."

Something mischievous danced behind his eyes as they met mine. "If it's not Bishop, then who would be able provide the Snatcher's real identity?"

Where was he going with this? I became frustrated, then realized what he meant. "Cindy Brolin. But she won't talk."

"She won't talk to us. But what if someone . . . more persuasive . . . asked her nicely?"

14

WE ARE HERE!!!!!!!!!!!!!

The text lit up my phone screen with thirteen exclamation points. Coming into the city on a Friday night might be mildly interesting to some kids. To Jupe it was like he'd been given shore leave. I untied my bar apron and told the new bartender that my half-shift was over. Amanda waved goodbye as I headed outside.

Just after ten and already freezing. I zipped up my coat as I climbed the belowground stairs to street level. Lon's SUV idled at the curb out front. Before I cleared the last step, Jupe jumped from the passenger seat and bounded across the sidewalk to greet me. "So this is what it's like at night, huh? Wow! The neon looks so cool lit up like that. How many people are inside? You look tired—is it busy in there? Who's working tonight? Is Kar Yee in there?"

"Hello to you, too. You think you could maybe ask me about thirty more questions before you let me answer any of them?" I said, poking him in the stomach.

He laughed. "Oops." Then he did the strangest thing. He leaned down and kissed me on the forehead. Just a casual peck. Something most people would expect from a brother or a friend. Only, I don't have a brother, and I certainly didn't have any friends who did that. Amanda often tried to hug me, but she once said I was unhuggable. That hurt my feelings, but not enough to start getting all free-love and touchy-feely.

Jupe, however, definitely had the potential to be excessive with PDA. He liked to hug—a *lot*—and that's fine, I suppose. We'd also cuddled up together and watched TV in his room, and yes, he fell asleep in my lap on the couch the other night. And once he'd tried to insert his big toe up my nose; if that's not affection, I don't know what is.

But he'd never *kissed* me.

And it was so casual, like he'd done it a billion times. I guess that's why he didn't seem to notice when I froze up on the sidewalk like some socially awkward recluse. He was too busy trying to peer down into Tambuku's stained glass windows from the top of the stairs. Meanwhile, I wasn't sure if I was mortified by the kiss, or if I was going to break down sobbing in some weirdo family-bonding moment. The horror of doing just that was enough to snap me back to reality. I tried to play it cool, like it wasn't a big deal. *This is what normal people do. It doesn't mean anything.* Thankfully, Lord Empath was in the car, out of range.

The door to Tambuku swung open and Kar Yee emerged, hiking up the steps. "You might need this," she called out, holding up my cell. "You left it in your apron." Her kohl-rimmed eyes fell on Jupe. "Well, well, well. Look who it is—my future boyfriend. What are you doing in the city? Couldn't stay away from me, huh?"

Jupe's eyes inflated into giant cartoon peepers in response. "I'm on a mission," he managed to get out.

"A mission?" Kar Yee's voice flattened in genuine

suspicion. "Is that a religious thing? You're not one of those irritating door-to-door people, are you?"

"No! I'm—"

"We're going to the grocery store," I said, covering up for Jupe's loose tongue as she handed me my phone. Not a lie, exactly. Dr. Spendlove wanted Jupe to practice his knack in supervised situations. I don't think what we were about to do was what he had in mind, but it *was* a situation. And we were supervising . . .

"Hey," Jupe said to Kar Yee. "You speak Cantonese, not Mandarin, right?"

"Yes."

"How do you say 'beautiful girl' in Cantonese?"

Oh, *brother*.

"Leng lui."

Jupe repeated it. She corrected his pronunciation, then added, "We would also say something more casual that translates to 'your beauty shatters the mirror.'"

"Really?" Jupe was definitely into that colloquialism. It had just the right dose of violence for his tastes. "How do you say that?" he asked with great urgency, then added, "I *have* to know."

"You say it like this: 'Your beauty shatters the mirror,'" she deadpanned.

"N-o-o-o," Jupe groaned. "In *Cantonese*."

"Does this look like Hong Kong to you? No. It's central California. I didn't travel halfway across the globe to speak Cantonese."

"Why did you move here, then? Hong Kong seems cooler than Morella, that's for sure."

"My father is American. He moved to Hong Kong and became a permanent resident a few years after marrying my mother. When I turned eighteen, I decided to go to college in Seattle. That's where I met her." She tipped her head in my direction. "I liked the States, so I stayed. Cady and I moved down here because it's sunnier and we wanted to make money. End of story."

"Your dad was American?" Jupe asked.

"A Jewish lawyer from Seattle."

"What? Wait a minute . . . is he white?"

"As a snowflake."

Jupe's mouth fell open. "You're biracial? Like me? Cady, you didn't tell me!" It was too much for him to process. Joy overload. Then his brow furrowed, as if he were checking himself; it was, surely, too good to be true. "You don't look it."

She crossed her arms over her middle and held her head high. "I got my mother's good looks and my father's knack."

"Wow," Jupe raved, his eyes pinwheeling in happiness.

A car door slammed behind us; Lon emerged from the SUV and then stood near it in a manner I can only describe as hulking—I wasn't sure if he was pissed about being forced to wait, or if he sensed his son's overactive hormones from the car. Kar Yee watched him as he approached. "So that's your dad, huh?"

"Yeah."

"Mmm-hmph. Better looking than my father," she observed.

I made introductions between Grunt and Glare, two people with some of the worst social skills on the planet. They eyed each other silently. For several moments. They'd heard all about each other; I wondered what they were thinking. Finally, Kar Yee remarked to Lon, "Your halo is almost as strange as hers." To me, she simply said, "Good for you." Then she retreated back down the steps to the bar.

Starry Market wasn't a chain. It was the largest and oldest independent grocer in the city as well as a hybrid of disjointed ventures—dry-goods liquidator (this summer's potato chip flavors that went nowhere), gourmet ingredient procurer, and international farmer's market. Amanda refused to shop there, claiming that all the produce was irradiated. I, on the other hand, had more to worry about than death by radioactive zucchini.

But we weren't there to buy vegetables. We were there to track down Cindy Brolin. Again. Though we'd failed the first time, we were determined to find out what she was hiding about the original Snatcher.

The market was in the middle of the university quarter. The squat, ugly building occupied a small block that also housed three businesses in a strip of leased storefronts on the sidewalk. The main entrance was inside the attached parking garage. Jupe was wary when we entered, remembering the last time we were in a city parking structure together, but I pointed out that the Starry Market garage contained only half the amount of hobo urine of the Metropark, which I have found to be a surprisingly accurate indicator of lower crime statistics.

Halloween candy, cinnamon brooms, and bins of pumpkins crowded the store entrance. Not many shoppers. Yacht rock from the 1970s floated over the aisles like a bad storm cloud, dumping torrents of Christopher Cross and of the band that gave me sweaty nightmares, Steely Dan. Once we'd meandered past the spicy scents of the seasonal display, the store's natural oppressive smell reared its head—day-old fish and transpacific shipping containers, dusty and perfumed with petrol.

Lon left me with Jupe while he combed the store looking for Cindy. We wasted time waiting for him while perusing a selection of unusual canned-good delectables from Russia. Jupe was enchanted. "A cartoon squid? What the hell is in here?" Jupe murmured, turning a dented can in his hand and trying to guess the Cyrillic letters. "Is it soup? It says 'herring' on the shelf label. That makes no sense. Squid-herring? *What is this?*" he whispered in wonder.

After he begged me to get a cart so that we could load up on grass jelly, silkworm pupae, and fish balls—which I refused to do—Lon stepped up behind me and spoke over my shoulder.

"Found her." He grabbed a can of congealed reindeer meat out of Jupe's hand and set it on the shelf. "Listen," he said in a low voice, heavy as steel. "This is serious—the first real thing I've ever let you do as an adult and not a kid. So stop screwing around."

Jupe's mouth scrunched up in embarrassment as he blinked up at Lon. "Okay."

"I'm having some serious doubts about pulling you into this," Lon admitted.

So did I, but we were desperate. The fruitless Polaroid had haunted him like a bad dream, while the origin of the strange markings on the seven magical circles I'd photographed in the cannery continued to elude both of us. Lon said Jupe's knack would probably be less traumatic on Cindy than dosing her with one of my medicinals. I agreed.

"I can handle it, Dad. I swear."

Lon frowned. "I hope so. This is not something I take

lightly. I'll say it one more time—you'll only use your knack exactly as we discussed unless one of us tells you otherwise."

"Yeah, I understand."

"And as you know," Lon continued, "Dr. Spendlove can get the truth out of you whether you like it or not, so if I even *think* you've been using it for the wrong reason, like cheating on tests or getting some girl to kiss you—"

Jupe feigned offense, his mouth forming an O. What a liar. He'd definitely already thought about using his knack for that. He'd better not have tried.

"—I will take you in to see him and he'll find out exactly how many times you've used your knack and why."

Jupe stuck a long finger into his curls, slowly scratching the side of his head. "All right, I get it for chrissake. What I *don't* get is why the two of you are doing all this. You aren't cops," he challenged.

Lon paused, staring at Jupe with fire in his eyes, then took a deep breath and answered in a calm voice. "You know the code? How we keep the demon talk quiet around savages?"

"Yeah."

"This is an Earthbound matter," Lon explained, then added, "Ambrose Dare is asking us to help."

"Mr. Dare? Whoa."

"Yeah, whoa. And if you can't handle it, then we'll just go back to testing your knack with Dr. Spendlove's 'favorite color' suggestion . . ."

"I can handle it!" Jupe insisted.

"And you can't breathe a word of this to people at school. You're going to want to brag—I know you. But you can't. Not even to your best friends."

"What about Mr. and Mrs. Holiday?"

Lon shook his head. "Only the three of us." He pointed for emphasis—one, two, three. "This is serious family business."

Us. Family. I was included. My mind raced back to the promises we'd made in the kitchen the other night and lumped it in with Jupe's casual kiss on my forehead . . . and now this. Something fragile cracked inside me. My chest felt warm. I blinked away emotion as Lon's eyes flicked to mine. *Get it together, Bell.*

"Can you promise me that you'll keep quiet?"

"I promise." Jupe held his head a little higher and added, "You can count on me."

"I know I can." Lon gave him a muted smile and squeezed his shoulder. And that was that.

We followed Lon to the back of the store. Cindy Brolin leaned behind the fish counter, hosing it down for the night. I puffed out my cheeks as we approached, trying to banish the stench. When she saw us, panic exploded over her face.

"Hello, Cindy," I said, holding my hands up like she was some skittish pony that might bolt out of the pen. "We only want to talk again for just a minute. Real fast, promise."

"I'm at work. I can't talk." With reddening cheeks and crazy eyes, she glanced around the area, maybe with hopes that her manager was somewhere nearby and could save her. The only person in sight was an old woman three aisles down pushing a cart filled with large multipacks of ramen noodles.

"Look, I'll come clean. We aren't really writing a historical book about La Sirena's schools," I said. "Surely you've heard there are now three kids missing."

She stiffened. Water dripped from the nozzle of the hose she held in one hand.

"More children might be taken," Lon said. "This is my kid

here, and I don't want him to be the next victim. The Snatcher took seven kids in the 1980s. We think you know something about it."

"Why . . ." Her voice cracked. "Why would I know something about that?" Wisps of dyed red hair clung to the sweat on her forehead. She wiped the side of her face on her shoulder.

Lon nudged Jupe. I glanced around, ensuring that we were still alone, then looked at Jupe. *Just like we rehearsed. Now or never, kid. You're on.* He took a deep breath, then balled up his hands into fists.

"Cindy," he commanded with confidence over the fish counter, like he did this for a living. His eyes were slitted, and Dr. Spendlove was right: they were flicking back and forth. "You trust us. You want to tell us everything you remember about the Snatcher. You're tired of keeping secrets and you want to be helpful. You aren't afraid anymore."

Cindy looked momentarily confused, just like the amusement park ride operator. Her face knotted up as if she might burst into tears. Then her shoulders sagged. She set the hose down and peeled off long black rubber gloves. "I don't know if what I remember will help," she said timidly. "I can take a short break, but let's talk outside."

We followed her down a tiled hallway past the swinging warehouse doors to a locked rear entrance. She entered a four-digit code and waited for the door to beep. It opened onto a deserted loading dock at the side of the parking deck. After a few steps, we huddled together under a covered walkway, next to an ashtray and a bench with peeling paint.

"So, what do you want to know?" she said, keeping her eyes on the cement as she fumbled around inside her Starry Market apron pocket for her cigarette case.

"Did the Snatcher take you?" I asked.

She took out a cigarette and paused, as if her brain was fighting Jupe's persuasion. At length, she finally said, "Not exactly. I got away."

I glanced at Lon. Bingo.

Cindy leaned against the bench. "I was fifteen at the time. My best friend had dropped me off at home. It was Friday, the day before Halloween. It wasn't too late, maybe nine or ten, but I knew my parents were asleep. I hung around outside on our front porch to sneak a cigarette. Next thing I knew, someone was hauling me up into the air and over the railing. He was hiding in the bushes, I guess. Yanked me from behind."

Jupe made a noise beside me. I touched his hand with the back of mine and he immediately held it.

"I tried to scream," she said, "but he got a hand over my mouth before I could. Kicked out my feet, dropped me to the ground, and held me down in the grass. For a second, I thought he was going to rape me or something. It didn't even cross my mind that it was the Snatcher."

"What made you realize it?" I asked quietly, squeezing Jupe's hand.

She shuffled one foot in front of her, tracing some invisible pattern on the walkway. "He whispered something to me. He said, 'Cindy Brolin, number seven.' I thought I was going to die of fright right then. Everyone was talking about the Snatcher those days. La Sirena was terrified. Every day we waited to hear if someone else had been taken. I knew the boy that got taken before me. Knew he was number six . . ." Her voice trailed off as she took a drag and her cigarette ashed; she flicked the filter roughly.

"What happened then?" Lon prompted.

"He mumbled something about needing a taste of me to be sure that I was 'viable.' Then he *bit* me."

"Bit you?"

Cindy nodded. "Yeah. Right on the arm." She pushed up the blue sleeve of her shirt, revealing a faded, crescent-shaped scar above her left elbow. "Had to have ten stitches. My parents told the doctor who sewed me up at the emergency room that it was a dog bite." She laughed nervously, then pushed her sleeve down. "I've been having nightmares about that bite ever since you both showed up at my apartment and told me that kids were going missing again."

"Sorry," I said.

She shook her head and looked away. "Anyway, he took the chunk out of my arm, then said something in another language."

"Any idea which language?" Lon asked.

"It was crazy-sounding. Kinda like—"

"Like what?"

"This is going to sound stupid, but it was almost like some alien sort of language from a *Star Trek* movie or something. Silly, right?"

Odd, but not silly. Lon was good with languages. He quizzed her, asking if what she'd heard sounded like Latin, speaking a few words in Latin for her to compare with her memory. Definitely not, she said. He tried a little Greek. Not that either, she said. Nor Egyptian, nor Enochian. That ruled out most of the basic spells. Dare was convinced that Bishop had been trying to re-create the transmutation initiation ritual, that the research notes were in the same journal with the list of the original missing kids. Notes in Latin. But if it wasn't Bishop who was taking the kids, then maybe the notes they found in Bishop's house were for the real Snatcher. Maybe he was forcing Bishop into helping him. Maybe he was another disgruntled Hellfire member who wanted the same power that the officers had. He could've turned on Bishop if the transmutation spell didn't work out. . . .

"Okay," Lon said, giving up on the mystery language, "what happened after he bit you and spoke strangely?"

"He still had one hand over my mouth, so I couldn't scream, but I saw my cigarette on the ground where I'd dropped it when he first grabbed me. While he was talking in that other language, I picked up the cigarette and shoved it into his face."

"Aww, shit," Jupe murmured.

She shrugged. "I only got his cheek. But it was enough to surprise him. He rolled off me, acting insane. Kicking and yelling. I didn't stick around to see what was going on, just jumped up and ran to my front door. He came after me, but I pounded on the door, and my parents woke up and let me in. He took off. I never saw him again."

"Your parents didn't go to the police?" Lon asked.

"My dad reported it anonymously from a phone booth at the emergency room. I remember my parents arguing about it in the car on the way to the hospital. This Snatcher had already managed to take six kids, and the police didn't have any leads. People were pissed off at them. Picketing outside the sheriff's department. And my mom didn't want to draw attention. All the other families were on the news, reporters camping outside their homes. Mom was too afraid that the guy would come back for me. Or my little sister. She was fourteen at the time, only a year younger, and she has a disability. She couldn't walk so good. Still can't. Mom said she was easy prey. My uncle came over and helped my dad search the neighborhood when we got back home. Mom was hysterical. Later that night, she had a nervous breakdown."

"I'm sorry," I said.

She sniffled, then wiped her nose. "It wasn't her first one. When I was younger, she stayed in a hospital for a couple of months after losing a baby. Anyway, if the police *did* catch him, I would've had to testify in court—and if he ever got out on parole, or if they screwed up the case, he might come after me in the future. That's what my dad said. A couple of weeks after my mom's breakdown, we packed up and moved to my uncle's house in Morella. My dad was just doing what he felt was best for us, you know?"

"That's all anybody can do," said Lon sympathetically.

"I know this might be an odd question," I said, "but at the time, were you experimenting with anything occult-related? Learning about magick, that kind of thing?"

"Huh? Like witchcraft? No. Why?"

"Just wondering," I said. Seeing Lon give me a strange look out of the corner of my eye, I changed the subject. "Can you tell us what he looked like?"

She licked her lips and stubbed out her cigarette. "Human. White. Dark hair. Really short. I was so mad at myself later that I let a puny little guy like that get the best of me, but I guess in the end I got away."

Dark hair and short. Definitely not Bishop, based on the photos I'd seen. But we already knew that. And there had to be hundreds of men with that description in La Sirena.

"Oh, and there's one more thing," she added. "His eyes. I'll never forget them. They were two different colors."

15

Mismatched eyes. One blue, one brown. Very unusual, indeed.

I was fired up when we left Starry Market. Lon was, too. His energy level zoomed from slow and steady to bright and bushy-tailed. But when Jupe wanted to play detective along with us, Lon flashed me one of his famous "not in front of the kid" looks. So I steered the conversation in a different direction and proposed a pit stop in Morella before we drove back to the coast—something to distract Jupe and give me time to speak privately with Lon.

The Black Cherry is an all-night diner that sits on a busy corner down the block from Starry Market. With its neon sign of blinking fruit outside and Miami art deco interior, the diner drew an eclectic crowd of hipsters, freaks, and geeks of all ages. But the real reason I suggested we stop there was because of their retro arcade room.

Our late-night dinner was mostly spent ensuring that Jupe wasn't too freaked out about what we'd all just heard. I was kinda proud of him, to be honest. Lon too. Cindy seemed to be okay when we left her, but I was concerned that Jupe's persuasion could wear off eventually, and she might regret everything that she told us. I left her my cell number, just in case she wanted to talk later.

After several minutes of chatting, Lon told him he'd done a good job and Jupe bounced away to the adjoining room, drawn to the bleeps and bloops of classic video games. The second his low-top sneakers squeaked around the corner of our booth, I turned to Lon to discuss Cindy Brolin's memories and found him grinning a smug, cat-ate-the-canary grin. His arm flew out and hooked me around the waist. With one quick tug, he slid me across the seat and planted a firm kiss on my lips. I nearly gasped for breath when he released me.

"What was that for?" I asked with a laugh.

"Because my son got us some damn good information."

"Oh, now you're loving his knack, huh?" I teased.

He snorted. "Still hating it. Still a little worried that it might not have been the best decision to bring him into this. But if what he did tonight helps to save some kids, then maybe I'm not the worst father in the world."

"You're far from that."

He smiled at me. I smiled back.

"So, the Snatcher was a biter," I said, clicking my teeth together.

Lon leaned backed in the booth. "She said he bit her arm to see if she was—"

"Viable," I finished. "Yeah, how weird was that?"

"Maybe he was using blood for some sort of spell with the kids, and was looking for something specific. The amount of Heka inside someone, possibly."

"I've never heard of anyone who could judge that by taste."

He absently traced his pirate mustache down around his mouth with his thumb and index finger. "Me either."

"Okay, apart from that, he identified her as number seven. And I'm still convinced the mandalas we found at the cannery had to be traps. He was holding the kids in there until Halloween. The circle of trees with their names at Sandpiper Park screams big-ass ritual."

Lon paused while the waitress filled our glasses and asked if we wanted dessert before she brought us our check. After she left, he continued. "What kind of ritual, I don't know. But I think we can safely rule out the theory that this was just Bishop experimenting with the transmutation spell. So what kind of ritual requires very specific kids?"

I shook my head. "I don't see how seven young teenagers without magical skills would be useful in any kind of working."

"That's why you asked Cindy about occult leanings?"

I nodded. "If all the kids were magically gifted, I could understand the Snatcher's choosing them to raise Heka. But he was tasting her blood as a qualifier for something more."

"Sacrifices?"

"No idea, but I hope to hell not." As an attempted-sacrifice survivor myself, I'd had about all I could handle of that bullshit. I twisted around in my seat. "All I know is that Bishop didn't commit suicide in that cannery, and whoever carved those mandalas knows some strange magick."

Lon groaned. "Yeah, and I can think of one local person who knows a lot of strange magick."

"Who?"

"The magician who conducted the transmutation spells on the Hellfire members in the eighties."

"You mean to tell me that the Hellfire Club hired a human magician to cast the transmutation spells?"

"More than one over the years. You thought we did it ourselves?"

"Well . . . yeah. You said your dad and Dare cast it on themselves when they first found the spell."

He stretched his back and grimaced, trying to get comfortable. "People who aren't naturally talented can't churn out magick. The early Hellfire members had the glass summoning circles designed for the Hellfire caves, but they didn't charge them when they were installed, Frater Karras did."

Who?

Frater Karras, Lon explained, was a member of a small esoteric organization until he and his brother left the order and went rogue. Did magick for hire in central California in the 1970s. The Hellfire Club used Frater Karras as a freelancer to conduct transmutation spells and perform other miscellaneous magical jobs. "They paid him exorbitant amounts of money for his magical work, and to keep quiet. He worked with them on and off for about ten years, until he had a car accident and physically couldn't work anymore. That's when his brother took over his duties—he worked for the Hellfire Club until he died in the 1990s. His brother was the one who cast my transmutation spell."

"Hold on. So you're telling me that this Frater Karras person was a skilled magician, and they hired him like a plumber?"

"Yep."

"His brother, too?"

"Uh-huh."

"But was Frater Karras employed by the Hellfire Club in the early eighties when the Snatcher was active? If Bishop wanted to undergo the transmutation spell so badly, what was to stop him from hiring Frater Karras on the side?"

"Good question."

"Is Frater Karras still alive?"

"Even better question. I don't know. He disappeared. Not all that uncommon for rogue magicians. They change names, move around. . . ."

"Like me."

"Like you. But you know how Cindy said the original Snatcher was a short man with mismatched eyes?"

I stared at him. "No way."

"Yes way. I nearly had a stroke when she said that. Fucking Frater Karras had one blue eye, one brown."

"Crap! If he was the person who tried to take Cindy, then—"

"Maybe he's the person taking the kids now."

The waitress returned briefly to leave our check. Lon always insisted on paying for dinner, so we had a standing agreement that I'd take care of the tip. I glanced at the check and counted out cash, lost in thought. We knew the original Snatcher's true identity. How were we going to find out if he was still alive? As I unwrinkled dollar bills and shuffled them into a neat stack, another nagging detail *almost* slid into place inside my head.

"Frater Karras," I said. "That name . . ."

Lon gave me a strange look. "Yeah?"

"Karras, Karras . . ."

Lon shook his head, not following my line of thought as Jupe bounded up to the table.

"I need dough, yo. Small bills or quarters. They've got all kinds of awesome stuff in there. Double Dragon, Altered Beast, Ghosts and Goblins—it's a freakin' gold mine!"

"I'm not a piggy bank," Lon complained. "Forget it."

"What do you want me to do? I'm too young to get a job working fast food after school. I can't just make money materialize." He lowered his head near mine and added in a hushed voice, "Or can I? There's not a spell for that, is there?"

"No, but I bet there's one to seal your mouth shut," Lon said grumpily. "Besides, I thought you were 'independently wealthy.' Use your fancy new savings account."

"I said small bills, Dad. Those games are ancient. I can't put an ATM card in them."

"Life is tough."

Jupe groaned then looked at me. "Why were you guys talking about *The Exorcist*?"

Lon's nose wrinkled. "Huh?"

"You were talking about Father Karras. I heard you when I walked up."

"That's it! *The Exorcist*!" My knees banged on the underside of the table in my excitement. "Father Damien Karras from *The Exorcist*!"

Jupe squatted down in front of the table and rested his chin on top of his folded arms. "Played by Jason Miller," he confirmed. "The younger Jesuit priest who threw himself down the steps at the end of the movie to get the demon out of his body."

"So what?" Lon said tersely. "It's just a name. Magicians don't use their given names when practicing." I knew he was referring to me, but as many promises as I'd made to him regarding Jupe, he'd made some to me too. Jupe would never know my real name. Never, never, never.

"That's right," I said, ignoring his accusing glare. "Magicians don't use their real names when practicing. And there's a crazy old magician who runs a Silent Temple somewhere in Morella. *He* goes by Frater Merrin."

"Oh!" Jupe exclaimed, not having any idea what we were actually discussing. "Father Merrin, played by Max von Sydow. He's the older priest in the movie who dies during the exorcism."

Lon sat up in his seat. Now he was paying attention. I pressed my hand over his knee and bit my lip in euphoric glee. I could be wrong—had been before. But this was an awfully big coincidence to ignore.

"Tomorrow's Saturday. Don't Silent Temples usually celebrate their Sabbath on Saturdays, not Sundays?" Lon asked in a low voice while Jupe continued to chatter with geektastic movie factoids about *The Exorcist*.

They did, and even if "Frater Merrin" wasn't working there anymore, maybe someone in the temple could clue us in to his whereabouts.

"What's a Silent Temple?" Jupe asked, suddenly interested in our discussion.

Mr. and Mrs. Holiday better be up for some Jupe-sitting, because I damn well wasn't hauling the boy along to a Silent Temple. Magicians in esoteric orders might be loopy, but those people were insane.

16

I had to make a few calls next morning to find out where it was. Silent Temples don't advertise, aren't in the book, and there's little talk of their locations online. Sure, you could find discussion boards populated with fringe people who post bizarre tales, told to them by a "friend." Rumors about temples in certain cities, that kind of thing. After surfing for an hour, you were more likely to have picked up some filthy virus from one of the web sites than to have discovered an actual location, which notoriously changes every few months.

That's when it pays to have friends like Bob. Though he hadn't quite gotten over the cannery terror, as long as he didn't have to follow me into dark abandoned buildings, he was willing to help—and did. It took him fifteen minutes to call me back with the current location of the temple in Morella: an old brick high school in the Eastern Foothills district.

The neighborhood was beyond sketchy. A shame, really. It had some killer views of the mountains in the distance. But no view was good enough to make up for the largest number of homicides in the city, or the fact that they made the national news last year because of an infestation of superlice that closed down every local school and motel in a five-mile radius.

The sprawling former high school that now harbored the Silent Temple had been split into thirty-plus separate apartments and dubbed the Mountain Lofts. Some people rented them for homes, others for businesses. And, from the looks of the boarded-up windows pasted with 4:20 stickers and psychedelically colored tribulation posters, I was guessing most of those businesses weren't exactly legal. Maybe Hajo got his sømna here.

We drove around the block twice looking for the temple's unit number, then decided to try on foot. After we weren't able to find a vacant parking space around the building, we parked Lon's SUV at a nearby gas station.

The rain didn't help matters. We huddled under an umbrella and hiked around the building, splashing through puddles. Lots of interesting sights at the so-called Mountain Lofts, such as a courtyard filled with brightly painted sculptures made from welded scrap metal . . . an overflowing city Dumpster being rummaged by three homeless people . . . a woman in a red-and-white-striped tube-top holding a soggy piece of cardboard over her head to block the rain, asking passersby if they'd seen her cat—which might've been some sort of prostitution code word. The whole place was classy with a *K*.

A few gutter punks sat lined up against a brick wall under a dripping cement eave that extended from one side of the building. This is where we finally found the unit number, painted sloppily on the brick. No temple sign. No sign at all, other than a ripped piece of brown paper bag taped above the handle. Scribbled on it in black marker was the instruction, *Door remains locked. Knock for service until 11 a.m. After that time, doors will not be opened. DO NOT KNOCK after 11!* An inverted pentagram served as a signature.

Lon glanced at his watch. "Not eleven yet."

I knocked three times in quick succession. A mini caduceus and a piece of red ochre chalk were both stashed in my jacket pocket. Inside Lon's was his loaded short-barreled Lupara. I could see the outline bulging through the worn denim. So could everyone else if they took a second look—which was the point, Lon said.

After a few moments, a metal square opened in the center of the door, revealing a grimy security window and a pasty face peering through slender iron bars.

"Yes?" A tinny voice floated through a small old speaker beneath the window.

"We're here for the service," Lon replied.

The face leaned closer to the window. Eyes roamed over Lon's fuck-you countenance, then flicked to my skunk-striped hair and tight jeans. That must have been enough to persuade him that we weren't officials from an esoteric organization coming to bust them, because we were let inside, no questions asked.

A small foyer was crowded with a motley assortment of templegoers. Goth kids mingled with old-money elderly Californians dressed in expensive cruise wear. All of them were speaking in hushed library voices, and most of them were Earthbound. Everyone looked up when we stepped inside. Cigarette smoke mingled with a cloying incense that was drifting in from the entrance to the main temple. The rain outside was churning it all into a foul-smelling stew.

We stood frozen in place for a moment, wondering what to do next. The man who'd let us inside tapped my shoulder, looking slightly oddball in a plaid dinner jacket and mismatched bow tie, with deep frown lines etched into his face and loose chicken-wattle skin drooping below his chin. He asked us if it was our first time attending. After we confirmed that it was, he instructed us to take seats inside.

We parted a beaded curtain and entered the main temple area. It was surprisingly spacious inside . . . wood floors, high walls lined with built-in bookshelves—the old school library, likely. The windows had been blacked out with thick coats of paint.

Mismatched furniture filled the center of the room. A collection of yard-sale loveseats, patio furniture, and armchairs that had seen better days were set in three rows facing the opposite wall. Lon and I claimed a stained love seat at the end of the back row.

Two sets of stairs hugged the front wall, both leading to separate loft areas. Between the stairs, a large marble sculpture stood—a winged, naked man with the head of a lion and a snake winding around the length of his body. Zodiac signs were carved into his skin. He held a set of keys in his hand.

"Leontocephalous?" Lon whispered, nodding toward the sculpture. I nodded in confirmation. An obscure Roman god associated with the Mithras mysteries. His keys were thought to open doors to other planes, Æthyric and otherwise. Two lighted metal torches were set into wall holders on either side of him.

The mood of the room was reverent and quiet, cut with a thin whisper of impending danger. You could see it in the way people held themselves, formal and wary, their eyes darting defensively as if they were hunters in the wild expecting to be attacked by a pack of wolves at any moment.

I grew up in an esoteric organization, so I had plenty of experience attending similar ceremonial functions. But they were never held in places as shabby and depressing as this. I thought about those local superlice outbreaks and found myself scratching under my clothes before I realized what I was doing.

Right before eleven, the remainder of the congregation filed inside and occupied the remaining seats. Someone dimmed the lights. Two altar girls lit torches on either side of the room. They wore long, red pioneer dresses, and their hair was braided and pinned to their heads. They could've been satanic stand-ins for the girls on *Little House on the Prairie*.

"If anything goes wrong, you banish it, you hear?" Lon whispered.

"Nothing's going to happen," I assured him. The Silent Temple put on this little freak show every week. Hopefully their casualty rate was low. "Wait until the ceremony's over before you go shooting a hole in the ceiling," I suggested, sneaking a quick scratch under my sleeve. Lice made me think of roaches, and that made me think of the cannery. I shuddered.

Epic, dark opera boomed over speakers near the altar. From Wagner's *Ring* cycle. I was pretty sure that was the equivalent of playing *Eye of the Tiger* at a wrestling match. The altar girls finished with their task and stood sentinel at the bottom of each set of stairs, their handheld torches held above their heads.

Two figures descended, one from either staircase. The first was a wiry boy, maybe early twenties. He wore a black T-shirt and matching pants, and had one too many pointy facial piercings. His booming voice didn't match his thin body as he announced the second figure descending the second set of stairs—

Frater Merrin.

"I'll be damned," Lon mumbled, tensing up as the man

greeted the congregation. Guess Frater Merrin really *was* his old Frater Karras. Ten points for Jupe's not so useless horror movie trivia.

The magician looked to be in his sixties. He was extremely short, balding like a monk, and dressed in standard gray ritual robes, with a hood lying against his back and zipper at his throat. Bare toes peeked out below the hem. Dark, pouchy circles gathered under mismatched eyes that swept across the congregation. He nodded occasionally at those who waved or called out to him.

"Welcome, Sisters and Brothers, to the Morella Silent Temple," he announced, holding out his arms while ambling by the front row. "For those of you who are first-timers, I hope you are enlightened by what you'll witness today. For those of you returning, I hope your faith will be renewed.

"Other churches," he continued, "talk a lot about miracles. But talk is cheap. I'm not saying that the beliefs that fuel other religions are wrong, I'm only saying that I can prove that our faith has substance. Our beliefs are grounded in what we can see and hear, not just what we're told."

The magician walked to a short table and picked up a small brass container with an elongated, skinny spout—somewhere between an Arabian oil lamp and a watering can. He carried the object to both sides of the altar and held it up for each of the girls in the red dresses to kiss in blessing.

A red circular carpet lay in the center of the altar. While the magician moved behind it, the girls rolled up the carpet and carried it off between them. And what do you know— where that carpet once lay was now an exposed summoning circle, though not as fancy as the glass tubes in the floor of the Hellfire caves. This one looked to have been constructed of a cement disk that had been recessed a couple of inches into a hollowed-out portion of the wood flooring. The edge was ringed with a dark stained channel, into which the magician poured oil from the spout of the brass watering can.

"From fire they are born, and to fire we all go. Let the sacred oil flow," Frater Merrin said. The congregation repeated these words in an off-key drone. After he made it all the way around, the prairie girls took their places at either side of the circle. The magician chanted something in Latin. His back to the congregation, he kneeled—with no small effort—in front of the sculpture of the lion-headed deity, and prayed.

"This is ridiculous," Lon complained in my ear.

"You think?" I hissed back. Pomp and show. A bloated ritual to impress the crowd.

The magician gave a signal to the girls. They held their dresses tightly around their legs and knelt by the oil-filled channel, touching their torches to it. A foot-high flame leapt up and spread, filling the entire circle in a flash. A ring of fire.

Yes, quite a production.

The humans who came to see it weren't savages. They believed in demons. They couldn't see the halos on the Earthbounds who sat alongside them, but they had proof, nonetheless: their church conjured up a living specimen every Saturday.

I crossed my arms, listening as the magician recited the *real* words to set the summoning circle.

If the occult organizations got wind of this place, they'd fan the flames licking around this circle and burn the whole temple to the ground. Especially my order—this was *so* against E∴E∴ policy. I mean, come on. A rogue magician conjuring demons in front of nonmagicians—conjuring demons to be worshipped, to boot. Such a big no-no.

Like most esoteric orders, the E∴E∴ believed Æthyric demons were to be summoned only for two reasons:

information and tasks. They should be tightly controlled at all times, and there should always be another magician present in case something goes wrong with the binding.

Of course, I never followed these rules myself. And in the big picture, what the Hellfire Club did every month—summoning Æthyric demons for heaping helpings of sex and violence—was far worse than what this guy was doing.

But I didn't really care about that either. All I wanted to know was whether the magician in front of us had kidnapped, and likely killed, seven human children in the early '80s, and if he was the one who'd been recently abducting Hellfire kids.

Merrin brought out a caduceus from under his robe. The wood was blackened at the bottom. He stuck it through the wall of flames and hit the inner ring of the summoning circle. The low lights in the room crackled and dimmed for a brief moment, throwing the room into near-dark, the only light coming from the torches on the wall and the ring of fire.

The summoning circle was set. Under the fire, it glowed with blue-white Heka, strong and stable.

Merrin whispered an incantation. An indistinct form solidified inside the circle. The temple was dark, and it was hard to see clearly, but what appeared in the circle was mostly human-looking. Male. Definitely male. His body was divine—perfectly sculpted, ropy muscle over long, pale limbs. A sleeveless white tunic clung to every hard curve. Long auburn hair was pulled back into a tight knot on the crown of his head, backlit by a dancing halo that took on a reddish hue in the firelight. At the front of his head were two gently curving horns, and from a slit in the back of the tunic, a long tail whipped back and forth, striking against the invisible circle walls.

He was startled . . . and *very* pissed off about being summoned.

17

A low buzz floated around the room as the congregation recited some ridiculous poetic nonsense at the trapped demon in the fire circle. Between their practiced lines, Frater Merrin was reading the summoned demon his Miranda rights, commanding it to obey. The demon didn't respond. He just scanned the congregation, searching the faces in the dark. He stopped when his gaze connected with mine.

Uh-oh. The last few Æthyric demons with whom I'd chatted seem to recognize whatever it was that my parents had bred into me. And pretty-boy demon in the fire circle was now eyeballing me with his head tilted in curiosity. Not good. I slouched lower in my seat and shielded my face with my hand.

More hive-speak from the crowd. More commands from the magician to the silent demon, who prowled the summoning circle, looking for a way out and occasionally pinning me with an angry stare that made my skin clammy.

"Now, for the querent," Merrin said to the crowd. "Brother Paolo won the query lottery this week. Where is Brother Paolo?"

A short Earthbound man raised his hand and stood.

The congregation applauded. Brother Paolo walked to the fiery summoning circle and stood next to Merrin, who laid his hand on Paolo's shoulder. "What is your question for the demon before us?"

The man cleared his throat. "I'd like to know if my brother will survive open-heart surgery next week."

You've got to be kidding me. The demon standing in front of him didn't have that kind of information. He wasn't an oracle, for the love of Pete. I expected Merrin to tell poor, misguided Brother Paolo this. Instead, he was rephrasing the question in Latin. Did the demon even speak Latin? He seemed to be listening to Merrin. His tail flicked lazily, but he remained silent. Merrin pressed him for an answer.

"*Pedicabo te*," came the demon's reply in deep voice.

Merrin's face tightened. Lon quietly snorted in amusement beside me.

"Yes," Merrin said hurriedly. "He says your brother will survive."

The congregation applauded.

"I don't recognize that verb," I whispered to Lon as Brother Paolo returned to his seat. He didn't look all that happy about the news. Maybe he was hoping to inherit his brother's bank account. "What did the demon say?"

"He threatened to sodomize the magician."

Frater Merrin's voice bellowed over the opera epic crackling from the speakers as he called out the banishing words to release the imprisoned demon, who immediately disappeared. A shame. I was starting to enjoy this ridiculous farce.

The altar girls poured black sand over the summoning circle, extinguishing the dwindling ring of fire. More applause erupted throughout the temple. A creepy hosanna-filled hymn followed. These people were one big, collective mess.

A potluck dinner, of all things, was announced. The congregation exited the temple into a room off the foyer. Lon and I stood up and hung to the side, nodding politely as people passed us. The last couple headed out of the beaded curtains. Lon tapped my arm. We strode to the front of the room, ignoring the weak protests of the altar girls, and marched up the set of stairs after the retreating figure of Frater Merrin, who climbed to a small loft room.

Stormy daylight filtered in through a window of glass bricks and cast a hazy light over a mussed up bed and a rack of clothes. An old theater makeup dresser stood against the wall, its mirror bordered with round light bulbs.

The magician turned around. "You're not allowed up here," he warned. Mismatched eyes—one blue, one brown. We were standing in front of the man who'd taken a big bite out of Cindy Brolin's arm. I felt a little sick.

"Don't remember me, Frater *Karras*?" Lon asked.

The elderly magician squinted, then picked up a pair of wire-rim glasses off the dresser, hooking the curved ends over his ears. "My goodness, is that Butler's kid? Well, I'll be damned . . . it's been a long time since I've set eyes on you."

"Since your 'accident,'" Lon confirmed. "The one that caused you to hurt your back so badly, you couldn't work for the Hellfire Club anymore. What year was that, again?"

"Oh, a long time ago, to be sure."

"Around the time of the Sandpiper Park Snatcher," Lon said, hand sliding inside his jacket.

I searched the magician's face for some spark of guilt, but he simply nodded and smiled tightly. "Yes, sometime after that. How's your father?"

"Dead."

"Oh? I'm sorry to hear that." The regret in his voice almost sounded genuine.

Lon unholstered the Lupara from inside his jacket.

The magician took a step back in alarm and held up his hands. "What is this?"

"Let's talk," Lon demanded.

"Talk? About what?"

"For starters, why don't you tell us about Jesse Bishop? We found your handiwork in the cannery. Was he your assistant? Did he help you snatch those kids, or did he catch you with your pants down?"

The magician's eyes remained steady, but his fingers curled up under the edges of his robe sleeves like snails retreating into their shells. It took him several moments to answer. When he finally did, he sounded exhausted. Demoralized, almost. "You don't have any idea what you're talking about."

"Why don't you explain," Lon suggested. "We've got time. Why don't you also tell us why you were biting the kids you kidnapped thirty years ago?"

That got the man's attention. A wave of surprise shadowed his face. "It's no use, because you won't believe me." He backed up another step and hit the dresser, steadying his fingers on the edge of it. "There's something far bigger going on that you can't comprehend. The best thing you can do right now is forget you ever saw me and leave it alone." His hand inched further back along the dresser top as he spoke. "Because it won't end. If he's not successful this time, he'll just keep trying. Thirty years are nothing to him."

"Who will keep trying?" Lon asked. "We saw Bishop's bones. We know he's dead."

Merrin sighed. "Bishop was in the wrong place at the wrong time."

"Then who are you talking about? Why are the children being taken?"

Did Lon see Merrin's hand moving? I stuck my own hand in my pocket, ready to retrieve my small caduceus.

The magician shook his head and looked away.

"We're not leaving until you answer me," Lon snarled, gesturing with the Lupara. He was too angry, not paying attention.

"Hey!" I shouted, my eyes on the magician's roaming fingers. I tried to yank my caduceus out of my pocket but it got stuck sideways, like a bone wedged inside a throat. That cost me. The magician's hand grabbed what he'd been seeking, some sort of engraved disk that fit into the palm of his hand.

The lights around the theater mirror flashed off and on as Merrin quickly pulled electricity and released kindled Heka through the disk, pushing it right into us. My hair blew back as charged Heka punched me in the chest so hard that it knocked me off my feet. I didn't even have time draw a breath before I was thrown backward into the wall.

My leg twisted painfully as I tumbled to the floor. Lon's head snapped to the side. The Lupara flew out of his hand—a deafening blast cracked the air when it hit the floor and went off accidently. The theater mirror shattered. Better it than me. The Lupara rotated near my feet like a lethal spin-the-bottle while the sharp scent of spent gunpowder blossomed.

And Frater Merrin was already racing down the steps.

I scrambled to pull myself up, afraid the vintage gun might go off again as Lon retrieved it. When I put weight on my twisted leg, pain flared. One of Lon's arms flew out and snagged me around the waist.

"You okay?"

"Goddamn knee," I bit out, testing it again. Better this time. Nothing broken.

"Can you—"

"Yes, go," I shouted, pushing him toward the stairs. I winced as we raced down to the altar, wondering just how fast a man in his sixties with a bad back could run. Halfway down the stairs, I got my answer. The beaded curtain swung in the distance as commotion surged behind it in the foyer.

"Call the police!" Frater Merrin cried out between heavy breaths.

Awesome. Just what we needed. We stormed through the temple and tried to catch up with him. Dear God, I was hurting. A sharp pain shot up and down my leg with every step. It was all I could do to push it out of my mind and plow forward, a few steps behind Lon.

I heard the front door crash open. He wasn't far ahead of us. A swell of angry cries rose up when we pushed through the beaded curtains and burst into the foyer. Lon flashed the Lupara and everyone backed up. Someone in the crowd echoed Merrin's instruction to call the police.

We darted out the open door and took a sharp left through the covered walkway. It was pouring rain now. I tore after Lon, nearly slamming into him when he stopped short. His torso whipped around as he quickly scanned the sidewalk behind me in disbelief.

"What?" I looked past him. No Merrin.

"What the hell?" Lon mumbled breathlessly. He turned to the street punks still huddled against the inner wall along the sidewalk, smoking cigarettes and sharing a case of Milwaukee's Beast. Only one of them was an Earthbound, a small boy with his hair dyed bright blue to match his halo, maybe sixteen. Lon singled him out, probably hoping for a little brotherly help. "Which way did he go?"

The blue-haired boy shrunk closer to the wall and shook his head nervously.

Lon repeated his demand to the rest of the punks, but was met with a sea of disinterested faces. No one said a thing.

With a growl, Lon shoved the Lupara back into his jacket and ran toward the street. I raced after him, cutting through a slippery patch of mud and dead grass. I bounded onto the cracked sidewalk half a block behind, but he wasn't running anymore, only turning around in circles, searching. Traffic raced by, splashing sheets of rainwater as we both surveyed the area. A few umbrellas danced along the sidewalk on both sides of the busy road, but no man in ritual robes.

Frater Merrin had disappeared.

Wet and miserable, we skirted around the side of the brick school trying to root out a place he might be hiding, even checking the Dumpster that the bums had been digging in earlier. It was fruitless. A man with his experience was probably well versed in concealment and warding magick. Hell, I'd figured it out on my own when I was eighteen—the spells were carved into my arm. Merrin could be standing right next to us and we wouldn't even know.

Crushing disappointment turned my limbs to cement. We were so close. We had him. The Snatcher himself. What were we going to do now? Sit out here in the rain and watch the temple in case he came back? Then again, if we left, he might. Maybe Dare could have some of his people watch it. We could stay until he sent someone.

A police siren wailed in the distance. *Shit.* Merrin had gotten his people to call the damn cops. I glanced back at the temple. Some members of the congregation were huddled beneath the overhang with the street punks, watching us. I could've cried in frustration.

"My gun has been illegally modified. I can't get caught with it," Lon lamented in defeat. With an open palm, he swooped back the dripping strands of hair matted against his forehead and blinked away rain. He glanced down at me. "You okay?" he asked a second time.

"Just pissed." Being outsmarted by a lunatic magician with one foot in the grave wasn't on my bucket list.

It wasn't on Lon's, either. He nodded once, sniffled, then slung his arm around my shoulders and urged me forward to the crosswalk. "Let's get back to the car and get the hell out of here."

"We should call Dare and—"

Lon stopped midstep. His arm grew rigid on my shoulder.

"What's wrong?" I asked.

"Oh . . ." He was watching a truck pull into a space across the street. "Oh," he said again.

"Lon?"

"The U-Haul . . ."

"Yeah?" I looked again. Nothing weird about it. I couldn't make out the person in the cab and doubted Lon could, either. The side of the truck was painted with bright graphics— a golfer in Augusta.

"Golf," he said with a dazed look as the Walk sign flashed. "Christ, Cady. I think I know where Bishop's Polaroid was taken."

18

It took us half an hour to get to the Redwood Putt-Putt Golf Center, located just off an old two-lane highway that once carried a good bit of traffic south of La Sirena before a shiny new bypass funneled it to a larger interstate in the mid seventies. By 1980, all the businesses that had grown up around the old highway had gone under, including two gas stations, the Lucky Roadside Diner, Maria's Fruit Barn, and poor old Redwood Putt-Putt.

Though the rain had passed, it left behind a threatening steel-gray sky. The industrial-strength heater in Lon's SUV had mostly dried our rain-damp hair, but I still wasn't all that keen on stomping around a muddy, abandoned miniature golf course.

Lon spent most of the ride over exchanging phone calls with Dare. His cell rang one more time as we pulled in. He answered and didn't say much of anything during the brief call. And all he said to me after hanging up was, "Dare's got people watching the temple."

Good. Maybe Merrin would be stupid enough to come back. A girl could dream.

Lon pocketed his phone and parked behind a crumbling

sky-blue wall that once hid the putt-putt course's garbage bin from street view.

"Was he lying?" I said as we exited the SUV.

Lon hit the alarm button on his key chain. "Who?"

"Frater Merrin." I trailed Lon around the backside of the building as he inspected a chain-link fence threaded with green plastic privacy slats that surrounded the property. "Was he lying when he was blabbering about everything being pointless because 'he' would just try 'it' again? Could you hear his emotions?"

Lon stopped at a locked double gate and bent to inspect it. "I read him. He wasn't lying."

"Then maybe he's not the Snatcher. Maybe it's someone else entirely."

"He definitely made it sound like someone else is involved, but he's not innocent, or he wouldn't have run from us."

True. "He said 'thirty years are nothing to him.' Thirty years isn't nothing."

Lon poked at the gate's lock and verbalized my thoughts before I could. "Unless you're an Æthyric being with a long life span."

"Exactly. I smell a rat. Or a demon. No offense."

"None taken." Lon reached inside his jean jacket pockets and retrieved gloves. "You got yours?" He nodded at my hands.

No fingerprints, right. I dug out my gloves and continued thinking out loud. "Merrin's a magician. Merrin summons demons. What are the odds that Merrin made some sort of deal with one thirty years ago?" Lon didn't answer. He was busy inspecting the fence. "Are you listening to me?"

"Always." The corners of his mouth briefly tilted up into

a gentle smile before he shook the fence several times. "A deal with an Æthyric demon usually means that the magician gets something out of it."

"So now we have two parties exchanging favors, and one of those favors involves kidnapping young teenagers. Was the bargain unfulfilled thirty years ago, and he's back to collect on it? Did Merrin try to worm his way out of a contract? And which one of them wanted the children and why?"

"Excellent questions. The only thing we know is that Merrin was snatching some of the children and biting them— or at least Cindy Brolin, anyway. Stay here." He trekked back to where we started, then returned with a dented metal garbage can and settled it upside down in the mud against the shorter fence near the gate. He placed a foot on top and tested his weight.

"O-o-oh, no," I said. "We are *not* climbing this fence."

"See where the top is bent? This isn't uncharted territory. We'll be fine."

"Just because someone else has done it doesn't mean we need to!"

"I'm the one with the shitty back—what are you worried about?" He picked up a damp cardboard box, shook it off, and broke it down.

"I . . ."

"Yes?" He cocked a brow in amusement then draped the flattened cardboard over the top of the fence.

"Can't you just shoot the lock off or something?"

"That only works in the movies. I'll go first." He balanced on the creaky garbage can, stuck a toe in one of the links, and pulled himself up, hesitating before going over the top.

"Be careful," I warned. "There are a few parts of you that are important to me. Please don't crush them."

"I'll let you check for damage once I'm over." And with a grunt he kicked a leg up and jumped over to the other side, making a sploshy noise when his feet hit the ground.

"You okay?" I called out.

"Right as rain. Come on, girl."

Following his method, I climbed the fence. But when I threw my leg over, my body froze up, midstraddle.

"Other leg now," Lon coaxed. "You can do it."

"I don't think I can."

"Well, then. Let me just find a long stick and prod you back over. You can wait in the car."

I grumbled under my breath. Once I got the leg over, I clung to the top of the fence, trying to get my shoe into one of the links. Then I felt his hands on my hips.

"Drop down. I've got you."

Not much of a choice there. My arms were starting to shake from holding myself up. I lowered myself down a few inches. He snaked a steely arm around my waist, so I let go and he caught me, setting me down on my feet.

"Would you like to check my parts now?" he asked, smugly holding his jacket open.

"Oww." I bent over and rubbed the heel of my hand over my jean zipper, wincing. "Maybe you should check mine instead. I need some fence-jumping lessons."

His lower lip pouted sarcastically. He slipped a gloved hand between my legs and pressed a finger into the bump in my jeans where all the seams converged. "Where? Here?"

"I'm not sure." I fought back a breathless laugh. "Keep it up and I'll tell you."

He patted me appreciatively, then pulled my coat back into place. "We can continue that later. Let's do this before it starts raining again."

We trudged through a marshy maze of tangled under-growth, fallen trees, and broken branches and emerged in a graveyard of dismantled course obstacles. An immobilized windmill sat on its side, tethered to the ground by vines. Just past it, a dinosaur was broken into ten sections of sun-faded, molded metal.

Tiers of synthetic putting greens lay just ahead of us, most of them choked with real weeds growing between the seams of plastic grass. A few others were flooded. All of it was sad and silent—no children, no cars passing in the distance.

"When I was a kid, my dad and I came here," Lon said. "Used to be an A&W next door. We'd get root beer floats after we played." A nostalgic smile lightened his face. "He'd always let me win."

"Do you miss him?" I asked, trying not to think of my own parents.

"Sometimes," he admitted at length. "Jupe was just a kid when he died. I wish he'd lived long enough to see him grow up. He was better at expressing his feelings than I am."

I was surprised to hear him admit this. "If you ask me, what you *do* is more important than what you *say*." Had I understood this a few years ago, my life might've been different. My parents lied to my face my whole life, then ditched me before I'd finished high school. I couldn't imagine Lon forcing Jupe to live on his own at seventeen—no matter the circumstances, not in a million years. "Besides, it's not like Jupe needs a role model for expressing himself. He's expressive enough for both of you."

He squinted down at me and suppressed a smile. "Maybe you're right."

We meandered past a gigantic Mother Hubbard shoe on hole twelve and a morbid decapitated crocodile on the tenth hole. The missing head was three holes down, its too-wide eyes mocking us atop the bank of a pinball obstacle.

After a few minutes of walking, Lon stopped at the seventh hole. The final resting place for the ball in this course was beneath a colorful castle. But that's not where Lon's eyes were. He was studying the cartoonish King and Queen statues that flanked a small bench at the beginning of the path: King Bull and Queen Cow, to be precise. They stood upright on two legs, both dressed in medieval finery, now faded and grimy. A miniature forest of weeds grew up around them.

Their frozen bovine faces stared back at us. The Queen's black fiberglass nose had broken off and been plugged with an orange golf ball.

Lon pulled out his phone and opened a JPEG of the scanned Polaroid, held the screen in front of him and squinted. "Look."

I slipped under his arm and compared the image on the screen with the dreary vista in front of us. The elusive dark shape in the foreground of the photo matched the outline of the Queen's torso—her molded blond hair, crown askew, and the sign she was holding on her shoulder that read: USE THE HONOR SYSTEM WHEN COUNTING STROKES.

Behind her, the same two palm trees stood in the distance, only taller. I squatted low to get a different angle. "How in the world did you remember this?"

"I broke her nose," Lon said, shoving the phone back into the front pocket of his jeans. "An accident. Was swinging my club around. Reared back and poked a hole through one of her nostrils with the grip. Looks like someone else punched the rest of it out."

We stood together in silent memorial for the defaced Queen.

"What now?" I finally said. "There must be something important about her."

"Important enough that Bishop either swallowed the photo to keep someone else from getting it—"

"Or someone shoved it down his throat in anger," I finished. "Trying to hide a secret."

And maybe that someone was Frater Merrin. He bit Cindy Brolin—as Lon said, the magician certainly wasn't innocent in all this—and may have even murdered the original seven kids taken in the '80s. Stands to reason that he could've done away with Bishop.

"Help me look."

As the sun shone intermittently behind shifting dark clouds, we circled Queen Cow, ripping away weeds to examine her for clues. No writing, no scratched message in any strange magical alphabet. But when I was inspecting her face, I brushed the Honor System sign she held in her hoofed hand. The sign was loose, and a dull pink light glowed from inside the sliver where her shoulder met the back of the sign.

"Lon! Here. Same pink charge that was in the cannery on that door ward."

"Dammit." Lon tried to pry the sign away, but his fingers slipped off once, twice. . . .

"Same spell, as well," I confirmed. "Keeps people away."

I took out the red ochre chalk and wrote out the counterspell I'd used on the door in the cannery, letting my spit dribble slowly into the hidden crevice. With a fizzle, the pink glow disappeared, but before I could pat myself on the back, the golf ball suddenly became dislodged and fell out of the cow's broken nose, bouncing as it hit the golf path. We watched in surprise as it rolled away.

A cracking noise brought our attention back to the

Queen. The fiberglass sign had split away from the body. The resulting dark crack gaped open; something shiny was down in there.

"Is it safe?" Lon asked, peering closer.

"I think so."

He reached a few fingers inside, twisted his hand, and slowly retrieved an object from the crevice—a tarnished silver tube, maybe a foot or more in length, a couple inches in diameter. Milky white glass capped either end, reminding me of a fancy kaleidoscope. A long leather strap suggested that it was intended to be worn around the body.

"What in the world is"—a louder *crack!* interrupted my words—"that?"

The Queen's entire body was splitting like a fissure on an ice-capped lake. The crack ran down the length of her side in one direction, up her shoulder, and across her face in the other. As it continued to deepen unnaturally, the hairs on the back of my neck rose. I *really* didn't like this magick. Didn't like it when we first encountered it in the cannery, and didn't like it out here in the abandoned putt-putt course.

With my hand on Lon's arm, I took a step back, attempting to pull him along with me. He wouldn't budge. The rigid muscle under his jacket might as well have been stone.

The front of the Queen buckled and swayed. I muffled the urge to yell "timber" as the crack ran across the base and the molded fiberglass shell began falling away from its inner wire armature.

"Move!" I shouted, yanking Lon. In a daze, he staggered backward as the fiberglass crashed into the cement in front of us and shattered into sharp pieces around our feet. At the base of the armature, the fissure grew. It radiated like a spiderweb and ran into the cement under the bench . . . then *up* and over it, across King Bull. Continued to spread down through the golf path, burrowing wide, ragged crevices into the ground. Mud seeped down into the dark spaces it left behind. I backed up and nearly tripped over the wood border than lined the course, righting myself on the muddy, synthetic grass.

"It's a spell," Lon said dazedly.

"Of course it's a spell!" What else would it be? The fissure spread up nearby trees, crackling the bark . . . it created a filigree pattern up the side of the castle obstacle.

We doubled back over the castle fairway and stopped at the next putting green as one of the smaller trees dropped branches and the side of the castle fell apart. The magical crack continued to spread.

"Do something," Lon snapped.

I cut him a dirty look. "Do what?"

Lon gave me a sidelong glance, his expression a mixture of alarm and anger. "What you did in the cannery!"

We jumped and cried out in surprise as the castle armature tipped and fell over with a boom, shaking the ground. The crack had destroyed everything around hole seven and was overtaking the surrounding greens.

He was right; I had to do something. I tried to will my Moonchild power, but nothing happened. It was dead. I couldn't understand why—how could it snap into action without my calling it up in the cannery, then refuse to surface when I tried now? Frustrated, I climbed a small hill on one of the courses, and tried again. Again, nothing.

"I can't!" I yelled as several trees split, the wood groaning in protest.

"Try harder."

"I'm trying, asshole—I told you, I can't!" Then something hit me. A big, gigantic *Duh*. "It's daytime! No moon! I need the moon to draw power." It had been night or near-night every time I'd used it in the past—in the Hellfire caves, when my parents were trying to kill me, and in the cannery. It was midafternoon now.

His face fell. He knew I was right.

"Can you manually cast the spell that you used at the cannery?"

"I'd have to circle the whole golf center with chalk. There's not enough time."

"Try again to use your ability," he suggested, panic in his voice. "Maybe it's possible when the moon's not out, just harder. Take a few breaths first."

Mumbling obscenities, I closed my eyes and attempted to calm myself enough to call up the power. Attempted to block out the image of the spell spreading through the town and destroying buildings like some sort of apocalyptic magical plague. Tried instead to visualize the experience of the blackness pushing away my surroundings and the blue pinpoint of light appearing.

"Come on, come on," Lon muttered.

Something clicked inside me; it crouched at the edge of my consciousness. I could *just* feel it connecting. Maybe I could pull it up if I tried harder. . . .

"Shit!" Lon yelled.

My eyes flew open. The entire park was cracking and crumbling as if a silent earthquake had hit. The fissure was spreading faster. I really didn't want to find out what would happen if it touched us.

Apparently Lon didn't either. "I think we're done here, witch."

He grabbed my hand and we fled like rabbits, hopping down terraces and cutting through the courses. Mud seeped into the hems of our jeans as we stumbled through under-brush and soared around the maze of dead course obstacles, past the unassembled dinosaur—

The ground suddenly cracked below my feet. My shoe snagged, midrun. I face-planted into the mud, the wind knocked out of my lungs.

Lon's yelp of surprise floated over my head. I couldn't breathe. Desperately I clawed at a puddle as my lower body sank. A horrific rumble shook my bones. Metal creaked behind me.

I couldn't see. Mud stung my eyes. I felt Lon's hands wrap around my wrists like steel bands. He pulled, but my foot was stuck in the earth. When the section of metal dinosaur came crashing down, it sounded like a bomb. An explosion. A car wreck.

Pain ripped through my leg.

I think I screamed, but I wasn't sure. I couldn't hear it. The ground was swallowing me. My leg was trapped under a metal dinosaur torso. Lon's hands slipped away from mine. I struggled—fought, pulled, thrashed. . . . I was feral. Completely out of my mind.

My body was sinking faster. The dinosaur was weighing me down. I stopped fighting and clung to a crumbling sliver of ground.

I was going down.

19

Buried alive. What a horrible way to die. I'd often imagined myself being torn apart by some primal Æthyric demon, or poisoned after testing a bad batch of medicinals—maybe even shot down while fleeing an FBI agent, come to collect me for my parent's heinous crimes.

But not this.

Not half-blind and suffocating in a whirlpool of mud.

Something pressed against my side. The steady vibration of the quaking ground was punctuated by three stronger thuds that reverberated through the metal dinosaur like a struck gong. It was Lon, kicking at it. On the fourth kick, the pressure lifted from my pinned leg. I yanked. Lon yanked. My knee found purchase on a tree root beneath the sinking ground, and I climbed, grasping fistfuls of wet grass above my head.

Lon grabbed the back of my jacket and hoisted me as I scrabbled to heave myself aboveground. My hip had barely cleared the unnatural sinkhole when I felt myself being sucked back down again. I wedged my fingers inside an expanding crevice. My jacket and shirt nearly slid over my head as Lon strained and yanked me forward.

"*Up!*" he yelled, not giving me a moment to rest.

Pain shot through my leg when I tried to stand. The earth shook and I wavered on my feet.

"Move—go!"

Lon gripped my waist and tugged me along. I faltered, then limped, then jogged, ignoring the pain. It only took me a few seconds to run without aid. We sloshed over the rumbling mud, outrunning the earthquake.

The fence was only a few yards away. Lon glanced back at the advancing fissure. "Climb," he instructed, securing the mudied silver tube inside his jacket.

No trash can on this side, so he boosted me up with his hands splayed across my ass. Under better circumstances, I might've appreciated this more, but it was all I could do to pull myself up and over the damn fence, even with his help.

Lon started climbing before I'd finished, pressuring me to drop. He slipped by my side and jumped down, then reached up to help me.

"Oww!" I cried out in pain. The leg of my jeans was torn and stuck on the fence.

The ground shook with crashing trees. The fissure was a few feet away. I twisted to jerk at my caught pant leg, grunted and tugged. The denim ripped, I fell into Lon's arms, and we tumbled, knocking over the trash can as we crashed to the ground.

Lon groaned as we untangled and pushed ourselves back to our feet, preparing to run again. Then everything went silent. No quaking. No sounds of destruction.

"It stopped!"

I glanced back at the park. The fence was still standing. A couple of aftershocks made us both jump, but when we were sure that it was really over, I warily peered through the chain link. Sure enough, the craggy fissures had crept all the way to the fence, then inexplicably halted. The entire property looked like it had been nuked and then swallowed by the earth. Nothing was standing but the brick entry building and the fence; the courses were just a mass of crumbled obstacles and fallen trees.

We surveyed the decimated land for a long moment, both of us breathing heavily. I squeezed my eyes shut, then reopened them, hoping to find everything restored. Maybe it was magick, like the cannery. That had been an illusion—the bugs had disappeared; they weren't real. This was.

"Did you use the Moonchild power?"

I shook my head, trying to catch my breath. "No. Wasn't me."

"What stopped it, then?"

"Hell if I know. The fence? Maybe it was just a ward that covered this property."

"I hate this magick," Lon mumbled.

Understatement of the day. Shock and relief mixed inside me. More than a little anxiety, too. Sure, I was thankful to be standing alive on this side of the fence, but the weird Æthyric magick—if that's what it was—was screwing with my head. It's hard to play the game when you didn't know the rules. I inspected the fence for markings, seeking something that might've been placed to contain the spell. Nothing.

"You're bleeding." Lon bent to inspect my leg, pushing back my torn jeans. Blood and mud swirled over pale skin. The cut was a couple of inches long and it throbbed. "We need to clean this."

We could both be dead right now, trapped underground. What would Jupe do without his dad? My heart clenched painfully at the thought of him being left alone if something happened to Lon. Things were simpler when I had only my-self to think about.

Cold wind bit through my damp clothes while the distant sound of a solitary car chugged along on the deserted high-way. "Can we please go home now?"

I limped to the SUV. Lon cranked it up and turned on the seat warmers. While the engine idled, he retrieved hand wipes from the glove compartment and helped me gently clean the mud from my cut. It stung something crazy, and it was sore. A bruise was already blooming on my shin.

Lon took the silver tube out of his pocket and turned it in his hands.

"Huh."

"What is it?" I leaned over the armrest for a closer look.

The tube was beautiful, engraved with a floral pattern that wound around hidden sigils. In the center was a single word constructed from the same foreign alphabet used on the mandalas in the cannery. Apparently Bishop's Polaroid really *had* been a threat to somebody.

"Look," he said, pointing to one end of the tube.

A small keyhole.

Lon opened the armrest compartment and dug through it, retrieving the box that held Bishop's key, which looked to be the right size.

"Is your leg okay? Can you make a few more minutes? I want to open it here," Lon said. "If it's got some weird spell attached to it, I'd rather it not destroy my house and kill my kid."

Outside the SUV on the rough parking lot I drew an antimagick spell, then kindled Heka with electricity that I pulled from the power lines above us. I couldn't feel any residual magick inside it, so Lon inserted Bishop's key. The lock snicked open. We backed up and waited for a few seconds. Nothing happened. No magical crack in the parking lot. No giant magical cockroaches.

Lon lifted the unlocked cap and cautiously peeked inside the tube. Inside was a scroll of parchment paper. Old paper, old ink. Lon's obsessions. He carefully withdrew it for inspection.

I whistled. "Look at that."

He blew out a long breath. "Vellum." He took one glove off to feel the paper, then sniffed it. "Iron gall ink, probably. See where it has caused the paper to disintegrate?" He unrolled the top of it with delicate precision, wincing as it crackled. We studied the handwritten text together.

It was a spell, written in a strange language, but not the same as in the mandalas and on the tube, and peppered with crude drawings of sigils and seals.

"Well, well . . . what do we have here?" Lon murmured.

My heart raced. "What is this? Do you know this language?"

"Looks like Old Nubian or Coptic. Maybe I can translate it at home."

"Most of this looks foreign to me, but this symbol here is a key," I said, pointing. "It's used with other symbols in spells to unlock doors."

Lon peered at it and tried to make sense of the surrounding symbols.

"I wonder if this is part of Merrin's bargain with his demon."

"I don't know, but the alphabet engraved on the tube isn't earthly," he said, "it's Æthyric. And we need to translate it."

"How?"

"Don't know. But if it means we've got to ask for help, then we ask."

"If I still had my guardian spirit, I'd just summon it and find out," I lamented, scraping my shoe across the asphalt to rub out my chalk marks.

"What about your caliph?" He carefully rolled the top of the vellum back in place and inserted it in the tube. "Could you call him and ask to borrow his guardian?"

"Maybe, but he's been having some issues with it since San Diego. When he sent me the check, he mentioned in a letter that he thought the spirit might be going senile. It might not be reliable."

Lon scratched his eyebrow and pursed his lips. "All this talk about bargains . . . what if we summon something ourselves and bargain for a translation?"

Summon a demon and barter for information? Great. That's the last thing I wanted to do.

Then a thought struck me. We might not have to barter at all. A demon owed me a favor. I'd saved his ass from the Hellfire caves. His ass, and other serviceable parts of his Æthyric body.

"Ha!" I cried out.

"What?"

"Mr. Butler," I said, suddenly energized, "how would you feel about summoning an incubus with me tonight?"

20

Lon watched me prepare the summoning circle. My aching leg was bandaged, and I'd changed into clean clothes, but it was nearly dark outside and getting colder every minute. I wanted to get this done pronto so we could head back to his warm house and watch monster movies with Jupe. It was also taco night. Lon's grilled *carne asada* would make everything better.

"If you really want to be impregnated by demon seed, I'd be happy to comply," he joked. "There's no need to call up an incubus for that."

I glanced up from a photocopy of the incubus seal. "Lord knows you're good at impregnating, but I'm gonna have to pass, thanks."

I'd already finished drawing a double-strong Æthyric-level binding triangle onto the floor of an old open-air workshop in the woods of Lon's property, a half-mile away from his house—a half-mile away from Jupe. It was really just a glorified carport on a concrete pad, with one full wall of metal siding that sheltered our work from the dirt road, and two half-walls. It housed a tractor that he used for clearing land and some miscellaneous tools locked up inside metal cabinets.

Not fancy, but it had the electricity I needed for kindling from a row of fluorescent lights above us.

The circle was finished. Lon let me borrow a full-sized caduceus. Good thing, because the miniature one I'd been carrying around all day in my pocket would have likely blown to smithereens with the amount of Heka I needed to kindle for securing this thing. I brushed off my hands and double-checked that everything was correct: the binding triangle, the summoning circle, and the incubus seal. All good. Time to start charging the triangle.

"Ready?" I asked.

Lon inclined his head and gestured for me to begin.

I took a deep breath and reached out for electrical current. It was nice and strong here, readily available. I pulled it inside and kindled Heka for several seconds. A firm push, and it rushed from me and ran through the caduceus. White light seared the chalked markings, solid and steady, no cracks or static. I didn't have time to fully appreciate it. The post-magick sickness came on the heels of the release, dropping my stomach to my feet. I closed my eyes for several seconds and counted breaths until it abated. Not too bad, but it would get worse after the next round.

"You could just do it with your ability. It's dark now. Moon's out."

"I've had about all the strange magick I can handle today." This way might take longer, but at least there wouldn't be any surprises.

The binding triangle had been charged. Next up was the circle. This time I had to focus harder to kindle more Heka. Summoning requires a big, big charge. When I pulled from the current, all the lights buzzed and flickered. Too big a pull and I'd short everything out; not big enough and I'd have to start all over again. I strained, carefully seeking the breaking point in the electricity. A sharp pop cracked the air on the other side of the shed when one of the fluorescent bulbs gave way and sent tiny shards of glass tinkling onto the floor.

Raw energy coursed through me, standing the hairs on my arms on end. Making my skin itch beneath the surface. Firing up every nerve in my body. My cells were rubber balls, bouncing off each other, erratic and frenzied . . . just a *little* further.

Lon murmured anxiously from the side. I ignored him.

The caduceus tip was poised at the chalked border of the summoning circle. Kindled Heka swirled inside me, begging for a release—I hadn't pulled this much current in a long time, and I couldn't hold it any longer. With a groan, I pushed it out in a smooth, heavy stream. Sweet, holy relief. The circle fired up so bright and strong, it hurt my eyes. I tried to laugh in victory, but it came out like a warped yelp.

If I'd been a surfer on a board, nausea would be the thirty-foot wave that broke too soon and knocked me down. The fall was surreal. Slow motion. I crumpled to the side, away from the circle. My shoulder hit the concrete. Pain ripped through me, but I didn't care. I was too busy trying to roll over before the vomit came . . . and it did. I retched violently. Mostly water and the crackers I'd eaten when we returned from the putt-putt center. I'd planned for it, so my skunk-striped hair was twisted up into a loose knot on the crown of my head: I'm a pro.

Lon's hands pulled me up, setting off a flare of pain in my injured shoulder. A cry broke from my lips. He jerked back, apologizing, then shifted his grip to my waist.

"Water and towel," I croaked, coughing from the stomach acid burning my throat. White terry cloth appeared in front of my face. I wiped my mouth, then swished bottled water and spat it out as Lon silently unrolled yards of paper towels. "I've got it," I complained. "I can clean up after myself." I briefly wondered how Frater Merrin managed to go through this every week at the Silent Temple. Maybe the nausea wasn't as bad when you were used to pulling that much Heka all the time. Or maybe he was just stronger than me, Moonchild or not.

Lon dropped the paper towels in a pile over the vomit. "Leave it. Go finish." His hand emerged from his pocket with a pack of gum. He offered me a piece with a whisper of a smile on his lips. I snatched it out of his fingers. "I'll brush my teeth before kissing you, don't worry."

"Small favors."

The circle was perfect. The binding was perfect. The seal inside the binding was perfect. All I had to do was call the incubus. There are several ways to do this, several calls in multiple languages. Some work better than others, depending on exactly what you're attempting to summon. But I always try their name first, without all the extra bells and whistles. For something as simple as an incubus, it should work.

"Voxhele of Amon!" I called out, pushing my will through the summoning circle as I paced around it. My legs were rubbery, still fighting the last waves of Heka-sickness. I anxiously smacked Lon's gum. Fiery cinnamon. It tasted like him; he loved cinnamon, hated mint.

A soft light pulsed in the middle of the binding triangle. It grew, filling out with the form of the incubus. Sallow-skinned and black-headed, the demon was the height of an average human, his body lean and wiry. His pleasant face featured heather eyes weighted with thick gray lashes. A matching patch of pale purple skin tipped his sternum. Rows of tight, gray scales trailed over his shoulders. Overall, fairly appealing, if a little feminine for my tastes.

He was sitting cross-legged inside the binding triangle, yawning and naked, like the first time I'd seen him. Not surprising—he *was* a sex demon. His head rotated in all directions when he realized he wasn't in Kansas any longer.

"Voxhele of Amon," I said in a mustered cheerful greeting, still fighting waves of nausea. "Remember me?"

A smile spread over his face. "Mother of Ahriman, a pleasant surprise. These aren't the Hellfire caves—how wonderful! Where are we, exactly?"

"Not far from the caves, geographically speaking."

He made a noise of disapproval and scratched the scales on his shoulder. "I owe you a favor, don't I?"

"Yes—"

"Oh, wait. I remember you, too," he said, speaking to Lon while looking him up and down with a lewd grin. "If this favor involves all three of us, I'm fine with that." He leaned back on the palms of his hands, displaying his wares. I wasn't sure if he was pierced in several places, or was naturally bumpy. I tried not to stare.

Lon mumbled something derogatory under his breath as he picked up the engraved silver tube and a stack of photos, enlargements of the cannery mandalas.

"I need information, not sexual favors," I said to the demon.

"Oh." He sounded disappointed. "Depending on what it is . . ."

I held up a hand. "I'm obligated to inform you that you are bound by me now, and must answer honestly."

"Yes, yes." He waved a dismissive hand in the air. "Ask

your question, and I'll weigh it to decide if it's an even trade for the favor I owe you."

From outside the circle, we showed him the silver tube and pointed out the engraving. His eyes widened. A few seconds passed as he glanced between us, then said, very carefully, "And wherever did you find that?"

"Can you translate it and give us the meaning?" I asked.

His eyes darkened as he considered, then he sighed heavily. "It's the name of a demon from my plane."

"What's his name?" Lon asked.

"It would translate loosely as 'Grand Duke Chora, Commander of Two Legions.'"

Never heard of him. "Two legions? Don't most of the dukes command like fifty legions or something?"

"I don't follow politics," Voxhele said as he inspected his fingernails.

Lon's face remained stoic. I couldn't tell if he recognized the name or not. I certainly didn't. There are, it is said, hundreds upon thousands of Æthyric demons, and only a smattering of those were cataloged in goetic texts and grimoires over the last century; when they were, many were listed with conflicting summoning names and half of them were dead.

"Do you know anything about this Grand Duke Chora?" I asked.

"I serviced a Duke Corelia last week," Voxhele said with a sly smile. "He was more than a mouthful, and let me just say—"

"Voxhele, please."

He sighed, great and long-suffering. "Chora commands a notorious battalion of Dragoons."

I glanced at Lon and wrinkled my nose. "Dragoons?"

"Mounted infantry," he clarified.

"They ride horses?"

A dark, slow smile lifted Voxhele's face. "Not exactly horses, no, but they are beasts of a kind. . . ."

"Anything else?"

"He's missing."

"From where?"

"From his command. Some say he's dead, but there are rumors that he's on assignment."

"What kind of assignment?"

"No one knows."

Huh. Looks like we just identified Merrin's demon. I elbowed Lon, requesting the mandala printouts. "What about the writing around these? Are they names too?"

Voxhele stood up, leaning close to the border of the binding, and studied each printout. "Yes, they're names."

"Who?"

"Not who. What. They're names of stars. At least I think so. This isn't a subject I've studied, Mother."

Stars. Interesting. We asked him which stars, but the answers he rattled off were foreign. He admitted that he didn't know their translation in English or in Latin. He also wasn't familiar with the old language used on the scroll inside the silver tube. Maybe it hadn't been the best idea to summon an incubus for assistance. I should've known that damn favor was worthless.

"What class of magick is this?" Lon insisted, referring to the mandalas.

"I'm afraid that goes beyond my simple knowledge. Only higher-level demons have been trained to wield magical talent. I'm not very savvy about such things, being the lowly prostitute that I am." He licked the corner of his mouth with a forked tongue while ogling Lon, who popped his jaw to the side in annoyance.

"What's this mean here?" I asked, pointing to an Æthyric word that was repeated on each of the mandalas.

"That means 'door.'"

"Door," I repeated, looking at Lon. Finally, something useful.

He stared at the photos thoughtfully. "Stars that open doors."

Oh, I *really* didn't like the sound of that.

21

GRAND DUKE CHORA

A clever and sly thinker, this Grand Duke uncovereth Hidden Paths and knoweth High Magics to Trap and Snare Enemies. He will maketh pacts with the Summoner to share his Wisdom, but will require Severe and High payments in trade. The Secret Science of War is etched upon his skin. He governeth two great Legions of the West with one thousand winged Dragoons. He appeareth from above as a Goodly Knight with a Cloak of Red Velvet.

—Ceremoniall Magics, John Gundye, 1498

The entry in Lon's goetic demon encyclopedia included a small etching of the demon, drawn as a handsome soldier riding a devilish-looking flying beast, something between an evil Pegasus and a dragon. And if the medieval magician who cataloged this entry was even partially correct—*He will maketh pacts with the Summoner to share his Wisdom, but will require Severe and High payments in trade*—then it would stand to reason that Merrin made a pact with Chora to learn Æthryic magick. The pink magick in the cannery and at the putt-putt course would definitely qualify as magick to "trap and snare enemies."

But what about the Æthyric spell in the tube? And the mandalas in the cannery—stars that opened doors? What doors, and who wanted them open—Merrin or Chora?

It won't end. If he's not successful this time, he'll just keep trying. Thirty years are nothing to him.

Chora definitely wanted something out of the bargain that he hadn't gotten yet, and if a new batch of children was being taken, then it stood to reason that he was the one who wanted these doors opened—not Merrin.

Merrin wasn't the only magician who could summon Æthyric demons. Chora's seal was listed in the goetic entry, so I figured I'd go straight to the source. But when I attempted to summon the demon later that night after dinner, he didn't appear.

There was a very short list of reasons why he wouldn't come when I summoned. So, assuming everything was executed correctly on my end—which it was—that meant the incubus was right when he said that Duke Chora was either dead, or here on earth.

We knew he wasn't dead, because Merrin suggested that he'd keep coming back until he was successful. But if he was alive on earth, he hadn't been just walking around, enjoying dips in the ocean, and sipping fruity drinks for thirty years. Æthyric beings can't survive on earth for long periods, certainly not for thirty years. If he was on this plane for a substantial stay, he had to be riding someone—and by that I mean old-school demonic possession, as depicted in the movie that inspired Frater Merrin's name . . . minus the green vomit.

Merrin showed no signs of possession when we found him at the Silent Temple. But if Chora was riding someone else, Merrin might know about it.

No getting around it: we had to track Merrin down again.

Once more I considered sending out a servitor, but it was just too dangerous. I toyed with the idea of reinforcing the Servitor Launch spell with wards, but magical experimentation could take days—or weeks. Plus, even with added protections embedded into a servitor, I still wasn't confident that someone like Merrin with more knowledge and skill than me couldn't reverse the spell, like Riley Cooper when she used my servitor to kidnap Jupe. I wasn't stupid enough to risk luring a child snatcher to a child.

There had to be another way to track Merrin down without using Jupe as bait, but for the life of me, I couldn't think of one. My mind just kept churning up spells that weren't viable, dead ends. It wasn't just frustrating, it was utterly dispiriting.

A small, selfish part of me wanted to just admit defeat. Hole up with Jupe in Lon's house and surround ourselves with extra warding magick and weapons. Ride things out until Halloween was over. I mean, I didn't know any of these families—why should I have to be the one to save more kids from being taken? Everyone knew the danger by now; Earthbound parents would be fools to allow their kids to be unsupervised after dark at this point.

I was contemplating this ugly thought as I emerged from the Tambuku kitchen the night after the incubus summoning. My leg still ached from the magical earthquake at the putt-putt course. Maybe being forced to stand on it through my shift was making me grumpier than normal. A normal person would take something for the pain, but I was trying to hold out. When I ducked behind the bar, a familiar face greeted me, but it wasn't Bob's.

Ambrose Dare sat on a barstool in an expensive suit, bald

head gleaming under the hanging strands of white lights that filtered through his green halo.

"Hello, Ms. Bell. Forgive me for barging in here without a warning." Funny, because he didn't really sound all that sorry. "I needed to discuss a couple of things with you, and I was in the area."

I glanced nervously around Tambuku. The backup bartender was serving a customer at the other end of the bar. A few booths were occupied, but we were slow tonight. No one seemed to notice that one of the most powerful Earthbounds in the area was sitting at the bar. I busied myself with shelving newly washed tiki mugs.

He tapped his fingers on the bar top. A few liver spots freckled over the bones in his hand. "A fourth child went missing tonight."

A mug nearly slipped out of my hand.

"She was taken two hours ago. It's not just Hellfire children that are being abducted, Ms. Bell. It's descendants of members who've undergone the transmutation spell."

"Oh . . . God."

"I might've been wrong at the beginning when I thought that Bishop was doing this, but I wasn't wrong about the motivation of revenge. Frater Karras—or Merrin, as he's calling himself now—was the magician who performed the transmutation spells on club members thirty years ago. I don't care what you and Lon found connecting Merrin with an Æthyric demon. Bargain or no bargain, that man is now going after the descendants of those members. This means my grandson and little Jupiter are now prime targets."

My stomach flipped. I forced panicked thoughts to quiet and considered the news rationally. "How many descendants of transmutated members are in their early teens?"

"Including both children and grandchildren, seventeen."

Seventeen? That seemed like a small and large number all at the same time. "Does Lon know?"

"My son, Mark, is parked outside, discussing this with Lon on the phone right now."

"Why did you come here to tell me in person?"

"Because I want to know what the hell you plan to do about all this."

You would think someone needing a favor would want to ask a little nicer. Indignation brought warmth to my cheeks, but I slid another mug into place and did my best to manage a calm tone. "This all centers on the bargain that Merrin made with the demon Chora."

"That's fine and dandy, but how is knowing this going to keep my kids safe?"

"If we can figure out why the spell—"

He interrupted me, raising his voice. "How is *this* going to bring the four children back home?"

I met his furious gaze and held it, listening to the tropical music and quiet conversations floating around the bar. "We need to find a way to track Merrin down again," I finally answered.

"I agree."

"Your people are still watching the Silent Temple?" I asked.

"Of course."

"I'm assuming they've seen nothing suspicious."

Dare made no comment, just studied my face like an artist memorizing shapes. I felt extremely uncomfortable. After a few seconds, he casually reached into his jacket on the chair next to him and pulled out a folded piece of paper.

"They are tracking every person who goes in and out of

the temple. So far this has proved fruitless. However, that's not the only tracking I've been doing. You'll forgive me, but I had someone do a little checking up on you after the incident in the Hellfire caves last month." He unfolded the paper and slid it across the table. "Magicians have a tendency to be loose wires. Imagine my surprise when we discovered an odd discrepancy in your origins."

My hand shook as I set down a mug. The paper was a photocopy of a handwritten birth certificate. *Arcadia Anne Bell. Born 1905.* Dare removed a second piece of paper. A copy of my modern birth certificate using her name. Forged, of course.

My pulse doubled . . . then tripled.

"It was old newspaper articles from the 1950s that got our attention. Cady Anne Bell, winner of several equestrian trophies. She was a fine rider. Only one of the articles listed her as Arcadia. That's the one that tipped us off, of course. We dug up the old certificate from a hospital warehouse outside Kirkland, Washington."

Airtight. That's what the caliph had told me about the identity years ago, before I started college. Something warm trickled down from my nose. I tasted copper. One watery, crimson drop fell and splashed on the bartop.

"Oh, my," Dare said, reaching across the table to hand me a paper napkin.

On instinct, I tilted my head back, then remembered that was wrong. Never back. The blood would slide down my throat and I'd vomit. I held my nose closed with the napkin and leaned forward, breathing hard through my mouth. I hadn't had a nosebleed since I was . . . I didn't know when. I tried to remember. A child? No. A teenager. When I parted ways with my parents. Breath was coming too fast, and my temples were throbbing. I was going to rupture more than a few vessels in my nose if I didn't calm down.

"Are you all right, dear?"

"No," I answered honestly. Brimming tears stung my eyes.

"I didn't mean to frighten you." He picked up the photocopies, stacked them together and refolded them, then slid them back into his jacket. "I've had problems with magicians in the past, Merrin being a prime example. If he is, indeed, the Snatcher, and if he gets away with it again, I'll never forgive myself. Never. The children's lives are my responsibility. I hired Merrin. He ate dinner in my home with me and my wife, and I never suspected anything. I blamed poor, stupid Bishop. And why? Because of a ridiculous argument."

I didn't care about any of this. My mind was racing, trying to put together my next move. What the hell was I going to do? All these years I'd been hiding from occultists who wanted me dead, and my fake identity had been ferreted out by some rich demon doing a standard background check? I pulled the napkin away from my nose, checking to see if the bleed was slowing. The printed Tambuku logo was obscured, soaked through with blood. I picked up a fresh napkin and clamped it back before the tiny trickle could fall.

Dare smoothed the lapels of his suit jacket and leaned back in his bar stool to squint at me. "Perhaps you and I can strike a new bargain concerning the Snatcher. If you stop him and return our children to us unharmed, then we'll keep this matter of your identity under wraps."

I bristled at his threat.

"Once you've completed that task," he continued, "you might be interested to know that the Hellfire Club can always use another rogue magician to help with our summoning and warding needs . . . and other matters." His lips stretched into a tight smile. "It pays handsomely."

Fury sliced through my flailing panic. I dropped the napkin on the table and leveled my gaze at him. "I couldn't give a damn about your money. I'm not summoning a bunch of low-level demons for your perverted parties."

"We've never had any complaints from the succubi."

"Oh, really? It totally surprises me that your *prisoners* aren't complaining to the people holding them against their will."

His brows shot up.

"I mean, who wouldn't want to screw an entire lot of wrinkly, stoned rich guys?"

"There are women, too. We aren't sexist."

"Even porn stars and prostitutes get a choice. They also get paid."

"Touché."

"For the record," I added, shoving my arm into a jacket sleeve, "I don't hire out my magick. I don't need money that badly."

"Lon's assets *are* nothing to sneeze at."

That sent me into orbit. I was fed up with feeling hunted, threatened, and living in the shadows. I was not about to be bullied by a man who thought he could slap his dick on the table and hold my life in his bony fingers. But to add insult to injury, he added, "You may want to plan for the future. When you're young, it's hard to see past tomorrow, but once Lon's midlife crisis wears off, he'll get bored with you. Then my financial offer might look more enticing. Especially to someone like you with a past you'd like to keep hidden."

His words felt like a slap in the face. I knew he was just goading me, knew what he was saying about Lon wasn't true, but the implication was a finger poking around in my insecurities. Insecurities about our age difference. About Lon's status in La Sirena versus the working-class life I'd created for myself. Dare's observation was worse than all the gossipy looks Lon and I got when we were out together in public.

A dark corner of my brain roared to life. Violent thoughts sprung from nowhere. I wanted to pound Dare's face into the table, make him take back the seed of doubt he'd just planted in my brain. And in that moment, I did something rash. My Moonchild power came to me like a loyal soldier following an order, fast and unquestioning. The bar fell into unnatural shadows and the blue dot appeared. I shaped it into a binding triangle and slammed it down over Dare before he could straighten his suit jacket.

The darkness fell away from my vision and the bar reappeared. Dare cried out in surprise as Heka trapped him where he sat. I could hear people murmuring in the distance, but I didn't care. If any savages were in the bar, they couldn't see the Heka anyway.

Dare's shock sluiced away. He laughed and gave me a rotten smile. "Impressive, Ms. Bell. Just splendid. How did you manage this without sigils?"

"You listen to me," I said, sticking my face in front of his, as close as I could get to the binding without breaking it. The Heka from the binding tickled my nose. "Lon and I will do our best to stop this goddamn Snatcher. But you're not going to bully me into doing Hellfire dirty work, and if you ever, ever imply that I'm some freeloading dinner-whore after Lon's money—"

Dare tugged at his tie, rocking it back and forth to loosen the knot at his throat. A bead of sweat dropped down his domed head, but his eyes fixed on mine with defiance. "You'll what, Ms. Bell? Follow me around and bind me every hour? This might scare the weaker Earthbounds that patronize this establishment, but it doesn't scare me. If you want me to keep your alias secret from Lon, you're going to have to do more than this."

I laughed. "Lon already knows my secrets. What he *doesn't* know, apparently, is what a despicable asshole you really are. He told me you were one of the few people he trusted in La Sirena—that you were a good person. But you're just like the rest of the Hellfire members, aren't you?"

"Despicable or not, I *am* Lon's family and have been since he was born into this community. Who are *you*, Ms. Bell? That's the real question, isn't it?"

Despite his bravado, Dare was turning a nasty color. The thought crossed my mind that the pressure from the binding could cause a heart attack in someone his age. I tugged at the binding with my mind, dissolving the magick and freeing him.

He crumpled into his chair, breathing heavily, then slowly stood up. "I don't know why you're using a fake name, but believe me when I say that I can find out. And Lon might know who you are, but I'm betting other people do not. Unless you want everyone knowing what you're trying to hide— a Ms. Kar Yee Tsang, perhaps—I suggest you refrain from binding me again."

Every muscle in my body tightened. Kar Yee was only a few feet away, behind the office door. She would never forgive me for lying to her all these years. Never.

Dare smiled like a man who knew he'd just won a small victory. "And regarding your future work with the Hellfire club? I don't think you're in any position to turn down my offer, so consider yourself officially moonlighting for me. You can start by recharging the summoning circle you broke in the caves last month. But first, you might want to try a little harder to stop our former magician from taking more of our children."

He turned to leave and my brain fired on again.

"Wait," I called out. "Are their homes warded? The seventeen kids?"

His head swiveled. He glanced at me over his shoulder. "No."

"Send me a list. I'll start in the morning."

22

The magical wards took me almost twelve hours to erect. Though they were temporary, unlike the massive wards that Lon and I had around our homes, at least they offered some protection.

It was just before nightfall when I pulled around the circular driveway in front of Lon's house to park behind his SUV and beat-up black pickup truck. The warding magick had taken everything out of me. I felt empty and frazzled, and though my stomach was currently attempting to calm, I had vomited several times throughout the day from post-magick nausea.

I unlocked the front door and ditched my coat and purse in the wide foyer before heading into the living room. Jupe's frizzy curls poked up over the couch when I called out his and Lon's names.

"How was school?" I asked.

"It blew chunks."

"Why? What happened?"

He grunted. "Everyone at school was in a shitty mood, including Ms. Forsythe, and she's *never* mean. How are we not supposed to be afraid of the stupid Snatcher when all the teachers are being jerks because they can't admit they're scared too?"

He didn't sound afraid. His tone was grumpy, more negative than usual. I leaned over the back of the couch and spotted Mr. Piggy curled up in his lap. "Everyone's on edge."

"This is my birthday week and everyone's ruining it." He scooped up Mr. Piggy and held him too close to his face, but the pygmy hedgehog didn't seem to mind. He snuffled around Jupe's neck, then made his hedgie happy noise, something between a whistle and a purr.

"You only get the one day for your birthday, you know—not a whole week. You aren't Elvis."

He grumbled an indiscernible reply while keeping his eyes on the television. His long legs were propped up on the coffee table, socked feet crossed. Beyond the living room, soft golden lights from the patio and deck spilled through glass doors. A row of black-and-white photos in modern metal frames hung above the doorway: Jupe as an infant and toddler—all beautifully composed, taken by Lon.

Jupe shifted his position on the couch, then moved the hedgehog in annoyance and groaned. "Ugh, I can't take it anymore."

"Take what anymore?"

He didn't say anything for several seconds, so I started to stand up and go find Lon. He put his hand on my arm to stop me. "Cady . . . I need to tell you something."

"Okay. Tell me."

His dramatic sigh was interrupted by Lon's muffled voice calling my name from the other end of the house.

"How does he know I'm here?" I whispered conspiratorially, trying to coax a smile.

"He knows everything."

"Tell me," I insisted again, leaning down to butt my forehead against his temple. He exhaled through his nose and traced his finger over Mr. Piggy's feet, stalling.

Lon called for me again, this time sharper.

"Go on." He picked up the remote and absently flipped through channels. "I'll tell you later. It's not important."

Though I was pretty sure that was accurate, it must've been important to him.

"I'll be back in a sec." I followed Lon's voice, Foxglove trailing at my heels, and walked past the scent of dinner wafting from the kitchen. My stomach grumbled indecisively. I was starving and felt shaky, but I wasn't sure if I could keep anything down just yet.

I continued on to Lon's library. He opened the door before I could knock. His faded T-shirt was dotted with cooking splatter and his hair had been hastily pulled back into a short ponytail, one wavy lock hanging free by his face. His brow furrowed as he looked me over.

"Jesus. You look like hell," he said. Scents of the library floated out from behind him—old leather, crumbling paper, parchment. Pleasantly musty.

"I feel like it, too. I never want to do that much magick in one day again. Ever."

"Maybe you won't have to. I think I found out why he's doing it now."

"Who?"

"Grand Duke Chora."

"Why?"

"Timing. Remember how the incubus said the words on the cannery mandalas were names of stars?"

"'Stars that open doors,' yep."

SUMMONING THE NIGHT   229

"It got me thinking about planetary alignments. Saturn takes thirty years to complete an orbit."

"Twenty-nine and a half," I corrected.

His eyes narrowed in frustration. "Did you already think of this?"

"Lon, I just set seventeen wards—my mind is mush and I can't stop shaking. I'm not thinking of anything right now."

He kissed the bridge of my nose, then herded me inside the library, glancing over my shoulder to make sure Jupe wasn't following. Foxglove threaded her way between us and trotted around the rectangular pillar of books in the center of the room, heading to the rug in front of the fireplace. I stepped over her and plopped down into an ochre armchair, kicking off my shoes.

"Look." He brought the Æthyric silver tube to me, pointing to a diamond shape etched on the opposite side of Grand Duke Chora's name. The diamond was filled with crisscrossing, seemingly random lines, like a wonky Spirograph. "Do you know what this is?"

"No."

"I didn't either, at first," he said. "Then I realized what it looked like—an astrological birth chart."

I held it closer, turning it to catch the light better. "If it was in a circle, maybe."

"Yes, if it was a chart from Earth, but what would one look like from another plane?"

He had my attention now, and he knew it. His brows lifted enthusiastically.

"Different plane, different planets? I've never considered it," I admitted.

"Why would you? Who cares about Æthyric sun signs?"

"I barely care about mine."

"Exactly." He strode to his desk at the other side of the room. "But one of my rarer books—"

"One of the Vatican's books?" I teased.

"Maybe."

I snorted. "Go on."

"This book has a strange chapter about planetary alignments. I never paid much attention to it—the planets are all wrong, so I thought it was just medieval hooey."

"Hooey?"

One corner of his mouth curled. "You know as well as I do that there's a lot of fucking hooey in thirteenth-century grimoires." He marched back with a photocopy from the book and handed it to me.

I pretended to be offended as I snatched the paper from his fingers. "You don't even trust me to look at the real thing? Is this from the *Liber Sacer*?"

"It's in the preservation safe—I wasn't going to leave it out until you came back home." Yes, I'd heard all his grimoire-geek talk about how that particular book, and a few others like it, could "under no circumstances" disintegrate away in the air like the bogus transcribed copy in the Sloan Collection.

I was too tired even to roll my eyes. "What am I looking at?"

"Æthyric astrology, I think. See the diamond here?"

"Holy shit," I muttered. He was right—had to be. The diamond was divided into quadrants and marked with small symbols that looked remarkably close to Earth's planetary symbols, just cleaner—and oddly familiar. I glanced at Chora's name etched into the silver tube, comparing. "The weird alphabet from the cannery!"

A proud smile spread across Lon's face. "There's more."

He handed me another photocopy of the spell from the silver tube. His finger moved across the paper, pointing out seven letters within the strange text. I never would've been able to pick them out myself, but when he put the cannery photos in my lap, I made the connection immediately.

"Seven stars," I murmured.

"Seven stars that open seven doors," Lon said. "This spell opens doors between worlds."

"Between earth and the Æthyr?" Definitely not good.

"They can only be opened during a planetary alignment."

"One that occurs when Saturn completes an orbit?" I guessed.

"It's not just about what's going on here. It's when Saturn's orbit conjuncts with a planetary alignment in the Æthyric plane."

"Alignments on both planes open doorways between." I stared at the photos in fascination. "But are these doors temporary? Only open during the alignment, or . . . ?"

"Even if they were only open for a few hours of the earth alignment, it could be disastrous. All of the goetic information I can find on Chora jibes with what your incubus told us when he claimed that the duke controls two legions of Dragoons in the Æthyr. You remember the etching of that nasty Pegasus? Can you imagine what would happen if hundreds of Æthyric demonic warriors broke into our world riding beasts like that? What about thousands of them?"

I remembered the pointy teeth and scales on Grand Duke Chora's winged horse and grimaced. "And if these are permanent portals between the planes . . . ?"

"Oh, we're screwed."

"So we know what the ritual is, and why it's happening now, and we know that the kids are part of it. What went wrong back in the eighties? Why didn't the doors open back then?"

"Maybe it had something to do with Cindy Brolin escaping."

"They had to go with a second choice."

"Maybe the second choice fouled up the ritual."

I tucked my legs sideways in the chair. "Merrin bit Cindy when he tried to take her. What if he made a pact with Chora to allow the demon to possess him back then? Maybe with Chora inside him, he was able to taste something in the blood that was needed to ensure the ritual's success."

"It's entirely possible. There's been blood at some of the recent crime scenes."

"Lon," I said, "if the ritual failed the first time, it stands to reason that the demon's going to try harder this time. That's why he's going after transmutated descendants. It's not revenge against the Hellfire Club—Dare's wrong again. There must be something stronger in the blood of those kids. You told Dr. Spendlove that your empathy is stronger than it was in either of your parents' knacks."

"Yes."

"Maybe it's because children of transmutated parents have fortified demon essence," I said quietly. "And maybe that's really why Jupe's knack is stronger."

Lon's face fell.

"It's just a theory," I said quickly. "But it might explain why the demon is choosing these kids this time around. And as much as all of this explains the 'why' of things—and no matter how much warding magick I did today—we need to find Merrin more than ever."

"He wasn't possessed at the Silent Temple," Lon argued.

"But I'd bet my last caduceus that he knows who is."

While Lon retreated to the kitchen, deep in thought and a million miles away, I tracked down Jupe, moping in his room. His mountain of dirty clothes had been cut in half since yesterday. Mr. Holiday must've gotten fed up and hauled some away to be washed. My hedgie was now lounging on Jupe's bed, gumming a hunk of banana.

"You just missed out on some projectile pooping," Jupe said, moving Mr. Piggy over.

"Oh, darn." Hedgehogs are sometimes overachievers. Mr. Piggy was trained to use a small litter box in my house, but was having trouble remembering it at Lon's. Luckily he spent most of his time in Jupe's room, who was totally fine with cleaning up hedgehog droppings. Score.

"So, taxicab confession time," I joked.

"Huh?"

"You have something salacious to tell me?"

A faint smile crossed his lips. "It's not that interesting."

I perched on the edge of his bed, moving his book bag to the floor. "Thank the gods for small miracles. Come on, now." I patted the mattress. "Tell me."

He bit his lower lip and made a sour face. "Promise me you won't tell my dad."

"I'm not lying to him."

"Okay, promise you won't tell him if he doesn't *ask first*."

I groaned. "Deal."

"Now promise you won't get mad."

"If you don't just go ahead and tell me, I'm going to get more than mad."

He shut his eyes, and for a second I nearly flipped out, thinking he was going to use his knack on me. But instead of straining with his fists, he merely grimaced and pulled the edge of his shirt up to reveal his stomach. Then he carefully tugged the loose waistband of his jeans down over his left hip, and I remembered his scratching problem.

For a second, I didn't know what I was looking at.

Then I did.

And it shocked me. Hard. Maybe worse than finding Bishop's bones in the cannery. I was horrified . . . and thoroughly embarrassed.

"Holy harlot." I murmured. "Oh, Jupe, what have you done?"

A soft choking noise drew my gaze upward to his face. Jupe's big green eyes flooded with tears that quivered at the border of his thick lashes, ready to spill. Goddammit. Seeing him broken was worse that just about anything. Like a contagious yawn, it jump-started waterworks for me that I had to wrestle to hold back. Apparently all the magick I'd done that day had also stripped away my immunity to kid-crying.

"I'm sorry," he squeaked. One tear dropped, snaking down over his sharp cheekbone before cascading down his cheek.

"Come here," I commanded in a soft voice. "Let me see what you've done—but for the love of Pete, keep your boxers on."

He hiccuped, holding back a sob, and unbuttoned his jeans, shimmying them down to expose his entire left hip. The tattoo was so badly infected that most people probably wouldn't have been able to make out the design. But I could.

It was my personal sigil. My identifying mark as a magician. About two inches in diameter, the occult rose-and-moon symbol with my given middle name was now branded into his *café au lait* skin.

"This is what you've been scratching at all week?"

He nodded.

"How long have you had it?"

"Since a few days before we got mugged in the parking garage. After I got my cast taken off." Which is exactly where he'd lifted the symbol—I'd sketched it onto his cast, feeling guilty that I'd been the one who inadvertently put him in the damn thing. It was one thing to casually mark it on his cast, but on his *skin* . . . You just don't screw around with magical symbols there. I should know. The white sigils tattooed on my forearm were not for show.

"Who the hell would tattoo a thirteen-year-old kid?"

"Fourteen, in two days."

I swiveled him so I could study it, pressing my fingers against the surrounding swollen skin. He winced, and his skin burned with fever. Yet, despite the inflammation and the disgusting oozing, the ink underneath looked precise and sharp. Better than my sketching on his cast, and pretty damn accurate. "Who did it? Did they use clean needles?"

"It's not a prison tattoo, Cady. I'm not stupid."

I lifted my brows. "Really? You're not? Because I'm having some doubts here."

He brushed away another tear, steeling himself. "It was Jack's cousin, Kenji. He works at Dragonfire Ink, in the Village. He's apprenticing, but he's been doing it for two years."

"Isn't there some law against tattooing minors?"

He mumbled something under his breath.

"I can't hear you."

"I *said*, I used my knack on him, all right? It was the first time I tried it on purpose. There were two times before, but I didn't know what I was doing."

"Okay, calm down." So it was professional, not done by a bum in a back alley with dirty needles infected with hep C. Best to focus on the positives. "Did he tell you how to take care of it?"

"He told me, uh, not to get it wet?" Jupe said this like he was guessing.

"Did you?"

"Just in the shower."

"That should be okay—"

"And I went swimming in Jack's pool once. The day after I got it."

I was pretty sure you were supposed to avoid swimming pools when you had a new tattoo, but still. "Have you been keeping it clean? What did you wash it with?"

"Regular soap."

"Not the soap in your bathroom, I hope."

He smiled nervously.

One time I almost used that soap to wash my hands then changed my mind when I saw all the grit and dirt packed around the pump. Probably teeming with boy-bacteria. Disgusting.

"Little red dots were breaking me out after I swam in the pool," he elaborated. "That's when the itching started. So I used stronger soap to kill any bad stuff."

Stronger soap?

"The stuff Dad uses outside."

"In the garage? Mechanic's soap? That's industrial heavy-duty grease cutter!"

"Well, I know that *now*. It made it worse. I couldn't stop scratching. It scabbed up and got all red and gross." He pulled his boxers back up, then cried out when the fabric brushed against it. "It *h-u-u-rts*, Cady," he whined dramatically.

I sighed just as dramatically in response. "Why *there*, Jupe? It's just inches away from . . ." Places I didn't want to think about on him. I wrinkled up my nose, trying to drive away the disturbing image of all his future girlfriends getting an eyeful of my symbol at inopportune moments.

"Where else was I going to get it without Dad seeing it?" He angrily kicked his book bag aside and flopped down on the bed next to me, morose and weary. "Better than on my ass."

True.

"But *why* did you do it?" I asked, angling to face him. "You barely know me, Jupe. You don't know anything about me."

He acted confused. "I know plenty about you."

"But not everything." *You don't know what was bred into me with magick, or that my parents were killers, or that my real name isn't Arcadia.*

"I know you hate ketchup. I know you make a weird dripping noise with your mouth when you fall asleep on your back. I know you always buy the wrong real estate when we're playing Monopoly."

"That's . . ."

"I know you lost your parents," he insisted quietly, "and I lost my mom. That makes us kinda the same in a way."

My voice caught in my throat. I started again. "My parents weren't very good people."

"Neither is my mom."

Our shoulders touched as we leaned against each other, both quiet for a long moment. I glanced across the room, spying the promotional Halloween Tambuku mummy mug on a shelf. It sat next to a small statue of Frankenstein's monster lying on an operating slab, a resin model he'd careful constructed and painted. He'd glued the legs on the slab backward.

"It's just that getting someone's name tattooed on you is like a death sentence," I finally said. "There's a good chance you're going to end up with a tattoo that you've got to get changed from Winona to Wino."

"But that only happens when you get your girlfriend's name tattooed on you," he insisted. "This is different. It'll be fine."

My mind roamed back to Dare's accusations the night before, when he said that Lon would get bored with me eventually. "Your dad and I are just dating, Jupe. What if we break up?"

His face fell. "What are you talking about? You live here. You can't break up with him."

"I don't live here, I just—" Dammit, he was making me flustered. "Look, no one's breaking up with anybody. I didn't mean now."

"You better not mean later either," he huffed, suddenly defensive. "My dad thinks this is serious."

"It is. Calm down." I didn't want to get into the messy business of relationships with him. He wouldn't understand. Hell, I barely did myself. "Just forget about all that. What worries me most is that my sigil is a magical identifier. Having real symbols on you is dangerous. You know the seals on my arm are real. You know what I can do with them, right?" I flipped my arm over, exposing the inner flesh.

He gingerly ran his fingertips over the raised scarring of the seals there, not for the first time. "That's where I got the idea to put your seal on me," he admitted. "You said this one"—he stopped above Priya's seal—"was for your dead guardian spirit and you use the others for protection. You told me your sigil would protect me when you put it on my cast, so when I got the cast taken off . . ." He swallowed hard and finished in a tiny voice. "I didn't want to lose your protection."

Oh.

Dueling emotions revved up inside me, slammed down on the gas pedal, and collided into each other in one glorious wreck. Before I knew what was happening, my arms were around him and he was crying on my shoulder. "It's okay," I murmured.

I couldn't really remember ever comforting someone before. I certainly was never comforted much myself growing up. My parents were never "hands-on"—big surprise in hindsight.

Despite my lack of experience, it somehow came naturally. As Jupe repeatedly told me he was sorry, I gladly absorbed his angst-ridden pain, selfishly appreciating that he was warm and his shampoo smelled good, and that his angular arms felt pleasantly familiar around me. Like Lon, but not. Same, but different. At that moment, it hit me like a ton of bricks that they were a package deal.

If I was fully committed to Lon, then I had to accept that Jupe was part of that. I knew this, of course, but Lon and I didn't exactly have a plan. One minute I was getting to know him, the next he was handing me a key to his house because "it's just easier." But even if Lon wasn't vocal about the future, Jupe was already jumping ten steps ahead, marking himself as mine. Sure, the tattoo was a stupid, impulsive teenage mistake, but it said loud and clear that he was expecting me to stick around.

It was easy to play house and enjoy the moment with both of them, not getting too close. But a person could do that only so long—could only test drive the car for so many miles before the dealer made you park it in the lot or buy it. There wasn't a rent-to-own clause when a kid was in the picture . . . even one who was fourteen years old in two days.

I rubbed his back and told him to hush, and he stopped clinging to me like we were in the middle of a whirlpool and he was saving me from spiraling away. He pulled back and sloppily wiped his wet face and snotty nose all over the front of his T-shirt.

"Hey, Jupe?"

"Yeah?"

"Have you ever used your knack on me?"

His response was fast and emphatic. "No way." Squinting up his tear-stung eyes, he added, "And you haven't used magick on *me*, right?"

"Of course not."

"Okay then."

Even without Lon there to evaluate his emotions, I believed him.

"Your dad is going to wring both of our necks when he finds out."

Panic flicked over his face. "You promised not to tell."

"And I won't, but you can't hide it forever. He's going to know. Besides, you should probably go see a doctor and get antibiotics. Or get a healer to pull out the infection. Did the Earthbound doctor who healed your arm when it was in a cast—"

"Dr. Mick? No way! We can't go to him. He's friends with my dad!"

"I know a healer who could probably take care of it, but if I took you to Bob, I'd have to tell Lon."

A low voice rumbled behind us, turning Jupe's muscles to rock. "We're not going to Bob."

Shit.

Lon stood in Jupe's doorway, slowly pushing the door all the way open with his fingertips.

"How much did you hear?" I asked while Jupe ducked behind my back, using me as a shield.

"All of it."

Ugh. That meant he heard me suggesting to Jupe that we might break up one day. I hoped he didn't take that the wrong way. He'd been listening to our emotions too, right?

Jupe peeped around my shoulder. "Are you mad?"

Lon glanced from Jupe to me, and when our eyes met, his were tender. A little puffy, even. You'd think that he, of all people, would be resistant to Jupe's infectious sobbing by now. Maybe not.

"I'll be mad if I cooked dinner for no reason," Lon said at length, then joined us by the bed. "Let me look at it. After we eat, I'll call Dr. Mick and see if he'll let us drop by tonight."

Dr. Mick was on duty at the ER. While Jupe got his infected tattoo squared away, Lon and I sat in the waiting room. I nearly dozed off in my chair until Lon's phone startled me fully awake. I watched his face while he answered the call. I knew it wasn't good news, but when he closed his eyes and his head dropped, worry crept into my chest.

He touched the screen to hang up, not bothering with good-bye, as usual.

"Lon?"

"It was Dare. A fifth kid, an hour ago. Mindy Greenburg."

I blinked, trying to remember the homes I'd visited earlier in the day. The Greenburgs—it was the last one on my route. I'd spoken with the father. "I warded her house," I protested. Had I screwed something up? Was this my fault?

Lon stared blankly across the waiting room. "She never made it inside the house. She was taken in the driveway. Her mother said that one second they were both getting out of the car; the next, she heard something in the bushes and her daughter was gone."

Outside the house. The ward didn't work unless you were inside it. All that work, and it didn't matter. I wanted to scream in frustration, but all that came out was a sob.

"She goes to the public school," he added in a fatigued voice. "She's one of Jupe's classmates."

23

Lon hesitated to send Jupe to school the next morning. He could've saved himself some trouble if he'd just kept the boy home, because it was only a couple hours later that he got a call from the principal's office: they were temporarily closing the school.

By the time we made our way over there, cars already filled the front parking lot and crowded the drop-off area, causing a traffic jam on the main road outside the school. Frustrated, Lon maneuvered his SUV through a gap and double-parked.

Inside was even worse. A total clusterfuck of parents waited outside the principal's office—mostly those complaining about the school's decision. They were shutting down for the rest of the week, until Halloween was over. The principal said it was a decision made by the school board, which didn't want to be held liable for any children being abducted from school. Even though no kids had gone missing during the day, they said they weren't taking any chances. They couldn't afford to hire additional security, and they were nervous.

Parents were scared and angry at being forced to take time off work and make other arrangements for their kids, teachers were upset, and the school staff was trying to maintain order and get everyone out. Total chaos.

Lon swore under his breath as we fought the crowd to Jupe's homeroom.

Ms. Forsythe's classroom was noisy. No one sat in their seats; they were grouped around the window watching the parking lot, huddled together in the corner, buzzing with gossip. Ms. Forsythe was standing in front of a chalkboard covered with lists of stars and astronomy vocabulary. A 3-D model of the solar system hung above her desk.

"Mr. Butler, Ms. Bell."

Though she was dressed in the same poncho she'd been wearing when I met her in the faculty parking lot, she now looked frazzled and run-down. Her eyes were bloodshot. She absently scratched her head, then tucked the ends of her unkempt bob behind her ears in exaggerated slow-motion.

"Bet you'll be glad to get out of here today," I said, having to speak up to be heard over the din.

"This has been a disaster," she said in a weary voice. "They called us in at five this morning to tell us what was going on. I've been cussed out by angry parents and it's like a war zone in here."

"I'm sure they understand it's not your fault."

"To be honest, I stopped caring about fifteen minutes ago."

Yikes. "The girl who went missing last night, Mindy . . . was she your student?"

"No, but I know her and her mother—not well, yet it's shocking nonetheless." She sighed heavily. "I think it's the right decision to close the school. I understand that it's hard on working parents, but most of the teachers are terrified something will happen on their watch, and no one's getting any sleep." She rubbed a temple and sighed. "My mother picked a fine time to get her stomach stapled—I was only supposed to stay with her for a few days while my house was being tented for pest control, but now I'm taking care of her, too."

"Not roaches, I hope." I thought of the cannery and shuddered.

"Termites," she said. "Costs me a small fortune every few years. And on top of all that, no one realizes what we've been having to do, sending the kids to the bathroom in pairs, watching their every move—it's been stressful."

"It's hard on everyone," I agreed. "Do you have kids of your own, or . . . ?"

"No. My husband died years ago. We never had children."

"I'm sorry."

"Don't be, my dear. I've got a wonderful family, friends, and my students. And I have the support of my church. I'm quite blessed."

Strangely, I could appreciate this, though not in any way she'd understand. When my parents left me and went into hiding after they were charged with murdering the leaders of rival occult orders, the only thing that kept me sane was the regular contact I had with my caliph, who is the head of the E∴E∴ and my godfather. Maybe that's one reason why, when I moved to Morella a couple of years back, I turned for friendship to Father Carrow, a local retired priest who lives down the street from me and who also introduced me to Lon.

Lon shifted his stance, antsy to leave. He hates crowds. "We're taking Jupe."

Ms. Forsythe nodded wearily. "Be my guest. He's over in the back with Jack."

As we elbowed our way through the crowded classroom, I couldn't help but wonder how many other of the seventeen descendants of transmuted Hellfire members were students here. I never thought to ask when I was doing the warding magick yesterday. So many kids in one place at one time. If the Snatcher operated in the daytime, he could take the rest of his victims in one fell swoop right here.

That's when it hit me. Maybe we'd been going about things all wrong. You couldn't summon an Æthyric demon who was already on earth, and you couldn't find a magician who didn't want to be found. But if I couldn't track down Merrin, then maybe I could draw the bastard out of hiding— or maybe even Duke Chora himself. . . . If I could get all the remaining transmutation descendants in one place, at one time, would he come?

24

The annual Morella Halloween Parade was a big earner for the city, with attendance that topped 100,000. It was dark, crowded, and one of the featured floats was sponsored by Dare Energy Solutions, Mark Dare's company in La Sirena. After a couple of hours of persuading, the senior Dare agreed to populate the float with the transmutation descendants. If that wasn't bait, I didn't know what was.

A couple of weeks back, when Jupe and I first made plans to attend the parade, it was just going to be me, him, and Lon, and the world was both Snatcher-free *and* anti–Halloween protester free. Now the protesters were out en masse, holding up handmade signs and shouting through bullhorns behind police barricades, and Jupe was one seriously unhappy boy, sitting at home with the Holidays, barricaded within the house ward. Both the housekeepers knew how to shoot—Mr. Holiday had been the one to teach Lon, when he was Jupe's age—and Lon had left them with loaded shotguns . . . just in case. I didn't feel guilty for refusing to offer up Jupe as bait along with the others. Lon either. Especially when we showed up before the start of the parade and discovered that Mark Dare's kid was also safe at home.

I wasn't, however, an unfeeling monster who didn't care about the other kids. I felt extremely anxious about this whole baiting plan. A little sick to my stomach, even. If anything went wrong, it would be my fault. So I told myself that nothing *could* go wrong. I wouldn't let it.

Halloween music pumped from portable speakers, but you could barely hear it over the clamor of the crowd. Every ten or twenty feet, food vendors and drink merchants were set up under tents and doling out smoked sausage, roasted nuts, gallons of beer and daiquiris. Hundreds of costumed revelers sauntered shoulder to shoulder up and down the packed sidewalks.

The Dare float was designed as a waterfall lit up with thousands of sparkling white lights. The float riders were divvying the free throws that they'd be tossing out to the crowd. Candy? Plastic spider rings? Small toys? No: flashing key chains with the corporate logo. "Way to advertise your business instead of promoting Halloween spirit," I remarked to Lon as we both donned parade badges and took our places at the rear of the float.

In addition to Lon and me, Dare had stationed a small army of plainclothes armed guards to walk in front and on either side. Everyone riding the float was dressed in white long-sleeved T-shirts, white jeans, and white gloves. Weird and creepy. The entire company must be drinking the Kool-Aid. Because of this, Mark Dare was easy to spot. He was standing on a platform at the foot of the sparkling waterfall wearing blue jeans—not white—and his T-shirt was the only one with printing. The front read, in *Frankie Goes to Hollywood*–style block letters, CLEAN AND LEAN. The back read, WE DARE TO POWER YOUR FUTURE. What a tool.

After a quarter of an hour, everyone was in place. The

Grand Marshal announced the official start of the parade over the loudspeakers, and the crowd broke out into even louder cheering, whoops, and whistles. Lon and I could see both sides of the float from our vantage point in back. We followed at a close distance, scanning the crowds on the sidelines for Merrin or anyone suspicious. Earlier in the day, Dare had made public announcements concerning the participation of junior high students on the float, spreading the word on TV, radio, and online. "We will not be bullied into hiding" was his catchphrase. If Merrin and/or Duke Chora were monitoring the children's whereabouts—and someone had to be, in order to pull off the kidnappings so flawlessly—they knew the kids were here.

Nothing remarkable happened along the parade route for the first thirty minutes, but somewhere along the route's halfway mark, the floats in front of us came to slow halt. We waited anxiously for several minutes, then overheard policemen along the sidewalks saying that some Halloween protesters had jumped the barricades a few blocks up and were standing in front of one of the floats with signs.

A few more minutes passed. Dare's twinkling float waited in front of us, and while Lon watched the left side, I continued to survey the right, a couple of yards away from him. My eyes tracked Mark Dare again. He was shrugging on a dark jacket. At first I thought the cold must've gotten the better of him, but then he slipped around to the back of the float's flatbed, glancing over his shoulder. In a series of quick movements, he jumped down to the road, squeezed through a gap in the barricade, and disappeared into the crowd.

Not exactly the behavior you'd expect from someone who

was helping to watch the kids on the float. It crossed my mind that Mark had been present at one of the kidnapping scenes— the Halloween carnival at Brentano Gardens amusement park. He was alone when he talked to us in line that day. Said his wife and kid were elsewhere in the park. Later that night, another kid went missing there.

But that was crazy, right? I mean, Mark Dare was an asshole, sure, but what reason would he have to be involved in the snatchings? Still, I couldn't help wondering why he jumped off the float in the middle of all this.

I glanced at Lon. He was still patiently watching to the left side of the float. I tried to catch his attention. He finally looked my way, but before I could get close enough to tell him about Mark's odd behavior, a bass-heavy rumble up the road drew everyone's attention.

Boom!

A column of fire shot straight up into the sky, flaming up past the second stories of the buildings that flanked the street. It was coming from the Little Red Riding Hood float: Grandmother's cottage was on fire.

An anxious roar fanned through the crowd as the police reacted quickly, helping people off the flaming float and herding them into the shocked crowd. Dare's plainclothes guards crowded closer to our float, all on full alert. Once Lon saw that they were in place, he ran to my side.

"What the hell?" he said.

"Electrical fire?" I suggested, craning my neck to see.

"Isn't it close to where the protesters were breaking through the barricades?"

People near the fiery float were struggling to retreat. A tower of flames rocketed into the sky. So strange, the way it burned in a neat, round column.

I squinted. Blue-white light fizzled where the column of fire met the float's cottage roof.

"Whoa!"

"What?" Lon demanded.

"Heka! That fire was set with magick."

His green eyes darkened with panic. We stared at each other, neither of us knowing what to do for several moments. Good news was, magical fire doesn't technically burn; it's a parlor trick. That meant the people on Red Riding Hood were likely unharmed.

Lon glanced back at the flaming float and the thousands of people who were watching it burn. "A diversion."

That's exactly what it was. A diversion set by a magician.

Lon informed one of the guards that we were going to the fire, then the two of us plunged into the rankled crowd and headed toward Red Riding Hood.

The column of magical fire might not have been real, but the heat it emitted sure felt believable. It toasted my skin with a preternatural warmth as we neared the barricade a few feet behind the float. No way we'd be able to get any closer. We fought the crowd just to stay in place and not be rolled along with the tide of people who were following police instruction to abandon the area. I spotted an empty sidewalk bench, the back of which advertised a demon-friendly restaurant near Tambuku.

"Up there!" I shouted to Lon.

We scrambled to the bench and stood on the seat to survey things from a better vantage point. Most of the crowd had thinned on the opposite side of the road, where the sidewalk was narrow. But on our side, where all the vendors were stationed and an empty parking lot made room for hundreds, it was still chaotic. Heads and halos bobbed in a sea of people moving in all directions as police and parade security did their best to herd them while also directing the nearby floats to move aside and make way for a fire truck that wailed in the distance.

I pulled Lon's face down and spoke in his ear. "Watch near the float—the magician will have to stop the spell or risk the firefighters discovering that they can't put out the fire!"

Together we scanned the float, looking for anyone out of the ordinary. But when I spotted something odd, it was a thing, not a person.

A hidden side door on the flaming cottage was cracked open several inches. Probably just access to a small stow area for extra candy, or jackets and purses. However, a glob of hazy white light was bobbing through the crack. The door shut by itself, then the ball of light moved a few feet, hovered, and stopped.

My pulse increased. All magick has a visual signature, a nebulous glow very similar to Earthbound halos.

The ball of light that hovered in the air outside the small cottage door looked to be the right level if it were, say, being emitted by a charged talisman. One that was hanging around someone's neck—especially if that someone was a magician using some kind of invisibility spell.

"Mother of Sorrows," I muttered.

"What?" Lon shouted in my ear.

I pointed. "That light. It's moving."

He watched it move with growing awareness. "Let's follow it."

"Hold on." Last time we'd gone up against him—if that was, indeed, Frater Merrin standing on the edge of the float—he'd bowled us both over with his weird little Heka weapon.

In my peripheral vision I saw the approaching fire truck,

slowly picking its way around the stalled floats ahead. I was still tracking the ball of light floating around the corner of the cottage. The magician was on the move, probably to get a look at the fire truck. He was going to wait until they turned hoses on it to break the spell, so it would appear like they did it. I'd bet my life on it.

"Can you charge one of your wards to cover us?" Lon asked.

"What?"

He tapped my arm. "Invisible Man."

And I wondered where Jupe got his love of horror movies? "My Ignore spell would be better in this crowd."

"Do it."

25

We jumped off the bench and settled our-
selves in the shadow of a low brick wall, giving people room
to walk by us on the sidewalk.

While I pushed up my coat sleeve, Lon whipped out his
pocket knife. One quick flick on my fingertip and I had blood
to charge the Ignore seal. I gripped Lon's arm and fired up the
spell to cover both of us.

The stomach-cramping nausea made me think I'd been
successful, but the fact that we could now push our way
through the crowd without people noticing our elbows in
their ribs proved it. Though my tattooed invisibility sigil
granted me greater visual cover, the Ignore spell forced people
to disregard sight, touch, and sound. Unless you punched
someone in the face or shouted at the top of your lungs, most
folks wouldn't give you a second look.

We made it to the edge of the float and stood a few feet
from the bouncing ball of light. The way it moved up close, I
had no doubt now that it was a talisman. With all the hustle
and bustle around, it could easily be dismissed as a trick
of light to any Earthbounds who might spot it, but I wasn't
fooled.

The firefighters jumped off their truck and barked out commands to one another. Before long, they were readying a hose. As the deluge of water hit the cottage roof, the ball of light dipped and the circle of Heka surrounding the fire fizzled. The fire receded, then went out completely like a candle being snuffed.

I *knew* it!

The ball of light dropped down off the float. We followed it, beelining through the dwindling crowd on the opposite side of the street. Two blocks down a side street, we trailed it into **Phở-Gasm** Vietnamese Soup Restaurant. Fragrant lemongrass, garlic, and unctuous pork hung heavy in the air as we trotted past mostly empty tables, and one lone person ordering takeout. The ball of light floated into a narrow corridor past the counter.

We stole down the hallway just in time to see the men's restroom door opening and the ball of light entering one of two tangerine Formica stalls, then the door closing behind it. The rasp of a lock sliding shut echoed around the tiled room. Our mystery magician wanted privacy.

A low grunt floated from the locked stall. Lon motioned to me. He wanted the Ignore spell removed. Before I could comply, the air shuddered with power. He was transmutating.

My chugging heartbeat increased its pace as Lon's halo flamed up. I dropped the Ignore spell and nearly collapsed with exhaustion.

Lon stood in front of the locked stall, menacing and furious, halo on fire and horns spiraling, as he listened with one palm splayed across the stall door. Reading the magician's thoughts, presumably. I squatted to peek under the stall and saw a pair of dark shoes and pants. The toilet flushed.

Lon's hard face wrinkled with puzzlement. He cut me a

look, but I couldn't figure out what he was trying to say. Was it not Merrin? What was going on? I hated being out of the loop. Hated feeling sick to my stomach with post-magick sickness and worry.

Inside the stall, the lock slid, metal on metal.

The moment it clicked open, Lon pushed the door into the stall, slamming it back with a disturbing crack, and threw himself shoulder-first inside the stall, charging like an aggressive ram. I jumped as a surprised shout burst from the stall.

"Frater," Lon's shifted voice rumbled, "what a coincidence."

Lon dragged Frater Merrin out of the stall, pinning the man's arms behind his back. The magician was red-faced and confused. I readied myself to use my ability, but paused when Lon spoke to Merrin in a calm voice. His voice of persuasion. The one Jupe had inherited. Kind of. Lon's persuasive effect on emotions required touch to work. No problem with that, because he was gripping Merrin like death.

"We saw your little magick show on the parade float. I'm sure you won't mind if we ask you a few questions."

At the mention of "we," Merrin's mismatched eyes darted around the restroom until they met mine. I gave him a little wave.

Lon towered over the balding, short man as he spoke with soft insistence. "There's no need for you to use any magick on us like you did last time. We just want a few answers, then we'll leave you alone. We're not a threat, and you want to help us, right?"

"Lon." Anger flashed over the magician's face, then faded; his body slumped in submission. "I won't fight you," he admitted at length. "I'm sorry about the incident at the Silent Temple. I panicked, you see . . ."

Lon turned the magician in my direction while gripping him from behind. And there it was, the source of the ball of light that had tipped me off—an invisibility talisman. Now uncharged, it hung around his neck on a rough cord, swinging against the placard of his button-up shirt. I yanked it over his head, nearly catching the cord on his wire-rim glasses, then stashed it in my coat. I checked his pockets for the Heka weapons but found nothing, so I took up a post against the restroom door. The last thing Lon needed was an unwary customer to stumble into the restroom and find a horned demon holding a man hostage.

"Let's talk," Lon said. "Tell us about the grand duke. How did you team up with him in the eighties? And what happened to Bishop?"

I'd seen Lon use his persuasive powers only a couple of times. Usually they completely transformed the recipient. Turned them into putty. Merrin wasn't aggressive, exactly, but he wasn't lying on the floor with his belly exposed, either. His willpower must've been strong as hell. A trickle of fear ran down my back. I really didn't trust this guy.

Merrin inhaled deeply through his nose, then sighed. "Thirty years ago, I was employed by the Hellfire Club. They paid me well and I enjoyed the work. During my time off, I became friends with Jesse Bishop."

"Yes, we found his body in the cannery," I said. Friend, indeed.

Merrin nodded in calm resignation. "Bishop was a young Hellfire member who had the rare knack of precognition. However, his ability was weak. His premonitions were hit-and-miss. A lot of Hellfire members didn't hold much stock in his visions, but they were idiots."

"You believed his visions?" Lon asked.

"I did, especially when he began seeing images of a spell that would open doors between the worlds and allow travel from either side."

The spell inside the Æthyric tube.

Merrin continued. "The idea of being able to cross into the Æthyr was an intriguing one, but it wasn't until Bishop had visions about the entity in possession of the spell that I became worried. Bishop described it as an Æthyric demon with pale skin, his throat covered in blackened symbols. He was dressed in armor and carried a blade shaped like a serpent. His halo was blood-red. Bishop had seen a demon that I'd conjured for information . . . Grand Duke Chora.

"I wasn't the first magician hired by the Hellfire Club, you know," Merrin continued wearily, as Lon continued to keep the man's arms pinned behind his back. "There was a magician named Frater Morrow. He was the first person to conjure the grand duke back in the seventies, and the first person the duke asked to aid him with the *Buné* spell."

"The spell to open the doors between the worlds?" Lon said.

Merrin nodded. "The duke is an old demon with a great deal of power. Frater Morrow made the mistake of refusing to bargain with him, and ended up dead. Chora laid a curse on him. I found that out from another Æthyric demon after I'd already summoned Chora and turned down his bargain. The curse was a tricky one that made it appear the mage had just experienced a simple heart attack—"

"So the duke had cursed this Morrow magician," I said. "And you realized after you'd summoned and rejected the duke that he could curse you too?"

"I didn't want to die," Merrin argued. "I realized my error after I summoned him, but I had no choice but to comply and let him ride me. So I called him again and made the bargain. He promised that he'd keep me blind during the possessions, so I wouldn't be aware of what was happening. All I knew is that he needed vessels to help open the doors. I agreed to invoke him into me eight times: seven to find the vessels, and once more to complete the *Buné* spell on All Hallows'. The summonings were temporary, a few hours each time, and only at night—he was stronger then. Once the alloted time was up, he would be banished automatically and leave my body."

He'd summoned the duke for short periods of time? Interesting.

"Bishop's visions of the duke became cloudy," Merrin said. "Bishop became obsessed with wanting to undergo the transmutation spell to increase his knack, in hopes that he'd be able to see his visions more accurately. He asked the Hellfire Club leaders, but they refused. Bishop begged me to help in secret, but I couldn't, of course. I didn't want him to realize that I'd already bargained with Chora."

"Because he would have tried to stop you," I said.

"The duke told me he needed vessels, but I swear, I didn't know they would be children."

"That means *you* took all those kids back in the eighties, didn't you? You bit them and tasted their blood?"

The accusation pulsed in the air between all of us.

"Answer her," Lon urged.

"I wasn't conscious during the abductions." Merrin tugged his shoulder back in a weak attempt to break from Lon's hold. The top button on his shirt popped out of its hole and a dark tattoo peeked out, black with a blue border. An eagle, I thought. It looked like a military insignia, maybe an army tattoo. "I didn't even know it was children until I heard it on the news and realized that we had done it, he and I. We were the Snatcher."

"You were the Snatcher," I said. "You."

"I didn't remember anything while I was possessed, but I couldn't stop invoking him or he'd kill me. You've got to believe me!"

"You also killed Bishop. When you realized that his visions might rat you out, you killed him with magick in the cannery, where you were keeping the kids."

Merrin flailed in Lon's grip, panicking. "I didn't! I swear! It was the duke! I woke up in the cannery after one of the possessions and Bishop was dead inside one of the duke's traps. The demon claimed that Bishop had found where we'd hidden the *Buné* spell. He'd taken a photograph—was going to send it to Ambrose Dare."

The Polaroid.

"Bishop was my friend," Merrin said softly. "I would never have harmed him."

Is he telling the truth? I asked Lon in my head. He looked up from Merrin and stared at me blankly, as if I was distracting him. If Merrin was Earthbound, I could just bind him and know for myself. So frustrating.

"What went wrong with the first ritual?" I asked impatiently. "Why aren't the doors open?"

Merrin blinked. His eyes became glossy with remembered emotion. "The planetary alignments were correct and the veil between earth and the Æthyr was thin on All Hallows' Eve. Everything should've been right. But there was a flaw."

"It was the kids themselves, wasn't it?" Lon said.

Merrin nodded. "The duke was seeking the strongest pubescent Earthbounds. He assured me they wouldn't be harmed. He just needed them to harness power and open the doors. But mistakes were made in the selection process. Some of them weren't strong enough to handle the energy of the spell."

Cindy Brolin was, but she got away.

"I woke up and the doors weren't open," Merrin said. "The spell had failed, and the children were piles of ashes in Sandpiper Park. I could barely see where they ended and the sand began."

No bodies. Would Hajo have been able to track them even if we'd given him an object of Merrin's instead of Bishop's?

"Is that why he's using descendants of transmutated Earthbounds this time?" Lon said. When Merrin didn't answer right away, Lon shook his shoulders, then spun him around to face him and shoved him against the wall. "I said, is that why he's using transmutation descendants?"

Merrin flattened against the wall and turned his face to the side to avoid Lon's angry gaze. "The duke wasn't aware of the Hellfire transmutation spell. When the first group of children failed, he thought it was my fault. I was human, and his possessions were taking a toll on my body. Little things, like my blood pressure. But he could tell when he possessed me that I was weakening. When I woke up in the park after the last possession, the duke had gained enough power during the ritual to leave my body and become semicorporeal. He was furious about the failure. I tried to tell him that it wasn't my fault. Told him about the transmutation spell, and how it strengthened Earthbounds. They would make better vessels. They might survive the ritual. But he didn't believe me—or he just didn't care at the time. All the current vessels were ashes, and the doors between the planes weren't open. He took it out on me physically. Forced himself inside one last time and tried to kill me from the inside out. I barely survived."

Lon grunted. "Your 'accident.' The reason you quit working for the Hellfire Club and left La Sirena."

"I was in the hospital for weeks. My back was broken. I just wanted to leave it all behind and forget it ever happened. Which I did, until I saw the news stories about the Snatcher returning. I knew it was him. He'd found someone else to possess. He'd try again."

Fury knotted Lon's face. He pushed a hand against Merrin's chest and held it there. "Liar. You're working for him again. Did you set that fire tonight as a distraction so that he could take another kid? Tell me."

"No, you've got it all wrong—I was paid by the anti-Halloween group. They wanted something spectacular to get trick-or-treating banned." His head dropped. "They paid me a handsome sum of money."

It made sense. Leave it to a bunch of misguided activists to put on a puritanical front and utilize whatever means necessary under the table to obtain their goals. Political sabotage was a big moneymaker for rogue magicians.

"You expect me to believe that this duke didn't come back looking for your help?" Lon said.

"Why would he?" Merrin said. "I failed him the first time, and he realized that he didn't need a trained magician to conduct the ritual. I summoned a few Æthyric demons later and inquired about him. Another demon told me that the rumor in the Æthyr was that the duke had managed to pierce the veil between the planes during our attempt at the *Buné* spell. Not a fully functioning door but a hole. If it was big enough, he could possess anyone in the La Sirena area without being summoned. Human, Earthbound—it could be anyone."

Oh . . . God.

"The person wouldn't know they were possessed. They wouldn't be conscious of what they were doing. Trust me, I know all too well."

If the Duke could possess anyone, how could we find him?

Lon let go of Merrin and folded his arms across his chest. "You don't have any idea where he'd be keeping the new kids?"

"Somewhere around La Sirena, I suppose," Merrin said. "Like I told you, the hole in the veil isn't a door—I don't think he can venture too far away from that area without losing power, even while he's riding someone. That's why I don't go back to La Sirena. I don't want him to find me again."

So, right at this moment, he could be possessing anyone, and keeping the kids anywhere. We were so screwed. Disappointment crushed any last bit of hope I'd had. No one said anything for a long moment.

What are we going to do with Merrin? I finally asked Lon in my thoughts. *Call the police and tell them that he confessed to us? That he was possessed by a demon?*

"Where do you live?" Lon asked.

"I abandoned my apartment when you found me at the Silent Temple. I was worried you'd get me arrested. Please, Lon. I was friends with your father—I'm begging you. I don't want to spend my last few years dwindling away in a prison. Not a day goes by that I don't feel guilty about my role in all of it, but I was just trying to survive. You've got to believe me."

Maybe he could help us find the duke, I suggested. *Then we can call the cops.*

Lon closed his eyes. When he opened them again, he looked exhausted. He used his persuasive voice when he spoke to Merrin again, clamping his shoulder. "If you know a way we can track the duke and stop him, you'll share that with us now."

Merrin considered this, then brightened. "I know a spell. It's one he taught me. The duke keeps himself warded with Æthyric magick, so you can't find him with the usual methods. But this spell should be foolproof."

"What kind of spell?" I asked.

"It calls him to you. Only takes a few minutes. And if you are able to keep yourself inside a sanctified circle when you perform it, I don't think he could enter you." He paused, then finished in a low voice bitter with regret. "If I'd only done that to begin with, I could've avoided a lifetime of guilt, but I was young and foolish, and thought I was a stronger magician than I really was."

Please. I was young and foolish, and I still wasn't stupid enough to make a pact with a demon like he did.

"I'll need to dig through some boxes to find my old spell books," he said.

"Where are you staying now?" Lon asked for the second time.

"Hotel Guinevere in Eastern Foothills. Room 213. I'll find the spell. You can pick it up. Just come by my hotel when you're ready. You probably have other things to do here. Better things than watch an old man dig through boxes, right? Just give me a couple of hours."

A couple of hours? Hell no, I thought to Lon. *Why don't we just go with him now?*

"The kids on the float," Lon said, searching my face with pleading eyes.

I'd completely forgotten about them. But still—

"You don't have to worry. I won't skip town," Merrin said.

"You have my word. Listen to me, Lon. You know I'm telling the truth." He reached out and gently touched my arm, staring at me with those strange mismatched eyes. "Meet me in two hours at my hotel, and everything will be okay. You can trust me. I've been through so much already. I'm ready for this to be over."

A sense of well-being flooded me, and for the first time all night, I felt relaxed and calm. I knew I shouldn't, but I believed him. Trusted him. He was just a little old man who'd been bested by a demon. I almost felt sorry for him.

"Maybe we should all leave now. That sounds like a good idea, yes?"

Yes, it did. It sounded like a good idea. I wanted to leave. My head suddenly didn't feel very good.

Lon nodded. "Two hours. We'll meet you at your hotel."

Something pushed against my back. The restroom door. "Lon!"

Releasing Merrin, he shifted down into his human form while someone knocked, trying to get inside the restroom. Merrin buttoned up his shirt, covering up the army tattoo. When the coast was clear, I opened the door. A man entered, eying me warily as Merrin passed between us.

"Sorry, dear," he said, bumping into me as he headed into the restaurant hallway. "See you in a couple of hours."

We followed Merrin out the front door, then immediately lost him in the crowd. Loud whoops and laughter echoed off the glass windows of the restaurant as drunken revelers galloped down the sidewalk.

"Damn, my head is killing me," I complained as we made our way back to the float. "I feel like I've forgotten something. Do think it was safe to let him go like that? He was telling the truth, right?"

"I guess."

"What do you mean, 'I guess?' You don't know?"

"I couldn't hear his emotions sometimes. I could at first, but later it was off and on. And his thoughts were muffled. I could catch glimpses of things, but I—"

This alarmed me. "Why didn't you say something?"

"Sometimes I can't hear certain people very well."

"But you didn't have problems hearing him in the Silent Temple."

"I don't think so, but I was pissed, and he was panicked."

"Wait, wait, wait—does that mean your persuasive emotional thing was working on him or not, Lon?"

"I think so." Doubt clouded his eyes. Embarrassment, too.

Dear God, my head! Blood pulsed in my temples. What had I forgotten? My mind fastened on a single detail: the tattoo on Merrin's chest, the one peeking out of the top of his shirt. It was awfully dark for an old military tattoo. And that was no army eagle, it was the top of an Egyptian symbol for strength, and it wasn't lined in blue ink, it was charged with Heka.

Shit! He'd constructed some sort of magical seal to ward himself, either from Lon's ability in particular, or from Earthbound knacks in general. Anxiety cleared a path through my fuzzy head.

"What?" Lon asked, suddenly panicking right along with me.

"My weird headache . . . Jesus, Lon. We just let Merrin go. He's not going to help us. He tricked us! He—"

"He was using my knack."

I glanced around. Thousands of paradegoers were swarming the streets. How would we find him now?

"You took his invisibility talisman," Lon said.

I patted my pocket, then thrust my hand inside. Empty. "Oh, no . . . He bumped into me on the way out. He . . ." I didn't bother finishing. Lon made a miserable sound. "How much of what he'd told us was true? Was he under your influence at all? Did he tell us enough to shut us up? Or—" I fished out my cell and ducked into an alcove to get away from the crowds.

"What are you doing?" Lon asked.

"Looking up Hotel Guinevere. Have you ever heard of it?"

His blank expression told me that he hadn't. I hadn't either. Not that I knew every hotel in the city. A million people lived here. "Hotel Guinevere," I said, reading from my phone's web browser, "closed in 1990. It was one of the oldest hotels in the city."

Lon's eyelids fluttered in disbelief. "How did I not know?"

"How did *I* not know? This must be what it feels like to be on the receiving end of Jupe's knack." My head still throbbed. "I wonder if he was lying about the possession details? He wasn't possessed himself—we'd know, right?"

"I wasn't touching him the entire time," Lon said despondently.

"Yeah, that's when I started trusting him—when he touched me."

"I think he was telling the truth at the beginning. Before his thoughts became muddled to me. But I don't know . . . I just don't know."

My mind flipped through everything he told us, then I suddenly remembered what had caught my attention before the magical explosion stole it. "Mark Dare."

Lon grunted.

"He jumped off the float less than a minute before Merrin's explosion."

Another grunt.

"He was at the carnival the night that the third kid was taken."

That got his attention.

"Mark and his father don't get along. Dare said they'd recently reconciled, but he'd also called his own son a prick—maybe Mark feels the same way about Dare."

"There's bad blood between them," Lon confirmed. "But enough for Mark to team up with Merrin?"

"They must know each other—if Merrin remembered you, then surely he remembered Mark, too. And teaming up certainly would allow Mark to get revenge on Daddy, by making it appear that Dare couldn't protect his own cubs from predators. If members were scared and pissed off, it might even get Dare impeached from the Hellfire Club and put Mark at the helm."

"Jesus fucking Christ, Cady."

"You were right to begin with—Merrin set that fire as a distraction. And it wasn't for the Halloween protesters. That was a load of crap."

Lon didn't answer. He just pulled me back into the moving crowd, and we plowed our way through to the float.

26

Police lights flashed red and blue on the parade route where the fire truck had been parked. But not all of the police were investigating the Little Red Riding Hood crime scene—several surrounded the Dare Energy float. A fresh rush of panic swept over me as I quickly inspected the area. The kids were all huddled at the front of the float with two police officers. Adults were being questions by other cops. I was searching for Mark Dare when his father stepped into our path.

"Where the hell have you two been?" Dare snapped. His face was red. His halo was bright and big, practically crackling. He wasn't happy.

Lon was unfazed. "Chasing after Merrin."

Dare was momentarily confused.

"I told one of your guards when we left," Lon added. "The fire on the float was magical—not real. Merrin's spellwork. We saw him and chased him down."

"Well, where is he then?"

Lon didn't answer.

"You fucking let him get away—*again*?"

"He used magick," I said. "He turned Lon's knack around on us."

Lon quickly explained what happened with Merrin, but his eyes were on the float the entire time, watching the cops. He finally stopped midsentence. "What's going on here?"

"Juanita and Ben's kid got taken right off the fucking float."

"No," I said weakly.

"That's right," Dare said, barely containing his anger. "Fifteen minutes ago, while you two imbeciles were being bamboozled by Merrin."

"But the guards . . ." Lon said. "How?"

"Everyone was watching the damn fire truck and the damn police cars and the exodus of the people from the Little Red Riding Hood float. The boy was standing near the back of the float. One of the guards felt movement behind him. By the time he turned around, the boy was gone. *Right under our noses!*"

I wanted to throw up. My voice was almost a whisper. "It wasn't Merrin, then."

"Where's your son, Ambrose?" Lon's voice was even and cool as ice.

Dare stared at him, not answering.

"I asked you a question. Where's Mark?"

"He was at the carnival the night the third teen was taken," I said quickly. "He slipped off this float right before the explosion. Merrin told us that back in the eighties, Duke Chora only possessed him for short periods of time. The person possessed this time around . . . you might not even realize . . ." I faltered as I watched Mark Dare approaching us.

"One of the police signaled him off the float," Dare said slowly. "He was asking about our weapons permits for the guards when the explosion happened. He returned immediately, and helped the guards search the barricades with the help of the police when the kid was snatched. My son has been right here the whole time, Ms. Bell."

My heart sank as Mark stopped in front of me, all blond hair and blue halo. He didn't look possessed. He looked royally pissed. Like he hated my guts.

"It was a logical leap," Lon said. "It looked suspicious. So let's all calm down and figure things out. No one saw the kid being dragged into the crowd? No one at all?"

For a moment, Mark continued to stare at me like I was trash, then he finally spoke. "Not a damn thing. It's as if the child just disappeared. No one spotted anyone with mismatched eyes, if that's what you're thinking."

Lon shook his head. "We chased down Merrin. It couldn't have been him."

"Tell me what happened. In detail, if you would," Dare said.

Lon doesn't do detail well. I listened to him recite a barebones account of what happened and had to stop myself from interrupting to add things, but the Dares got the gist of it well enough. Lon tried to pinpoint the exact points in Merrin's interrogation that he had trouble "hearing" him.

I thought about it, trying to make sense of it all.

If we assumed that the beginning of Merrin's story was at least half true, then maybe Merrin really *hadn't* been aware of the duke's final plans for the "vessels" when he was puppeted into snatching the kids for the demon. But Merrin was a talented magician; an experienced magician. And he'd snooped around after the *Buné* spell failed, asking other Æthyric demons what the duke was up to. He found out that the veil had been pierced by the spell, and knew that the duke could come back in thirty years to try again.

And if *I* were unscrupulous and egotistical, like Merrin,

and an Æthyric demon had not only used me to kill a bunch of kids but had also nearly killed me from the inside out after it was over, *I* would want revenge against the duke. I would do whatever it took to kill the duke, or at the very least, banish him permanently. I would *want* me and Lon to track him down and help me get rid of the demon.

So why didn't Merrin?

He had to be working with the duke again. It was the only thing that made sense. He set the magical fire on the float to divert attention away from the Dare float. He was helping whoever was possessed. The getaway driver, so to speak.

I knew damn well that I didn't trust that asshole the moment Lon pulled him out of the restroom stall. I should've trusted my instinct and used Moonchild right then. But I didn't. And now look what happened. Another kid gone.

Dare's fury-laden voice plowed over Lon's account of what transpired with Merrin in the restaurant. "What you're telling me, then, is that you don't know jack shit. Merrin may or may not have lied the entire time."

I'll admit, Lon's account sounded pretty dubious even to me. And I could see that it was killing him to lay the whole messy thing out in front of Dare. It was killing me, too. But all I could think about—what repeated over and over in my head—was that another kid was taken. This was my idea, bringing the kids here. It could've been Mark Dare's kid here tonight; could've been Jupe. In the end, the kid who was taken tonight was innocent, just like the others, but this time it was my fault. I forced Dare into the baiting plan. Me.

Tears welled. I couldn't stop them. I was shaky and

exhausted and I wanted to crawl into a hole and die. But I couldn't. I had to fix things. I needed to get home, or someplace private, where I could try to summon Duke Chora again. If he was riding someone right now, and if Bishop had been telling the truth about the possessions being timed and temporary, then maybe I could summon him in a few hours. At dawn. A long shot, but it was all I had.

"This is a disaster," Dare said, looking between me and Lon. "And tomorrow is Halloween night, so let me tell you what's going to happen. All of the remaining kids are going to be locked up in a room inside my house at noon. I'm putting a hundred armed guards inside and outside that room. And tomorrow night, I'm going to send a hundred more people to patrol the streets of La Sirena. The two of you are going to help them. And you're not going to sleep until you bring me back every single one of the missing kids, and Merrin's head on a fucking pike."

Lon and I said nothing. Mark Dare turned and shook his head as he walked back to the police officers near the float. His father marched toward me until he stood an inch away. I tried to step back, but he got in my face and spoke in an angry whisper—"I am not happy"—so close I could feel his hot breath on my face. "You have failed me, and you are now mine. I own you. You will spend the rest of your life repaying me for the lives that have been stolen from my community under your watch."

My heart was beating so fast I thought it might break through my chest. I could hear Lon behind Dare, telling him to leave me alone, but his voice might as well been a mile away.

Dare's head dropped lower. He spoke directly in my ear. "A lifetime of service. I own you now. Me, Ambrose Dare, and the Hellfire Club, not your occult order, the E∴E∴ Do you understand me . . . *Sélène Duval*?"

My skin grew cold. My pulse was faster than a hummingbird's wings. The sound of the crowd receded. There was nothing but Dare's voice in my ear, even as it lowered to the barest whisper: *"I know who you are now."*

27

Halloween.

Our busiest night at the bar, and I wouldn't be there. Kar Yee wasn't happy. Neither was Jupe as he dumped Mr. Piggy's crate on my coffee table late that afternoon and shrugged his backpack off his shoulder. "Worst birthday, *ever*," he grumbled.

I had to agree. I pocketed my phone and ran a hand through the back of Jupe's frizzy hair. Foxglove's sleek black form trotted around my living room, sniffing every corner and cataloging all the strange scents that her keen Lab nose encountered; it was her first visit here. Last night after the parade disaster, Lon and I drove back to La Sirena and took turns checking on Jupe while he slept. Today we made a new plan and filled the SUV like Noah's Ark, loading up every person and beast, minus the Holidays, and drove here to my place.

I hadn't slept or eaten. My stomach was still twisted in knots from an attempted summoning earlier in the day. Two attempted summonings, actually, both of them failures. Chora didn't appear, which meant that he wasn't in the Æthyr during the daytime. Merrin had lied. Big surprise. I wondered if he really had an Æthyric spell that could call Chora on this plane, or if that was just a lie, too.

When I caught my reflection in the window, I couldn't believe it was me. Then again, maybe I didn't recognize myself because I didn't really know who I was anymore. Sélène was supposed to be buried in my past, along with my dead parents. The only connection I had to that life was through E∴E∴, and that was minimal at best these days.

Hadn't I suffered enough? I just wanted it all to go away. I wanted a nice, normal life. No Moonchild, no FBI, no serial-killer parents. No looking over my shoulder and being constantly afraid. But Dare wouldn't let that happen now.

"Trick-or-treating is banned throughout the entire county? How can that be legal?" Jupe complained.

Lon ignored him. "There are too many windows in here. The house ward will keep Merrin from coming inside, but it won't stop a bullet if he shoots through the window."

"Your place has twice as much glass," I argued.

"Either way, I'm *not* going to Dare's house," Jupe said as he opened the door to Mr. Piggy's crate and pulled out the hedgehog. "No way. I hate all those kids. I'm not gonna sit around in some rich guy's panic room all night like a sitting duck."

"I already told you that you didn't have to," Lon said. "He can kiss my ass."

"Good," Jupe said. "Besides, Foxglove will warn us if anything comes. If she can see ghosts, she can see anything."

Lon smoothed a thumb down one side of his mustache. "We could leave town. We've got a good four, five hours of daylight left."

"You know I can't do that," I said. "And I don't want you and Jupe to be unprotected halfway down the coast. We stick to our plan—you stay here with Jupe, and I'm going to get far away from both of you and meet up with Dare's people."

"And then what? I know you're planning something."

I darted a glance at Jupe.

"Go to the kitchen," Lon said. "Cady and I need to talk in private."

"I can hear you in the kitchen," Jupe argued. "It's still daytime. I'll just go outside."

"*No,*" Lon and I said in unison.

He crossed long arms over his chest. "I'm the one who's the damn target. You might as well say what you're going to say in front of me."

"He's right. No secrets," I said, giving Lon a soft smile. I wilted onto the couch and curled up on my side like a cooked shrimp. "I'm taking Hajo with us to track down the kid who was taken off the Halloween float last night."

"Hajo?" Jupe said. "Who's Hajo?"

"Are you kidding me?" Lon said. "Absolutely not. Is that who you were on the phone with earlier?"

"No. I was on the phone with Bob and then Dare. Bob already arranged things with Hajo. He's coming here to pick me up—"

Every muscle in Lon's neck strained in anger. "You're inviting a junkie into your house—"

"Junkie?" Jupe said.

"—who wants to get in your pants—"

"Wait, *what*?" Jupe's interest was now fully piqued. "Who wants to get in your pants?"

"Will both of you please shut up?" I said in exasperation. "Bob is coming to take me to Hajo. He will stay with me the entire time, along with a couple of Dare's men." I glanced at Jupe. "No one's getting in anyone's pants. Your dad is being dramatic."

"My dad? Dramatic?" Jupe snorted. "The Æthyr just froze over."

"Cady," Lon pleaded.

"I don't want to do this—believe me. But if there's a chance that Hajo can track the kid's energy—"

"He tracks dead things. How do we even know he can track someone alive? What if he was just bragging?"

"He says he'll try. Do you have a better idea? Because if you do, I'll call him back right now and cancel the whole thing."

"What about Cindy Brolin?"

I looked at him in confusion.

"At Starry Market. She said she was having nightmares, remember? Maybe they weren't just old memories. She was the one who got away—what if Chora has been possessing her against her will, without her knowledge?"

Jupe gave Lon a questioning look. "Cindy Brolin could be the Snatcher?"

"She works night shift at the market," I said. "Which means she sleeps during the day. The demon is possessing someone who's taking the kids during the night—when she's at work."

"Maybe she did it on her days off," Lon said, but without much conviction.

"Call the market and give the manager some legitimate-sounding reason for him to tell you when she worked the last two weeks," I said. "If her off-time overlaps with the snatchings, then Hajo and I can start looking there."

Silence fell.

"What does he want in payment this time?" Lon asked quietly.

"I didn't ask."

After a few moments, Lon walked around the sofa and slouched next to me. He pulled me closer. I laid my head against his chest and closed my eyes. "Think about boarding up some of the windows or holing up in the basement. I need to rest now. Wake me if you discover anything damning about Cindy Brolin's schedule."

Lon agreed and I took a restless nap on the couch. He didn't wake me after calling the market; Cindy Brolin had worked during all six kidnappings—she wasn't involved.

Bob was late. He pulled up in my driveway just before twilight. Foxglove barked her head off, circling his legs. "Oh! I don't like dogs," he said, jumping to the side.

I tugged Foxglove's collar. "Dogs don't seem to like you either. Get inside."

Upon entering my house, Bob greeted Lon in a cheerfully strained voice. "Mr. Butler."

Lon didn't answer.

Bob's smile cracked. He looked beyond Lon. "This must be your son."

Jupe paused *The Mummy*—"The good one from 1932, with Boris Karloff," he had told me, when I mistook it for the newer franchise—and inspected Bob with curiosity. "Are you the junkie?"

"No, this is my friend Bob," I said. "I know him from Tambuku. He's a healer," I added, just to make sure Jupe disconnected Bob from the junkie thing.

"Oh, cool," Jupe said. "I like your shirt."

More hula girls. At least it was PG and not an R-rated one—Hawaiian leis covered their breasts.

"It's vintage," Bob said.

"That's pretty cool. I like old stuff."

Bob cleared his throat. "Uh, Cady said it was your birthday. I brought some Halloween candy." He offered Jupe a plastic bag shaped like an upside-down witch hat.

Jupe gave him a toothy smile. "Wow! Thanks, man."

Lon's face told me everything he was thinking, namely that this was a violation of Jupe's no-sugar rule, and that he was considering the possibility that Bob had filled the candy with razor blades. I put a hand on Lon's arm and shook my head. It was the boy's birthday, for Pete's sake.

"Hey, do you know Kar Yee, too?" Jupe asked.

"Sure. I see her every day."

"Every day? Do you work there or something?"

"He likes tiki drinks," I said.

Jupe eyed him suspiciously. "You must like them a lot."

"Cady's the best bartender in the city," Bob said proudly.

"She makes good smoothies," Jupe said matter-of-factly. "But my dad's a better cook."

Don't spare my feelings, kid.

Bob leaned against the sofa while I got my jacket. "So," he said, still attempting to woo Lon's good grace through his son, "I heard all the schools had closed in La Sirena. What about yours?"

"Yep. Good thing, too. It was getting crazy stressful up in that place."

"Oh?"

"The teachers turned into tyrants. I've got this one teacher, Ms. Forsythe, who's really cool, but she's super-religious, and she's always giving me extra homework for cussing in class, because she says it's wrong." Jupe rolled his eyes. "But she was so stressed out the day the school closed that she said 'I don't give a damn' in front of one of the parents." Jupe gave a single, loud laugh. "I almost lost my shit. It was awesome. I wonder if she'll have go to confession for that?"

"Jupe," Lon warned halfheartedly.

Bob shifted. Foxglove started barking again.

"Hush, you damn mutt," Jupe complained. "We're in the city tonight. You can't act like that here."

Bob moved away from the dog as she quieted. "What did you say her name was?"

"Foxglove," Jupe said as he forced her to sit.

"No, your teacher."

"Oh. Ms. Forsythe. Why? You know her?"

I zipped up my jacket. My ear was ringing. I tilted my head to the side and jostled it. "Bob lives here in Morella, Jupe. He doesn't know her."

"Ms. Forsythe lives out here in Morella, too," Jupe argued. "She just works in La Sirena."

Bob had a strange look on his face. "Grace Forsythe?"

"Yeah, Gracie. That's what the other teachers call her," Jupe said.

"That's weird," Bob said to me. "When he said she was religious, I thought he meant traditionally. But"—he glanced back at Jupe and lowered his voice, speaking to me conspiratorially—"Grace Forsythe goes to that, uh, temple you were asking me about the other day."

I stared at him in disbelief.

"She used to be a patient at my father's clinic before he died. All the Silent Temple members went to him."

I have the support of my church. I'm quite blessed.

"Oh . . . God," I murmured as I blinked at Lon. "Could it be?"

"No," Lon insisted. "I know Grace. I can read her. If she's involved, she has no idea."

She was being used. Merrin was the getaway driver. Ms. Forsythe was unknowingly possessed by the duke.

Thirty years ago, Bishop was the getaway driver and Merrin was possessed by the duke. Only, Merrin was willing. Merrin struck the deal with the demon, but he was too weak to host him; too human. Merrin found someone stronger. Bishop's old house was near the school. Ms. Forsythe worked at the school. She knew all the Earthbound kids. She was a member of the Silent Temple.

She was easy prey.

"Dad, what's going on?"

Lon grimaced. "We can't be sure, Jupe. I know she's innocent—"

"No—that sound. Can't you hear it? Foxglove's whining. Where is that coming from?"

My ringing ears.

A shadow darkened the living room window, blocking out the setting sun.

Someone was testing the wards.

28

The shadow shifted out of sight. The ringing continued intermittently—softer, then louder.

"Oh, hell," I said.

"Hasn't reached the house ward yet," Lon said. "No blue web."

Lon and I set that ward together, strong magick that incapacitated anyone who crossed it with the intent to do harm. When tripped, it became visible, a network of bright blue lines. However, my own personal wards didn't do that. Most of them alerted me with instinctive warnings that popped up in my mind, but I'd put up so many over the last few months, the windows and walls were covered with invisible ink, symbols from different traditions. One of them must issue an audible warning, and now was not the time I wanted to discover this detail.

Foxglove rocketed to the side door and barked her head off. My pounding heart mirrored her warning.

"Did you lock it when Bob came?" Lon said.

"Both locks."

Lon grabbed a 12-gauge shotgun off the dining room table.

"Is it the Snatcher?" Jupe said, then squeaked out, "Ms. Forsythe?"

"Everyone upstairs," I shouted. "My bedroom is the safest room in the house. Go!"

Jupe scooped up Mr. Piggy. "Foxie, come!"

The dog obeyed, darting up the stairs alongside Jupe. Once we were all inside my room, Lon slammed the door shut and locked it. "Help me move this, Bob."

Bob scrambled to Lon's side. Then they dragged my chest of drawers across the room and wedged it against the door. Jupe and I retreated into a corner and watched the door. If the main house ward was tripped, we'd all know. That's what I kept telling myself as Foxglove paced the room, panting, alert. The ringing in my ears stopped.

I crept to the window and peeked through the curtains. Not much light left outside. The line of trees that created a privacy screen at the front of my lawn cast long shadows. I couldn't see any movement below. My street was quiet. No one walking, no cars passing by. No trick-or-treaters, thanks to the countywide ban.

Jupe whispered in my ear, "I can't hear the noise any-more."

Foxglove snarled.

A dark shape bobbed outside the edge of the window. Jupe jumped back. Foreboding chills slithered down my back as the shape glided fully into view. It was a face. Grace Forsythe's face. She was floating in the air like a balloon.

Her gentle blue halo was now fireball-red. It rippled around her head and shoulders like a wind-whipped cape. A fragment of Duke Chora's goetia entry popped into my mind: *He appeareth from above as a Goodly Knight with a Cloak of Red Velvet.*

Not a cloak, but a halo, from above: Chora could fly without wings. That's how he was snatching the children unnoticed.

Ms. Forsythe dipped and rose, peering into the window with a foreign intelligence behind her eyes—the hippie teacher who encouraged Jupe's wild imagination was no longer home. Her gaze flicked around my bedroom until it lit on Jupe. Then something changed. Her face twisted unnaturally like she was in pain. The red halo pulsed and disappeared. I saw a dim circle of her old blue halo shimmer around her bobbed hair as her eyes fluttered shut.

Her shoulders sagged and without further warning, she went limp as a rag doll and plunged downward—no floating or gliding, just a limp weight being dropped from the sky like a bag of discarded garbage. The fleshy thud her body made when it hit the ground was muted and distant.

We all gasped in horror. I pressed my face to the glass to see if she was moving below, but I jerked back when a blinding ball of light exploded next to me and Bob screamed. I crashed into Lon as my eyes focused on what was now, inexplicably, standing in my bedroom—a towering demon dressed like a colonial soldier in a long, trailing gray coat with rows of gold buttons. His face was pale, his horns dark and burnished. He carried the impressive build of a warrior and held himself with a dignified posture that came with power and rank.

Despite the change in attire, it was, without doubt, the same beautiful demon that Merrin summoned into the fiery circle at the Silent Temple.

My memory from that day suddenly overlapped with the engraving of the demon who commanded two legions of Dragoons. . . .

Grand Duke Chora had materialized inside my bedroom.

All my wards went off at once and blared inside my head as a network of fine blue lines bloomed in the air around us. The demon wailed in pain; a scaled tail whipped out from beneath the hem of his military coat. He growled a single foreign word, and the blue lines transformed to pink—the same pink that had lit the Æthyric wards at the cannery and the putt-putt course. The ward shattered into fragments and disappeared.

A clever and sly thinker, this Grand Duke uncovereth Hidden Paths and knoweth High Magics to Trap and Snare Enemies.

Someone who knows how to set traps knows how to get around them. And once he'd disabled the main house ward, Chora didn't hesitate. His arm swung and slammed into Jupe's head with terrifying force. Jupe cried out as his body snapped sideways and crumpled to the floor at an awkward angle. He didn't move. I shrieked and dropped to my knees beside him. A groan slipped from his mouth when I touched his face. But only for a moment. He flew out from beneath my fingertips when Chora seized him by the leg. With one violent tug, the demon dragged Jupe across the floor and effortlessly slung him over his shoulder.

Lon bellowed and lunged at the demon. His arms grabbed air. Chora had already disappeared with Jupe's limp body in his arms.

Shocked silence fell as we stared at the spot where Chora had just stood. Having summoned and banished Æthyic demons for years, I mistakenly thought for half a second that the demon was taking Jupe back to the Æthyr. Then my brain unknotted and I ran to the window, just in time to see Ms. Forsythe's body reanimate and float up from my lawn.

In one arm, she grasped Jupe's doubled-over body by the waist. Her other arm dangled strangely and was covered in blood that had seeped down from a large wound in her head. Her body was half broken from the fall but Chora was using it anyway. She rose higher, clearing the trees lining the front of my lawn.

Why was he back inside an injured body? He had just been solid in his own body inside my house—surely that was preferable. I recalled Merrin telling us in the restroom of the Vietnamese restaurant that Chora had gathered enough strength to become temporarily corporeal after the ritual. Clearly he had done just that, right here in my house . . . in order to slip inside my wards. He must not be able to remain in that state, or he wouldn't be using Ms. Forsythe's damaged body again—Chora needed it to move around.

We all watched in horror as the silhouetted shapes of Jupe and his teacher glided over the rooftops of the houses across the street and disappeared with the last slice of daylight.

Lon's anguished cry echoed around my bedroom, shattering my heart into a million pieces. I didn't know what to do. My mind didn't want to accept it—utter disbelief. It took every ounce of willpower I had to shut down my out-of-control emotions and focus.

"He's still alive," I blurted, knowing this was little consolation. "Chora needs a vessel for the ritual, not a dead body. Hajo will find Jupe's trail. It'll be even easier for him than the kid from the parade float, because I just touched Jupe, and we have lots of Jupe's things here for Hajo to use as dowsing objects. Strong energy. Fresh."

Lon wasn't listening. He was shoving the chest of drawers away from the door; Bob stood by in shock.

"Wait—*oh!*" I said as a loose thought congealed. "Ms. For-sythe's house is being tented for termites. Remember? She told us when we picked up Jupe from school. What if the termites aren't real? Think about it—if the Æthyric magick in the cannery could produce gigantic magical cockroaches, magical termites would be a breeze. And it would keep Ms. Forsythe out of her home."

He heaved away the drawers just far enough to get the door open.

"Don't you get it?" I said. "They could be keeping the kids there!"

Lon's hand paused on the door's lock.

"Where does she live in Morella?" I asked. "Bob?"

"No idea, but I can call and find—Cady!" Bob said, his voice panicky. "What's that?"

He pointed at a fine thread of light stretching across the room. It shimmered in the air and languidly floated out the window like a single strand of spiderweb spun from gold. Lon approached it and hesitantly reached out. His finger passed through the thread. It wasn't solid; like a laser beam, it didn't break when he waved his hand back and forth across it. His eyes followed the wispy line, looking for the source. He picked up my left hand. Right there, the golden thread was spooling out of the tip of my index finger.

"What the hell?" Lon continued to hold my hand up like it was science experiment ready to boil over and positioned me toward the window. He unlocked it and pushed it up; stuck our heads out and leaned over the sill. He waved my hand in the air. The thread moved with a corresponding ripple. I could see it better now, especially in places where it glinted in the streetlights. It shimmered over the road, across the rooftops, stretching in the same direction that the demon had floated away with Jupe.

The realization struck me like lightning.

"The tattoo on Jupe's hip—my sigil!"

He'd marked himself as mine. He was in danger—and magick linked us. I'd never seen anything like it, but when I concentrated, I could feel my Heka draining and funneling into the thread.

"Does it go through any object?" Lon asked, tugging me back inside and shifting me in front of a wall. He looked through the window. "Right through the damn house," he said. "We don't need Hajo. We can track him through you."

Lon slammed the window and locked it. "Bob, change of plans," he said as we raced out of the bedroom and down the stairs. "Stay here at Cady's and watch my dog. Call that bastard junkie and tell him we don't need him. We'll call you if we need backup."

Bob was sweating again. "What if the demon returns?"

"Tell Foxglove 'Squirrel.' That's her command to attack. Don't feed her, and stay out of Cady's underwear. I'll know if you're lying."

"I wouldn't—"

"Right. Keep your phone turned on," Lon said as he grabbed his coat on the way out. "If we make it back with my boy, I'll cook you dinner."

And with that, we raced across the driveway and loaded into Lon's SUV.

"Keep your hand on the dash so I can see which way it's pulling," he said as he slammed the car into gear. We both fixated on the taut line of gold that passed through the windshield and pointed upward into the night sky. It was astounding.

"Is it part of your Moonchild power, or what?" Lon asked as he sped down my street fast enough to get pulled over. Luckily no one was around to stop him.

"No idea, but it if leads us to Jupe, I don't care."

"Agreed."

Lon ran a four-way stop and swerved around a corner, following the thread.

"You watch the road," I suggested. "I'll watch the thread and call Dare." I continued to hold my hand over the dash as I dialed Dare one-handed and updated him. He didn't say much. Only that he would send people to Ms. Forsythe's address in Morella and an instruction to call him if we ended up somewhere else. Good enough. I hung up the phone and gave Lon Ms. Forsythe's address, 623 Monte Verde Street in the Rancho District.

"The Rancho District is out this way, isn't it?"

"Yeah." I didn't want to assume anything, so I just watched the thread. I was really noticing the loss of Heka now. I wasn't outright nauseous, but I was starting to feel a little low-blood-sugary. I kept the complaint to myself. If I passed out, Lon could just prop me up and continue to use me as a GPS.

After a few blocks flew by my window, Lon mumbled, "I think someone's following us."

He pointed out a dark sedan trailing a few car lengths back on the four-lane. When a white compact changed lanes to move behind us, the sedan went out of its way to speed up, weave around the small car, and slide into place again at our tail.

"Looks like an older model. Seventies or something. Dark green." If Jupe was with us, he'd be able to identify it. My chest tightened.

"Can you see the driver?"

"No," I admitted. "Too far away. Would Dare have sent someone local in Morella? Someone he's hired?"

"Don't know."

We were on the outskirts of downtown, and traffic wasn't heavy here, so I suggested he run the red light up ahead. Why not? He'd already violated a kajillion traffic laws and the intersection was clear. Almost. He slowed down, feigning a stop as he let a lone car cross, then slammed on the gas and ran the light. I gripped the armrest and briefly closed my eyes as someone honked at us.

"Where are they?" Lon asked as he sped away from the intersection.

"Shit! They went through the light!"

This was no friendly follower.

"Watch the gold thread and hold on." He took a sharp right. The SUV's wheels protested as we rounded the corner. I swiveled to peer out the back window. As we sped down the block, a pair of headlights made the same sharp turn.

"Still following!" I said.

"What the hell?" Lon mumbled. "How many people in the car? Can you tell?"

"Just a driver, I think. You think it could be Merrin?"

My head bounced as Lon raced across railroad tracks. The golden thread stretched straight ahead, but the sedan was gaining on us. We were going to have to do some fast maneuvering to lose it. I blurted out heated instructions to Lon. He ignored everything I suggested and cut across two lanes of traffic without warning, scaring the hell out of me.

We made another sudden turn and tore down a busy street filled with strip clubs and seedy restaurants offering $4.99 steak dinners. A few adults in Halloween costumes dotted the sidewalk as we wove in and out of traffic, nearly clipping off a car door that was swinging open on a parallel-parked van.

"Still following."

"I've got eyes," Lon snapped.

I ignored that—you know, his son being snatched by an evil demon and all. Besides, I was too busy feeling woozy, either from the loss of Heka or the crazy driving. I tried to watch the golden thread but was terrified to take my eyes off the road. Then I recognized a cross street. Lon did, too. We were in the Rancho District. He caught the tail end of a yellow light through a busy intersection and turned. *Don't follow*, I thought, as if that would help.

Lon took a couple of quick turns, and traffic became sparse. We sped through the edge of a residential neighborhood, then the four-lane dropped to two. Woods lined either side of the road. It was a straight shot, but hilly. My stomach lurched. Memories of Jupe speeding up the Halloween ride at Brentano Gardens filled my head.

As we headed toward a short bridge that stretched over a dry riverbed, one car flew past us in the opposite direction. Then we were alone. Just us and the green sedan. Lon could outrun it in the SUV out here on the straightaway. Easily. You don't pay six figures for German engineering without some perks. So when he yelled, "Brace yourself!" I didn't expect him to stop.

Brakes squealed on asphalt. Both my palms hit the dash. The green sedan sounded like a flock of screeching harpies as the car slid across the pavement behind us. Time slowed. I saw Lon watching the rearview mirror intently. I silently thanked providence that we were in a vehicle built like a tank and not in my tiny car.

Without warning, Lon hit the gas and whipped into the opposite lane. He stopped on a dime, right before the bridge. The green sedan rotated sideways as it skidded past, their front bumper missing my door by an inch. An angry face stared back at me through the windshield. The sedan's back wheels flew off the pavement and it slammed into the concrete road barrier, then careened backward over the bridge into the dusty riverbed below.

Lon jumped out of the car. I hustled out to join him and peered over the siderail. The drop to the riverbed wasn't far—ten, fifteen feet, tops. The green sedan sat at the bottom, haloed by a cloud of dust. It was too dark to see much, but I was pretty sure the engine was smoking. The back end of the car was smashed against a concrete girder below the bridge.

The driver's door opened with a squeal. A short figure stumbled out.

"Merrin, you demon-fucking piece-of-shit warlock!" Lon shouted, then pulled up the shotgun, nestled the butt against his shoulder, and took aim.

29

I lurched sideways a couple of feet and covered my ears as the blast went off. All this time we'd been trying to find the magician and now he was hunting *us* down? That figured. When I peered down into the riverbed, he was ducking behind his car door. I knew Lon wouldn't really shoot him. We might need the guy. Or maybe not . . .

The golden thread caught my eye. It wasn't pointed above the treeline anymore. It had lowered and leveled out, and it was much, much brighter. Jupe was close. They must have landed just ahead. I squinted at the quiet intersection in the distance.

"Monte Verde!" I shouted at Lon, maybe a little too loudly, because my ears were ringing again. First the damn wards, and now the shotgun blast. I was going to be deaf before the night was over.

Lon glanced where I pointed, then gauged it against the gold thread.

We both peered down at Merrin. He was drawing something on the hood of his busted-up sedan. "He's doing magick," I said.

Lon racked the shotgun and blasted it over Merrin's head.

He flattened against the ground. Good enough. Someone would be calling the cops after hearing all that. Lon and I retreated to the SUV and took off. I knew which way to turn on Monte Verde due to the line of gold light, and there was no need to check house numbers once we got closer. Situated at the end of cul-de-sac in a heavily wooded lot, the small two-story home stood out like a circus tent, striped yellow and red. And the golden thread was heading straight for it.

Hiding in plain sight. No abandoned cannery, no deserted warehouse—just a house in the suburbs, tented for pest control. Brilliant.

Lon sped down the block and braked hard in the short driveway, slamming the SUV into a plastic trash can as we came to a sliding stop. I threw off my seat belt and pushed the door open. A tall wooden fence lined with trees shielded Ms. Forsythe's backyard from the neighbors on either side, one of which had a For Sale sign staked out front. Big lot. Lots of trees. Very private. A great place to hide kids. Even better when you'd traced out spells over the tent to keep things quiet and ignored—I could see the Heka all over it.

Now that we were here, the golden thread was *much* tighter, and the angle wasn't as level as I thought it should be. I dashed to the side of the house. Lon unlatched the gate. The hinges squeaked when it he pushed it open. We craned our necks, looking upward in the night sky, searching the trees. No, not there. The roof.

We crept inside the fenced backyard and skirted the house. Streetlights provided little illumination here, casting lacy shadows on the damp grass. At the back of the home, where it was even darker, Ms. Forsythe's possessed body stood on the edge of the sloping tent-covered roof, one broken arm wrapped around Jupe's shoulders. Blood soaked through her poncho and stained Jupe's shirt. Her free hand—the one that wasn't damaged in the free fall onto my lawn—was clamped over Jupe's mouth.

A single loud sob escaped my mouth when I saw him.

He was conscious, standing on his own, to my great relief. And a bright golden light shone from beneath the waist of his jeans, just over his hip. My golden line of magick was connected there. He squirmed and tried to break away from the demon, who bent to speak into Jupe's ear. Whatever was said, it stilled him.

I held up my finger and showed Jupe the golden thread, smiling tightly. I tried hard to sound braver than I felt. "You left bread crumbs, Motormouth."

Lon raised his shotgun. The ghoulish specter of Ms. Forsythe shifted position, just slightly. Enough to show us that she could snap Jupe's neck. "Please lower your weapon," the demon said in the teacher's voice. It didn't sound quite right. The accent was rough and stilted. But it was English, not the Latin that he'd spoken to Merrin inside the Silent Temple.

Lon hesitated, considering for a moment, then lowered the gun. He spoke to the demon. "That's my son. I know you want him for the ritual. If I bring you a substitute, will you release him?"

Lon's attempt at negotiation surprised me, but I didn't comment.

"I am not able to make such allowances," the demon said stiffly.

"He's afraid," Lon whispered against my hair.

At first I thought he meant Jupe, and wondered why he was telling me something I'd already guessed, but he meant the demon—Chora was afraid. He certainly hadn't seemed frightened when he punched Jupe's lights out in my bedroom and spirited him away into the darkening sky. But I had to trust that Lon could hear the demon's emotions. I just didn't know what to do about it. Maybe the neighbors were home. Surely someone down the block had heard Lon's shotgun blasts. I quickly scanned the house and looked for a way to climb, but the striped tent made that idea an impossibility. Nothing to hold on to.

Lon whispered to me again. "Can hear the children, too. Inside the house."

Before I could process any small bit of comfort over that good news, the gate creaked. Merrin's silhouette limped our way. He was panting and sweating. Running down the block must have been a feat for him. I shifted my position, moving into a shadow with the golden thread. Two steps and it wasn't glinting quite so brightly in the dim light that spilled over the roof. If Merrin hadn't noticed it, I wanted to keep it that way.

"I'd advise you to drop that gun if you value your boy's life. The duke is stronger than he appears." Merrin might be gasping for breath and limping in pain, but his mood was giddy.

"Why would he kill someone he needs for his damned *Buné* spell?" Lon asked.

"I didn't say the duke would kill him."

"Do not speak for me, mage."

I looked toward the roof, surprised to hear the demon again. Surprised to hear a sharp note of animosity under Ms. Forsythe's strained tones. Then I remembered how the demon had spoken to Merrin in the Silent Temple. This was not a happy partnership.

Merrin ignored him and spoke to Lon. "I'm guessing that the boy could withstand an incredible amount of pain and remain alive for our purposes. Put the gun down, if you would, please."

Lon measured his options and tossed the shotgun on the grass. Merrin smiled and canted his head politely. Then he held out his arm, revealing something round and shiny in his grip—the metal instrument he'd used to throw Heka against us in the temple, maybe, or some other magic weapon. He stepped toward us and hastily retrieved the gun and with a grunt, heaved it over the fence into the neighbor's yard. Lon groaned under his breath.

I knew he was probably panicking about losing his weapon, but it didn't matter to me—I was trying to keep my eyes on both Merrin and Jupe while I considered my options. How could I use the Moonchild ability to bind the demon inside Ms. Forsythe's body without binding Jupe along with him? "How much of what you told us was true?" I asked the magician, stalling for time.

Merrin shuffled back a few steps and pocketed the metal disk as he glanced at the roof. "In the restaurant? Almost everything. It was a close approximation of the truth, anyway. I'm betting that you've already guessed the white lies."

"You're the one who killed Bishop," I said. "Not the demon."

"First Bishop stole the key to the *capsa*, then he took a photo of me hiding it."

"The silver tube at the putt-putt course?"

"Bishop was planning to blackmail me with that photo. He was running to Dare and Butler, trying to get me stripped of my Hellfire paycheck. Chora had taught me some new magical skills, so I practiced them. You found the body at the cannery, so you already know how well they worked."

I wondered if I could sneak a phone call to Dare. Probably not. "Other lies . . . you were conscious when the duke was riding you?" I guessed.

"Quite."

"Grace Forsythe is not." Lon said.

"No, not Gracie. She's a vegetarian who insists on organic pesticides. Do you think she'd agree to kidnapping children?"

"The termites aren't real," I said.

"Of course not. Termite extermination doesn't take two weeks. I just moved some things around in her brain." He adjusted his glasses, rehooking them over his ears. "I've known her since she was a teenager. She's a gentle soul but a strong vessel. Ideal for possession. We take her for a little ride every night, and she has vivid dreams. No harm done."

"The demon's broken half her bones," I argued.

"She can go to a healer." He glanced at the roof again and stepped back a couple of paces. "If she makes it through the night," he amended.

A wave of nausea hit me and the tent's stripes swam in my vision. *Crud.* There wasn't an unlimited supply of Heka, so I knew it had to come sooner or later. Maybe I could hold on a little longer. The golden thread was becoming dull—not good. I steadied myself and considered pulling electrical current to fortify my Heka, but I was more than a little worried that it would flow into Jupe and fry him.

"You aren't afraid of Chora," Lon noted.

Merrin grinned. "Why would I be afraid of a demon bound to serve me?"

"And there was never any curse," I guessed. "You were never afraid of him, were you?"

"Why should I have been? Chora is the Æthyric James Bond," Merrin said with a smile. "He can move in and out of wards, set traps, elude capture. He flies by night and steals secrets. He's no terrifying general or gifted warrior—he's a demonic spymaster."

Merrin unzipped his jacket. "I asked around the Æthyr. Discovered that he was in possession of the *Buné* spell. He'd stolen it, apparently, on one military mission or another. I trapped him, and we made a deal—I wouldn't sell his secrets to his enemies, and he would help me with the ritual. We would be partners. A simple pact. Everything was going smoothly, up until the last child chosen for the ritual. She was tricky."

"Cindy Brolin."

He shrugged. "I don't remember her name. I went on with the ritual anyway, hoping it would work with a substitute, but it failed."

"What were you testing for, biting the children?"

"Ratio of demon to human. Chora can taste it in the blood. Demon is sweeter."

"Oh," I said weakly, my vision blurring around the edges again.

"We made a couple of errors," Merrin continued, "but I'm not one to just give up on something this big. And my deal with the demon was contractually binding until the doors between the planes were open. Once we got past our disagreements—"

Chora swore indecipherably from the rooftop, giving Jupe an earful of Æthyric curses intended for Merrin.

"—we made better plans. I kept Chora bound in the gap between the planes until we were ready. And now we are. Because this time, I've gone to great lengths to ensure our success. And wouldn't you know, the biggest mistake thirty years ago wasn't merely the substitute vessel. The stronger the vessels, the longer the doors stay open, you see, but they never opened at all—not even a crack. The vessels just turned to dust. Over the years, I realized the real problem. Timing."

"Timing? You mean the overlapping alignments?"

"Conjunctions, alignments . . . here and in the Æthyr. It only granted a short window of time, and I was a few hours too late. I've never been very good at calculations." He nodded to the roof. "Luckily, Ms. Forsythe is mad about astronomy. She's far too knowledgeable for a junior high teacher, she just never had the drive to do anything more. But when I gave her the problem to solve, she was more than happy to help, even without magical coercion or understanding why I needed it—imagine that!"

What did he want? Applause?

"It was a long wait," he said, "but once the doors are open, I will be able to cross into the Æthyr."

"And what will you do there?" I asked. "What's worth waiting thirty years for?"

"I've learned the secrets of possession, my dear. I will ride Chora like he's ridden me. Do you know how old he is? Nearly a thousand years. And he's barely hitting the middle of his life span. I can either die here in this miserable excuse for a body—bald, short, and half crippled—or I can live for decades inside the body of a demonic knight."

"I thought you said he nearly killed you when the ritual went wrong the first time? What makes you think that you won't do the same when you're inside him? Bodies weren't designed for two separate occupants, Frater."

"I'm willing to take that chance. And if he can't hold me, I will find someone else in the Æthyr who can. You can sit around demurely and wait for your reward in heaven, if there is one, but I'm seizing mine while I'm able."

Merrin ripped open his shirt, baring his withering chest and paunchy gut that ballooned below the blue ink of the tattoo I'd spied when we cornered him in the restroom. It wasn't the only one. A smaller tattoo was etched on the sagging skin over his heart; God only knew what other tricks he'd learned, and this smaller seal was already dimly glowing with charged Heka. Not a good idea to have two tattoos charged at once. I knew this from experience. Merrin didn't seem to be worried, though. He retrieved the metal disk from his pocket and sliced it across a palm. Blood welled. He pressed the Heka-rich fluid over the tattooed sigil on his chest. It lit up with a bright blue charge, then sank back into an ink tattoo.

"No need to be frightened of me," he said to Lon. "How I pity you, being forced to hear all this emotional garbage, day in and day out. A useless knack, much like your father's."

Lon was a patient man, but lately I'd seen him reach his snapping point more times than I could count. He barreled toward Merrin before I could stop him, charging the elderly magician like a bull. But it was pointless. Merrin wasn't lying—he had no interest in Lon's knack. He wanted Chora's ability, and with his tattooed sigil now freshly charged, he absorbed it.

The magician leapt out of the path of Lon's charge and floated into the darkness just above us. Lon jumped and swatted at the magician's feet, but they were already out of reach. His shirttails fluttered behind him as he rose to the roof and landed near Jupe and Ms. Forsythe. He stumbled, not quite competent with the whole flying thing, then righted himself.

"Now, *this* is a knack!" Merrin shouted breathlessly. "And your son's new ability isn't half bad, either. Thank you for telling Gracie about it, or I never would have guessed," Merrin yelled down to Lon, yanking Jupe away from the demon.

Jupe, God bless him, wasn't going gently. He kicked the living daylights out of Merrin and the volume of his muffled shouts increased, but then the magician hissed something to him that I couldn't hear. After that Jupe went quiet. Merrin kept one hand clamped over Jupe's mouth, just as Chora had done.

Come on, Chora. Take one step back, I thought, watching the three of them on the roof. I calmed myself and searched inside for the Moonchild power, willing it to the surface.

"What's this?" Merrin peered at the fading golden glow emanating from Jupe's tattoo. The trailing thread was becoming difficult to see in the darkness, but the mark itself still pulsed with Heka. "Have you warded the boy?" he yelled down at me. "You'll tell me the truth."

"No," I answered, before I could even consider an answer. I covered my mouth in alarm. Jupe's damned knack! But I'd only told the truth—I hadn't warded him. Jupe had put that mark on himself.

"It doesn't matter. The duke can break it later." He turned to the demon. "Chora, right now you will kill both of them below. Quickly, if you would, please."

The demon didn't hesitate. Still wearing Ms. Forsythe's skin, he glided to ground, heading straight for us. I yelped and turned to Lon, but he wasn't there. Gone! Any crumb of calm I'd accumulated in readying myself to wield the Moonchild power dissipated as panic seized my chest. I whipped my head around, searching the shadows for him, and the demon landed several yards in front of me. Ms. Forsythe's crushed arm hung limply beneath her poncho, and her hair was matted with blood. But the demon didn't seem to care about her injuries. When her leg quivered as if it might buckle, he just groaned and hobbled toward me.

"Lon!" I called out.

Angry grumbling filtered from beyond the fence, over which Lon had climbed and was now leaning across the top, tugging at a nearby tree branch in the neighbor's yard. One strong wrench and something loosened. "Aghh!" he cried out in victory before he leapt to the ground, shotgun in hand. Lon shouldered the butt of it and aimed it at Ms. Forsythe's stalking figure.

"Gracie, if you can hear me, try to fight him," Lon said between labored breaths. "I'd hate like hell to kill you."

If the teacher *could* hear him, she sure didn't show it. The person striding toward us had a purpose. Lon aimed low and squeezed the trigger. *Boom!* If no one had called the police about the shots at the scene of Merrin's wreck, they would surely be dialing now. Ms. Forsythe's body tilted, then faltered. The shot had landed just above a kneecap.

Although a good chunk of her lower thigh was gone and dark blood splattered across her pant legs, she attempted to take another step and stumbled. Lon pumped the shotgun and fired at the opposite leg. Her knee exploded. That did it. The teacher's entire lower body fell out from beneath her and she went down like a rock, her face slamming into the grass.

Movement on the roof tore my attention away. Merrin was tightening his hold on Jupe as he stepped to the edge of the roof. "Too much noise," Merrin said, looking over the roof to the street below. "Chora, finish up quickly and join me. That's a command."

The magician jumped off the roof and descended several feet. While floating in place, he shifted his grip long enough to slice through the striped tenting with his metal disk. A flap fell open, exposing a second-story window. He murmured something to Jupe, who struggled to push the window open. They were going inside.

I took one look at the teacher's body on the ground and figured she wasn't going anywhere, then raced across the yard and stopped beneath the window. Merrin was stuffing Jupe inside, legs first. The golden thread vibrated. It was taut and glowing brighter. My finger throbbed as if there was an actual piece of string tied to the tip.

Magick is directed energy. It can be formed, shaped, and molded. I took a chance, acting on instinct. With gritted teeth, I made a fist and pushed Heka into the golden line, then tugged on it. Resistance. Weak, but it could be enough . . . if only my body didn't feel like a gas tank running on fumes. I needed more juice. Had to risk it.

I reached out and siphoned electricity from the house—not much, just enough to kindle what little Heka reserves I had left—and sent it down the thread. Raw, burning Heka.

"Brace yourself!" I called to Jupe as the thread lit like a fuse.

30

Jupe yelped. Merrin shouted in fear as gravity suddenly weighed him down and he plunged, dropping Jupe.

I tugged on the golden thread as hard as I could. Jupe's body jerked and sailed toward me like an angel—long arms and legs and a mass of volcanic hair whizzing through the darkness. I held out my arms and braced myself for collision: his elbow knocked my jaw sideways and he crashed into my ribs as he body-slammed me to the ground.

Everything hurt except my heart, which was thundering with surprise and relief.

Jupe let out a dopey groan. His eyes opened. He blinked rapidly. "Cady," he murmured with a scratchy voice.

"Got you." I scrambled to shove him off and hauled us both to our feet. The kid might've saved his own damn life with that stupid tattoo.

Merrin howled in pain a few feet away, writhing in the grass. I couldn't tell how badly he'd been injured from the fall, but if he recovered his wits and hijacked Jupe's knack again, we'd all be in trouble—how far was far *enough* away to ensure we were outside the knack-stealing sigil's range? I didn't have a clue.

Jupe cried out in surprise at something he saw over my shoulder. I spun. Across the yard, Ms. Forsythe's limp body remained sprawled on the ground. Unmoving. But that wasn't the cause of Jupe's anxiety. Chora now floated above her, dressed in his military coat, tail whipping.

And that wasn't all.

Lon stood in the same place I'd left him, but his green-and-gold halo danced like a crown of gilded flames over his head and spotlighted the two spirling horns that jutted from his hairline.

He looked devastatingly menacing and shockingly demonic—

And Jupe had never seen him transmutated.

"Dad?" he croaked.

"It's okay," I assured Jupe, squeezing the back of his neck. "He's still your dad, it's—I can't explain now. I need to help him. Stay behind me."

I raced my heartbeat across the shadowed lawn with Jupe dogging my heels. When we got closer, Lon, without taking his eyes or the aim of his gun off Chora, yelled, "Stay back!"

We came to a sliding stop.

Chora was staring at Lon, sizing him up. "The mage told me of this magick, this transmutation. He chose vessels for the ritual who were born with this magick inside them. He believes this will help them live long enough for the doors to open between the planes. Their blood is sweeter."

"Why doesn't he just summon seven demons from the Æthyr?" Lon asked.

"They must originate on this plane for the doors to open from this side."

Chora looked weary. I guess if I'd spent thirty years trapped in some crazy gap between the planes, I'd be weary, too.

"The ritual matters little to me," he said. "I only wish to fulfill my contract with the piggish mage and return home."

Chora held one palm up, as if he were asking for a handout, and used a finger to trace an invisible mark over his open palm as he mumbled something foreign. The air crackled. A pink glow lit his hand from the inside out. Then his skin turned translucent and I could see veins and bones beneath it. Jupe made a wary noise behind me. I could feel his labored breath against the top of my head. I tugged him closer.

Chora floated down and landed on the grass. "If we were back in my homelands, I would not chose to battle you, Kerub," Chora said, referring to the class of demon from which Earthbounds are descended. "Nor you, Mother." He looked at me with the same familiarity that I had glimpsed in the Silent Temple. "But I do not have that choice. I am sorry."

The demon's scaly tail flicked as he held out the hand glowing pink with magick. He pushed back the cuff of his colonial coat, exposing his wrist, then sank two fingers into the flesh there. Slick, sucking noises made me grimace as he dug around inside his own skin. He extracted something skinny and straight. Once he was able to get several fingers around it, he tugged with more force.

A thin, whispery blade the length of a small sword glinted in the moonlight. He unsheathed it from the scabbard of his forearm. The grip of the weapon was ivory, and might've been constructed from bone, but the dripping blood made it hard to be certain. The blade was metal, though. And he wielded the disgusting weapon with determination as a new noise stole my attention.

Merrin was on his feet. Shoulders dropping, head lowered, he bowled toward us, only slightly impeded by his awkward limp. He was disoriented and pained, and his glasses were gone—lost in the fall. But he squinted into the dark and his eyes caught mine.

Chora raised the bloody blade, murmuring under his breath. It sounded calm and peaceful. Maybe a prayer. Lon racked his shotgun and fired. Chora jerked to the side. The shot hit his free shoulder, he cried out in fury, and dark blood flowed over the gray fabric of his coat. His tail whipped furiously around his legs.

Lon groaned and cracked his jaw. Despite the shot, he wasn't happy. He'd been aiming for the heart, I realized, and missed his mark, not expecting the demon to move so fast. Worse, that was his fifth shot. Four rounds plus one in the chamber makes five total. He lowered the gun and held it by the barrel as he fished inside his pocket. *More shells*, I thought, *thank God*. When he pulled out his phone instead, I wondered if he'd gone loopy. His fingers danced over the screen. He spoke a single word into the phone, then tossed both it and the shotgun on the grass beside him. Maybe he was calling Dare. Or the police. I'd take either at this point.

Chora groaned and tilted his neck to inspect the damage Lon had inflicted. Just a glance. His eyes refocused on Lon, who held up his hands in surrender. I silently called out for the Moonchild power. Not a request, a command. The telltale pinpoint of blue light manifested in my vision. It was ready, waiting to be used. But, like Lon, I might have only one shot to change things, and I didn't want to miss.

I could either conjure up the *Silentium* seal I'd used in the cannery to negate Merrin's knack-stealing magick, or I could bind Chora.

Merrin was now halfway across the yard.

Chora repositioned his blade to strike, ignoring the weeping wound in his shoulder.

Jupe's hands were shaking on my back—from fear? Or was he readying his own power? If he used his knack, he'd use it to help his dad. A guess, but I was willing to gamble, and there was no time left to do anything else.

Merrin's mouth opened and began to form a command.

Silentium.

The pinpoint of light flattened into a disk. The lines of the magick seal formed in blue light. Heka and moon energy zigzagged in and out of me and poured into it, then I used every ounce of willpower I had to thrust the seal at Merrin's galloping body.

Blinding white light whooshed around the magician. He hollered and tripped, thudding to the ground as Jupe yelled, "Stop!"

Chora's eyes darted in our direction. He'd heard Jupe's persuasive command, but it didn't come fast enough. Though he faltered, his blade was already arcing through the air. As Lon ducked, the blade's tip sliced, nicking Lon's neck where it met his jaw.

Lon grasped his throat and fell to his knees. Blood seeped between his fingers and stained the neckline of his shirt.

"Nooooo!" Jupe screamed as he hurtled to Lon's side.

Chora's arm went limp, his hand still gripping the bloodied blade. A look of regret darkened his eyes. Regret and pity. The wound he'd delivered wasn't deep, but it was precise. He looked like someone who'd just killed a stranger in a duel over honor. He looked human.

Merrin's husky voice burred from behind me. "Finish him off, Chora!"

He was on his feet again, but the knack-stealing sigil was dead. And it wasn't the only sigil diffused by my *Silentium* spell. The smaller tattoo over his heart that I'd glimpsed earlier? That was dead now, too. The ink was faded—the tattoo was much older than the knack-stealing sigil—but now that Merrin was bowling toward me like a peg-legged sailor ready to throw me to the sharks, I recognized its purpose. Egyptians marked their dead with a symbol to keep their mummified bodies from being invaded by evil spirits. I reckoned that Merrin used it to keep Chora from entering him. A little insurance, I supposed, after the demon nearly killed him during the first possession thirty years ago.

Partners. Chora and Merrin. That's how Merrin described their relationship. I hardly agreed, but since Chora hadn't realized that Merrin was now wide open and unprotected, I'd give him a little push.

Darkness blanketed my mind. The yard and everything in it faded to black, and the breezy night air stilled. I willed the moon power into action once more, conjuring the blue light, expanding it into a simple binding triangle, clear and strong. Moon-kindled Heka flowed as I tossed it like a lasso and slammed it over Chora's body.

As I'd done with Jupe's golden thread, I reached out with magick and pulled. Darkness receded. Sound and sight returned to me in a flash as the binding snagged the demon. Furious and unhinged, Chora howled as his body sailed through the air like a bullet headed for Merrin's chest.

"Ride!" I commanded as he blurred by me.

I released the binding. Chora's body slammed into Merrin's without a sound, without the expected thud of flesh hitting flesh. Chora merely melted into the magician's skin and disappeared like a specter.

Merrin's eyes widened in horror. His body twitched, bristling with additional life. His torso jerked. A low rumbling started in his legs and spread upward. What little hair he had remaining on his balding head stood on end.

Then the shaking halted and his eyes rolled back in his head. Flesh ripped. A thin, bloody blade, glowing with pink light, poked out from his stomach. The blade quivered, then sliced upward, dissecting Merrin from the inside. His organs spilled out in a dark, shiny tumble half a second before a bright pink light exploded and geysered up into the air. Merrin's body erupted along with it, sending up a grisly shower of blood and flesh that fell back like rain and splattered over the wet grass.

Merrin was gone. Decimated. Torn to shreds.

Chora was gone, too. No trace of pink magick remained. Whether he was dead or banished, or had slipped back into the gap between the planes, I didn't care. I turned my back on the gore and raced to Lon, dropping to the ground beside him.

He lay on his back, his horns and halo gone. His hand still gripped his neck. Both of Jupe's hands were pressed on top. So much blood . . .

I tore out of my jacket and ripped a strip of the lining, balling it up. "Let go, Jupe!" I said as my hands hovered over his with the cloth.

"I can't!"

"On three, okay? One, two . . ."

Jupe jerked his hands away. I pressed the fabric against Lon's neck, his hand still clamped and wedged under my makeshift compress. I saw the fear in his eyes as I pulled his hand away. "Let me, please," I said. His blood-slicked hand drooped into the grass.

My arms shook. Blood had soaked through the gray fabric way too fast. I pressed harder, using both of my hands.

How long did it take someone to bleed to death? Minutes? How long had it been already? "Nine-one-one, Jupe," I said with a strained voice.

He struggled with his cell phone. "I can't dial," Jupe answered frantically between sobs. "My hands are slippery!"

I heard noise behind us—traffic, brakes, car doors slamming . . . Jupe's shrill voice carried in the darkness. "Help! Help us, please!"

I chanced a quick look over my shoulder. Several people were rushing into the front yard.

"Mr. Dare!" Jupe called out to one of the approaching silhouettes. "Help! Call Dr. Mick. My dad needs help!"

Dare jogged toward us. "Dear God," he said. "Mark, get an ambulance here!" Dare yelled back at his son.

"No. Dr. Mick," Jupe insisted. "It's bad."

"Can he speak?"

"Don't you even try!" I barked at Lon as blood oozed between my fingers. "Stay still."

Dare glanced at the carnage in the yard. "Are the kids—" Dare started.

"In the house," I said. "Lon heard them."

"Move away, miss," one of the Dare's people said, an Earthbound with a green halo. He kneeled beside Lon and tried to take over.

"No! He'll bleed out."

The Earthbound looked at my hands and winced. "Keep pressure on it."

Any more pressure and I'd be choking him. I tried to keep my hands steady. Lon's eyes were glassy and kept fluttering shut. His breath was becoming shallow.

"Stay awake," I croaked. Hot tears welled and spilled down my cheeks. I dipped my head to his and pressed a shaky kiss to his brow. "I need you, Lon," I whispered. "You're the only family I have. Don't leave me."

His lips moved. He looked up me, dazed, and blinked.

"Police will be here soon," Dare said. "I'll handle them."

Another car drove up. I heard talking outside the fence, commotion. I could spy a little of it through the open gate. A lone figure was arguing with Dare's people, who were managing a growing crowd of neighbors on the sidewalk. Someone raced through the gate.

"Cady!"

"Bob?"

"Lon called me," he yelled. *The phone call before he surrendered,* I remembered. Not Dare, but Bob? The Earthbound dashed out of the shadows, chest heaving, face red. "Oh, no," he lamented when he spotted Lon.

"You're a healer," Jupe said.

"Yes, but not a good one," Bob said. "I can't . . . this is . . . it's too big."

"Yes, you can," I pleaded. "You can help. *Please,* Bob."

"Cady"—he shook his head—"I really can't. I'm not my father. Small wounds, Cady. Not this."

"Jupe, Bob is a good healer. He just doesn't believe he is. Can you please persuade him?"

Jupe wiped away tears. "What?"

"Tell him how good he is, Jupe. You dad needs someone *now.* Dr. Mick is too far away."

Realization cracked Jupe's miserable expression. He swallowed hard, squeezed his eyes shut, and shouted, "You're a good healer, Bob. Good enough to help my dad. Please fix him!"

Bob swayed on his knees.

Lon's green-and-gold halo was shrinking. His eyes fluttered closed.

Jupe choked on a sob and tried to persuade Bob again. His body shook as he balled up his hands into fists. "Heal him!" he cried out. "Stop the bleeding!"

"I trust you, Bob," I said, smiling and crying at the same time. "Please."

He stared at Lon for a moment, then nodded once and took a deep breath.

Bob's fingers touched mine and prodded. I didn't want to let go. He prodded me a second time. I sobbed and jerked my hands away. *I trust you, I trust you, I trust you. . . .*

Bob removed the soaked compress from Lon's neck and slid his fingers over the wound. He mumbled something to himself and closed his eyes.

I waited, talking to Lon in a whisper and gripping his limp hand. Jupe's squatted next to me, his shoulder pressed against my arm as he nervously rocked on his heels.

I waited longer, barely breathing, as Dare's people worked in the distance, rescuing the kids from the house.

Then Bob gasped.

His shoulders strained.

My heart pounded.

And as Bob let out a long, labored breath, Lon's halo pulsed brighter. An ambulance wailed in the distance, and Lon's fingers, slick with blood, flexed around mine.

His eyes opened.

31

Mr. and Mrs. Holiday walked into Lon's house hauling a homemade cake scattered with multicolored birthday candles. It was a week late, but when the actual birthday sucked as much as Jupe's did, it was only fair to get a do-over. Banana-and-chocolate layer cake with peanut butter frosting was definitely *not* my first choice, or second. But it was Jupe's favorite, and they'd gone to so much work. When I tasted it, though, I was pleasantly surprised. "Mmm," I said, smiling.

"Told you. It's good, right?" Jupe shoveled an enormous bite into his mouth.

"Slow down," Lon said. "You'll make yourself sick."

"It takes three pieces to make me throw up," he argued, then waggled his eyebrows in my direction. "I put that to the test last year."

"I remember," Mr. Holiday said sourly.

"You're a disgusting little animal," Mrs. Holiday echoed.

He grinned and licked crumbs off his fork.

As Lon grumbled, Jupe plucked out a chunk of banana from his slice and fed it to Mr. Piggy under the dining room table while he recounted stories from past birthdays, enlightening me as to why both saltwater aquariums and slumber parties were forever banned at the Butler house. Good to know.

Though he'd already unwrapped several gifts, Jupe's big birthday present came while we were clearing away the remains of the cake. I agreed to distract Jupe while Lon went outside and took care of the delivery.

"I'm sorry your real birthday stunk," I said as we waited.

"You and me both. I always thought flying would be cool, but I was *this* close to pissing my pants," he admitted with a weak smile.

"That's a habit of yours, isn't it?" I teased.

He snickered, then we both fell silent.

"Do you think Ms. Forsythe will ever teach again?" he asked after a time.

"I don't know."

She was currently healing in the hospital after reconstructive surgery on her knees. Unlike Lon's neck wound, her shattered bone and cartilage couldn't be mended by a healer, not even one as skilled as Mr. Mick. At Lon's insistence, Dare was making arrangements for Ms. Forsythe to be checked into some place up the coast, the Golden Path Center, a "voluntary" mental health retreat for Earthbounds. I hoped she found a way to deal with her very *involuntary* role in all this, but I wasn't sure if that was possible.

"Hey, Cady," Jupe said in a low voice, "how long have you known about my dad?"

I hesitated. "The transmutating?"

He shifted uncomfortably on the sofa. "Yeah."

"A couple of months, I guess. But only because of all that stuff he was helping me with when we first met."

"I can't believe he lied to me," he said softly.

"He didn't want you to know because he doesn't want you to undergo the spell that allows him to do that."

"Why?"

"Because you're strong enough without it, and it's caused him a lot of problems. If he had to do it all over again—if he had the choice—he wouldn't undergo the spell. That kind of power can be a burden. You might not understand that now, but you will. Your knack isn't going to be roses, either. With or without a spell to boost it."

"Maybe," he said after a few moments. "But I'd kinda like to have the horns."

I slanted a glance his way. He was smiling. I elbowed him and he chuckled.

"All right," Lon called from the foyer. "Get your ass out here, Motormouth."

Jupe leapt off the sofa and raced outside.

The departing tow truck was circling the driveway when I got to the door. I trailed Lon and Jupe across the gravel to the garage—a really nice, three-car one, with a polished floor and custom cabinets lining the walls. They almost never used it because Lon parked his beat-up truck and SUV in the driveway. The sleek silver Audi we'd taken to the Hellfire caves last month sat covered on the far side—he only drove it a few times a year—and the rest of the garage was usually empty. Right now, however, a rusted-out jalopy occupied the wide space.

"What the hell is this?" Jupe said, half horrified, half intrigued.

It wasn't the prettiest thing, and I could only imagine what Jupe was seeing: no tires, the busted-out rear window, and a spring poking through a large slit in the backseat.

"This," Lon said proudly, "is a 1967 Pontiac GTO. A legendary muscle car. It used to be called 'The Great One.'"

Jupe carefully treaded around the car, looking up at Lon like he was certifiable.

"The Ramones sang about it," I offered.

Lon added, "Bruce Lee's car in *Return of the Dragon*."

The kid's face lit up ever so slightly, then fell again. "It's . . ." Jupe screwed up his face, trying to find the right words. "It's dead."

"Neglected," Lon corrected.

Jupe squinted at his father, a dubious look on face.

"It needs to be restored," Lon said. "But the V-8 engine is original, and it's only got fifty thousand miles on it. Things will need to be stripped and replaced, but that's minor."

Jupe shuffled to the other side of the car. "It doesn't have any wheels!"

"That's the least of your problems."

"It will cost a fortune to fix this thing up," Jupe argued.

I smiled. "Lucky for you, you're independently wealthy."

"The savings account?"

"You wanted to save it for a car—"

"One that *worked*," he said. "One that didn't look like someone dropped it in the Pacific with a body in the trunk!"

Lon picked up a stack of books and photos from a shop table in the corner and tossed them on the rusted hood. "After it's fixed up, it could look like this . . ."

Jupe studied the photos that Lon was spreading out for his inspection. I peeped over his shoulder. Beautiful GTOs gleamed, fully restored and sitting pretty at car collector shows. All of them had sleek, two-door bodies fronted by curvaceous hoods with chain-link grilles.

"Whoa," Jupe said, touching a photo.

Lon pulled out a small, square card, a sample of auto paint in high-gloss, metallic red-violet. I was afraid to look at it for too long—like staring into the sun, it might do some eye damage. "The car could be any color you wanted," Lon said. "This is Plum Mist. It's one of the original colors."

"No way." Jupe picked up the paint sample and held it up to the light. "No one in La Sirena has a purple car."

"You could. Or black, silver, or red," Lon encouraged.

"Purple is my favorite color." Jupe smiled, turning around to hand me the sample. "Who's going to fix it up? When can they start?"

Lon scooted the restoration books in Jupe's direction. "You are."

Jupe's jaw dropped. "What? I can't rebuild a car."

"Sure you can. You're smart, good with details."

"Good at taking apart things and putting them back together," I added, remembering how he'd fixed the vacuum cleaner a couple of weeks ago when Mrs. Holiday sucked up one of Mr. Piggy's tiny spines and gummed up the works.

"This is crazy! I can't do this!" Jupe's eyes were frantic, darting up and down the car. "I'm just a kid!"

Lon set two keys down on the hood, along with the bill of sale. "I thought you were fourteen."

"Yeah, I don't even know how to *drive* a car—how could I restore one?"

"You read these books, look up stuff online. Take a class after school. My friend Danny teaches auto shop at the high school, and he's a member of the La Sirena GTO Association. He'll help you with the hard stuff, locate parts for you, that kind of stuff. We'll find someone who can reupholster the seats."

Jupe eyed the keys on the hood. "Even if I could, it would take me, like, forever."

"You've got a year until you can get your learner's permit," I said.

"And you can take over the garage," Lon suggested. "Haul over a couch from Grandpa's old house in the Village. Maybe even put a TV in here."

Jupe pulled his face away from the passenger window and looked between us, then spoke to Lon in a small voice. "You really think I could do it?"

"Why not? And when you're done, you'll know all about cars. Mechanics make decent money. It'd be nice to have a skill like that."

After a few moments of doubt, Jupe smiled, like he was starting to believe it himself. Then he scrunched up his face, thinking two steps ahead. "Can I put posters up on the walls in here?"

"No naked women."

"What about a nude *calendar*? All mechanics have them."

"That's just in the movies," Lon said. "No one makes those anymore."

"Please! You shot—"

Lon made a loud chastising noise. "That was a long time ago."

"You shot what exactly?" I asked. "And *how* long ago?"

Jupe grinned. "It was—"

"So do you want this thing or not?" Lon said quickly, cutting him off.

Jupe snatched the keys off the hood. "Hell yeah! This is the best birthday present ever!"

He took a couple of laps around the car, opening both doors and crawling around inside, only to complain about the "dead fish" stink. Lon lifted the hood, and after they peered inside, Jupe finally calmed enough to call his friend Jack and brag about his new prize.

Lon and I leaned against the GTO.

"Good job," I whispered to Lon.

"It was your idea." He slung an arm around my shoulder and kissed me lightly on the top of my head.

I smiled up at him and traced the small scar on his neck. Much smaller than the scar on his ribs, and I was glad this one was there. It meant he was alive. Warm and breathing and whole. I would never stop being thankful for that. And, truthfully, I couldn't be happier about Lon's owing Bob a favor. Maybe Bob's newfound confidence would lead him to spend less time on a barstool in Tambuku and more time putting his knack to better use.

"If the kid can't restore this thing, don't blame me," I said.

Lon pushed long strands of tawny hair away from his face. "Danny said he'd do it for parts if Jupe helps him out after school a couple of days a week. Even then, it'll take months."

I laughed. Probably more like years.

"Hey," Lon called out to Jupe after he ended his phone call. "It's almost six. You ready to do this?"

Jupe ambled through garage, threading the GTO keys onto his Wolf Man key ring. "Oh, yeah! I almost forgot."

I frowned at Lon. "What's going on?"

"Nothing. I made a quick phone call earlier."

"What kind of phone call?"

Jupe gleefully dangled his newly ringed keys in front of my face. "Let's just say that you're going to owe me big-time."

"*Pfft.* I owe you zilch," I said. "I helped pay for this junk heap already." Okay, only a couple hundred dollars, which barely covered the tow up the cliff, but still.

Lon whistled merrily.

I glared at him. "Explain."

"We're taking a little trip down to the Village. Got a meeting at the Singing Bean."

"With whom?"

Lon grinned. "Your death dowser pal Hajo has agreed to meet us. Jupe's going to get your vassal potion back."

"What?"

"That's right." Jupe arched his back and stretched like a cat, then smugly pretended to crack his knuckles. "Step aside and watch the master go to work, people."

Lon brushed his fingers across mine. "Dr. Spendlove said we should teach Jupe how to use his knack for good, not evil," he reminded me. "This qualifies as good in my book."

"So this is all for Jupe's education, huh?" As if he didn't get enough education last week. How in the world Lon planned to ensure that the kid didn't go bragging to his friends about demon horns was beyond me. I was pretty sure Lon was doing this to keep Jupe happy and quiet.

"Please," Lon pleaded, lifting my chin. "Hajo's a bum. Am I wrong?"

"No," I admitted.

"Woot! I get to meet a real-live junkie!" Jupe exclaimed.

Lon flashed me a triumphant smile. As he walked by, he smacked my ass, coaxing a reflexive jump out of me. "Come on, Cadybell. We're gonna be late."

Jupe sneaked me a mischievous look, then reared back with his palm, ready to follow Lon's example. I grabbed his hand midswing. "You do, and I'll break it."

He snickered, wiggling free of my grasp, then threw down an alternate gauntlet. "Race you to the SUV."

Challenge accepted. I scraped an invisible line across the garage floor with the side of my shoe.

Things weren't perfect. Even if we got the vassal back from Hajo, I had the binding debts hanging over my head. My house wards had been disabled by Chora, and though they could be fixed eventually, I wasn't sure I'd ever feel one hundred percent safe inside them again. And though Dare was relieved to have all the Hellfire kids back, he still had me over a barrel with my identity. Official Hellfire Club magician . . . I really didn't like the sound of that.

And on top of all that, a detail from Halloween night nagged me: Merrin's death. He was a despicable person, and he got what he deserved. But I couldn't stop obsessing over it, and this unnerved me. At first I thought that I was having guilt issues, but after a few days of replaying his death inside my head, I finally identified the real problem: I didn't kill Merrin with my own hands. I used Chora to kill him. My parents did the same thing years ago—summoned a demon to do their killing for them. Logically I knew that the circumstances weren't the same, but I couldn't stop making the connection, and it troubled me more than I liked.

But there was only so much worrying you could do before you just had to accept what life throws at you and move on, because some things were going to be out of your control, and others can't be fixed or changed. And for everything I'd lost over the last couple of months, I still had a lot. More than I expected, actually.

Lon turned and watched us with amusement as Jupe lowered himself into a runner's crouch at my side. "First one there gets to ride shotgun. On your mark, get set . . ."

Go.

ACKNOWLEDGMENTS

Thank you to my agent extraordinaire, Laura Bradford, for her frankness, good humor, and unshakable belief in my storytelling; Jennifer Heddle, for pointing out a better path (may the force be with you!); Brian, for his creative problem solving, endless patience and ideas, and unflagging support (love you); Tony Mauro, for bringing the cannery to life on the cover; to everyone behind the scenes at Pocket (including Julia Fincher, Esther Paradelo, Sarah Wright, Anne Cherry, and Erica Feldon); the bloggers, reviewers, and tweeters who gave Arcadia a shot and spread the word (special shout-outs to Synde Korman, Jess Turner, Julie Walsh, Natasha Carty, and Pamela Webb-Elliott). Many thanks to Ann Aguirre, Carolyn Crane, Marta Acosta, Moira Rogers, Suzanne McLeod, Kelly Meding, Karen Chance, Juliana Stone, Anya Bast, and Karina Cooper; Ben and Tripp, for the emergency MacBook; Carrie and Dave, for their feedback (step away from that cat!); Jen and Bill, for their friendship and support; and to my wonderful family for pretending to understand paranormal fantasy (Demons? Magic? What is this crap?) and for rolling out the red carpet whenever I visit (love you, Gee).

But mostly, I'd like to extend genuine gratitude to all my readers. I adore each and every one of you.

Fantasy.
Temptation.
Adventure.

Visit PocketAfterDark.com,
an all-new website just for Urban
Fantasy and Romance Readers!

- Exclusive access to the hottest
urban fantasy and romance titles!

- Read and share reviews on
the latest books!

- Live chats with your favorite
romance authors!

- Vote in online polls!

More Bestselling Urban Fantasy from Pocket Books!

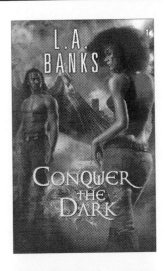

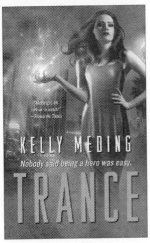

Walk these dark streets... if you dare.

Pick up a bestselling Urban Fantasy from Pocket Books!

Printed in the United States
By Bookmasters